A SUMMER TO REMEMBER

A Summer to Remember

Remember

Mary Balogh

DELACORTE PRESS

Published by
DELACORTE PRESS
Random House, Inc.
1540 Broadway
New York, New York 10036

Delacorte Press® is a registered trademark of
Random House, Inc., and the colophon is a trademark
of Random House, Inc.

ISBN 0-385-33535-0

Manufactured in the United States of America

A Summer to Remember

1

*L*ondon's Hyde Park was decked out in all the splendor of a
May morning. Sunlight beamed down from a clear blue sky
and twinkled off a million dewdrops, giving a fresh, newly
washed appearance to trees and grass. It was a perfect setting for the
customary promenade along fashionable Rotten Row, the riders cantering along the wide stretch of turf that ran from Hyde Park Corner
to Queen's Gate, the pedestrians strolling on the footpath beside it,
separated from the equestrians by a sturdy rail.

Perfect except for one discordant detail. In the middle of an open
stretch of grass well within sight of the Row some sort of commo-
tion was rapidly drawing a crowd of the curious. That it was a fight
became quickly evident. Not a duel—there were four participants
instead of two and the morning was far too well advanced—but an
indecorous outbreak of fisticuffs.

Gentlemen, and a few ladies too, rode closer to see what was tran-
spiring. Many of the gentlemen stayed to watch the progress of the
fight, their interest in the morning considerably piqued. A few, those

unfortunate enough to be escorting ladies, were obliged to ride hastily onward since it was most certainly not a genteel sight for female eyes. Some pedestrians too approached the scene along the path that ran close by and either hurried on past or drew closer, depending largely upon their gender.

"Scandalous!" one haughty male voice declared above the hubbub of the crowd gathered about the empty square in which the brawl was proceeding apace. "Someone ought to summon a constable. Riffraff should not be allowed into the park to offend the sensibilities of decent folk."

But although the shabby garments and generally grubby, unkempt appearance of three of the participants in the fight proclaimed them to be undoubtedly of the very lowest classes, the elegant though scant clothing and general bearing of the fourth told an entirely different story.

"It is Ravensberg, sir," the Honorable Mr. Charles Rush explained to the outraged Marquess of Burleigh.

The name was apparently explanation enough. The marquess raised a quizzing glass to his eye and from the vantage point of his position on horseback peered through it over the heads of those on foot at Viscount Ravensberg, who was stripped to the waist and at that particular moment was having much the worst of the encounter. He had an assailant clamped on each arm while the third pummeled him with hearty enthusiasm in the stomach.

"Scandalous!" the marquess declared again, while all about him gentlemen cheered or jeered, and two or three were even engaged in laying wagers upon the outcome of such a seemingly unequal contest. "I did not believe I would live to see even Ravensberg stoop so low as to brawl with riffraff."

"Shame!" someone else called as the red-haired giant who was doing the pummeling changed the direction of his assault and planted a fist in his victim's undefended right eye, snapping his neck back in the process. "Three against one is no fair odds."

"But he would not accept our assistance," Lord Arthur Kellard protested with some indignation. "He made the challenge—and insisted that three against one suited him admirably."

"Ravensberg *challenged* riffraff?" the marquess asked with considerable disdain.

"They dared to be insolent after he rebuked them for accosting a milkmaid," Mr. Rush explained. "But he would not simply chastise them with his whip as the rest of us suggested. He insisted—*oh, I say!*"

This exclamation was occasioned by Lord Ravensberg's response to the punch in the eye. He laughed, an incongruously merry sound, and suddenly lashed out neatly with one slim leg and caught his unwary assailant beneath the chin with the toe of his boot. There was a loud cracking of bone and clacking of teeth. At the same moment he took advantage of the astonishment of the two who held his arms and twisted free of them. He spun around to face them in a half crouch, his arms outstretched, his fingers beckoning. He was grinning.

"Come on, you buggers," he invited profanely. "Or do the odds suddenly appear less to your advantage?"

The opponent whose jaw had just been shattered might have thought so. But although his eyes were open, he appeared more intent upon counting stars wheeling in the morning sky than considering odds.

There was a roar of appreciation from the ever growing crowd of spectators.

Viscount Ravensberg showed to far better advantage without his shirt than with it. A gentleman of medium height and slender grace, he had doubtless appeared an easy mark to the three thugs who had taken him on with a collective smirk of insolent contempt a few minutes before. But the slim legs, encased in fashionable buff riding breeches and top boots, showed themselves to be impressively well muscled now that he had descended from the saddle. And his naked chest, shoulders, and arms were those of a man who had exercised and honed his body to its fullest potential. The white seams of numerous scars on his forearms and chest and one the length of the underside of his jaw on the left side proclaimed the fact, as his clothes did not, that at one time he had been a military man.

"Atrocious language to use in a public place," the marquess remarked disdainfully. "And an unseemly display of flesh. And all over a *milkmaid*, you say? Ravensberg is a disgrace to his name. I pity his father."

But no one, not even Mr. Rush, to whom his remarks were addressed, was paying him any attention. Two of the bullies who had thought to amuse themselves by coaxing unwilling kisses from an unaccompanied milkmaid in the park were taking turns rushing at the viscount, who was laughing and repulsing them with his jabbing fists every time they came within range. Those who knew him were well aware that he spent a few hours of most days at Jackson's boxing saloon, sparring with partners far his superior in height and weight.

"Sooner or later," he said conversationally, "you are going to put together your two half-brains to make one whole and realize that you would stand a far better chance against me if you attacked simultaneously."

"This is *not* a sight for ladies," the marquess said sternly. "The Duchess of Portfrey is walking past with her niece."

But although one gentleman detached himself hastily—and perhaps reluctantly—from the crowd at mention of the duchess's name, his lordship's disapproving voice was largely drowned out by a roar of enthusiasm as the viscount's remaining two assailants took his advice and charged him in tandem, only to find their progress checked when he reached out his arms and cracked their heads together. They went down as if their four legs had turned to jelly, and they remained down.

"Bravo, Ravensberg!" someone called above the chorus of whistles and cheers.

"'E's bloomin' broke my jaw, 'e 'as," the third young man complained, clutching it with both hands and turning over on the grass to spit blood and at least one tooth onto the grass. He had abandoned counting stars but did not look as if he were about to resume the fight.

The viscount was laughing again as he wiped his palms on his breeches. "It was too easy, by Jove," he said. "I expected better sport from three of London's choicest laboring men. They hardly merited my getting off my horse. They were definitely not worth stripping down for. If they had ever been in my regiment in the Peninsula, by thunder, I would have put them in the front line to shield the worthier men behind them."

But the morning had one more incident of interest to offer—both for him and for the cheering spectators. The milkmaid who had been the unwitting cause of the fracas came hurtling across the grass toward him—the crowd parted obligingly to let her through—flung her arms about his neck, and pressed her person against his.

"Oh, thank you, *thank* you, your worship," she cried fervently, "for saving a girl's virtue. I'm a good girl, I am, and they would of stole a kiss or p'raps worse if you 'adn't 'appened along to save me. But I'll kiss *you*, I will. For a reward, like, being as you earned it an' all."

She was plump and shapely and ruddily pretty and drew shrill whistles and admiring, bawdy comments from the spectators. Viscount Ravensberg grinned at her before dipping his head and availing himself of her offer with lingering thoroughness. He tossed her a half sovereign along with a wink from his good eye when he was finished, and assured her that she was indeed a good girl.

There were more whistles as she made her unhurried departure, all dimples and saucily swaying hips.

"Scandalous!" the marquess said one more time. "In broad daylight too! But what can one expect of Ravensberg?"

The viscount heard him and turned to sketch him an ironic bow. "I perform a public service, sir," he said. "I provide topics for drawing-room conversation that are somewhat more lively than the weather and the state of the nation's health."

"I believe," Mr. Rush said with a chuckle as the marquess rode on, his back ramrod straight and almost visibly bristling with disapproval, "you are barely whispered about by the more genteel, Ravensberg. You had better come to White's and get a beefsteak on that eye. That rascal gave you one deuce of a shiner."

"Hurts like a thousand devils," the viscount admitted cheerfully. "Egad, life should always be so exhilarating. My shirt, if you please, Farrington."

He looked about him after taking it from the hand of Lord Farrington, to whom his clothes had been entrusted at the start of the fight. The crowd was dispersing. He raised his eyebrows.

"Frightened all the ladies away, did I?" He squinted off in the direction of Rotten Row as if searching for one in particular.

"It *is* an alarmingly public place, Ravensberg," Lord Farrington said, laughing with him. "And you *were* bare to the waist."

"Ah," the viscount said carelessly, taking his coat from his friend and shrugging into it, "but I have a reputation for wild living to live up to, you see—though I believe I must have done my duty by it for one morning." He frowned suddenly. "What the devil are we to do with these two slumbering bodies, do you suppose?"

"Leave them to sleep it off?" Lord Arthur suggested. "I am late for my breakfast, Ravensberg, and that eye is crying out for attention. The mere sight of it is enough to threaten one's appetite."

"You, fellow." The viscount raised his voice as he drew another coin out of his pocket and tossed it onto the grass beside the only one of his opponents who was conscious. "Revive your friends and take them to the nearest alehouse before a constable arrives to convey them elsewhere. I daresay a tankard or two of ale each will help restore you all to a semblance of good health. And bear in mind for the future that when milkmaids say no they probably mean no. It is a simple fact of language. Yes means yes, no means no."

"Bloody 'ell," the man mumbled, still holding his jaw with one hand while setting the other over the coin. "I'll never so much as *look* at another wench, guv."

The viscount laughed and swung himself up into the saddle of his horse, whose bridle Mr. Rush had been holding.

"Breakfast," he announced gaily, "and a juicy beefsteak for my eye. Lead the way, Rush."

A few minutes later Hyde Park in the vicinity of Rotten Row was its usual elegant, *ton*nish self, all traces of the scandalous brawl van-

ished. But it was one more incident to add to the lengthy list of
wild indiscretions for which Christopher "Kit" Butler, Viscount
Ravensberg, had become sadly notorious.

"I cannot tell you," the Duchess of Portfrey had been saying to her
niece a few minutes earlier, "what a delight it is to have your company, Lauren. My marriage is proving more of a joy than I ever expected, and Lyndon is remarkably attentive, even now that I am in
expectation of an interesting event. But he cannot live in my pocket
all the time, the poor dear. We were both pleased beyond words when
you accepted our invitation to stay with us until after my confinement."

The Honorable Miss Lauren Edgeworth smiled. "We both know,"
she said, "that you are doing me a far greater favor than I can possibly be doing you, Elizabeth. Newbury Abbey had become intolerable
to me."

She had been in London for two weeks, but neither she nor the
duchess had touched upon the underlying reason for her being here
until now. Elizabeth's supposed need for Lauren's company while she
awaited the birth of her first child two months hence had been
merely a convenient excuse. Of course it had.

"Life does go on, Lauren," Elizabeth said at last. "But I will not
belittle your grief by enlarging upon that theme. It would be insensitive of me, especially when I have never experienced anything to
compare with what you have suffered—and when I have finally found
my own happiness. Though that fact in itself may be of some reas-
surance to you. I was all of six and thirty when I married Lyndon last
autumn."

The Duke of Portfrey was indeed attentive to his wife, with whom
he was clearly deeply in love. Lauren smiled her acknowledgment of
the words of intended comfort. They strolled onward through Hyde
Park, as they had done each morning since Lauren's arrival, except for
the three days when it had rained. The broad, grassy expanses on either side of the path looked enticingly and deceptively rural despite

the frequent glimpses they afforded of other pedestrians and riders. It was as if a piece of the countryside had been tossed down into the middle of one of the largest, busiest cities in the world and had survived there, untainted by commerce.

They were approaching Rotten Row, from which Lauren had shrunk in some alarm the first time Elizabeth had suggested they walk there two weeks before. The morning gathering was nothing like the crush of the fashionable afternoon promenade in the park, it was true, but even so there were too many people to see and—more significant—to be seen by. She had thought she would never find the courage to face the *beau monde* after the fiasco of last year.

Last year half the *ton* had been gathered at Newbury Abbey in Dorsetshire to celebrate the wedding of Lauren Edgeworth to Neville Wyatt, Earl of Kilbourne. There had been a grand wedding eve ball, at which Lauren had thought it was impossible to feel any happier— and how horrifyingly prophetic that thought had proved to be! And then there had been the wedding itself at the village church, which had been packed to the doors with the crème de la crème of the *beau monde*—a wedding that had been interrupted just as Lauren was about to step into the nave, on her grandfather's arm, by the sudden appearance of the wife Neville had thought long dead and of whose very existence Lauren and his whole family had been totally unaware.

Lauren had come to London this spring because she could no longer bear to be living at the dower house with the dowager countess and Gwendoline, Neville's sister, while Neville and his Lily lived at the abbey a mere two miles distant. Unfortunately, there had been few avenues of escape. She had grown up at Newbury Abbey with Neville and Gwen after her mother married the late earl's brother and went off with him on a wedding journey from which they had never returned. She had read Elizabeth's letter of invitation, then, with enormous gratitude. But she had come on the assumption that since Elizabeth was increasing, they would not be taking part in any of the social activities of the Season. She was right about that, but Elizabeth did like to take the air.

"Oh, goodness," the duchess said suddenly as they topped a slight rise in the path and came within sight of Rotten Row, "I wonder what the reason is for that crowd. I do hope no one has been taken ill. Or been thrown from a horse."

There was indeed a large gathering of horses and people on the grass beside the path, directly on their route to the Row. They were mostly gentlemen, it appeared to Lauren. But if someone had indeed been hurt, the presence of ladies might be welcome. Ladies could be far more practical in emergencies than gentlemen. They both increased their pace.

"How absurd of me," the duchess said, "to be remembering that Lyndon went out riding this morning. Do you suppose . . ."

"Indeed I do not," Lauren said firmly. "And I do not even believe there has been any accident. They are *cheering.*"

"Oh, dear." The duchess touched Lauren's arm to slow her down again and sounded suddenly on the verge of laughter. "I do believe we have stumbled upon a fight, Lauren. I think we must walk on past as if we had noticed nothing untoward."

"A fight?" Lauren's eyes widened. "In such a public place? In broad daylight? Surely not."

But indeed Elizabeth was quite right. When they drew closer Lauren confirmed it with her own eyes before she could avert them and hurry decently by. Although the crowd of men and horses was really quite dense, one of those inexplicable gaps appeared for a moment, allowing her a view of what was happening in the hollow center of the square. A shockingly clear view.

There were three men there, although she thought there might have been a fourth too, stretched out on the grass. Two of them were dressed decently, if shabbily, in the clothing of laboring men. But it was upon the third that Lauren's eyes riveted themselves for a few startled moments. He was crouched ready for action and was apparently taunting the other two by beckoning with both hands. But it was not his actions that startled her as much as his state of dress—or rather, his state of undress. His supple top boots and his form-fitting buff riding breeches proclaimed him to be a gentleman. But above the waist he was quite, quite naked. And very splendidly and alarmingly male.

Before she looked sharply away in blushing confusion, Lauren became aware of two other details, one visual and one aural. He was fair-haired and handsome and laughing. And the words he spoke to accompany the beckoning hands fell unmistakably upon her ears despite the hubbub of voices proceeding from the many spectators.

"Come on, you buggers," he said without any apparent shame at all.

She hoped fervently, even as she felt the uncomfortable heat of a blush spread up her neck to blossom brightly in both cheeks, that Elizabeth had not heard the words—or seen the half-naked man who had uttered them. Rarely had she felt such embarrassment.

But Elizabeth was laughing with what sounded like genuine amusement. "Poor Lord Burleigh," she said. "He looks as if he might have an apoplexy at any moment. I wonder why he does not simply ride on by and leave the children to their play. Men can be such foolish creatures, Lauren. Even the slightest disagreement must be settled with fists."

"Elizabeth," Lauren said, truly scandalized, "did you see . . . ? And did you hear . . . ?"

"How could I not?" Elizabeth was still chuckling.

But before either of them could say more, they were distracted by the appearance of a tall, dark, handsome young gentleman, who stepped onto the path before them, bowed with hasty elegance, and offered an arm to each of them.

"Elizabeth," he said, "Lauren. Good morning. And what a lovely morning it is too. It bids fair to being unseasonably warm later today. Allow me to escort you to Rotten Row and earn the envy of every other gentleman there."

Joseph Fawcitt, Marquess of Attingsborough, was a cousin, nephew of the Dowager Countess of Kilbourne. He had been one of the spectators of the fight, Lauren realized, but had seen them and had come to hurry them away. She took his arm gratefully. Actually, she thought, hearing the echo of his words, it was probable that there *was* no other gentleman on Rotten Row. Surely they were all clustered about the brawling men.

"How provoking it is sometimes to be a lady, Joseph," Elizabeth said, taking his other arm. "I suppose if I were to ask you who that gentleman is who is fighting and why he is doing so, you would not answer me?"

He grinned down at her. "*What* fight?" he asked.

Elizabeth sighed. "As I thought," she said.

"For my part," Lauren assured him fervently, "I have no wish to know." She was still flushed at the memory of the gentleman fighter, naked from the waist up. And of his words—*come on, you buggers.*

Joseph turned his head to look down at her, a twinkle in his eyes. "Mother intends to call at Grosvenor Square this afternoon," he said. "She has *plans* for you, Lauren. Be warned."

Some rout or concert or ball, doubtless. It was proving extremely difficult to convince Aunt Sadie, the Duchess of Anburey, Joseph's mother, that she simply did not *wish* to join in any of the activities of the Season. Having seen her daughter, Lady Wilma Fawcitt, eligibly betrothed to the Earl of Sutton before the Season even began in earnest, Aunt Sadie had turned her well-meaning matchmaking eye upon Lauren.

Joseph turned to address a remark to Elizabeth, and Lauren, despite herself, looked back over her shoulder. She had heard a loud cheer a moment before. The fight was over. The crowd had parted along her line of vision, and she could see that the gentleman with the naked torso was still on his feet. But if she had been shocked before, she was doubly horrified now. He had a *woman* in his arms—his were right about her waist and hers were wrapped about his neck—and he was *kissing* her. In full view of a few dozen spectators.

He lifted his head just as Lauren looked, and in the fraction of a second before she could whip her head about to face front again, his laughing eyes met hers.

Her cheeks were on fire again.

"You are looking thoroughly blue-deviled, Ravensberg," Lord Farrington commented late the following night, crossing the room to the sideboard and replenishing the contents of his glass before resuming his seat. "Foxed, are you? Or is it the eye? It has turned marvelous shades of black, purple, and yellow. Not to mention the bright scarlet slit through which you are peering out at the world."

"I tell you, Ravensberg," Lord Arthur added, "I could scarce swallow the kidneys on my plate this morning for looking at that eye—or do I mean yesterday morning?"

"If I could just be sure," Charles Rush said, "that this mantel would stay upright when I push away from it, I would pour myself another drink. What the devil time is it?"

"Half past four." Lord Farrington glanced at the clock six inches from his friend's head.

"The devil!" Mr. Rush exclaimed. "Where has the night gone?"

"Where all nights go." Lord Arthur yawned. "Let's see—I believe I started the evening at m'aunt's rout—a deuced flat affair, but family duty and all that. I did not stay long. She looked over m'shoulder to see if Ravensberg was with me and then, even though he wasn't there, read me a lecture on the company I keep and the nasty tendency rakish reputations have of rubbing off on a fellow's companions. It seems I ought to stay away from you, Ravensberg, if I know what is good for me."

His friends shared the joke by roaring with hearty mirth. All except Kit, that was, who was sprawled with casual elegance in a deep chair beside the fireplace in his bachelor rooms on St. James's, gazing vacantly with his one healthy eye into the unlit coals.

"You won't have to put up with my wicked influence for much longer," he said. "I've been summoned to Alvesley."

Lord Farrington sipped his drink. "By your father? Redfield himself?" he asked. "A *summons*, Ravensberg?"

"A summons." Kit nodded slowly. "There is to be a grand house party this summer in honor of the seventy-fifth birthday of the dowager, my grandmother."

"An old dragon, is she, Ravensberg?" Mr. Rush asked sympathetically. "*Do* you suppose the mantel would collapse if I stopped holding it up?"

"You are three sheets to the wind, old chap," Lord Arthur informed him. "It's your legs, not the mantel."

"I have always had a soft spot for the old girl, you see," Kit said, "and my father knows it. Oh, for God's sake, Rush, just look down into your glass, will you? It is still half full."

Mr. Rush looked with pleased astonishment at the glass in his hand and drained off its contents. "What I really need," he said, "is my bed. If my legs would just carry me there."

"Egad," Kit said, his gloomy stare back on the unlit fire. "What *I* really need is a bride."

"Go to bed," Lord Arthur advised him hastily, "and sleep it off. The feeling will go away by morning—guaranteed."

"My father's birthday gift to my grandmother is to be the betrothal of his heir," Kit said.

"Oh, I say! *You* are the heir."

"Jolly rotten luck, old chap."

Lord Arthur and Mr. Rush spoke simultaneously.

"A pox on all fathers!" Lord Farrington exclaimed indignantly. "Does he have someone picked out for you, Ravensberg?"

Kit laughed and draped his hands over the arms of his chair. "Oh, yes, indeed," he said. "Along with everything else, I am to inherit my late elder brother's betrothed."

"Who the devil is she?" Mr. Rush forgot his inebriated state sufficiently to straighten up and stand unassisted.

"Bewcastle's sister," Kit said.

"Bewcastle? The *Duke* of?" Lord Arthur asked.

"I have obliged my father by withdrawing from the Peninsula and selling my commission," Kit said. "I'll oblige him further by going back to Alvesley after almost three years even though I was banished for life the last time I was there. I'll even oblige him on the matter of the birthday gift. But I'll do it all on my terms, by Jove. I'll take with me a bride of my own choosing, and I'll be married to her before I go so that there will be nothing Redfield can do about it. I have been sorely tempted to pick some vulgar creature, but that would not do. It is just the sort of thing Redfield would expect of me. I'll choose someone above reproach instead. That will gall him more than anything else because he won't be able to complain about her. She is going to be dull, respectable, prim, and perfect." He spoke with grim satisfaction.

For a moment his friends regarded him in fascinated silence. Then Lord Farrington threw back his head and laughed. "*You* are going to marry a dull, respectable woman, Ravensberg?" he asked. "Just to spite your father?"

"Not wise, old chap," Mr. Rush said, treading a determinedly straight path toward the sideboard. "You would be the one married to the woman for life, not your father. You would find such a wife insupportable, take my word on it. The vulgar wench might afford you more amusement."

"But the thing is that one has to marry sometime," Kit explained, cupping one hand over his aching eye for a moment. "Especially when the death of one's elder brother has made one the reluctant heir to an earldom and vast estates and a fortune to boot. One has to do one's duty and set up one's nursery and all that. Who better to do it with than a quiet, dull, worthy woman who will run one's home competently and without fuss and will dutifully present one with an heir and a few spares?"

"But there is a very real obstacle to such a scheme, Ravensberg." Lord Farrington was frowning when he spoke the words, but he grinned and then chuckled outright before continuing. "What respectable woman would have you? You are a handsome enough devil, it is true, or so I understand from the way females look at you. And of course you have your present title and your future prospects. But you *have* established an impressively notorious reputation as a rakehell since you sold out."

"And that would be stating it mildly," Lord Arthur muttered into his glass.

"As bad as that, is it? What a devilish stuffy world we live in," Kit commented. "But egad, I am serious about this. And I *am* Redfield's heir. That fact alone will outweigh all else when it is perceived that I am shopping in earnest for a wife."

"True enough," Mr. Rush admitted, seating himself on an upright chair after refilling his glass. "But not necessarily the sort of wife you are looking for, old chap. Parents with lofty principles and daughters to match steer clear of gentlemen who mill with foul-smelling laborers within sight of Rotten Row and then kiss milkmaids without their shirts on for all the world to witness. And men who on a wager drive along St. James's in their curricles past all the gentlemen's clubs, a painted doxy squeezed onto the seat on either side of them. And men whose names appear in all the betting books in connection with every disreputable and outrageous dare anyone cares to wager on."

"Who are the possibilities?" Kit asked, ignoring this dire prediction and returning his attention to the coals in the fireplace. "There must be hordes of new arrivals in town now that the Season has begun in earnest. Hordes of hopeful misses come shopping for husbands. Who is the dullest, most prudish, most straitlaced, most respectable of them all? You fellows will know better than I. You all attend *ton*nish events."

His companions gave the matter serious thought. Each threw out a few names, all of which were rejected out of hand by the others for a variety of reasons.

"There *is* Miss Edgeworth," Lord Arthur said at last, when they appeared to have run out of suggestions. "But she is too long in the tooth."

"Miss Edgeworth?" Lord Farrington repeated. "Of Newbury Abbey? The Earl of Kilbourne's abandoned bride? Lord, my sister was at that wedding. It was the sensation of last year. The bridegroom waiting at the front of the church, the bride in the porch ready to make her grand entrance. And then the arrival of a ragged woman claiming to be Kilbourne's long-lost wife—and telling nothing short of the truth, by gad. The Edgeworth chit fled from the church as if the hounds of hell were at her heels, according to Maggie, who is not normally prone to exaggeration. Is she in town this year, Kellard?"

"Staying with Portfrey," Lord Arthur said. "The duchess is Kilbourne's aunt, y'know. And Miss Edgeworth is connected to her too in some way."

"I had heard she was in town," Mr. Rush admitted. "But she doesn't go about much, does she? Hedged around by the Portfreys and dozens of other relatives, I daresay, all trying to get her married off quietly—and *respectably*." He snickered. "She is doubtless dull enough to set one to yawning at the mere thought of her. You don't want *her*, Ravensberg."

"Besides," Lord Arthur added with what proved to be the fatal challenge, "you would not get her even if you did want her, Ravensberg. Portfrey, Anburey, Attingsborough—*none* of her relatives would allow someone of your reputation within hailing distance of her. And even if you did slip past their guard, she would give you the cut direct. Turn you into an icicle on the spot, I daresay. You are *just* the sort none of them would want for her, least of all the lady herself. We will have to think of someone else for you. Though why you would want—"

But Kit was laughing gaily as he turned his face from the fire again. "Was that a challenge, by any chance?" he asked, cutting his friend off midsentence. "If it was, you could scarce have made it more irresistible if you had tried. I will not be allowed within hailing distance of Miss Edgeworth, you say, because I am the sort of rake and rogue from whom such a delicate and aging bloom must be protected at all costs? And she would freeze me with a single glance from her severe, maidenly eye, would she? Because she is incorruptible and I am corruption incarnate? By Jove, I'll have her." He slapped the arm of his chair with one open palm.

Lord Farrington flung back his head and shouted with laughter. "I smell a wager," he said. "A hundred guineas on it that you cannot do it, Ravensberg."

"And a hundred more of mine," Lord Arthur added. "She is very high in the instep, Ravensberg. Someone just last week, though I can't for the life of me remember who, likened her to a marble statue, except that she came out the colder of the two."

"I might as well throw in my hundred too," Mr. Rush said, "though I should know better where Ravensberg is concerned. It was Brinkley, Kellard, who is forever scouting out prospective new mothers for his orphaned brood. That's how I knew she was in town—I remember now. She told Brinkley right straight out as soon as he broached the subject of wedlock with her—when he was strolling with her on Rotten Row one morning, if you can imagine it—that she has no intention of marrying anyone ever. He believed her. Apparently she is not the sort of lady whose word one doubts. That was when he made the remark about marble statues. Brinkley is eminently respectable, Ravensberg."

"And I am not." Kit laughed again. "Well, for three hundred guineas and to annoy my father into the bargain I'll have to change her mind, won't I? Shall we say by the end of June, when I have to leave for Alvesley? A *marriage* before the end of June, that is. Between Miss Edgeworth and yours truly, of course."

"Less than six weeks? Done." Lord Farrington got resolutely to his feet. "Now I am for my bed, while I can still find it and convey myself toward it unassisted. Come along, Rush, I'll steer you in the direction of yours at the same time. I would not begin the campaign for at least another week if I were you, Ravensberg. Any delicately nurtured female would swoon outright at the sight of that eye. That will give you approximately five weeks." The thought amused him considerably.

"A marriage to Miss Edgeworth by the last day in June, then," Lord Arthur said, summing up the wager as he joined his friends on their way out of the room. "It cannot be done, Ravensberg. Not even by you—*especially* not by you. This will be the easiest hundred guineas I have made this year. But of course you *will* try."

"Of course." Kit grinned at his friends. "And I will succeed. With what event shall I begin the campaign? What is happening a week or so from now?"

"Lady Mannering's ball," Lord Farrington said after a moment of consideration. "It is always one of the grand squeezes of the Season. Everybody attends it. Miss Edgeworth may well not, though, Ravensberg. I have not seen her at any balls—or any other entertainment for that matter. Not that I would recognize her if I saw her, of course, but someone would surely have pointed her out. She is still news."

"Lady Mannering's ball," Kit said, hoisting himself out of his chair in order to see his friends on their way. "I must find out if she will be there. Is she a beauty, by the way? Or is she an antidote?"

"Now that," Lord Farrington said firmly, "you must discover for yourself, Ravensberg. It will serve you right if she resembles a gargoyle."

2

*L*auren arrived at Lady Mannering's ball the following week in company with the Duke and Duchess of Anburey and the Marquess of Attingsborough. After much initial resistance, she had agreed to attend even though she was fully aware that almost the whole of the *beau monde* would be present. Or perhaps it was *because* of that fact. She had made her decision to go for sheer pride's sake.

She was in London during the Season, and she was a member of the *ton*. If she maintained her decision to live a retired life as Elizabeth's companion, she might give the lasting impression that she was afraid to appear in public, that she was afraid of being laughed at, scorned, shunned as a poor rejected bride. She was indeed afraid, mortally so, but above all else she had been raised to be a lady. And ladies did not allow fear to master them. Ladies did not abjure society merely because they were embarrassed and unhappy, merely because they felt unattractive and unwanted. Ladies did not give in to self-pity.

And so she had taken her courage in both hands and agreed to appear before the *ton* on one of the *ton*'s favorite playgrounds—a

London ballroom during the Season. She would go and hold her head high and confront the demons that had shadowed her ever since that most dreadful of all mornings in the church at Newbury. She would remain in London until after Elizabeth's confinement—the duke had brought his duchess to town so that she would be close to the best physicians—and then she would do what she had decided she really wanted to do. She would take her modest fortune and set up her own establishment, perhaps in Bath, and she would live a quiet, retired life with a small circle of select friends. She would endure this ball, because when she did, no one was going to be able to call her a coward.

The Duke of Anburey's crested carriage took its place in the line of coaches depositing guests outside the Mannering mansion on Cavendish Square. Lauren could see that every window was ablaze with candlelight. Light spilled out from the double doors, which stood open, and illumined the red carpet that had been rolled down the steps and across the pavement. Even above the snorting of horses, the stamping of hooves, and the rumbling of wheels, she could hear the festive sound of voices raised in greeting and laughter.

It was a nerve-wracking moment and made her understand fully how much she had changed in the fourteen months since her wedding eve ball. Then she had felt very comfortably ensconced in her own milieu, perfectly at ease, perfectly assured of her own worth and her own place in the ranks of the *beau monde*. It was time she took that place again, not as Neville's prospective bride and countess, it was true, but as the Honorable Miss Lauren Edgeworth. She raised her chin, an unconsciously arrogant gesture that masked her desire to jump from the carriage and run and run until Cavendish Square and Mayfair and London and her very self were far behind her.

And then it was their turn to alight. A footman opened the carriage door and set down the steps, the gentlemen descended, Uncle Webster handed Aunt Sadie down, and Joseph was reaching up a hand to assist Lauren. She took it and made her own descent to the red carpet, paying particular attention to her posture and facial expression as she did so. She knew she was looking her best. Her gown had been specially made for the occasion by Elizabeth's own modiste, and Elizabeth had helped her choose both the fabric and the design, as well as all the accessories to wear with it. The Duchess of Portfrey was well known for her exquisite taste. But then so was Lauren Edgeworth.

Lauren smiled as her aunt and uncle made their way indoors and she laid her hand on Joseph's offered sleeve.

"That's it, Lauren," he murmured approvingly, smiling at her and even winking. "You imitate a queen, my girl. Indeed you look lovelier than any queen I ever saw."

"And how many would that be, Joseph?" she asked, picking up the front of her skirt with her free hand and walking gracefully up the steps into the crowded, brightly lit hall. She quelled the sudden panicked conviction that she must have forgotten something essential— like her gown.

"Hmm, let me see." He pretended to consider his answer. "One actually. Our own Queen Charlotte. You are a hundred times lovelier than she."

"Keep your voice down," she advised him. "You will have your head chopped off for treason if anyone should overhear you." But she slanted him a quick, grateful smile. He clearly understood something about the flock of butterflies dancing frantically in her stomach and was doing his best to distract her.

He led her toward the staircase and the slow-moving queue of guests ascending it. She drew a few deep, steadying breaths and resisted the urge to look at things rather than people. How many of the guests on the stairs, and how many guests in the ballroom above, had been at her wedding and witnessed her humiliation?

The answer was, of course, a significant number of them. But a lifetime of training can be a marvelous thing, Lauren soon discovered. It took her up the stairs, along the receiving line, and into the ballroom, which was already crowded with people who for the moment had nothing better to do than watch and comment upon the arrival of fellow guests.

She tried to concentrate upon the magnificence of the ballroom,

which was lit by hundreds of candles set in three great crystal chandeliers overhead and in numerous wall sconces, and upon the sumptu-
ous floral arrangements that filled the room with their delicate pastel
shades and their perfume. And she tried—with some success—to
look calmly about her, making eye contact with numerous other
guests, inclining her head politely to those she recognized.

But it was her own family who killed any remote chance that she
might enjoy the evening—killed it by kindness. Almost before
Lauren was fully inside the ballroom, still on Joseph's arm, her uncle
and aunt close by, Wilma and Lord Sutton came along, all gracious
condescension, a thin, reedy young man in tow, and made the introductions. Mr. Bartlett-Howe earnestly solicited the hand of Miss
Edgeworth for the second set, it being understood that the Marquess
of Attingsborough had already bespoken the first. And only a minute
or so later Lord Sutton, who had wandered away, returned with yet
another gentleman, who had apparently conceived a burning desire to
reserve the third set with Miss Edgeworth.

It seemed that her family, concerned that she might be a wall-
flower at her first ball in over a year, had spent the few days since she
had agreed to attend lining up prospective partners for her—and
prospective suitors too?

Just a little over a year ago she had danced at her wedding eve ball,
secure in her own attractiveness, the cynosure of all eyes, the admired
and envied bride of the Earl of Kilbourne. Tonight she was an aging,
faded beauty, unable to attract her own partners, in dire danger of declining into a permanent and irrevocable spinsterhood. Or so her
family made her feel.

Lauren felt the depth of humiliation. Even Joseph's kindness in
offering to escort her to the ball was—well, it was just *kindness.*

Lauren smiled her unconsciously arrogant smile and plied her fan
with slow grace.

When Kit and Lord Farrington arrived in Cavendish Square, the ball
had been in progress for some time. But it was a clear, moonlit

evening, unseasonably warm for the middle of May, and the front doors were still open wide. The merry noises of conversation and laughter spilled outside from the hall and stairs. The sound of an orchestra playing a vigorous country dance wafted down from the ballroom above.

"A squeeze indeed," Kit said, handing his opera cloak and silk hat to a liveried, bewigged footman and looking about the entrance hall with open interest. "Do you suppose the ballroom is as crowded, Farrington?"

"Sure to be. More so, in fact." His friend relinquished his own cloak and hat and checked the immaculate folds of his neckcloth. "We had better go up and find out."

Kit nodded affably to a few acquaintances, mostly male, as they ascended the staircase. This was the first ball he had attended since Lisbon. He could not even remember quite how long ago that had been. He had had invitations to several here in London, of course. His wilder exploits might have caused the highest sticklers to raise disapproving eyebrows and the most conscientious parents of young ladies to gather them more protectively to the family bosom, but he was after all Viscount Ravensberg. More important, he was the son and heir of the Earl of Redfield. And this was the Season, the great marriage mart, when everyone of any consequence at all was invited almost everywhere.

"You are quite sure she is going to be here this evening?" he asked as they reached the top of the stairs and turned in the direction of the ballroom. The crowd became denser and there was a noticeable swell in the noise level. Kit was aware of increased heat and the heavy scents of a thousand flowers mingled with the expensive perfumes worn by guests.

"As sure as I can be." Lord Farrington paused in the doorway of the ballroom and gazed unhurriedly about the milling crowds. "Sutton said she was coming and he ought to know—betrothed to Lady Wilma Fawcitt, you know. Of course, she might have contracted some deadly disease or broken a limb or simply changed her mind. Ah." He raised his quizzing glass to his eye.

"You have seen her?" Kit asked.

He might have been feeling self-conscious since this was his first appearance in years at a grand *ton* entertainment, and there was no doubt that he was attracting considerable attention. A number of those not dancing were looking quite pointedly his way. Lorgnettes and quizzing glasses were raised to inquisitive eyes. Heads were moving closer to other heads as confidences were exchanged. More than a few young ladies were stealing covert glances his way, especially those who had been apprised of his identity—the shocking, forbidden Lord Ravensberg! But Kit had never been much concerned with what others thought or said of him and tonight was no different.

"The delectable Miss Merklinger," Lord Farrington murmured, his quizzing glass trained upon one of the dancers. "All dimples and bouncing golden curls. Not to mention the bosom."

Kit chuckled and favored the beauty in question with a long scrutiny through his own glass. "And not a day over eighteen," he said. "Definitely not an object for your particular brand of gallantry, Farrington."

"Lord, no," his friend agreed with a sigh. "More is the pity. That is the attraction, I suppose. Now then, Miss Edgeworth."

He resumed his unhasty perusal of the room and its occupants even as the set came to an end and the dancers moved off the floor to further crowd the sidelines.

"Kellard pointed her out to me in the park just three or four mornings ago," Lord Farrington said. "I am quite certain I will recognize her again."

"But you were not presented," Kit said, "so cannot now introduce me to her."

"I would not make matters that easy for you anyway," his friend assured him. "I have a wager to win, if you will remember. Ah, there she is. Just being escorted to Attingsborough's side by Stennson. Oh, hard lines, old chap. Anburey and his duchess are hovering over her too. She is quite hedged about with formidable gaolers." He grinned.

"Stennson? *That* dry old stick?" Kit followed the direction of his friend's gaze. He knew both the Marquess of Attingsborough and

George Stennson and soon picked them out in the crowd some distance away. The older couple with them must be the duke and
duchess. And the lady standing between the two gentlemen had to be
the one he had come to meet. His future bride. Kit raised his glass to
his eye again.

She was on the tall side and slender, he could see, but not without
pleasing feminine curves. He would wager that beneath the flowing skirt
and train of her high-waisted gown her legs were long and slim. She had
a graceful bearing, with the sort of arch to her spine that invited a guiding male hand to nestle against the back of her waist. Her dark hair was
glossy in the light of the candles. It was dressed high on her head, held
there with jeweled combs, and fell about her neck and temples in soft
curls. Her face was oval with high cheekbones and straight nose and large
eyes—he could not see their color from where he stood. She was elegantly and fashionably dressed in a shimmering satin gown of deep violet, which she wore with silver gloves and slippers and a pale violet fan.

She was nothing short of a beauty. Kit's lips pursed in a silent
whistle.

She was conversing with her companions, but she was fanning herself and looking about at the same time. For a few moments Kit was
pleasantly surprised by the smile on her face. It gave the lie, seemingly,
to the notion that she was as cold as a marble statue. But the expression, he noticed as he kept watching, did not once change as she continued to converse and look about. Then it struck him that perhaps it
was not so much a smile as a haughty, condescending look of contempt for all the lesser mortals within her orbit.

"A diamond of the first water," he murmured, lowering his glass.

"Indeed," Lord Farrington agreed. "And an impregnable fortress if
ever I saw one, Ravensberg. She looks as if she considers anything
short of royalty quite unworthy of her notice." He obviously found
the thought amusing.

"But then," Kit said, looking about for their hostess, who by happy
chance was making her way toward them, a smile of welcome on her face,
"I always did have a weakness for impregnable fortresses, Farrington.
And for other assorted impossible challenges."

"Lord Farrington, Lord Ravensberg." Lady Mannering was all gracious charm as she presented each of them with a gloved hand to bow over. "How delightful that you have seen fit to attend my ball. And how provoking that you have arrived so late. You cannot know what a headache it is to a hostess to have to provide all the young ladies with partners for the opening set when all the young gentlemen persist in being fashionably late."

"But it is not with the *very* young ladies that I came to dance, ma'am," Lord Farrington said with his most disarming smile. "I knew the partner of my choice would be busy for the first few sets finding partners for her guests. It was my hope that by now you might be free to honor me with your hand for a set."

Lady Mannering laughed as she tapped his arm sharply with her closed fan. "You are a rogue, Farrington," she said. "It would serve you right if I clung to your arm for the rest of the evening. Now, how did you succeed in luring Lord Ravensberg here? It was my understanding that he is always too busy racing his curricle to Brighton and engaging in other such fascinating manly activities to attend dull events like balls. However, his notorious presence will guarantee the unqualified success of mine." She tapped Kit in his turn on the arm with her folded fan.

He inclined his head. "How could I resist, ma'am," he said, "when I saw that the invitation came from one of my mother's dearest friends?"

"I have not set eyes on your mama in years," Lady Mannering said bluntly. "She stays in the country. Now, permit me to find partners for you both. Though if all the fond mamas do not grab their daughters and run with them the moment they see the infamous Viscount Ravensberg in my ballroom, I will be agreeably surprised."

"Perhaps, ma'am," Kit said, favoring her with his most engaging smile, "you would present me to Miss Edgeworth of Newbury?"

Lady Mannering's eyebrows rose. "I believe there are younger ladies who are far more desirous of handsome, roguish partners than Miss Edgeworth," she said. "And it is her family, rather than I, who have been choosing her partners this evening. However, if it is your wish."

"It is, ma'am." Kit bowed again.

"And is it also your wish?" Lady Mannering asked Lord Farrington.

"Thank you, ma'am," he said, "but I see some acquaintances across the room to whom I must make myself agreeable—since you are to be otherwise engaged."

Kit followed his hostess across the ballroom while the crowds parted to let them through. His appearance had definitely caused a buzz, he noticed with rueful amusement, though whether it was a buzz of indignation or one of speculation he neither knew nor cared. He was noticing that by a stroke of good fortune the Duke and Duchess of Anburey were engaged in conversation with a couple behind them, Stennson had disappeared, and Attingsborough was directing his attention and his gallantries toward a blushing, giggling young lady who had just stepped off the dance floor. Miss Edgeworth stood virtually unattended for the moment, still looking about her, still wearing that fixed half smile.

"Miss Edgeworth." When Lady Mannering addressed her by name, she turned her gaze toward the newcomers, and her eyebrows arched above her eyes even as the motion of her fan was suddenly arrested. "Viscount Ravensberg has asked for the honor of an introduction."

She regarded him with large, dark-lashed violet eyes, the exact shade of her gown—surely the most beautiful feature in an extraordinarily beautiful face. Quite a perfect knockout, in fact.

But it was a face he had surely seen before, Kit thought—and recently too. For a moment the exact occasion eluded him. But then he remembered last week's fight in Hyde Park and the embrace with the milkmaid. When he had looked up after kissing her, he had found himself locking eyes with a shocked beauty—clearly *not* of the milkmaid class—some distance away and wishing fleetingly and naughtily that it was she who was caught within his embrace. But before he had been able either to grin or to wink at her, she had whipped her head about to present the back of an elegant bonnet to his gaze. When he had looked for her a short while later, she had disappeared among the crowds strolling on Rotten Row.

He had not thought of her since—until now.

Kit executed his most elegant bow.

Lauren felt a shock of recognition the moment she set eyes on him, even though he looked very different tonight—he was *clothed* from the neck down. He was dressed with impeccable elegance, in fact, in a black, form-fitting evening coat, cream silk knee breeches and embroidered waistcoat, and pristine white linen and lace.

He was not outstandingly handsome. And he was no more than two or three inches taller than she, Lauren was surprised to discover. Yet there was an aura of confident vitality about him that gave the illusion of extraordinarily attractive good looks. His face was tanned and good-humored, and his gray eyes smiled with some inner light.

He was the sort of man whose acquaintance she should avoid at all costs, Lauren thought in the few seconds that elapsed after Lady Mannering's introduction, while Lord Ravensberg bowed and she curtsied. Even if she had not been a witness to his unseemly behavior in the park, she surely would have sensed the indefinable air of raw masculinity that he somehow exuded. There was something very different indeed about him from the eminently respectable parade of gentlemen Wilma and Lord Sutton had been presenting to her thus far this evening. She felt an unexpected wave of amusement as she realized that her aunt and uncle and Joseph were bringing their attention back to her and looking concerned—as if she were a green girl who was quite incapable of taking care of herself. And Lord Sutton was approaching purposefully from a short distance away with a portly, earnest-looking young man—as if she were a dull, aging creature quite without the charms to attract any gentleman who was not coerced.

Viscount Ravensberg had not been coerced.

"My lord," she murmured.

"Miss Edgeworth? Charmed." The smile lurking in his eyes spread to the rest of his face to reveal very white teeth and laugh lines at the outer corners of his eyes. Lauren revised her first impression that he was not particularly handsome. "I begged for the introduction since I simply had to get close enough to discover if your gown really does match the color of your eyes. It does."

Lauren fanned her cheeks slowly—the ballroom was surely over-warm even though both sets of French windows leading out onto the balcony on the other side of the ballroom were wide open. Did he expect her to blush and simper at such blatant gallantry—when she had heard very different words on his lips last week? *Come on, you buggers.*

Joseph was purposefully clearing his throat.

"May I hope you are free to dance the next set with me, Miss Edgeworth?" Viscount Ravensberg asked while Lady Mannering smiled benevolently at his side.

"I was about to escort my cousin to the refreshment room," Joseph said smoothly but with a firm edge of dismissal in his tone. He offered his arm for her hand. "Miss Edgeworth is thirsty and needs a rest from dancing. Lauren?"

But Lord Ravensberg did not look away from her. He raised his eyebrows inquiringly while laughter danced in his eyes. He awaited an answer from her own lips. No true gentleman would have done so. And there was no necessity for her to reply when Joseph had done so for her. She had merely to place her hand on his arm, smile disdainfully, and walk off. It was a quite unexceptionable way in which to deal with unmannerly pretension. But she did none of those things.

Lord Ravensberg had not been coerced. He had complimented her eyes, however foolish the flattery. And he was undeniably attractive.

"Thank you, Joseph," she heard herself saying, "but perhaps I have the energy to dance one more set before taking refreshments."

She stepped forward, set her hand on the viscount's sleeve, and allowed him to lead her onto the open space of the dance floor. Would she have done so if Joseph had not spoken up to protect her? Or if Lord Sutton had not been bringing her another partner? She did not know. But she did realize suddenly, now that it was too late to change her mind, that the next set was to be a waltz—the intimate dance, still considered slightly scandalous by the highest sticklers, that she had once considered wondrously romantic. But that had been when she had danced it with Neville at her wedding eve ball. And never before or since.

"Such a grave look," the viscount murmured as she turned to face him. "*Are* you tired? Would you prefer after all that I escort you to the refreshment room?"

"No. Thank you." It was strange how such a small rebellion had lifted her spirits. And she was actually glad that the dance was to be a waltz. Perhaps she could lay to rest more than a few ghosts tonight.

The orchestra began playing the opening bars. Lauren raised her left hand to his shoulder and set her other hand in his. She could feel his right hand come firmly to rest against the arch of her back. His height made their positioning seem more intimate than it had felt with the taller Neville. She could not easily avoid gazing into his face. She could not avoid feeling his intense physical presence. She could feel the warm strength of both his hands. She could smell the subtle musk of his cologne. She drew a slow breath and looked into his eyes.

They smiled warmly, knowingly back into her own—as if he felt her discomfort and was amused by it. A dangerous man indeed, she thought. She had never been comfortable with such men. She had avoided them all her life.

He led her into the waltz.

For a while the bitter memories of her wedding eve ball and the day that had followed it threatened to overwhelm her. She calmed herself by deliberately counting her steps and concentrating on the rhythm of the music and the movement of her feet. But it did not take long to realize that she was partnered by a man who was an accomplished dancer. It was easy—it felt almost like second nature—to fit her steps to his lead and to follow the graceful, twirling pattern he set about the perimeter of the ballroom floor. It was easy to feel comfortable with his height, to appreciate the fact that she could look over his shoulder and see her surroundings.

She had not enjoyed the evening so far—and that was an understatement. But she had consoled herself with the knowledge that her appearance at such a squeeze had served a useful function. Now, suddenly, unexpectedly, she *was* enjoying herself. The lavish floral displays and the gowns of the other lady guests all merged into a glorious kaleidoscope of color. The candles in the chandeliers became swirling bands of light. And there was something undeniably exhilarating about waltzing with a man who not only knew the steps but also surely felt the magic of the dance as she did.

But that thought brought Lauren firmly back to reality after several minutes. She was dancing about Lady Mannering's ballroom in the arms of a stranger whom she had first seen just a week ago in shocking, scandalous circumstances. Joseph had tried to prevent her from dancing with him this evening. Was the viscount not respectable, then, despite his title and his presence at a *ton* ball? Had her first instinct about him been correct? Was he a rake?

Part of her did not care, was even surprisingly titillated by the possibility, in fact. But it was a part of herself with which she was thoroughly unfamiliar, a part of herself that must be reined in.

"Do you attend many balls, my lord?" She concentrated her mind upon making polite conversation and setting some sort of safe social distance between them. "I must confess this is my first this year."

"No, I do not," he replied. "And yes, I know."

She was indignant at the brevity of his answer. Did he know nothing about polite conversation? And then she was struck by its oddity. What did he mean—*yes, I know.* If he did not attend many balls himself, how did he know that she had attended none?

"It is a grand squeeze," she said, trying again, clinging to cliché. "Lady Mannering must be well pleased with the success of all her efforts."

"Successful indeed." His laughing eyes did not waver from hers.

"The flowers and other decorations are both lovely and tasteful," she said, laboring onward. "Do you not agree, my lord?"

"I have not looked to see, but I will take your word for it."

He was *flirting* with her, she realized in sudden shock. He was implying that he had eyes for no one but her. And indeed, he was matching action to implication. She felt an uncomfortable and unfamiliar rush of physical awareness—and then indignation again.

"Now it is *your* turn to choose a topic of conversation," she said, her voice deliberately disdainful to mask her discomfort.

He laughed softly. "A man does not need to converse when he is dancing with a beautiful woman," he said. "He can be content merely to *feel*. To indulge all his five senses to the full. Conversation is a mere distraction."

It was not just the outrageous words that made her heart beat faster. It was the way they were spoken. Softly. In a low, velvet voice that wrapped itself about her as if she were somehow naked to its touch. As if the two of them were alone together in the ballroom— or perhaps somewhere altogether more private.

And then suddenly they *were* alone and in relative darkness. She had not noticed that they were dancing close to the French windows until he had twirled her right through them and they were alone—or almost so—on the balcony beyond the candlelight.

Lauren was shocked to the depths of her soul.

"And light can be a distraction too," he said, tightening his hand at her waist so that for a moment she became even more aware of his nearness and feared that her bosom would brush against his chest. His head dipped closer to her own as he spoke so that she felt the warmth of his breath kiss her cheek. "As can crowds of people."

How dared he! She had been quite right to suspect . . . No gentleman . . .

But he had not stopped dancing, and with one more twirl they were back in the ballroom, having entered it through the other French windows less than a minute after leaving it. The withering setdown that was forming on her lips died unspoken as she met his laughing eyes and was once more caught up in the magic of the dance with a virile, attractive partner. Her little rebellion was proving undeniably enjoyable, she admitted ruefully to herself. He was a practiced charmer, of course. Lauren Edgeworth was not the sort of person with whom men flirted. She never had been even when she had been young and happy.

Now for the first time in her life she was being flirted with. And it felt rather pleasant—provided she did not for a moment allow herself to be beguiled by it.

She did not attempt any further conversation. Neither did he.

When the waltz was over, Viscount Ravensberg offered his arm to escort her back to her own party.

"I will not suggest leading you to the refreshment room, Miss Edgeworth," he said, the laughter in his voice now as well as his eyes, "even though I daresay you are *very* thirsty by now. Your family would not approve. They can scarce wait for you to return to their midst so that they can inform you that you have just risked your reputation by waltzing with London's most notorious rakehell."

"And have I?" she asked him.

"Waltzed with a rakehell? Oh, undoubtedly," he murmured.

"Thank you, my lord," she said politely when he had returned her to Aunt Sadie's side. She regarded him with deliberate, cool hauteur. He was not even *ashamed* of his own reputation?

"The pleasure was all mine, Miss Edgeworth," he told her, and before she could realize his intent, he had possessed himself of the hand she had just removed from his sleeve and raised it to his lips. Her hand was gloved, but even so the gesture seemed starkly, shockingly intimate. She resisted the urge to snatch away her hand as if it had been scalded and so draw unwelcome attention to herself. There was nothing so very improper about such a gesture, after all.

And then he was gone—not just from her side, but from the ballroom itself. She watched him go with considerable relief—and with a strange, unwilling awareness that the rest of the evening was going to seem very flat indeed.

Perhaps even the rest of her life, she thought with uncharacteristic hyperbole.

3

*D*espite the lateness of her return home from the ball, Lauren was up at her usual time the next morning to accompany Elizabeth on her daily walk in Hyde Park. The air was brisk and chill, though it promised fair for later in the day.

"Exercise *does* feel good," the duchess said as they approached the house on their return. "I feel remarkably fit despite a growing ungainliness, and I am quite sure it is the walking and fresh air that does it, despite Lyndon's anxieties."

Marriage suited Elizabeth, Lauren reflected. She had wed for the first time just seven months before. Pregnancy suited her too. There was a new glow about her.

The footman who opened the door to their knock bowed deferentially as he stood aside to allow them in. "A bouquet has been delivered for Miss Edgeworth, your grace," he said. "Mr. Powers had it carried into the salon."

"For me?" Lauren asked in some astonishment.

But Elizabeth was laughing as she took Lauren's arm and turned her in the direction of the visitors' salon, which led off the hall. "A bouquet the morning after a ball?" she said. "Goodness me, Lauren, you have a *beau*."

"Nonsense!" Lauren winced. "I daresay it is from Mr. Bartlett-Howe. He danced with me twice last evening and led me in to supper. But I *did* try not to encourage him. How very embarrassing."

"A gentleman's admiration need never embarrass you, Lauren," Elizabeth said, "even if you cannot return it."

Lauren bit her lip when she entered the salon and saw the handsome bouquet of at least two dozen red rosebuds amid lavish sprays of fern, already arranged in a crystal vase. She crossed the room and picked up the card that was propped against the vase. She hoped fervently he had not made a cake of himself with extravagant sentiments.

"They are quite lovely," Elizabeth said from behind her. "Roses must have been difficult to find this early in the year. And exorbitantly expensive, I daresay. Poor Mr. Bartlett-Howe. He is so very earnest and worthy." But there was a tremor of laughter in her voice.

"Alas," the writing on the card said, "I could find no violets to do justice to your eyes." The signature was scrawled in a bold, careless hand. "Ravensberg."

His laughing gray eyes, his devil-may-care smile, his slender grace, his male vitality, the indefinable air of danger that clung about him— Lauren had seen them all behind her closed eyelids as she had tried to fall asleep after the ball. And she had pictured the same man half naked in his skin-tight breeches, uttering shocking profanities. And holding a young woman in his arms and kissing her with obvious enthusiasm.

"The flowers are not from Mr. Bartlett-Howe," she said. "They are from Viscount Ravensberg. I waltzed with him last evening."

The duchess looked over her shoulder at the card. "Oh, goodness," she said gaily, "he is smitten indeed, Lauren. He has complimented your eyes. Who is he? The name is not familiar."

"He told me," Lauren said, replacing the card against the vase, "that he sought an introduction to me to discover if my gown matched my eyes in color. Have you ever heard anything more absurd?"

"He does not sound like the sort of gentleman the Earl of Sutton would present to you." Elizabeth's voice still shook with amusement. "It must have been Joseph, the rogue."

"It was Lady Mannering," Lauren said. "Aunt Sadie and Wilma almost had the vapors. They told me after I had danced with him that I must cut his acquaintance if he should presume upon it again. Uncle Webster called him a black sheep. Joseph told me he was a cavalry officer until recently. He is heir to the Earl of Redfield."

"Ah." Elizabeth nodded. "Yes, of course. The earl's eldest son died a year or two ago, I remember."

"Elizabeth?" Lauren turned to look at her, and she could feel her cheeks grow hot. "He is the gentleman who was fighting in the park last week."

"Oh, dear." But Elizabeth, after the first moment of surprise, chose to laugh again rather than blanch with horror. "Poor Lauren. You must have felt trapped indeed when Lady Mannering presented him and good manners forced you to dance with him—to *waltz* with him, did you say? And now he is sending you flowers. I did notice on that infamous occasion, of course, that he is a remarkably handsome young man."

"Not extraordinarily handsome." Lauren flushed. "Next time I see him, if there *is* a next time, I shall incline my head just so, thank him for the roses, and make it perfectly clear that I desire no further acquaintance with him."

"You depress pretension so well," Elizabeth said, her eyes dancing with merriment. "There is no more perfect lady than Lauren Edgeworth." She linked her arm through her niece's. "Now, let us go for breakfast. I shall have a footman carry the vase up to your sitting room so that you may be reminded for the next few days that there is a gentleman in town who is so lost in admiration for your eyes that he searched for flowers to match them in beauty—and was forced to settle for roses instead."

"It is no laughing matter, Elizabeth," Lauren said reproachfully, though she smiled despite herself and then chuckled.

Kit jumped down from the high seat of his curricle in Grosvenor Square and tossed the ribbons to his tiger, who had already scrambled down from his perch behind and rushed to the horses' heads. Kit approached the front door of the Duke of Portfrey's town house and rapped the knocker. He had ascertained ahead of time that this was one of the afternoons on which the duchess was regularly at home to callers.

At least Lauren Edgeworth was beautiful, he thought. Extremely lovely, in fact, even if one discounted those extraordinary, almost smoky violet eyes. She was no young girl, of course, but then the dignity of extra years enhanced her good looks rather than detracting from them. He was almost thirty himself and was not remotely interested in simpering young misses. Miss Edgeworth bore herself with proud grace and wore on her face the sort of perpetual half smile he had seen on certain Greek statues. Last evening she had given the distinct impression that she was immune to charm and humor and even the mildest attempt at flirtation. He had been somewhat disconcerted by her chilly demeanor, if the truth were known.

But therein lay the challenge.

The door opened, the ducal butler bowed with such stiff hauteur that the uninitiated might have mistaken him for the duke himself, and Kit tossed his card onto the silver salver the man held.

"Viscount Ravensberg to call upon Miss Edgeworth," he said and stepped boldly into the hall.

It was to be easier than he had expected. Perhaps so few visitors were turned away on these at-home days that it did not even occur to the butler to carry the card upstairs first to ascertain that the lady was willing to receive him. Or perhaps the butler recognized his name as the sender of roses this morning and assumed his visit in person would be welcome. Or perhaps it had not occurred to Portfrey—as it doubtless would have to Anburey—to leave instructions that he was to be denied admittance if he called.

"Follow me, if you please, my lord," the butler said with another bow before leading the way to the staircase.

The sound of voices engaged in polite conversation wafted from the drawing room as soon as a footman opened the doors at their approach. The butler stepped into the doorway.

"Viscount Ravensberg for Miss Edgeworth, your grace," he announced.

An unnatural silence fell as Kit strode into the room. He recognized Sutton and Attingsborough in one swift glance about the room. And he saw too that Lauren Edgeworth, seated in the middle of a group close to the window, was rising to her feet, a look of astonishment on her face. A handsome lady of regal bearing—despite the visible evidence that she was breeding—was hurrying toward him, her right hand outstretched, a smile of polite welcome on her face. Kit bowed to her.

"Your grace," he said and took her offered hand in his.

"Lord Ravensberg. How delightful." If she was shocked at his appearance in her drawing room or chagrined with her butler for allowing him up without question, she was too well bred to show it.

"Ravensberg?" The Duke of Portfrey, whom Kit knew by sight, had come to stand beside his duchess. He was rather more poker-faced than she.

"I have come to pay my respects to Miss Edgeworth. She was gracious enough to dance with me last evening," Kit explained. The room, he was aware, was half filled with visitors. Most of them were still gaping at him rather as if Portfrey's butler had just committed the faux pas of ushering the chimney sweep into their presence. This moment, he suspected, would be discussed with some relish in a few more drawing rooms before the afternoon was out.

Miss Edgeworth came toward him herself, then, and the duke and duchess returned their attention to their other visitors. Those same guests had recovered their manners and were resuming their interrupted conversations.

"How kind of you to call, my lord," she said. "Thank you for the roses. They are exquisite."

If the roses were in front of her face at that particular moment, he thought, they would surely freeze upon their stems, her gaze was so cold.

"It was not merely the reflection of your gown, then," he said softly, dipping his head a little closer to hers. "Today you wear green, but your eyes are still unmistakably violet." She looked every bit as lovely as she had last evening even though her dark, glossy hair was dressed with a great deal more simplicity today.

She showed not the slightest pleasure in the implied compliment.

"Do have a seat, my lord," she said with gracious condescension— a stranger would surely have mistaken *her* for the duchess. She turned and indicated an empty chair in the midst of the crowd of young people among whom she had been sitting. "I shall fetch you a cup of tea."

When she took her place again, he noticed that she sat very straight, her spine not quite touching the back of her chair. She launched into conversation about music, and a spirited discussion of various composers and the relative merits of different solo musical instruments followed.

Kit did not attempt to participate but amused himself by observing the other members of the group. His appearance had obviously discomposed several of them. The red-haired Lady Wilma Fawcitt was looking prunish, Sutton haughty, Attingsborough watchful and faintly amused. The skeletal young man whose name had escaped Kit for the moment was looking irritated, George Stennson openly hostile. Miss Edgeworth seemed the only one who was serenely unaware of his very existence. Kit sipped his tea.

"Miss Edgeworth," he said at last, taking advantage of a brief lull in the conversation, "would you allow me the honor of driving you to the park in my curricle later this afternoon?"

He was gazing directly at her and so was fully aware of the momentary widening of her lovely eyes and parting of her lips. The next moment she was looking coolly back at him, her expression politely

bland. He was sure she was about to refuse him. Perhaps he had proceeded too precipitously. How would he win his wager if she said no?

"Oh, I say," the skeletal, still unidentified young man said indignantly, "I came to ask the same favor, Miss Edgeworth, but thought
to do the correct thing and wait until I could speak privately with you
when I took my leave. I was here before Viscount Ravensberg," he
added feebly.

Kit raised his eyebrows. "I do beg your pardon," he said. "Did I do
the *incorrect* thing? Having spent so many years of my adult life away
from England, I must confess myself unsure of the finer points of
etiquette." With his eyes he laughed at Lauren Edgeworth.

"Oh, I say!" The anonymous gentleman sounded distinctly uncomfortable. "I did not mean to imply—"

"I believe," Attingsborough said smoothly, "it might have been for
this afternoon that you and I made our appointment to drive to the
library together, Lauren. You will refresh my memory if I am wrong."

"Sutton has quite set his heart on taking you and me for a turn in
his new barouche after tea, Lauren," Lady Wilma said with a toss of
her red curls. She tittered. "I am quite counting on you to act as my
chaperone."

Kit continued to smile into Lauren Edgeworth's violet eyes, which
had not wavered from his own. There was not the faintest suggestion
of an answering smile there.

She looked away. "No, you are wrong, Joseph," she said. "It was
not for today. And you certainly do not need a chaperone when riding in an open carriage with your betrothed, Wilma. Perhaps some
other day, Mr. Bartlett-Howe? Thank you, Lord Ravensberg. That
would be very pleasant."

He had the other members of the group to thank, of course, Kit
realized as he rose to take his leave. He was quite certain she had been
going to refuse him until they had all rushed in so gallantly to rescue
her from the horror of being obliged to drive out with a notorious
rakehell. She might be cold and imperturbably self-contained, his intended bride, but she was not immune to a challenge.

It was an intriguing thought.

"Until later, then, Miss Edgeworth," he said, bowing to her, nodding affably to the group at large, and then strolling across the room to take his leave of the Duchess of Portfrey.

He grinned as he ran down the steps outside the house a few minutes later and summoned his tiger, who was walking the horses about the square. Breaching the formidable defenses of Miss Lauren Edgeworth was going to be a challenge worthy of his best efforts. He must hope, perhaps, that all her relatives and friends would come to his assistance by persistently warning her against him and attempting to shield her from him—the idiots.

But for a while at least later in the afternoon he would have her all to himself.

Lauren sat straight-backed beside Viscount Ravensberg, holding her parasol over her head with both hands to shield her complexion from the harmful rays of the sun. She was unaccustomed to riding in a sporting curricle, and she felt very far above the ground and alarmingly unsafe. But it would be unladylike to show a lack of trust in the skill of the gentleman plying the ribbons by clinging to the rail beside her.

The gloved hands that held the ribbons were slim. They were also demonstrably capable of controlling his high-spirited and perfectly matched pair of grays. His legs, encased in tight, biscuit-colored pantaloons and supple, highly polished Hessian boots, were slender but shapely and well muscled in all the right places.

Shocked at the direction her thoughts had taken, Lauren flexed her hands on the handle of her parasol and looked determinedly away from him as he turned his team with effortless skill between the gateposts into the park. It was the fashionable hour, the time of day when the *beau monde* turned out in large numbers to parade on horseback, on foot, and in a variety of different carriages, intent upon seeing and being seen, upon imparting and ingesting all the latest gossip.

Lauren was about to provide them with a new topic, if Wilma was to be believed. She had raised a number of eyebrows by consenting to waltz with the infamous Viscount Ravensberg last evening. Yet now, just the day after, she had agreed to drive with him in the park. In a sporting vehicle, no less. Without a maid. Wilma had quite untruthfully declared herself speechless and had called upon Joseph, Lord Sutton, and Elizabeth to talk sense into Lauren. Only Lord Sutton had complied with her request. Miss Edgeworth must invent some indisposition and send down her regrets when Viscount Ravensberg came to fetch her, he had advised. She would not, after all, he was certain, wish to put her spotless reputation in jeopardy simply because she was too courteous to give a rogue the cut direct.

"If anyone has anything to say on the subject of Lauren's reputation," the Duke of Portfrey had said with languid hauteur, directing his quizzing glass at Wilma's betrothed, "he may address himself to me."

Lauren's lips quirked with unexpected amusement at the memory. But really, would she be here now if everyone had left her alone to make her own response to Lord Ravensberg's invitation? She had never thought of herself as a willfully stubborn person. *Was* she? Certainly she had avoided the parade in the park since her arrival in London. But there was no need to continue to do so. She had faced the *ton* last evening. And it was unexceptionable to drive out in public places with a gentleman who had been properly presented to her, even if he was a notorious rake.

"Well, Miss Edgeworth." Having negotiated the tricky turn into the park, the viscount turned his head to look at her. "We seem to have exhausted the topic of the weather."

Lauren twirled her parasol. She *had* been unmannerly enough to allow their conversation to lapse. She wondered briefly if he had practiced that particular look before a glass until he had perfected it—that laughter-filled expression that started in his eyes and sometimes did not even reach his mouth to become a proper smile. It was quite disconcerting and interfered considerably with her thought processes. It was one of those things that made a rake appealing to women, she supposed.

"Your father is the Earl of Redfield, my lord?" she asked.

"I am his heir," he replied, "the elder of his two surviving sons. My elder brother died almost two years ago."

"I am sorry," she said.

"So am I." He flashed her a rueful glance. "The last time I saw Jerome I broke his nose and my father banished me from Alvesley and told me never to return."

Gracious! Lauren was intensely embarrassed. That it might be true was shocking enough, but why would he air such very dirty linen before a stranger—and a lady, at that?

"I have shocked you." The viscount grinned at her.

"I believe, my lord," she said with sudden insight, "you fully intended to do so. I ought not to have asked about your father."

"Let me return the favor," he said. "You have lived most of your life at Newbury Abbey, but you have no blood relationship to the family there. Who is—or was—your father?"

"He was Viscount Whitleaf," she said. "He died when I was two years old. Less than a year later my mother took me to Newbury and married the Earl of Kilbourne's brother."

"Indeed?" he said. "And does your mother still live?"

"They left on a wedding journey two days after their nuptials," she told him, "and never returned. There were occasional letters and packages for a number of years and then . . . nothing."

The smile was gone from his face when he glanced at her this time. "You do not know, then," he asked her, "whether your mother lives or has died? Or your stepfather?"

"Certainly they are both dead," she said, "though where or when or how I do not know." It was something she almost never spoke of. She had locked away the hurt, the sense of abandonment, the feeling of incompletion, a long time ago.

They were drawing closer to the press of carriages and horses and pedestrians that were making the slow circuit of the daily parade.

Lauren determinedly changed the subject. "Do you come here often?" she asked.

He laughed across at her. "You mean apart from the mornings," he asked in his turn, "on or close to Rotten Row?"

She could feel herself flush and twirled her parasol again. More and more, she was convinced that he was no gentleman. He *had* seen her, then? And was not ashamed to admit it? No gentleman . . .

"You ride there in the mornings?" she asked.

But he was unwilling to have the subject turned. "That kiss," he said, "was a milkmaid's way of thanking me for felling the three thugs who had accosted her and demanded certain favors she was unwilling to grant."

Was *that* what the fight had been all about? He had taken on *three* men in order to defend a milkmaid's honor?

"It was *ample* reward," he said before she could frame the words with which to approve his motive even if not his actions. He was deliberately trying to shock her—again, she realized. Why? He touched his whip to the brim of his hat as two ladies rode by with their grooms, their eyes avid with curiosity.

"A gentleman," Lauren said with prim reproof, "would not have asked any payment at all."

"But how ungallant," he said, "to refuse a reward freely offered. Could a gentleman do such a thing, Miss Edgeworth?"

"A gentleman would not so obviously enjoy himself," she said and then glared at him indignantly when he threw back his head and laughed—just when they were close enough to a vast crowd of their peers to draw attention. She twirled her parasol smartly, but there was no chance of further conversation on the topic. Why had she allowed herself to be drawn anyway?

The following fifteen minutes were spent driving at a snail's pace around the circuit taken by other carriages and riders, smiling and nodding, stopping every few yards to converse with acquaintances. Wilma and Lord Sutton were there, of course, as was Joseph. There were a few other people Lauren knew, Elizabeth's friends whom she had met during the past three weeks, and others to whom she had been presented at the ball last evening. And there were a number of Lord Ravensberg's friends, who rode up beside the curricle to exchange pleasantries with him and to be presented to her.

It was not a difficult occasion to endure. Having made a public appearance last evening, she no longer felt the dread that had kept her in virtual hiding for over a year. It was a bright, sunny day and she was enjoying herself far more than she ought—and far more than she would have in Mr. Bartlett-Howe's company, she thought treacherously. But how could the viscount have openly referred to that scandalous fight in the park when he should be properly mortified to realize that she had witnessed it? He had fought in a woman's defense—in a milkmaid's defense. Most men would not even have noticed the distress of a woman so far beneath them in rank.

Most gentlemen within hailing distance acknowledged him and seemed genuinely pleased to see him. Most ladies either openly ignored him or nodded to him with distant hauteur. But many of them, old and young alike, stole covert glances at him. He was indeed a gentleman whom it was impossible not to notice. He exuded vitality, laughter, and a careless disregard of sober propriety. And *she* was the only woman with whom he had danced last evening. *She* was the one he had invited to drive with him this afternoon. She, Lauren Edgeworth, the very personification of sober propriety.

The thought ought not to be flattering at all.

Viscount Ravensberg steered his curricle clear of the crowds before they had made the complete circuit. Soon, she thought, disappointed despite herself, they would be back in Grosvenor Square and she must make clear to him that she would not welcome any further attempt to make her the object of his gallantry. But there was a question she could not resist asking, unmannerly as it might be.

"Why did you invite me to dance last evening?" she asked him. "And why only me? You left immediately afterward. Why did you send me roses on the strength of that single encounter? Why did you ask me to drive with you this afternoon?"

Oh, dear. More than one question, all of them unpardonably rude. And she had plenty of time in which to realize the fact and feel increasingly uncomfortable. So uncomfortable that she did not immediately notice that he had turned his curricle, not onto the main thoroughfare leading out onto the streets of London but onto another path that led deeper into a less traveled, more wooded area of the park. By the time she did notice, it was too late to protest. *This* would certainly be remarked upon, she thought—first she had waltzed with a notorious rakehell, then she had driven with him, and now she was allowing him to drive off alone with her.

"Perhaps you have not looked at yourself in a glass lately, Miss Edgeworth," he said at last.

"But Lady Mannering's ballroom was filled with ladies lovelier than I," she said. "And most of them considerably younger."

"I cannot answer for your youth," he said, "but I can for your beauty. If you did not realize that you were by far the loveliest lady at the ball, then indeed you have not looked at your reflection lately."

"How absurd." She had never had a great deal of patience with flattery. Or with ladies who fished for compliments. Was that what she had just done? If so, she had been served well. The loveliest lady at the ball, indeed! The path dipped into a hollow bordered on either side by giant oak trees, whose branches met in an arch overhead.

"It is your eyes that make you uniquely lovely, of course." He slanted her a look. "I have never seen any others of quite their color or beauty."

This was all highly improper. But she had only herself to blame.

"You knew who I was, I suppose," she said. "Someone had pointed me out to you. You knew what happened to me last year. Was it curiosity, then?"

He angled a penetrating look at her. "To dance with a bride who had been abandoned at the altar?" he said. "I hope the park at Newbury is a large one. My guess is that Kilbourne must be constantly whipping himself all about its perimeter at his foolishness in having married someone else, doubtless on a momentary impulse, and so having lost the chance of having you."

She despised herself for taking comfort from his words. For longer than a year she had felt so . . . unattractive. "Well, you are wrong, sir," she said. "His marriage to the countess was and is a love match." They were driving in a cool, verdant shade. Lauren lowered her parasol to her lap though she did not close it.

"And yours to him would not have been?" Again that swift, penetrating look.

Lauren raised her chin and stared straight ahead. How had she trapped herself into this? "That is an impertinent question, my lord."

He chuckled softly. "My humblest apologies, ma'am," he said. "But Kilbourne's loss is my gain. I asked you to dance because even across Lady Mannering's ballroom I was struck by your loveliness and felt compelled to discover who you were. I sent the roses because after waltzing with you I could do nothing else but return home and lie awake half the night thinking of you. I called upon you this afternoon and invited you to drive with me here because I knew that if I did not see you again you would haunt my waking thoughts and my sleeping dreams for the rest of the summer."

Lauren's eyes widened with shock, but by the time he had finished speaking she was glaring at him in speechless anger. How foolishly gullible did he think she was?

"My lord," she said with all the cool dignity with which she had armed herself for most of her life, "no *gentleman* would so mock a lady. But then I have been warned that you are no gentleman, and with my own eyes I have beheld that it is true. Now my ears tell the same story. I would be obliged if you would return me to Grosvenor Square without further delay."

He had the gall to look across at her and chuckle softly. "You *did* ask, you know," he said, rearranging the ribbons so that they were in his right hand. With his left he possessed himself of one of her hands and raised it to his lips. "It would have been ungentlemanly of me to lie to a lady, would it not?"

"I suppose," she said with icy dignity, "you expected me to be easy prey to this blatant gallantry, Lord Ravensberg, since I am an *abandoned bride.* You thought to have some sport with me. You have failed. I came to town to offer my companionship to the Duchess of Portfrey, who is awaiting a confinement. I did not come to parade myself in the marriage mart. I am not in search of a husband and never will be. And even if I were, I would not fall an easy prey to such as you."

"To such as I." They were headed back in the direction of the park gates, she realized suddenly. "Have they told you very dreadful things about me, then, Miss Edgeworth? But of course they have. And with your own eyes you have seen me brawling half naked in the park and kissing a milkmaid. I have confessed to breaking my brother's nose and suffering the indignity of banishment from my boyhood home. I perceive that my chances of pursuing an acquaintance with you are remote indeed."

"Absolutely nonexistent." They drove clear of the shade of the trees and the sun beamed down on their heads as if in mockery.

"You have broken my heart." He turned his face to her again and gazed soulfully into her eyes—except that even now she could see laughter lurking in the depths of his.

"I doubt you have one to break," she retorted.

Neither of them spoke again after that. When the curricle came to a halt before the duke's door several minutes later, Lord Ravensberg's tiger came darting across the square, where he had been left earlier, and ran to the horses' heads. Lauren had no choice but to retain her high seat until his lordship had descended and come around the vehicle to help her alight. But even this he did not allow her to do with dignity. He set his hands on either side of her waist and swung her down to the pavement. He did not, as she expected for one horrified moment, allow her body to slide down his, but even so she was a mere few inches away from him when her feet found the ground. She looked at him, her face tight with indignation again.

"Thank you for the outing, my lord," she said with icy politeness. "Good-bye."

His smile lit his whole face with merriment and devilry. "Thank *you.*" He released his hold on her waist and made her an elegant bow. "Au revoir, Miss Edgeworth."

The front door was already open, Powers having noted her return home. Lauren walked up the steps and into the hall with unhurried dignity. She did not look back as the door closed behind her.

4

*S*utton?" Lord Farrington said. "Yes, I know him well enough, Ravensberg. We were up at Oxford at the same time. Cut up a few larks together. That was before he inherited the title and became head of the family and pillar of the community and intolerably stuffy."

"You are going to invite him to join a party of friends in your box at the theater next week," Kit told him. "With his betrothed, of course."

"Am I?" Lord Farrington replied. They were on horseback, cantering along Rotten Row rather earlier in the morning than usual. It was still almost deserted. "Am I permitted to ask why?"

"Because Lady Wilma Fawcitt is Miss Edgeworth's cousin," Kit reminded him. "Or stepcousin, to be precise. You are also going to invite her."

"Miss Edgeworth? Ah." His friend's voice was full of sudden comprehension. "And I suppose I am going to invite you too, Ravensberg. Or have you already invited yourself? And why, pray, should I help you win your wager when I stand to lose a hundred guineas?"

"Because you will be unable to resist your curiosity to watch the progress of my courtship," Kit said with a laugh. "And my chances are looking woefully slim, you will be delighted to know. I heaped gallantries upon her the day after the Mannering ball, when I drove her in the park, and instead of blushing and simpering, she did that icicle thing I was warned about and accused me of mocking her. I felt distinctly as if I were perched on top of the North Pole with no way down and no way home."

"You failed to charm her?" Lord Farrington threw back his head and laughed. "Are you losing your touch, Ravensberg?"

"In the week and a half since then," Kit continued, "I have looked in at a whole dreary array of balls and soirees and even a concert or two and have caught nary a glimpse of her. It is time to take a more active hand in my own fate. We have to entice her to the theater."

"*We?*" Lord Farrington turned his horse at the Queen's Gate end of the Row and headed back up it.

"And I think you should invite another couple or two as well," Kit said. "We must not appear too obvious, after all. Eminently respectable couples, I need scarcely add."

"Of course. And I am to forget to mention in the invitations that the infamous Lord Ravensberg is to be one of the party, I suppose?" his friend asked.

"No, no," Kit protested. "I would not win by foul means. She will be determined not to come when she knows I am to be there. Sutton and his betrothed, when they know it, will exert all their considerable influence to dissuade her from accepting. So will Anburey and his lady. And Attingsborough. Probably Portfrey and the duchess too, though I am not at all sure that I don't have an ally in that particular lady—she has a twinkling eye. Anyway, I count upon the discouraging chorus about Miss Edgeworth being loud enough to persuade her to come just to spite them all."

"Tut, tut. You may as well pay your debts now and resign yourself to your father's choice of a bride." Lord Farrington shook his head before prodding his horse to a gallop and leaving his unwary friend in his dust for a moment.

But winning his wager had become an appealing as well as a necessary challenge, Kit realized before going in pursuit. She was prim and proper and apparently without even a glimmering of a sense of humor. At the same time she was hauntingly beautiful, and she was not immune to a challenge. Certainly she did not allow her relatives to rule her. And she had shown some intelligence as well as spirit in spurning his deliberately blatant flatteries in the park. What would such a lady be like in bed? he wondered suddenly. It was an intriguing thought.

He needed to see her again. For the sake of his wager. For his chance to go to Alvesley on his own terms. And for the personal challenge of somehow penetrating that cool, ladylike façade—if there was anything beyond the façade to penetrate to, that was. There might well not be.

The roses had wilted after a few days. But one bud was still pressed between several heavy volumes a footman had carried up to Lauren's sitting room from the library below. It was too perfect to be allowed to die and be forgotten, she had told herself.

She had refused all further invitations to *ton* events after the Mannering ball and the drive in the park. She had gone shopping and walking for exercise. She had read several books from both the duke's collection and Hookham's subscription library. She had worked diligently at her embroidery and at her tatting. She had written almost daily letters to Gwendoline and Aunt Clara, Gwen's mother. She had even written one to Lily and had the duke enclose it with his daily missive—Lily was his daughter. If there was a certain boredom in her days, a certain restlessness—well, that was a lady's lot in life.

But on this particular evening she was riding in the Earl of Sutton's town carriage with the earl and Wilma. They were on their way to the theater at the invitation of Lord Farrington to watch a performance of Shakespeare's *King Lear*. Viscount Ravensberg was to be a member of the party.

"You must sit between Sutton and me when we arrive, Lauren,"

Wilma instructed, not for the first time, as the carriage drew up behind a couple of others close to the theater doors.

Wilma had been vociferous in her determination not to accept her invitation, and she had had a firm ally in her betrothed. But a couple of weeks ago Lauren had discovered a hitherto unsuspected side to herself—a stubborn disinclination to have her activities ordered for her by others, however well meaning. All her life she had behaved the way she believed a lady ought to behave. And look where it had got her. She had informed Wilma that she was accepting her own invitation even though she had never met Lord Farrington. She was still not sure what she would have done if Wilma had not considered it her duty to accompany her with Lord Sutton.

The carriage inched forward and a doorman opened the door and let down the steps. A gentleman stepped forward from the throng about the theater doors and reached up a helping hand.

"Miss Edgeworth?" Viscount Ravensberg said. "Allow me."

He looked incredibly dashing and handsome in his swinging black opera cloak and silk hat. Lauren set a hand in his even as Wilma and Lord Sutton murmured ineffectual protests.

"Thank you, my lord." She stepped down to the pavement.

"A violet cloak," he said, "with a matching gown beneath. But the shade is paler than your eyes this time—and less lustrous. I have missed you. I have looked for you everywhere and not seen you. I had to descend to this stratagem." He led her through the crowded foyer of the theater toward the staircase up to the boxes.

"Why?" she asked.

He countered with another question. "Why did you accept?"

"Perhaps," she said, "because I admire the work of Mr. Shakespeare."

He chuckled.

"Lauren," Wilma called from behind them, "do remember to sit between Sutton and me. I need you to tell me what is happening on stage. I am such a dunce. I never did understand all that archaic language."

"There," Lord Ravensberg murmured. "Your excuse to escape my lascivious clutches has just been presented to you, Miss Edgeworth. If you sit beside me, as you are invited to do, you may find me whispering naughty nothings into your ear all evening and touching you in places I ought not to touch you under cover of the darkness."

His words were shockingly outrageous. They were meant to be, she realized, just as his lavish praise of her beauty had been meant to provoke rather than deceive her that day in the park. She would not show her indignation. She would merely be playing into his hands and affording him amusement, she suspected. Though why it should amuse a man like him to goad someone like her she did not at all understand.

"If I had wished to escape your clutches, my lord," she told him, "I would have remained at home."

"Provocative words indeed," he murmured before stopping outside one of the boxes and opening the door.

A couple of minutes later, having been introduced to Lord Farrington, Miss Janet Merklinger, and Mr. and Mrs. Merklinger, the young lady's parents, Lauren seated herself on a velvet-covered chair at the front of the box even though Wilma, still in conversation with Mrs. Merklinger, tried to snatch at her arm to detain her.

Viscount Ravensberg took the seat beside her.

Despite all her good intentions Lauren felt a prickle of awareness along the arm closest to him and a stirring of anticipation that felt very like excitement. If he should be forward or impertinent or otherwise outrageous, she would deal him a sharp setdown. She almost looked forward to pitting her wits against his.

Life was usually so very dull and predictable.

She sat, as he expected, without touching the back of her chair with any part of her spine. But it would be inaccurate to describe her posture as ramrod straight. There was an elegant arch to her back. Indeed, there was grace in every line of her body. A disciplined grace, that was. And perhaps an unconscious one. Certainly she watched the play with all her attention, her hands motionless in her lap, her closed fan clasped in one of them.

Kit watched her.

Did she realize that he did so? Had she noticed the considerable stir of interest their entry into Farrington's box had aroused in the pit and the other boxes? Numerous quizzing glasses and lorgnettes had swung their way, and heads had moved together in that way people have when exchanging gossip. There had been a flurry of talk, of course, when he had driven her in Hyde Park the day after dancing with her at the Mannering ball—particularly, according to Rush, over the fact that he had borne her off along one of the shadier paths instead of completing the social circuit with her. But two weeks had passed since that occasion with nothing to fan the flames of speculation.

She seemed oblivious to the interest she had aroused. She turned her attention away from the stage only when the first act ended.

"I had forgotten," she said, "what it is like to watch a live performance of a play. One forgets one's very existence, does one not?"

"I have not been watching the play," he confessed, deliberately lowering his voice.

Her lips compressed in an almost imperceptible expression of annoyance, and she opened the fan in her lap. Clearly she understood his meaning. Equally clearly she still did not approve of his form of light flirtation. He did not approve of it himself. He was capable of far more effective subtleties. But he found it amusing to discover how far he could push her before she lost her cool control over her temper—and to discover too what would happen if ever he could push her so far. Was there anything interesting behind the cool façade?

Everyone else in the box had risen. Farrington was bearing Miss Merklinger off in pursuit of a glass of lemonade. Her parents, very correctly, were following closely behind.

"Lauren." Lady Wilma Fawcitt touched her cousin on the shoulder. "Sutton has offered to escort us across to Lord Bridges's box to pay our respects to dear Angela. Do come along." She smiled graciously at Kit. "Goodness, you will feel quite abandoned, Lord Ravensberg. But we will be back for the second act."

Lady Bridges was Sutton's sister, Kit recalled. He got to his feet. Miss Edgeworth did not. She fanned her face slowly and set one slim arm along the velvet rest at the edge of the box.

"I believe I will remain here, Wilma," she said. "Do please convey my respects to Lady Bridges."

Interesting!

Sutton and his betrothed had little choice then but to proceed with their visit to the Bridges's box, which was at quite the opposite side of the theater. Miss Edgeworth looked down into the pit and continued to fan her cheeks as Kit resumed his seat.

"You were a reconnaissance officer in the Peninsula, Lord Ravensberg," she said without turning her head to look at him. "A spy."

She had been learning things about him, then? "I prefer the first appellation," he said. "The word *spy* conjures up images of cloaks and daggers and hair-raising exploits of reckless derring-do."

She turned to look at him then. "I would have expected such a life to appeal to you," she said. "Was it not like that?"

He thought of the long, solitary journeys, sometimes on horseback, more often than not on foot, over hostile terrain no matter what the season. He thought of the endless wild-goose chases, of dodging French scouting parties; of making painstaking contact with partisan groups in both Portugal and Spain; of having to deal patiently and tactfully with petty dictators and wild hotheads and cruel, fanatical nationalists; of the unspeakable atrocities that happened far from the battle lines—the torture, the rapine, the executions. Of the weariness of body and spirit and the constant drain on the emotions. Of his brother . . .

"It was far more mundane and dreary, I'm afraid," he told her with a laugh.

"And yet," she said, "you were singled out for commendation in several dispatches. You saved your country on numerous occasions. You are a military hero."

"My country?" He considered. "I doubt it. Sometimes as a military man one wonders exactly what it is one fights for."

"Surely," she said, "one fights for what is right. One fights on the side of goodness against the forces of evil."

If that were so, why was insomnia such a problem for him? And the frequent nightmares when he *did* sleep?

"Do you believe, then," he asked her, "that every Frenchman—and every Frenchwoman—is evil, that every Briton and Russian and Prussian and Spaniard is good?"

"Of course not," she said. "But Napoléon Bonaparte is evil. Anyone who fights for him is evil by association."

"I suppose," he said, "France is full of mothers with sons slain in battle who believe the British soldier to be evil incarnate."

She opened her mouth to speak but closed it again.

"It is *war* that is evil," she said at last. "But then wars are provoked and fought by men. Did you acquire the scar beneath your jaw in battle?"

It ran from the hinge of his jaw on the left side to the point of his chin. "At Talavera," he said. "I did not complain too loudly about it even at the time. Two inches lower and I would have been playing a harp for the rest of eternity." He grinned at her and ran one knuckle lightly down the arm that held her fan, from the edge of her short, puffed sleeve to the top of her glove. Her skin was silky and warm.

All around them was a loud hum of conversation as members of the audience visited one another and shared impressions of the play and other gossip. And yet suddenly the two of them seemed very alone. He felt a totally unexpected stirring of sexual desire for this woman who did nothing whatsoever to arouse it. She possessed beauty in abundance but no overt femininity. He had not even seen a genuine smile on her face. Yet his body wanted hers.

She drew her arm away from him. "I have given you no permission to touch me, my lord," she said. "In fact, I have given you no encouragement at all. Why did you arrange this . . . stratagem tonight?"

"I was tired of attending every interminable social event of the

Season," he said. "I have been becoming alarmingly respectable. How dull for the *ton* to have had no outrageous exploit of mine with which to titillate its conversations during the past week or so. I have been compelled to take action."

"If I had smiled and fawned over you at Lady Mannering's ball," she said, "and if I had simpered and giggled during the drive in Hyde Park, you would have lost interest in me in a moment, Lord Ravensberg."

"Good Lord, yes," he agreed. Perceptive of her.

"I would thank you not to take the Lord's name in vain," she said so primly that he was momentarily enchanted. "I see that I have behaved in quite the wrong manner with you. I should have *encouraged* you."

"There is always time," he suggested, moving his chair half an inch closer to hers, "to mend your ways, Miss Edgeworth."

"You mock me," she said. "You laugh at me—constantly. Your eyes never stop laughing."

"*Smiling*," he said. "You do me an injustice. My eyes smile with delight because every time they behold you they see a woman so beautiful that no one after her is worth looking at—or thinking of or dreaming about."

He was enjoying himself enormously, he realized—and wooing her in quite a different way than he had planned, with a quite blatant lack of subtlety. But there *was* no conventional way of wooing this woman, he suspected.

"I rest my case," she replied, a faint blush coloring her cheeks. "There is no common ground between us, my lord, upon which any sort of meaningful relationship might be built—if that is your intent. We are as different as night and day."

"And yet night and day meet fleetingly at twilight and dawn," he said, lowering his voice again and narrowing his eyes and moving his head a quarter of an inch closer to hers. "And their merging sometimes affords the beholder the most enchanted moments of all the twenty-four hours. A sunrise or a sunset can be ablaze with brilliance and arouse all the passion, all the yearning, in the soul of the be-holder." He grinned wickedly at her and touched his fingertips to the back of her gloved hand.

She moved her hand sharply away and then, seeming to recollect that they were on public view, raised it gracefully in order to fan her flushed cheeks. "I know nothing of passion," she said. "You are wast-ing your time with me, my lord. I am not the sort of woman on whom words like these will have any effect whatsoever."

"The theater is certainly overwarm," he said softly, his eyes on her fan.

She ceased her movements abruptly and turned her head to look directly into his eyes. He expected her to move back when she saw how close they were, but she stood her ground, so to speak. He could sense anger hovering behind her control, and willed it to burst forth, even in this very public setting. Especially here, perhaps. They would instantly become a spectacular *ondit*. But he could almost see her rein-ing in her temper before she spoke.

"You would be well advised not to continue pursuing me after tonight," she said. "I will not accept any future invitation that in-cludes you, my lord. I am accustomed to moving in circles where gen-tlemen are unfailingly gentlemanly."

"How intolerably dull for you," he said.

"Perhaps," she said, plying her fan again, "I like a dull life. Dullness is much underrated. Perhaps I am a dull person."

"Then perhaps," he suggested, "you should marry someone like Bartlett-Howe or Stennson. Every time they move they are lost to view within a cloud of dust."

He thought for an intrigued moment that she was going to laugh. Then he was convinced that she was drawing breath in order to de-liver the blistering setdown he had been trying his damnedest—Lord knew why!—to provoke. But dash it, the door of the box opened be-fore she could either laugh or explode, and she turned her head away sharply to gaze down into the pit again.

Kit rose and bowed to Mrs. and Miss Merklinger, helped them re-sume their seats, and asked them how they had enjoyed the first act.

He grinned and winked at a poker-faced Farrington, and resumed his seat beside Lauren Edgeworth only moments before Sutton and Lady Wilma returned and regaled everyone with a résumé of every topic of conversation they had pursued with Lady Bridges and her party.

The second act of the play rescued them all from death by boredom.

5

*I*t rained intermittently for five days straight. It was impossible to walk any farther abroad than the back garden of the Duke of Portfrey's house during the brief intervals between heavy downpours of rain. Lauren would have been perfectly content to remain quietly indoors, keeping Elizabeth company and busying herself with her needle and her pen, but everything around her seemed to conspire against any such hope.

The Duchess of Anburey came the morning after the theater visit with gentle reproof for Lauren's having agreed to remain alone with Viscount Ravensberg when Wilma had very properly tried to draw her away to call at Lady Bridges's box. Even when Lauren pointed out that she had stayed in Lord Farrington's box from choice and that their tête-à-tête had been conducted in full view of any of the theater patrons who had cared to look, her aunt informed her that a lady could never be too careful of her reputation. Especially Lauren, under the circumstances, she added significantly.

She invited the Duke and Duchess of Portfrey and Lauren to dine the following evening. It would have been a reasonably pleasant family event, Lauren thought afterward, if it had not been for the presence of the lone outsider, another of the Earl of Sutton's worthy, dull friends, who was seated next to Lauren at dinner and scarcely left her side all evening. It was most provoking to be six and twenty years old, a jilted bride, so to speak, and the object of all the determinedly well-meaning matchmaking efforts of several of one's relatives.

Viscount Ravensberg did not remain without a mention. Lord Sutton regaled the company in the drawing room after dinner with an account of the viscount's latest scandalous escapade. He had made a spectacle of himself the day before by going for a swim in the Serpentine in Hyde Park in the middle of the day between rain showers, wearing only—well, the earl did not care to elaborate on *that* topic in the presence of ladies. Lord Ravensberg had been laughing merrily when he got out of the water and revealed himself in all his shocking dishabille—he had not even been wearing his boots! He had sketched a deep, mocking bow to Lady Waddingthorpe and Mrs. Healy-Ryde, who had stopped, despite the mortification of being witness to such a shocking sight, to do their duty and inform him that he was a disgrace to his name and his family and the uniform he had worn until so recently. It was they who had spread the story, of course, beginning in Lady Jersey's drawing room no more than an hour later.

The worthy young man assured Lauren with hushed solemnity that some gentlemen were not deserving of the name.

There were letters to and from home during that week, including one from Gwendoline, Lauren's cousin and dearest friend—more sister than either cousin or friend, in fact. They had grown up together and had been virtually inseparable for most of their lives. Gwen referred to a letter her mother, the dowager countess, had received from Aunt Sadie.

"It is evident that she is surrounding you with a veritable army of eligible suitors," Gwen had written. "Doubtless worthy and impossibly stuffy to a man. Poor Lauren! Is there anyone special—anyone *you* consider eligible? Oh, I know you have no wish for a beau, eligible or otherwise, but . . . *is* there?"

Lauren could picture the bright, mischievous grin Gwen would have worn while writing those words. But of course there was no one. Did he deliberately court notoriety? she wondered, her thoughts going off at a tangent. Swimming half naked in the Serpentine, indeed!

Gwen's letter ended with a sentence written in slightly darker ink, as if she had sat at the escritoire for a long time before adding it to the rest, dipping and redipping her pen into the inkwell as she did so.

"Lily and Neville called at the dower house this morning," the sentence read, "to bring the happy news that Lily is increasing."

That was all. No details. No description of how Lily must have been glowing with joy and Neville bursting with pride. No description of how Aunt Clara must have wept with delight at the prospect of holding her first grandchild—or of the pang of grief Gwen must have felt at the memory of losing her own unborn child in a miscarriage following the riding accident that had left her permanently lame.

Just the bare fact that Lily was going to have a baby. Lily and Elizabeth both—newly married and increasing and as happy as the day was long. While Lauren was planning to set up her own very lone spinster establishment later in the summer and convincing herself that it was what she wanted most in life.

Lily had written to her father with the news, of course. Lauren was with Elizabeth in the morning room when he brought the letter to share with his wife.

"Oh, has it happened, then, Lyndon?" Elizabeth asked, clasping her hands to her bosom. "Lily was quite convinced she was barren." Then she bit her lip and looked at Lauren, her eyes troubled.

Lauren smiled with all the warmth she could muster. "You must be very happy, your grace," she said.

"Indeed I am, Lauren." But he laughed ruefully. "Or I was until I recollected but a moment ago that now I will be plagued with anxieties for both my wife *and* my daughter."

Lauren put away the embroidery she had been working on and got to her feet to leave Elizabeth and the duke alone together.

And then on the sixth day a card was delivered to Lauren at breakfast. It was an invitation from Mrs. Merklinger to dine the following evening and then proceed with their party to the private box Mr. Merklinger had reserved at Vauxhall Gardens, where there was to be dancing as well as fireworks.

She had spoken very little with the Merklingers at the theater. She had no other acquaintance with them. The only explanation for their invitation to join what must be a small, select party was that Viscount Ravensberg was to be another of their guests. Somehow he had maneuvered this.

She had told him quite firmly that she would have nothing further to do with him. For six days it had seemed that he must have accepted her dismissal. She had been relieved. Oh, whom was she trying to deceive? The past six days had been almost intolerably tedious, though they had been no different from much of her life before them. She must refuse the invitation. It just would not do to fall prey to Viscount Ravensberg's mocking flatteries and deliberate attempts to shock her. They were so obviously insincere. She must refuse. And yet . . .

And yet Vauxhall Gardens of an evening were said to be enchanting.

And she had a curiosity to know how he meant to proceed with her now that she had made it quite clear that she was not susceptible to his flatteries.

And Aunt Sadie, Wilma, and Lord Sutton disapproved so very strongly of him. That was almost a recommendation in itself, she thought with guilty self-reproval.

And soon now Elizabeth's confinement would be over and Lauren must move on to . . . well, to the life she had chosen as the most desirable for herself.

And Lily was increasing. Neville was a married man, soon to be a father.

"What ought I to do?" She showed the invitation to Elizabeth, who read it through and handed it back.

"You are assuming Lord Ravensberg will be of the party?" she asked.

"Yes."

Elizabeth looked kindly at her. "What do you *want* to do?"

"He is an infamous rakehell," Lauren said. "Why would he feed gossip by swimming in the Serpentine and then laugh about it when caught and scolded?"

"He is also a remarkably attractive young man," Elizabeth said. "Attractive to *you*, Lauren. What are your wishes? I cannot tell you what to do. Is your disapproval of Viscount Ravensberg stronger than your attraction to him? That is the real question that needs answering."

"I am *not* attracted to him," Lauren protested.

"Then there is no harm, surely, in taking advantage of an opportunity to enjoy an evening at Vauxhall," Elizabeth said. "Unless you are actively repelled by him, that is."

"I am *not* repelled by him."

Elizabeth set her folded napkin beside her plate and rose from the table, spreading a hand over her swollen abdomen as she did so. "Lauren," she said, "both Lyndon and I are distressed for you that Lily's news has followed so soon upon your arrival here that you must wonder if you will ever escape your painful memories. No." She took Lauren's arm and led her in the direction of the morning room. "You must not deny it. I am perfectly well aware of how deeply attached you were to Neville. But please—oh, dear me, I have sworn to myself that I will not make the mistake Sadie is making and try to order your life for you." She sighed. "But I cannot altogether resist. Please, Lauren, do not imagine that your life is over or at least your chance for a happy, productive life. Only you can know what will make you happy, and if a quiet retirement from society is what will do it, then I will support you against all the Sadies of this world. But . . . No, I will positively say no more. Do you *really* want my advice concerning that invitation?"

"No," Lauren said after a moment's consideration. She smiled ruefully. "It was unfair of me to ask. I shall go. I have always wanted to see Vauxhall. And I am neither attracted to nor repelled by Lord

Ravensberg, Elizabeth. It is quite immaterial to me that he too will be one of Mrs. Merklinger's guests."

Elizabeth patted her arm.

Alone in her room a few minutes later, Lauren was suddenly struck by a memory—of words to which she had not been given a chance to respond at the time.

Then perhaps you should marry someone like Bartlett-Howe or Stennson. Every time they move they are lost to view within a cloud of dust.

How incredibly rude! How cruelly unkind! How absolutely delicious!

Lauren suddenly grabbed a cushion from a chair within reach and stuffed it against her mouth as she went off into whoops of laughter. Then she had to drop the cushion in order to find a handkerchief with which to mop at her brimming eyes.

He ought not to be encouraged, she told herself severely, even by this secret laughter.

It was already dark when they approached Vauxhall Gardens by boat. There was a bridge that could take them across the Thames by carriage, Merklinger had explained at dinner, but why waste a perfectly good opportunity to do the romantic thing and cross by boat, especially as all that infernal rain seemed to have ceased at last and it looked to be a bright night with all the stars out and the moon approaching the full?

Why indeed, Kit thought as he handed Miss Edgeworth into the boat and took his seat on the bench beside her. He had sat beside her at dinner too, Mrs. Merklinger having apparently made the assumption that they were a couple—just as she was determinedly making it about Farrington and her pretty little chit of a daughter. Farrington was being roundly ribbed about it among their circle of acquaintances.

"And so," Kit said, "they sailed away over the edge of the world to a land of wonder and enchantment. And carefree dalliance."

"We are merely being rowed across the River Thames to Vauxhall Gardens, my lord," she said. "A journey of ten minutes or so, I daresay."

At least she was speaking directly to him. She had avoided a tête-à-tête during dinner, pointedly directing most of her conversation to Merklinger on her other side.

"Ah, but Vauxhall *is* a wonderful, enchanted land," he told her. "And famous as a setting for dalliance and other romantic capers. Have you been there before?"

"No. And your conversation borders upon the offensive, my lord."

He wondered if she knew how delectable she looked when she was at her most prim and indignant, as she was now. Her already upright posture had taken on a distinct resemblance to a poker at the mention of dalliance. Her chin had lifted an inch. She gazed disdainfully off across the water instead of looking back at him. She was wearing the lavender cloak she had worn to the theater, its wide hood pulled halfway over her dark curls for the river crossing, though the evening was balmy. Beneath it she wore a high-waisted, long-sleeved gown of ivory lace over silk. He had wondered, when he first set eyes upon her earlier in the evening, how she could always appear to be the best-dressed lady at any gathering despite the comparative simplicity of her dresses. But the answer had come to him almost immediately. To add to her other ladylike perfections, she was also a woman of exquisite taste.

The realization somehow made this evening's task more daunting. There were ten days of his wager remaining. He was to be married to her within ten days or else be three hundred pounds the poorer. *Married* to her? Within ten days? Was it possible? But the word *impossible* had never been part of his vocabulary.

Kit listened to the babble of voices around them. Miss Merklinger and her cousin, Miss Abbott, were commenting on everything they saw with bubbling, youthful enthusiasm. But Lauren Edgeworth, having allowed plenty of time for her last scolding words to sink home, was speaking again, her face still half turned from him.

"Why were you swimming half clad in the Serpentine?" she was asking. "Why did you make such a public spectacle of yourself? Do you enjoy giving outrage wherever you go?"

"Ah." He chuckled. "You have been told about that, have you?"

"And yet you expect me to allow myself to have my name linked with yours?" she added.

"You would not wish for the acquaintance of someone who makes a spectacle of himself in public places?" he asked her. "Someone who courts notoriety? I am desolate. But the child was wailing pitifully, you must understand, and his nurse was at the very tail end of her tether. I do believe she was rapidly coming to the conclusion that her only remaining option was to smack him."

"*What* child?" She turned a frowning face toward him.

He chuckled. She looked beautiful even when she was cross. "I might have guessed," he said, "that those old tabbies would tell only part of the story. The child had a new boat, you see, which set off boldly and proudly for the distant horizon and held its course for all of one minute while he jumped up and down with glee and yelled loudly enough to do an infantry sergeant proud. And then it sank ignominiously without leaving so much as a bubble on the surface. It was several yards from shore by that time."

"And you dived in to retrieve it." Her tone held a mingling of incredulity and scorn.

"Not immediately," he explained. "I waited until the nurse's total incompetence to deal with the crisis became evident. It *was* a crisis, you see. What self-respecting captain can watch his ship go down without him and not throw a massive tantrum, after all? When there was no other course open to me but to witness a justifiably hysterical lad being cuffed by his insensitive nurse, I removed as many of my clothes as I decently could—though I understand there are varying opinions upon just how many that is—and dived in. I recovered the boat from its muddy grave. I thought my actions were rather heroic. So did the lad."

She stared at him, obviously speechless.

"You see," he explained, tipping his head to one side, "I was a boy once myself."

"Once? You mean you have grown up?" She bit her lip—to hold back a smile? But there was telltale laughter in her voice.

"Lady Waddingthorpe and Mrs. Healy-Ryde swelled with outrage, like two hot-air balloons," he said abjectly.

For a moment, even in the moonlight, he could see her eyes light with merriment. But—damn it!—before she could express it the exclamations of Miss Merklinger and Miss Abbott drew the attention of everyone in the boat to the fact that it was drawing in to the bank. Light shivered across the water from the many lamps strung in the trees of Vauxhall Gardens.

"Oh!" Lauren Edgeworth said.

"You see?" he said gently. "It *is* an enchanted land, is it not?"

"Magical," she agreed with such warm fervor that he guessed she had forgotten her eternal—or infernal—dignity for the moment.

He handed her out, and they followed the others into the pleasure gardens, whose enchantment could weave its spell even over such jaded tastes as his own. The long colonnades, the extensive groves of trees, and the wide avenues would have made for pleasant strolling even during the day, he guessed. But during the evening all was transformed into a glorious wonderland by the colored lamps waving from the colonnade and from the tree branches, the moonlight and starlight like twinkling lamps in a distant black ceiling. The music of the orchestra wafting from the direction of the open-air pavilion wrapped itself about them and muted the sounds of voices and laughter from the dozens of merrymakers.

It was the perfect setting for dalliance.

And for a marriage proposal.

They took their places in the box Merklinger had hired for the evening, close to the orchestra and the wide open space before it where the audience stood during concerts and other spectacles and where the dancing would take place tonight. They ate strawberries and cream and drank wine and enjoyed the evening air. Miss Abbott flirted with Mr. Weller. Mrs. Merklinger courted Farrington for her daughter with single-minded devotion. Merklinger hailed almost everyone who passed in front of their box and engaged anyone who stopped in hearty conversation. Kit turned to Lauren Edgeworth.

"Will you waltz with me?" he asked.

"Oh, *yes!*" Miss Merklinger exclaimed, clapping her hands. "Let us all waltz. *May* we, Mama?"

Fortunately, Kit discovered when he looked at the young lady, rather startled, she had not mistaken the object of his invitation. Her sparkling gaze was fixed upon Farrington, who was climbing indulgently to his feet while the girl's mother beamed benevolently upon them.

"A waltz," she said. "You have not yet been given the nod of approval by any of the patronesses of Almack's to dance it, my love, and neither has Amelia. But in Vauxhall I daresay the rules are not so strictly observed. Off you go and enjoy yourselves."

And so they waltzed, Kit and Lauren, and the other two couples too, beneath the stars and beneath the swaying lamps, the evening breeze fluttering the lace of Lauren's overdress and tousling Kit's hair. The delicate arch of her spine had been made to fit his hand, he discovered again. And the waltz might well have been invented for her to dance. She performed the steps with elegance and grace. And she was more beautiful than he had had any right to hope.

She would make a perfect countess when the time came. His father could have no greater objection to her than the fact that she was not Freyja. How very different they were. . . . But he did not choose to pursue that thought. This woman would suit him well enough.

"Can there be anything more romantic than waltzing beneath the stars?" he asked her, his voice lowered for her ears only.

She had been gazing about at the trees and lamps, but she looked directly at him when he spoke. "I suppose," she said gravely, "one's answer to that must depend upon one's partner."

He chuckled. "I tremble to ask," he said. "Can there be anything more romantic than *this* waltz beneath the stars?"

"There can be few activities more *pleasant* than this, my lord," she said. A setdown if ever he had heard one.

"I could think of a few." He deliberately dropped his gaze to her mouth and tightened his hand at her waist. And what the devil was he about, trying to annoy her when he should be wooing her?

"Why do you persist in flirting with me?" she asked him. "Have I not made it abundantly clear to you that I will not succumb to flattery? Does my reluctance amuse you?"

Her *primness* amused him—surprisingly. It should be annoying, he supposed, but it was not. He found her grave dignity almost endearing.

He twirled her without answering, drawing her closer when he saw another couple perilously close. But she was having none of it. She set the correct distance between them once more and looked into his eyes with steady reproach.

"There was a large bumpkin about to mow you down," he explained. "That one. Oops." The large young man he indicated had just collided with another couple. Kit chuckled. "I will take you strolling when the waltz is over. And before you say the very firm no you are drawing breath for, I plan to make all proper by suggesting that the others accompany us."

She closed her mouth and looked warily at him.

"It would be a shame," he said, "to come to Vauxhall and not see as much of it as possible, would it not? The paths are wooded and rural and unutterably romantic."

"I did not come here for romance," she said.

"There are other alternatives." He smiled wickedly at her and twirled her again, and her neck arched back as she gazed up at the wheeling colors of the lamps. "Why *did* you come?"

When she did not immediately answer, he sighed soulfully. The music, he sensed, was about to end.

"Come strolling with me," he said. "With the others for propriety, of course." If he could not escape their chaperonage once they were away from the environs of the pavilion, then he would have lost his touch indeed.

The music drew to a close, and they stood facing each other while all about them couples made their way back to the boxes.

"You hesitate because I swam in the Serpentine wearing only my pantaloons?" he asked her.

"You make a joke of everything," she said. "I wonder if anything is serious to you."

"Some things," he assured her. *Ah yes, some things.* "Walk with me."

"Very well," she said at last. "Provided everyone else agrees to accompany us, my lord. But I will not tolerate either flirtation or dalliance."

"I promise neither to flirt with you nor to dally with you," he said, smiling, his right hand over his heart.

She looked unconvinced.

"Very well," she said again.

6

*L*auren had always loved beauty. The park at Newbury Abbey was beautiful, especially on a sunny summer's day when the wind off the ocean was not too blustery. It was the inner lawns and flower gardens that she loved best, though, those parts of the park that had been tamed and cultivated. Those parts that were civilized. She had never really liked the wilder valley and beach, which were all a part of the park. They were untamed and disordered. Sometimes they frightened her in a way she could never quite explain. They reminded her, perhaps, of how little control humankind has over its own destiny. Of how close we always are to chaos.

She was terrified of chaos.

Vauxhall Gardens was a sheer delight. Nature had been tamed here and made lovely. The forest was lit by lamplight and traversed by wide, well-illumined paths with sculptures and grottos to add interest and elegance. The paths were crowded with strollers, all of whom were behaving in a perfectly civilized manner.

And yet she was aware of danger. Miss Merklinger and Lord

Farrington, Miss Abbott and Mr. Weller, walked ahead of them, talking and laughing among themselves. Lord Ravensberg made no attempt to join in their conversation even though Lord Farrington was a personal friend of his. And every minute set the two of them at a slightly greater distance behind the other four.

Every so often narrower paths wound away into the trees. They were darker, lonelier than the main thoroughfare.

Lauren could almost read Lord Ravensberg's mind. He intended that they take one of those side paths. Just the two of them. She shivered. She could increase her pace and close the distance with the others. She could herself join in their conversation. Or she could, when the time came, firmly refuse to leave the main path. He would hardly try forcing her to comply with his wishes, after all. The fact that she was even having this inner debate with herself bewildered her. Lauren Edgeworth had always known what was what, and it would certainly not be the thing to go off with a virtual stranger along a deserted path when he could have nothing but dalliance on his mind.

But she was horrifyingly tempted. What was it like—dalliance? It must be different from simple flirtation, certainly. One could flirt in company with other people. One needed to be alone with another in order to dally. She had never wondered about it before. She had never been even faintly curious.

But tonight she was.

"The path grows crowded," Viscount Ravensberg said, dipping his head closer to hers. "Perhaps you would like a quieter, more leisurely stroll along one of the side paths, Miss Edgeworth?" His eyes, dancing with merriment, mocked her. He knew, of course, that she *knew*. Did he know too that she was tempted?

She felt as if she had come to some crossroads in her life. She could and should say no and there would be an end of the matter. Or she could say yes. She could simply say yes and risk . . . what? Detection? Exposure? Scandal? They would be unchaperoned. Did he intend to steal a kiss from her? It was a shocking thought. She had only ever been kissed by Neville. She was six and twenty and had only ever been kissed—chastely—by a former betrothed. Perhaps he intended more than kisses. Perhaps . . .

"Thank you," she heard herself say before she could talk herself into making an acceptance impossible. "That would be pleasant."

He turned without further ado onto a narrow path to their left. The other two couples strolled onward, unaware that they had been abandoned.

The path was narrow—only just wide enough for two people to walk side by side if they were close together. Lord Ravensberg pressed her arm firmly against his side so that she had no choice but to rest her shoulder just below the level of his. It was the *path* that gave her no choice—the path and the tall, silent trees that grew to its very edge and met overhead, almost totally blocking out the moonlight. The only light came from the occasional lamp in a tree.

She ought not to have agreed to this, Lauren thought. There was a feeling of even greater aloneness and intimacy than she had expected. The sounds of voices and music seemed to grow instantly fainter. There was no one else on this particular path.

Why *had* she agreed? Curiosity? A desire to be kissed?

She wished he would say something. She thought of all sorts of things *she* might say—she was adept at making polite social conversation, after all, but any topic that came to mind would have sounded ridiculous under the present circumstances.

"I want to kiss you," he said in a voice that was so calmly conversational that for a moment his meaning did not quite penetrate her mind. It was her *heart* that comprehended first as it thumped uncomfortably against her rib cage, half robbing her of breath.

What would it be like, being kissed by a man who was not Neville? Being kissed by a notorious rakehell? By Viscount Ravensberg? And why had she not spoken up instantly with a firm and frosty refusal?

"Why?" she asked instead.

He laughed softly. "Because you are a woman—a beautiful woman—and I am a red-blooded male," he said. "Because I desire you."

Lauren wondered if her legs would continue to support her. They seemed suddenly turned to jelly. *This* was dalliance?

. . . I am a red-blooded male.

Because I desire you.

His choice of words paralyzed her mind with shock. Yet they strolled onward as if they had just exchanged comments on the weather. He did not just wish to kiss her. He *desired* her. Could she possibly be desirable? Was she really beautiful? Was it possible after all that this was not simply dalliance? Or was she turning into the mindless dupe of an experienced rake?

They stopped walking as if by mutual consent, and somehow they were standing facing each other. The faint light of a distant lamp danced across his shadowed features. He lifted a hand and ran the backs of his knuckles feather-light down one side of her jawline to her chin.

"Let me kiss you," he whispered.

She closed her eyes and nodded—as if being unable to see and giving no verbal answer somehow absolved her from responsibility for whatever would follow.

She felt his hands coming to rest on either side of her waist. They drew her forward so that, even though she did not move her feet, her bosom brushed against his chest and then pressed closer. For balance she lifted her hands to grasp his shoulders—and felt again the strange intimacy of being with a man who was no more than two or three inches taller than she. She opened her eyes and saw his face very close to her own, his eyes intent upon her mouth. And then his own covered it.

His lips were parted. She felt with shock the moist heat of the inside of his mouth and the warmth of his breath against her cheek. For a few moments she was lost in wondering contemplation of sensations more carnal than she had ever suspected possible. And then she became aware of two other things simultaneously. His *tongue* was tracing the seam of her lips, causing a terrifyingly raw sensation to rush aching into her throat and down into her bosom and down . . . And one of his hands was spread firmly behind her waist—no, below it—and had drawn her against him so that her thighs rested against his and . . .

She pushed away from him and fought the chaos of unfamiliar sensations and emotions that whirled through her brain. How much sense it made that unmarried ladies were never allowed to be alone with a man until they were betrothed. But she had felt none of these things with Neville. Neville had been . . . a gentleman.

"Thank you, my lord," she said, relieved at the calm coolness of her voice, quite at variance with the turmoil of her emotions. "That will be quite enough."

"Miss Edgeworth." He was regarding her closely, his head tipped a little to one side. He made no attempt to grab her again. He was not even touching her. His hands were clasped at his back. Even so she would have taken a step back to set more distance between them if the trees had allowed it. "Would you do me the great honor of accepting my hand in marriage?"

What? She stared at him, speechless. His question was so unexpected that her mind could not grapple with it for the moment. *This* was not dalliance, surely. He had asked her to *marry* him.

"Why?" The question was out before she could curb it.

"I saw you across Lady Mannering's ballroom," he said, "and knew that you were the woman I would marry—if you would have me."

It was every girl's dream, surely, to be singled out across a crowded room, Cinderella one moment, the love of Prince Charming's soul the next. There was no more romantic myth. And despite herself, Lauren was not immune to it. But she was no girl. There was all the difference in the world between myth and reality. Life had dealt her enough doses of reality that she felt no doubt of that. She did not believe in love at first sight. She did not even believe in romantic love.

"Since then," he said, "my regard for you has deepened every day. Every hour."

"Has it?" She almost wished for the foolish girlhood she had never known—for the gullible belief in fairy-tale romance. She almost wished she could believe. "Why?" It was a question she seemed to have asked a great deal lately.

"You are beautiful," he said. "You are elegant and graceful and dignified. You are a perfect lady, in fact. I have fallen head over ears in love with you."

Those were the words that released her from her mental torpor. Men simply did not fall head over ears in love. Young girls might, but if love happened at all for men, it did so far more slowly and pragmatically. Lord Ravensberg was not the type to fall violently in love with any woman. He loved himself far too much, she suspected. And Lauren Edgeworth was not the type of woman to inspire soaring flights of emotion in any man.

"My lord," she asked him, looking him directly in the eye and wishing there were more light, "what is your game?"

"Game?" He leaned a little closer and she turned sharply away and took a few steps along the path. She stood with her back to him.

"Is it my fortune?" she asked him. "Do you need to marry money?"

"I have all the wealth I need," he said after a short pause. "And I am heir to a great deal more."

"Then why?" She gazed ahead along the path and absently noted the shifting patterns of bluish light and shade cast across it by the distant lamp. "Why did you attend Lady Mannering's ball? I have been told that you had been to no other before it this Season. Why did you dance only with me? You went there with that specific intention, did you not? You intended to offer for me before you even saw me. Am I right?"

"I had seen you in the park before then," he said. "Remember? You are hard to forget."

London during the Season was the great marriage mart. Viscount Ravensberg must be in his late twenties, perhaps older. He was heir to an earldom. It was perfectly conceivable that he had decided it was time to take a bride. But why her? And why sight unseen? She did not believe for a moment that he had conceived a passion for her during that brief meeting of their eyes in the park while he was holding and kissing the milkmaid. She did not believe he had conceived a passion for her at all. She turned to look back at him. From this angle his face was more in the light. There seemed less laughter there than usual.

"Your pretense of passion is insulting, my lord," she said. "Lies are surely unnecessary. Why not simply the truth?"

His features looked hard and chiseled without the customary expression of good humor. She could imagine him now, as she had never been able to before, as a military officer.

"Insulting," he repeated softly. "I have insulted you. And indeed you are right. I have."

She had the distinct impression that her heart plummeted all the way down from her chest to her feet. She was right, then. He felt nothing for her. Of course he did not. And she did not want him to, anyway. She did not want his love or any man's. Especially not his. But she felt suddenly chilled. She was *not* beautiful. She was *not* desirable. She was simply Lauren Edgeworth, perfect lady and eligible bride for an earl's heir—as she had been all her life, unless the man happened to find a more appealing bride before it was too late. She turned her head to confirm what her eyes had seen earlier without really noticing—a rustic seat. She walked toward it and seated herself, arranging her skirts carefully about her so that she would not have to look at him. He moved closer, but made no attempt to seat himself beside her.

"Honor has always been enormously important to me," he said, his voice so devoid of laughter that she scarcely recognized it. "There was a time—while I was commissioned—when honor meant more to me than life itself, even the lives of those I loved. But—" There was a short silence before he continued. "In all my dealings with you I have acted completely without honor. I am deeply ashamed and I beg your pardon. Perhaps you will allow me to escort you back to Mrs. Merklinger?"

She gazed up at him. Without honor? Merely because he had pretended a love he did not feel? And why did that fact make her feel so very bleak? She had never believed him.

"I believe you owe me an explanation first," she said though she was not sure she wanted to know.

For a long time it seemed to her that he would not answer. Footsteps approached along the path, accompanied by soft whispers and laughter. But whoever it was must have spotted them from a distance and turned to go back. The music of another waltz intruded from what seemed to be a long distance away.

"Suffice it to say," Lord Ravensberg said at last after inhaling audibly, "that I have wagered against three other men that I will have wooed you and wed you by the end of this month."

Lauren imposed control over herself by trying—and failing—to describe her feelings to herself with one word. Shock? Anger? Bewilderment? Hurt? Humiliation?

"A wager?" She was whispering.

"You were chosen," he said, "because you have a reputation for unshakable dignity and gentility and respectability. For being the perfect lady, in fact. My . . . friends considered you to be the lady least likely to accept my proposal."

"Because you are a rake? This was all a game, then?" Her tone, she realized, matched his own in flatness. "But a remarkably foolish one. What if you had won? You would have been stuck for life with a prim, respectable wife. A perfect lady. A perfectly *dull* lady. That is what I am, Lord Ravensberg."

The sharpness of her pain was ridiculous. She had never respected this man or believed his preposterous flatteries. She respected him even less now. What did it matter that he had made a wager concerning her only because she was dull, dull, dull? For that was what dignity, gentility, and respectability added up to for him. And he was quite right. She was exactly what he thought her to be. She had always been proud of being a lady. She was *still* proud. So the pain was not valid. She was not really feeling it. Only anger—against herself more than against him. She had known from the start who and what he was. She had deliberately chosen not to listen to her family. She had wanted to assert her independence. And all the time she had been persuading herself that she was immune to his charm.

"No," he said. "You do yourself an injustice. And it was not just a game. I really did—*do*—need a bride. Someone like you. But I should not have courted you with such . . . insensitivity. With such careless disregard for you as a person. I should not have allowed you, or any other lady, to become the object of a wager. You may be the perfect wife for me, but I would be just the worst possible husband for you."

She should have risen to her feet then, the explanation given, and made her way back to the main path and the box where Mr. and Mrs. Merklinger waited. For very pride's sake she should have left—and refused his escort. But she did not move.

"Why do you need a bride by the end of June?" she asked him. "That is less than two weeks away. And why a—a perfect lady?" She could not quite keep the bitterness from her voice.

"I had better tell you everything." He sighed and took a step closer. But he did not sit down beside her. He set one foot on the wooden seat instead and draped an arm over his raised leg. His face, only inches from her own now, was as serious as she had ever seen it.

"I have been summoned to Alvesley for the summer," he said. "My father's principal seat, that is. My brother's death almost two years ago made me his heir and forced me to sell my commission since he pointed out to me that I was no longer free to put my life at risk every day. My life was suddenly valuable to him, you see, even though he banished me forever the last time I saw him."

"You did not wish to sell out?" she asked, noting the unusually bitter tone of his voice.

"As a younger son, I was brought up for a military career," he said. "It was what I wanted anyway. And I enjoyed it, all things considered. It was something I did well."

She waited.

"There is to be a house party in celebration of my grandmother's seventy-fifth birthday this summer," he told her. "My banishment has been revoked. The prodigal is to be allowed home after all. He is to learn his duties as the future earl, you see. And one of those duties is to take a bride and set up his nursery. It is my father's intention, in fact, to make my betrothal the central event of a summer of festivities. It is to be a birthday gift to my grandmother."

All was beginning to make sense. Her respectability, her reputation as a perfect lady, made her a good candidate. She had been chosen with cold calculation. As most brides of her class were, of course.

Had he been open about his intentions from the start she would not have been offended. There was nothing intrinsically offensive about them.

"The Earl of Redfield has instructed you to choose a respectable bride?" she asked. "Was it he who suggested my name?"

"No." He tapped his free hand against the leg on which he stood. "Actually he has another prospect in mind."

"Oh?"

"My dead brother's betrothed."

"Oh." Lauren clasped her hands tightly in her lap. How very distasteful for both Lord Ravensberg and the poor lady, who was being handed from one brother to the next like a worn inheritance.

"And my own before him," he said after a slight pause. "But when given the choice three years ago, she chose the heir rather than the second son, the mere cavalry major. Ironic, is it not? She might have had both me and the title. But I no longer wish to marry her. And so I decided to choose my own bride and take her with me when I go as a fait accompli. I wanted a bride to whom my father could not possibly object. Your name was suggested to me—not as someone who would surely accept, but as a lady of perfect gentility who probably would not. Hence the wager."

Lauren looked at her hands in her lap. She was not sure he spoke the strict truth. She thought it more likely that she had been named as someone who would almost certainly accept his proposal with alacrity. Was she not a jilted, abandoned bride, after all? A woman past the first blush of youth who would surely grab with desperate gratitude the first man who asked? But if that were so, why would three gentlemen have wagered against his success?

But did it matter?

"I beg your pardon," he said. "You have been the victim of my unpardonable lapse of honor. I owed you honesty from the start. I should have approached the Duke of Portfrey with my offer and been content with whatever he might have said. But it is too late now to court you the right way. You have done nothing to deserve such shabby treatment. Please believe me to be truly contrite and most humbly your servant. May I escort you back to the box?" He returned his foot to the ground and offered his arm.

She continued staring at her hands while he waited. Another crossroads. Yet there was nothing further to decide, nothing more to say.

Because you are a woman—a beautiful woman—and I am a red-blooded male. Because I desire you.

All a lie. And she was undeniably hurt by it. It had all been a ruse to lure her into accepting him and winning his wager for him.

But still . . . a crossroads.

"No, wait," she said softly, even though he was already doing that—waiting to escort her out of his life. "Wait a moment."

Kit watched her spread her fingers in her lap. She did not speak again for a long while. He felt damnably wretched. All he wanted to do, if the truth were known, was take her back to Mrs. Merklinger's side and wait out the evening with all the patience he could muster. And to seek out his three friends in the morning to pay his debts before taking himself off to Alvesley.

He was deeply mortified to realize that in consenting to make a lady—a perfectly innocent lady—the subject of a sordid wager he really had tainted the honor he held so dear. It had seemed faintly amusing at the time, before she had become a person to him.

Another group was approaching along the narrow path, this one more boisterous than the couple before them. And they came right along even when they saw that they were interrupting a tête-à-tête. Kit sat down beside Lauren, and the four revelers walked past in loud silence, their eyes carefully averted, and then laughed and snickered before they were quite out of earshot. Kit stayed where he was.

"Will you go to Alvesley, then," Lauren Edgeworth asked, "and betroth yourself to your former fiancée after all?"

"I hope I may avoid that fate," he said.

"Does *she* wish to marry *you?*" she asked.

"I very much doubt it," he said. "She preferred Jerome to me three years ago." Though one never quite knew with Freyja.

"I will make a bargain with you, Lord Ravensberg," Lauren Edgeworth said, her voice quite steady and calm, "if you will agree to it."

He turned his head to look at her, but her eyes were still directed downward at her spread fingers.

"I will go to Alvesley with you," she said very deliberately, "as your betrothed."

He sat very still.

"As your *temporary* betrothed," she explained. "I will go with you and be presented to your family and be everything you hoped I would be. I will be there while you establish yourself again as your father's son and while you take your rightful place in his home as his heir. I will be there so that a distasteful engagement will not be pressed upon either you or the lady who once chose your brother rather than you. I will give you some breathing room, so to speak, during the house party and the birthday celebrations. But I will not marry you. At the end of the summer I will leave Alvesley and break the engagement. I will do it in such a way that no censure will fall upon you. By that time it is to be hoped that your family will have accepted your right to choose your own bride in your own time."

He could not possibly be misunderstanding her. She spoke very precisely. But what the devil?

"You would *break* the engagement?" he said, frowning. "Do you realize what a scandal that would cause? You would put yourself beyond the social pale."

"I think not," she said with a faint smile for her hands. "There would be those who would congratulate me upon having freed myself just in time from marriage to a rakehell. But I care little anyway. I have told you that I am not in search of a husband, that I have no intention of marrying. What I have realized only very recently is that I need to break free of my well-meaning relatives, who treat me as if I were both a green girl and excessively fragile goods. In reality I am a woman who long ago reached her majority, and I have a comfortable independence. I intend to set up my own home, perhaps in Bath. After spending the summer at Alvesley, supposedly as your betrothed, and then breaking the connection, I will find it far easier to do what I ought to have done a year ago. None of my relatives will argue with me. I will be demonstrably unmarriageable."

What the devil? He stared at her profile and realized fully what he should have realized long ago—that he did not know this woman at all. Yet he had been prepared to marry her within the next two weeks.

"Were you deeply attached to Kilbourne, then?" he asked her.

Her head dipped a little lower. Her fingers closed and then spread again.

"I grew up with him at Newbury Abbey," she said, "from the time I was taken there at the age of three. In some ways he seemed like my brother as much as he was Gwen's. But I always knew too that we were intended for each other when we grew up. I shaped my life to the expectation that one day I would be his countess. Even when he bought his commission and went away, telling me not to wait for him but to feel free to marry someone else if I wished, I remained loyal. I waited. But while he was gone he married secretly and then watched his wife die in an ambush in Portugal—or so he thought. He came home and would have married me after all. It seemed as if life would proceed in the direction I had always expected it to take. But Lily did not die. She came home to Neville—on my wedding day."

He was not deceived by the lack of emotion in her voice. This story had been the sensation of last year. But almost all the gossip, he guessed, had focused upon the glorious love story that was Kilbourne and his lady's. Lauren Edgeworth had been pitied, spoken of, no doubt, in hushed, shocked whispers. How many people, himself included, Kit thought, deeply ashamed, had really considered the pain the woman must have suffered and must still suffer? She had been within a few minutes of fulfilling a lifetime's dream only to have it shattered most cruelly.

"You loved him?" he asked. Though he was not sure the past tense was strictly appropriate.

"Love," she said softly. "What is love? The word has so many meanings. Of course I loved him. But not in the way Neville and Lily love each other. Love of that sort is a disordered, undisciplined emotion, best avoided. I would have remained loyal and faithful and . . . Of course I loved him." She sighed. "I will contemplate no other marriage, Lord Ravensberg."

He gazed at her, deep pity—and guilt—holding him silent. But she appeared to read his thoughts.

"I am not asking for your pity," she said. "Please do not offer it or even feel it. I need only to be accorded the privilege that men expect as a natural right—to be allowed to live my life my way without having those who claim to love me forever knowing better than I what it is that will make me happy. I want to be alone and independent. If I ruin my reputation this summer, I will achieve that for which I ought not to have to fight."

"Good Lord," he said, running the fingers of one hand through his hair and then leaning forward to rest his forearms across his legs. "How can I agree to this? Having spoken of honor just a few minutes ago, how can I now agree to deceive both my family and yours? And how can I leave all the burden of breaking our betrothal to you? You do understand, do you not, that as a gentleman I could not possibly break it myself?"

"And therein is your answer," she said. "To you the betrothal would have to be a real one, my lord, would it not? If I were to behave dishonorably, you see, and refuse to break it off even after striking a bargain with you, you would have no choice but to marry me. And so you would be involved in no deception if you were to agree to my suggestion."

He tried to find a flaw in her argument. But really there was none. Of course if he agreed to her strange proposal the betrothal would be a real one for him. And perhaps—yes, perhaps he could redeem the honor he had lost in the past few weeks and persuade her after all during the summer to marry him. Perhaps he could persuade her that what he had to offer was slightly more appealing than a life alone. Women, even those with the means to live independent lives, had very little real freedom.

He did not love Lauren Edgeworth. He did not even *know* her, he admitted ruefully. But of one thing he had grown painfully aware during the past half hour or so. She was a very real person with very real feelings. And she was one for whom he felt a certain regard. And one to whom he owed a debt.

"Are you sure a large house party would be to your taste?" he asked her, sitting upright again.

For the first time she turned her head to look at him. "I believe it would suit me admirably," she said. "I was brought up to be a countess, remember? I was brought up to expect to run Newbury Abbey one day, to be the lady of the manor. Going to Alvesley as the betrothed of the Earl of Redfield's heir would be something I could contemplate with the greatest confidence and ease. You would not be disappointed in me."

He frowned into her eyes. "But why would you do all this merely to convince your family to leave you to your chosen way of life?" he asked. "Pardon me, but you are no timid or easily dominated female, Miss Edgeworth. All you really need to do, surely, is tell them that you have made up your own mind about your future and they might as soon save their breath to cool their porridge as seek to change your mind."

She looked away again—to the dark trees at the other side of the path, to the sky above, just visible through the branches of the trees.

"Your confession tonight confirmed me in all the bad things I have thought or been told about you," she said. "For a while I could think of nothing but getting away from you and never seeing you again. But..."

For a while it seemed that she would not continue. He waited.

"My life has been quiet and decorous," she said. "I have only recently realized that it is also dull. Its dullness suits me. It is what I know, what I am comfortable with, what I will live with quite contentedly for the rest of my life. But recently I have felt a craving to know just once what it would be like to have some sort of adventure. To... Ah, I do not know how to put the feeling into words. I think that spending a summer in your company, masquerading as your betrothed, would be rather . . . adventurous. This all sounds very lame put into words."

But she was saying much more than the words themselves conveyed. She was, obviously, a woman who had never known joy, who had long ago repressed all her potential for spontaneity and happiness.

"What I would get out of this bargain," she continued, "would be your promise, Lord Ravensberg, to give me a summer I would not forget for the rest of my life. Adventure and . . . well, *adventure*. It is what I want in exchange for extricating you from an unwanted marriage."

He thought she was finished, but she held up a staying hand when he would have spoken. She was looking at her other hand again, spread palm-up in her lap.

"There was a morning," she said. "At Newbury just a few days after my wedding—the wedding that never was. I was walking early and alone down toward the beach—three things I almost never do. When I was descending the hill into the valley leading to the beach, I grew aware of voices and laughter. It was Neville and Lily, bathing together in the pool at the foot of a waterfall there beside a little cottage Neville's grandfather built for his wife. The door was open. They had spent the night there. They were . . . Well, I believe they were both unclothed. And they were . . . I think the only suitable word is *frolicking*. It was the moment when I realized that she had won in more ways than one. He was blissfully happy, you see. And I could never have done that. I could never have behaved with such total . . . abandon. At least, I do not believe I ever could. It was passion I witnessed for a mere few seconds before I ran away as fast as I could."

She drew breath to continue but shook her head and stopped.

"Are you asking," he said, "for a summer of passion as well as adventure?"

"Of course not." She seemed more herself for a moment, straightening her spine and lifting her chin, looking shocked. "I just want to know what—what it feels like to throw off some of the shackles that bind me. Just fleetingly. I am not a person made for wild, passionate emotions. Or for vivid happiness. I just want a summer to remember. Can you give it to me? If so, I will come to Alvesley with you."

Good Lord! He sat back on the seat and looked at her averted face. She was a far more complex person than he had ever dreamed. A wounded person. One who for some reason he did not understand had never been whole, and never free. Even if she had married Kilbourne, he suspected, she would have lived a half existence hidden behind her mask of perfect gentility. What exactly was she asking of him? To bring her out from the shadows in which she had dwelled all her life? To teach her spontaneity and passion and laughter? Joy? So that she could then abandon him and proceed with the lonely spinster existence that was all that remained of her dreams?

Did he want to take on such a challenge and responsibility? What if he could not do it? Worse, what if he could? But a good challenge had always been the breath of life to him. And if he agreed to this bizarre proposal, he would, of course, go into it full tilt, determined to win her as his wife. She loved Kilbourne—always had, always would. He was not looking for love. But could he . . . bring her out into the light?

"I can give you a summer to remember," he said.

She turned her head sharply in his direction. "You agree, then?"

He nodded. "I agree."

It was the precise moment at which the first fireworks exploded with a series of loud cracks. Even within the shaded grove where they sat they could see the night sky suddenly lit up with great arcing rays of dazzling color.

7

*L*auren was on her way to Alvesley Park. The long journey into Hampshire must be almost over, in fact, she thought. The afternoon was well advanced.

More than two weeks had passed since the evening at Vauxhall when all this madness had begun. And madness it surely was. At the time she had imagined—if she had stopped to think at all—that she would simply ride off with Viscount Ravensberg on their masquerade, that they would proceed the very next day to Alvesley and her summer of adventure.

It had not turned out that way. *Of course* it had not. Even before she had tossed and turned her way through a sleepless night after the Merklingers had conveyed her home, she had realized that what she had agreed to—no, what she had suggested—was not just a carefree fling for the two of them but a huge lie that was to involve a large number of people. Common sense and a regard for propriety almost prevailed at that point. She almost dashed off a note to Lord Ravensberg, canceling all their plans.

Almost. But she had gone down to breakfast first, and Elizabeth had asked her about the evening at Vauxhall.

"It was very enjoyable," she had replied—and after a moment's hesitation, "Elizabeth, he asked me to marry him and I said yes."

Elizabeth had risen hurriedly to her feet despite her bulk and hugged Lauren and laughed with delight and assured her that she had made a wise choice despite anything that Aunt Sadie and her ilk might say to the contrary.

"You have chosen to go with your heart after all, Lauren," she had said. "I am so very proud of you and happy for you."

Lord Ravensberg had called only an hour or so later to speak with the Duke of Portfrey, though he was not in any way Lauren's guardian. It was a visit Lauren had not expected him to make, but one that Elizabeth had commented upon with approval.

Suddenly it had seemed out of the question simply to ride off for Alvesley with her betrothed. How could *she*, Lauren Edgeworth, have thought for a single moment that it might be possible? Suddenly everything had become very formal and correct.

Announcements had had to be made—to Lord Ravensberg's family to expect her, to her grandfather in Yorkshire, to her family at Newbury Abbey, to her relatives in London, to the *ton* at large.

The betrothal—the *fake* betrothal—had become alarmingly real and no carefree adventure at all. Uncle Webster had rumbled with displeasure and called the viscount—in his absence—an impudent puppy. Aunt Sadie had called for the hartshorn, and Wilma had volubly declared herself speechless. Joseph had looked faintly amused but had offered no comment beyond a wish for Lauren's happiness. The Duke of Portfrey had given it as his opinion that Lord Ravensberg's notorious exploits amounted to nothing more than a sowing of wild oats. His military record told its own impressive story, he had added. He and Elizabeth had hosted a grand family dinner in celebration of the event the day before Lord Ravensberg left for Alvesley to break the news to his parents and two days before the announcement appeared in all the morning papers.

It had been impossible to come to Alvesley alone or with only a maid for company, of course, even though the journey could be made in one day. And impossible too to make the journey with Lord Ravensberg's escort. Such behavior simply would not be proper—they were not wed. Elizabeth was within a month of her confinement and quite unable to travel. Lauren would not even ask Aunt Sadie to accompany her.

It was Aunt Clara, the Dowager Countess of Kilbourne, who was doing that. And Gwendoline, the widowed Lady Muir. They had come all the way from Dorsetshire to London in order to cry over her and laugh over her and hug her until her ribs felt bruised—and to accompany her to Alvesley at the invitation of the Countess of Redfield.

All was very formal, very proper.

Lauren felt weighed down by the hugeness of the lie she had set in motion. She had not told even Gwen the truth. And there had been no word from Lord Ravensberg to tell her how well—or how ill—his announcement had been received at Alvesley. Only the letter of formal invitation from his mother.

"Ah," Aunt Clara said now, waking from a doze that had kept the two younger women silent and had left Lauren alone with her thoughts and her conscience, "this must be it. I will not be sorry to see the journey at an end, I must say."

The carriage—the Duke of Portfrey's, complete with all the pomp of ducal crest and splendidly liveried coachman, postilions, and outriders—had just passed through a small village and was slowing to turn between massive wrought-iron gates, which a porter was throwing wide. He stood aside, glanced up into the carriage, and dipped his head, pulling respectfully on his forelock.

"Oh, Lauren." Gwen leaned forward to squeeze her cousin's knee. "This looks very impressive indeed. You must be bursting with excitement. You have not seen Lord Ravensberg for almost two weeks."

"I am eager to make the young man's acquaintance," Aunt Clara said. "Despite Sadie's disapproval and Wilma's foolish vapors, I am prepared to like him. Elizabeth does, and she is invariably sensible in her assessment of character. And he has won *your* regard, Lauren. That must override any possible doubt I might feel."

Lauren curved her lips into a smile—they felt remarkably stiff. She did not want to be doing this—deceiving the two people who were dearest to her in the world, deceiving the Earl of Redfield and his family, bowling along through a shaded, heavily wooded park toward a charade of her own making. But of course it was too late now *not* to be doing it.

How could she have made that irresponsible suggestion at Vauxhall? What on earth had possessed her? She was *never* impulsive. And she did not even *like* Lord Ravensberg. Did she? Certainly she did not approve of him. His dancing eyes and his frequent laughter suggested altogether too careless an attitude to life. He positively delighted in doing and saying outrageous things that were simply not gentlemanly. At this precise moment, she thought with some alarm, she could not even remember exactly what he looked like.

Suddenly the carriage interior was flooded with sunlight again. Lauren moved her head closer to the window beside her and gazed ahead. They had drawn clear of the forest and were approaching a river, which they were going to cross via a roofed Palladian bridge. To her far left she could see that the river emptied its waters into a lake, which was just visible among the trees. Beyond the bridge, well-kept lawns sloped upward to the classical elegance of a large, gray stone mansion. The lawns were dotted with ancient trees. On the lake side of the house were stables and a carriage house.

"Oh," she said, and Gwen pressed her face to the window too, turning her head to look backward.

"Splendid," Aunt Clara said. She was looking through the opposite window. "That must be a rose arbor beside the house with flower parterres below it."

Then Gwen was patting Lauren's knee again and smiling, her eyes sparkling with excitement.

"I am so *happy* for you!" she exclaimed. "I *knew* that sooner or later you were bound to meet the man who was created just for you. Are you *very* deep in love with him?"

But Lauren only half heard. The carriage had turned past the stables, and its wheels were crunching over a wide graveled terrace toward the steep flight of marble steps leading up beyond massive fluted pillars to the mansion's great double doors, which stood open. There were people on the steps—two, three, no, four of them. And at the foot of the steps, dashing and elegant in a form-fitting coat of blue superfine over tight gray pantaloons and shiny, tasseled Hessian boots, a sunny smile on his face . . .

"Ah, yes," Lauren said, though whether in answer to Gwen's question or her own foolish fear that she would not recognize him, no one thought to ask—least of all Lauren herself.

Kit had been restless all day. He had ridden for hours, alone, across country, following no particular route, trying to kill the hours until she could reasonably be expected. Then, back at the house, he had paced in and out of front-facing rooms, peering out through the windows long before the carriage could possibly roll into sight unless it had left London in the middle of the night. He had even walked briskly down to the lodge shortly after luncheon to chat with the porter for a while.

He wished this whole thing were not happening. He wished, now that it was too late to do things differently, that he had simply written to his father earlier in the spring with a firm refusal to have any marriage arranged for him. He should have refused even to come home until he felt more ready to do so. He should not even have sold out last year. He could be with the armies now, doing what he did best. He should have written to his father . . .

But the trouble was that he was Ravensberg. He was the heir. And as the heir he had responsibilities, which he had shirked for almost two years even though he *had* ended his career. It was his duty to be at home, to make his peace with his father, to learn what the future Earl of Redfield needed to know, to take a wife, to father sons—yes, preferably plural.

But was he fulfilling those duties even now? With a sham engagement? And a homecoming that would have been difficult even under the best of circumstances? His father had been predictably furious when, after the first awkward exchange of greetings following his arrival, he had made his announcement. The situation, he had then discovered, was far worse than he had realized. A marriage settlement had been discussed and fully agreed upon by his father and the Duke of Bewcastle, Freyja's brother. They had even signed a contract. It had apparently not occurred to either of them that it might be advisable to consult the wishes of the prospective bride and groom first.

Kit doubted that Freyja's wishes had been consulted.

His mother had been dismayed and then tearful. The tight hug with which she had greeted him had not been repeated since. Even his grandmother had shaken her head at him with unspoken reproof. She was unable to say a great deal, having suffered an apoplexy five years before from which she had never quite recovered all her faculties. She still treated him with affection, but he knew that he had disappointed her.

And Sydnam—well, he and his younger brother, who had shaken hands awkwardly and without making full eye contact on Kit's arrival, had had a nasty falling out that same night and now scarcely spoke to each other. Kit had found him in the steward's office after everyone else had retired to bed, writing laboriously in a ledger with his left hand.

"So this is where you disappeared to after dinner," Kit had said. "Why here, Syd?"

"Parkin retired before Christmas last year," Sydnam had explained, looking at the worn leather cover of the ledger rather than at his brother. "I asked Father if I could take his place as steward of Alvesley."

"As steward?" Kit had frowned. "*You,* Syd?"

"It suits me very well," his brother had told him.

Kit had assumed that Syd was living a life of enforced idleness here without his right arm and with only his left eye out of which to see and with no possible way of doing what he had been created to do. They had exchanged no letters in three years. He had assumed that Syd could not write any, and he had written none of his own because . . . well, because there had been nothing to say.

"How are you?" he had asked.

"Well." The single word had been spoken abruptly, defiantly. "I am perfectly well, thank you."

"Are you?"

Sydnam had opened the top left-hand drawer of the desk and placed the ledger inside it. "Perfectly well."

They had been unusually close when they were younger, despite the six-year gap in their ages. He had been Syd's hero, and in his turn he had adored his young brother, who had possessed all the qualities of character that he lacked—steadiness, sweetness, patience, vision, dedication.

"Why did you tell me to leave?" Kit had blurted suddenly. "Why did you join the chorus?"

Sydnam had not had to ask what he was talking about. After their father had banished Kit three years before, Syd had got up from his sick bed and come down to the hall, looking like a ghost and a skeleton combined, clad only in his nightshirt, his valet and a footman hovering anxiously in the background. But instead of offering the expected sympathy, he had told Kit to leave, to go, not to come back. There had been no word of farewell, no word of forgiveness . . .

"You were destroying all of us," Sydnam had said in answer to his questions. "Yourself most of all. You had to go. I thought you might defy Father. I thought you might go after Jerome again and kill him. I told you to go because I wanted you gone."

Kit had crossed the room to the window, from which the curtains were drawn back. But he had been able to see nothing outside—only his own reflection thrown back at him, and Syd's, still seated at the desk.

"You did blame me, then," he had said.

"Yes."

The single word had pierced his heart. He would never forgive himself for what had happened, but without Syd's forgiveness there was no hope of any kind of lasting peace. Only more of the restless search for forgetfulness, which he had been able to achieve with a measure of success while he had still been commissioned, but which had been impossible to find since he sold out. He had tried. He had hardly rested, day or night.

"Yes, I blame you," Sydnam had said. "But not in the way you think."

It had not been worth pursuing.

"Do you think," Kit had asked, "that I would not have taken all your suffering into my own body if I could? I wish it had been me. I wish I had made that choice. If you could be made whole again, do you not think I would give my life to make it happen?"

"I'm sure you would," his brother had said. "I am quite certain you would, Kit." But there had been no forgiveness in his voice. Only harsh bitterness. "I do not want to talk about this. It was *my* suffering and these are *my* deformities and this is *my* life. I ask nothing of you, nothing whatsoever."

"Not even my love?" The words had been almost whispered against the windowpane.

"Not even that, Kit."

"Well." Kit had turned and smiled, feeling as if all the blood in his body were draining downward, making him rather light-headed. He had crossed the room toward the door with deliberately jaunty strides. He had let himself out and closed the door behind him before bowing his head, his eyes closed.

No, no one had been made happy by his return to Alvesley, least of all himself. He felt like a stranger in his own home—an uncomfortable, unwelcome stranger. He felt useless—he, who had always been active and brilliantly successful and highly respected in his career. His father had made no move to educate him in the duties of the heir or to include him in any activities of his daily routine. Perhaps he was waiting until after the house party and the return of normality to the household. And Kit too felt as if he were waiting for the next phase of his life to begin—yet the very next phase was to be a charade. A lie. Unless, that was, he could persuade her to marry him after all and redeem some of his honor by doing what was right by her.

He had not been sleeping well—again. And when he *did* nod off from sheer exhaustion, the old nightmare kept rearing its ugly head. Syd . . .

By the middle of the afternoon he found himself in the drawing room in company with both his mother and his father—who rarely spent his afternoons there—as well as his grandmother. The others sat in quiet conversation while Kit made no pretense of doing anything but standing at the window waiting, his eyes fixed on the point of the driveway just beyond the bridge at which a carriage would first come into sight. They were all waiting, of course, for the unwanted, unwelcome arrival of their guests—though none of them had been discourteous enough to put it quite that way.

Kit's betrothal had caused an awkward rift with their neighbors at Lindsey Hall six miles away—the Duke of Bewcastle and the Bedwyns, his brothers and sisters. Kit had ridden over there on his first morning back and had asked to speak with his grace. Bewcastle must have assumed, of course, that the call was a courtesy one for the making of a formal offer for Freyja. Kit had been shown into the library almost immediately.

Wulfric Bedwyn, Duke of Bewcastle, was not the sort of man anyone in his right mind would deliberately cross. Tall, dark, rather thin, with piercing gray eyes in a narrow face, a great hooked nose, and thin lips, he bore himself with all the unconscious arrogance of his breed. He had been brought up from the cradle for his present position and so had always held himself somewhat aloof from his brothers and his brothers' friends, even though he was only a little more than a year older than Kit. He was a cold, humorless man.

He had not exploded with wrath when informed about the betrothal. He had merely crossed one elegantly clad leg over the other, taken a sip from his glass—the very finest French brandy, of course—and spoken softly and pleasantly.

"Doubtless," he had said, "you are about to explain."

Kit had felt just as he used to feel during his boyhood years when hauled up before the headmaster at school for some mischief—caught out, in the wrong, on the defensive. He had prevented himself only just in time from acting accordingly.

"And you will explain," he had replied just as pleasantly, "why you would negotiate a marriage contract for your sister with my father rather than with me, her proposed husband."

He had found himself being regarded steadily from cold, inscrutable eyes for long, silent moments.

"You will excuse me," his grace had said softly at last, "for not offering my felicitations on your betrothal, Ravensberg. You do, however, have my congratulations. You have a fine sense of revenge. Better than you used to have. Less brash, shall we say?"

He had been referring to three years before, of course, when after breaking Jerome's nose Kit had galloped hell-for-leather over to Lindsey Hall and banged on the outer door for half an hour—it had been late at night—before Rannulf, Bewcastle's brother and Kit's particular friend, had opened it and told him not to make an ass of himself but to go on home. When Kit had demanded to hear the truth of her betrothal to Jerome from Freyja's own lips, Rannulf had come outside and they had stripped down and engaged in ferocious fisticuffs for all of fifteen minutes before a burly footman and Alleyne, another brother, had dragged them apart, both bruised and bloodied, both snarling and struggling to continue. Bewcastle, standing outside the door silently observing the fight, had then advised Kit to take himself off back to the Peninsula, where his rage could be put to better use. Freyja had stood at his side, her head thrown proudly back, a smile of open contempt on her lips as she stared at Kit. She had not uttered a word.

Now, three years later, Kit had been framing an answer to the duke's words when the library door behind him was suddenly flung back against the bookshelves and his grace's eyes had gone beyond Kit's shoulder, his eyebrows rising haughtily.

"I fail to recall," he had said, "inviting you to join me here, Freyja."

But she had stridden into the room regardless and approached Kit's chair, ignoring her brother. Kit had risen to make her a bow.

"You have certainly taken your time about leaving the pleasures of London behind," she had said, tapping a riding whip against her skirt. "I am on my way out for a ride with Alleyne. If you wish to call upon me, Lord Ravensberg, you may make an appointment with Wulf and I will see if I am free that day." She had turned to leave without waiting for his answer.

She had not changed in three years. Of slightly below medium height but generously endowed, she carried herself with proud grace. No one, even in her infancy, had ever called Freyja pretty. She was one of the fair Bedwyns and wore her thick golden hair as she had always liked to wear it, quite unfashionably, in long, loose waves down her back. Like the other fair Bedwyns, she had startlingly dark eyebrows and a dark-toned complexion. And the family nose. As a child she had been ugly to the point of freakishness. Then she had blossomed into young womanhood, and ugliness had been transformed into a startling handsomeness. She had always, from infancy on, been a spitfire.

"Lady Freyja," Kit had murmured.

"If you had simply gone riding, Freyja," her brother had said, still in his soft, pleasant voice, "instead of feeling constrained to announce in person your intention of not receiving Viscount Ravensberg, you might have been spared having to learn thus publicly what he has come here to inform me. He has recently become betrothed to Miss Lauren Edgeworth of Newbury. She will be coming to Alvesley within the next week or two."

Freyja was not his sister and a Bedwyn for nothing. After a moment's silence, she had turned her head back over her shoulder to smile at Kit—a baring of the teeth that bore a resemblance to a smile, anyway.

"Oh, well done, Kit," she had said softly. "Well done indeed. You have learned subtleties you used not to know."

She had left the room without another word.

Three years before, Kit had conceived a sudden, all-consuming passion for the woman who had been his playmate all through their childhood—she had always flatly refused to be excluded by her brothers and their friends even from their wildest exploits. She had seemed to return his sentiments in full measure. He had talked of marrying her and taking her back to the Peninsula with him to follow the drum. She had said nothing to discourage him. He had believed that summer that he would willingly die for her. And then, when Jerome had suddenly, without warning, announced his betrothal to her, Kit had thought he might well die of her betrayal. But that had been three years ago. Much water had passed beneath the proverbial bridge since then.

"Ah," he said now, his mind back in his father's drawing room, his eyes on that point just beyond the bridge where the deer forest ended, "here it comes."

A carriage, unmistakably grand, drawn by four perfectly matched horses and escorted by outriders, had come into sight. There was no possibility that it was merely a neighbor come to call on his mother or grandmother.

Everyone was rising, he saw when he turned toward the door, even his grandmother with the aid of her cane. But of course. They would all do what was proper and come down to welcome the unwelcome guests with formal hospitality. He wished suddenly that it was a *real* betrothal, that it was a love match, that at last he would be able to convince his family—and keep them convinced—that he had done something that was right and responsible and good for the whole family when he had chosen the Honorable Miss Lauren Edgeworth to be his viscountess.

He would have offered his grandmother his arm, but his father was before him. He gave it to his mother instead, and they descended the stairs, walked through the echoing hall, and went out onto the steps together, without exchanging a word. He had always been the most troublesome of her three sons. If ever there were mischief to be got into—and there always had been—he had invariably been at the center of it, the instigator and main participant. But she had always loved him anyway. Sometimes she had even shed a tear over him after his father had finished with him in the study. Since his return—except for her first warm hug—he was not sure she loved him at all any longer.

The carriage was almost at the stables. Portfrey had sent them in his own coach, then, and surrounded them with all his ducal pomp. It was all so very damnably proper and ceremonial. Had he really imagined during that mad hour at Vauxhall that he could simply load her into a hired carriage the very next day and bring her here to surprise his parents with their announcement?

He moved away from his mother's side and ran down the steps to the terrace. Deuce take it but this felt strange. He was about to see her again. Their grand masquerade was about to begin. Was she nervous?

And then the carriage rolled to a halt, one of the postilions jumped down to open the door and set down the steps, and Kit stepped forward, smiling and stretching up a hand. He was half aware of the other two ladies, but it was Lauren Edgeworth who leaned forward and set her gloved hand in his.

He had half forgotten how very beautiful and elegant she was. Her dove-gray traveling dress and bonnet, both with violet trim, appeared quite uncreased by the long journey. She looked fresh and lovely and perfectly composed.

"Lauren." He handed her down and bent his head to kiss her cheek, though somehow he caught one corner of her mouth as well.

"Kit."

They had agreed at Vauxhall—or rather he had persuaded her—that they should use each other's given name, but they had not done so until now. He squeezed her hand, still clasped in his own, and grinned at her. Suddenly a two-week-long depression lifted like a physical weight from his shoulders and he felt a surge of confidence and exhilaration at the prospect of the days ahead. Lauren really had been the right choice for him, even if only for the summer. And there was to be all the challenge of getting her to change her mind about the summer's ending. He loved challenges.

"Aunt Clara," Lauren said as he turned back to the carriage and gave his hand to the older of the two ladies within, "this is Kit, Viscount Ravensberg. My aunt, the Dowager Countess of Kilbourne."

She was a smart, handsome lady with shrewd eyes and proud demeanor.

"Ma'am," he said, making his bow to her after handing her down. "And Gwendoline, Lady Muir, my cousin."

He handed down the younger lady, who was very small, very blond, and very pretty. She looked at him with sparkling, frankly assessing eyes as he bowed to her.

Then it was time to turn and make the introductions to his family, who were waiting on the steps. All was accomplished in a manner that was perfectly smooth, perfectly civil. If Lauren was feeling any misgivings, any nervousness, she certainly was not showing it. Neither were his parents showing in any way at all that their son's betrothal was anything but perfectly acceptable to them. His grandmother, when they were introduced, even took Lauren's hand in her good one and drew her down for a kiss.

"Pretty," she said, nodding in that way she had of indicating that she would say far more if she could. "Might have . . . known . . . Kit would choose a . . . pretty one."

Lauren showed no discomfort at having to wait an inordinately long time for the short sentence to be completed. She was smiling— yes, actually—and giving his grandmother her full attention.

"Thank you, ma'am," she said.

But Kit had suddenly noticed Sydnam standing on the top step, inconspicuous in the shadow of one of the pillars, half turned so that his left side faced out. Kit took Lauren by the elbow.

"There is someone else I want you to meet," he said and led her up the steps. He half expected Syd to flee through the open door, but he stood his ground. "My brother Sydnam. Lauren Edgeworth, my betrothed, Syd."

If she felt shock as she saw him fully, she gave no sign, not even a stiffening of her elbow against his hand. When viewed from his left profile, Syd was as extraordinarily good-looking as he had been all his life. But as soon as he turned, the beholder could see his empty right sleeve pinned neatly against his coat, the purple marks of the old burns discoloring and immobilizing the right side of his face and neck, and the black patch over his right eye socket. Beauty and the beast occupying the two halves of the same body.

Syd held out his left hand, and she did not hesitate to take it in her left so that they could exchange a handshake that was not awkward.

"Mr. Butler."

"Miss Edgeworth, welcome to Alvesley," Syd said. "Has your journey been very tedious?"

"Not at all," she replied. "I had the company of my aunt and cousin, you see, and the knowledge that Kit would be here waiting for me at the end of it."

Kit looked at her appreciatively. She sounded so warmly convincing that he felt a foolish lurching of pleasure in the region of his heart.

But his mother was, as always, the perfect hostess. She would accompany the ladies to their rooms, she told them, coming to join them on the top step, so that they might have an opportunity to freshen up before tea was served in the drawing room. She took Lauren's arm, drawing her away from both her sons, and led the way inside while Lady Kilbourne and Lady Muir followed behind. Lady Muir limped, Kit noticed.

8

*G*wendoline was playing the pianoforte while the Earl of Redfield stood behind the bench, turning the pages of the music for her. The countess and Aunt Clara were seated side by side on a love seat nearby, alternately listening to Bach and conversing with each other. Sydnam Butler was sitting on the window seat at the opposite end of the drawing room, where he had been ever since they had moved here from the dining room following dinner, slightly turned so that his right side was in the shadow of the heavy velvet curtains. *What had happened to him?* Viscount Ravensberg—Kit— moved about the room, smiling, genial, occasionally interjecting a remark into a conversation, but not becoming a part of any group, and never approaching his brother.

He looked restless, rather like a caged animal of the wild.

Lauren had spent almost the whole evening seated beside the dowager countess, Kit's grandmother, close to the fire, though she had obliged the company by taking her turn briefly at the pianoforte. She had told the old lady about Newbury Abbey, about the weeks she had recently spent in London, about the few entertainments in which she had participated there. She had also listened. It was not easy to do when the dowager's speech was halting, punctuated by long, painful pauses as she tried to form words. It was tempting to interrupt, to supply the words she knew were about to be spoken, to complete sentences whose endings she could guess long before the words were out. It was what the earl and countess tended to do, Lauren had noticed both at tea and at dinner. Perhaps they were embarrassed for her in the company of guests. Perhaps they thought they did her a kindness. But it seemed unfortunate to Lauren.

She listened, giving the old lady her full attention, keeping her expression bright and interested. Nevertheless there was a great deal of time in which to think and observe. She had been welcomed to Alvesley with meticulous courtesy but perhaps without warmth. But she had not expected warmth. Courtesy was enough. Kit had played his part well. He had looked so delighted to see her, in fact, that Gwen had been totally beguiled. She had come into Lauren's room before they went down to tea together, hugged her, and beamed at her.

"Lauren," she had said, "he is quite gorgeous. That smile! And when he kissed you for all to see as soon as your feet touched the ground, I could have quite swooned with the romance of it." She had laughed merrily. "You *said* he could be quite outrageous."

That last remark had not been a criticism, though the kiss, brief peck though it had been, had almost robbed Lauren of her poise.

There had been almost no communication between him and his parents since her arrival, she had noticed. All three of them had spoken with her, with Aunt Clara, with Gwen. But not with one another. They were very upset with him, then, over this betrothal when they had hoped for another for him? And perhaps none of them could forget that he had fought with his elder brother three years ago, presumably over the woman they had both wanted to marry, and that afterward the earl had sent him away and told him never to return. How bitter an experience it must have been for the earl to see his eldest son die and suddenly to have his exiled second son as the new heir.

And how doubly bitter to Kit to know that his banishment had been revoked only because of his elder brother's death.

Kit and his younger brother both behaved as if the other did not exist. And yet Kit had made a point of introducing them on her arrival, and it had seemed to her at the time that he was fairly bursting with affection for his horribly wounded brother. *What had happened?*

The Earl of Redfield's family was certainly not a close or a happy one, she concluded. Suddenly the task ahead of her, the task she had taken on so glibly that night at Vauxhall, seemed daunting indeed. How could she help reconcile Kit with his family when the wounds were apparently both deep and long-standing? And when she was responsible for widening the gap, deepening the wounds? And when she was going to break off the engagement . . .

But her thoughts were distracted by the dowager countess, who had grasped her cane with the obvious intention of getting to her feet. Lauren restrained her first impulse to jump to her feet to help. She had not been asked for help, and any intrusion on her part might be resented. She smiled instead.

"Going to bed, Mother?" The earl was striding toward them. "Allow me to summon your dresser."

"I am . . . going to . . . walk first," she said.

"The evening air will not be good for your lungs, Mother," the countess said, raising her voice. "Wait until the morning."

"I'll . . . walk now," the old lady said firmly, waving her son away with her free hand. "With . . . Kit. And Miss . . . Edgeworth."

"She *will* insist that fresh air and exercise are good for her," the countess was explaining to Aunt Clara. "Though I am sure rest would do her more good. She insists upon walking along the terrace and back every day, rain or shine. But usually it is in the morning."

Kit meanwhile had come to draw his grandmother's free arm through his own while she leaned on her cane with the other hand. He was grinning his usual sunny smile.

"If you wish to walk now, Grandmama," he said, "we will walk now. If you wish to dance a jig, we will dance a jig—until you have worn me out. Will you come too, Lauren?"

"Of course," she said, getting to her feet.

And so five minutes later they had donned cloaks for warmth and were strolling slowly along the terrace, away from the stables, Kit's grandmother on his arm, Lauren on her other side, her arms clasped behind her.

"Tell me," the old lady said in her habitual slow, laborious manner, "how you . . . two met."

Kit's eyes met Lauren's over the top of her head, his eyes dancing. "Grandmama is an incurable romantic," he explained. "*You* tell her, Lauren."

But he was so much cleverer at such stories than she, Lauren thought. Gazing across a crowded ballroom, eyes alighting on her, heart skipping a beat, knowing that she was the one woman in this world meant for him—he could make it all sound quite soulful. Besides, it needed to be told from his perspective. She could, of course, describe . . . Her smile was entirely an inward one.

"It was in Hyde Park one morning," she said and watched the laughter arrested in Kit's eyes before she turned her head away and continued. "Lord Ravensberg—Kit—was in the middle of a fistfight with three laboring men while half the gentlemen of the *ton* cheered him on. He was stripped to the waist and he was swearing most vilely."

She listened to herself in some amazement. Lauren Edgeworth never told such sordid tales. And she was *never* motivated in either speech or action by a sense of mischief.

The old lady surprised her with a bark of laughter.

"The men had insulted a milkmaid," Lauren continued, "and Kit had ridden to her defense. He knocked them all down and then kissed the milkmaid as I was passing in company with my aunt and cousin."

"Actually, Grandmama," Kit said meekly, though Lauren could tell from his voice that he was enjoying himself, "it was the milkmaid who kissed me. It would have been ungallant to have taken the moral high road and turned my head away."

His grandmother chuckled.

"And then our eyes met," Lauren said, lowering her voice, "and it happened. Just like that."

She had never suspected that she had acting abilities. She was almost convincing herself that there had been an element of fate in that first shocking encounter.

"Every . . . woman," the old lady said, "loves a . . . rogue." She chuckled again.

"Well, I *was* warned against him, ma'am," Lauren said. "He has the most shocking reputation, you know. But when we met again at Lady Mannering's ball and he wangled an introduction and asked me to dance with him, how could I resist? It was a waltz, you see."

They had arrived at the end of the terrace. The daylight had gone, but the moon and stars prevented it from being a dark night.

"That is a rose arbor just ahead of us," Kit explained. "I will show it to you tomorrow, Lauren."

"I can smell the roses even now," she said, inhaling their heavy, sweet scent appreciatively.

"The formal gardens are below it," he said. "Beyond them are the trees. But there is a wilderness walk there with several pleasing prospects—all carefully planned, of course."

"I look forward to seeing it all," she said as they turned to stroll back to the house.

But when they had arrived there and climbed the steps and entered the hall, the old lady lifted her cane to summon the footman who was on duty.

"Your arm," she told him, relinquishing her grandson's. "Kit, you . . . must show . . . Miss Edgeworth . . . the roses."

He bent his head to kiss her cheek, his eyes alight with laughter, Lauren could see.

"A tryst all carefully orchestrated in advance, Grandmama?" he asked. "Morning *is* your usual time for walking, after all. But we will not disappoint you. I will take Lauren to the rose arbor. Just so that she may smell the roses, of course."

Lauren felt as if her cheeks were on fire.

Kit was laughing as they descended the steps to the terrace again, her arm drawn firmly through his. "I warned you that she is a romantic," he said. "She sat there in the drawing room all evening observing her grandson and his newly betrothed, who have been apart for two weeks, constrained by a roomful of relatives and good manners into exchanging no more than the occasional polite observation and yearning glance."

"I did *not* give you any yearning glances," she protested.

"Ah, but I did you," he said, turning in the direction of the rose arbor. "And of course, Grandmama had to devise a way to give me an opportunity to kiss you thoroughly before sending you off to bed."

She was intensely embarrassed. "I hope," she said primly, "I did not give the impression—"

"That you are deep in love with me?" he suggested. "I believe you did—to Grandmama at least. And then you told her that story of our meeting to confirm her impression. I did not expect that particular one."

"My lord." They were halfway along the terrace. "The charade is necessary only when we are in company with others. We need not go into the rose arbor. Your grandmother has gone to bed, I daresay, and will not know if we return immediately to the house. It is improper for us to be alone together like this. We are not really engaged."

"Oh, but we are." He moved his head a little closer to hers. "Until I hear otherwise, you are my betrothed. And what is this nonsense about our game being played only for the benefit of others? And why have I become 'my lord' again? I promised you adventure, did I not? And passion? We need to be alone together if I am to keep the promise. We are going to begin tonight in the rose arbor. You are going to be kissed."

"Kit!" she said sharply. "I did *not* ask for passion. At least, not for kisses. I would never dream—"

"You asked for adventure," he said, his mouth so close to her ear that she felt the warmth of his breath there. "For passion. In many ways they are interchangeable terms."

"It would be most improper," she said, truly alarmed. She did not like to remember their kiss at Vauxhall. She had tried to block it from her memory. It had been so very alarmingly . . . physical.

"I will try my best to see that it is," he said with a soft laugh as he led her down off the terrace and through a trellised arch into the arbor, where the scent of roses instantly assailed their senses.

"Kit!" But the more indignant she became, the more on her dignity, the better he would like it, of course. She had learned that about him. He loved to tease. He would never take her seriously. She changed the subject. Perhaps he would forget this nonsense. "Was your father very angry when you came home?"

"Oh, Lord, yes," he said. "He and Bewcastle—the lady's brother, that is—had actually signed a marriage contract. I am more in your debt than you realized, Lauren."

"The lady has been jilted, then," she said, wincing. "I know how that feels. Is she hurt?"

"Freyja?" he said. "She had her chance three years ago. She is doubtless annoyed, which is a little different from being hurt. She is good at annoyance. All the Bedwyns are. But they have no right to be annoyed. My father had no right to plan a marriage for me without waiting for me to come home to give my consent."

"Do they live far away?" she asked.

"Six miles."

He led her to a rustic bench and she sat down. "Our betrothal has caused dissension, then, between neighbors," she said. "That is unfortunate."

He set one foot on the bench beside her and draped an arm over his raised leg—just as she remembered his doing at Vauxhall.

"But unavoidable under the circumstances," he said. "I really did not want to be forced into that marriage, Lauren."

"And yet," she said, "you must have loved her three years ago." She wondered if she would have a chance to meet Lady Freyja Bedwyn.

"Sometimes," he said, "love dies."

She did not believe that. Certainly it was not true in her case. But there was no point in feeling guilty. He *did* have a right to choose his own bride, and she could see that without this temporary betrothal he would be trapped indeed. This was the very reason for their bargain.

"What happened to your younger brother?" she asked.

He abruptly lowered his foot to the ground and turned away to bend over a nearby bloom as if he were examining it closely.

"War happened," he said after a lengthy silence. "He insisted, against everyone's advice and pleas, including my own, that our father purchase a commission for him in my regiment so that he could follow me to the Peninsula. The military life is the very last thing Syd was cut out for, but he can be remarkably stubborn when he chooses to be. I promised my mother faithfully—and foolishly, of course— that I would look after him and protect him from harm. Less than a year later I brought him home more than half dead after the surgeons and the subsequent fever had finished with him. It was touch and go whether he would survive the journey. But I was determined that if he was going to die, at least it would be at home. I can be stubborn too."

She could just imagine how dreadful he must have felt. "But surely you do not blame yourself in any way," she said. "In the heat of battle it must have been impossible for you to protect him."

"It did not happen in battle," he said curtly.

She waited for him to explain, but he said no more.

"Did anyone else blame you?" she asked. "Did *he*?"

"Everyone, including me. The judgment was unanimous." He turned toward her suddenly and she saw the flash of his teeth in the darkness. He took her hand and drew her to her feet. "But that is all ancient history, Lauren, best forgotten. Syd survived. So did I. All is well that ends well, to coin a phrase that someone else must have coined before me. In the meantime we are wasting a perfectly decent moonlit night and the opportunity for romance that Grandmama has sanctioned."

Best forgotten. But it had not been forgotten by either brother. Or resolved. It must have happened the same summer he had fallen in love with Lady Freyja and then fought his elder brother when she had accepted his offer instead. Little wonder he had been so upset, if both his brothers had turned against him. And his father too. Yet it was understandable that the earl had sent him away—he had caused both his brothers physical harm.

Now he had come back to Alvesley, and as far as she could see all the old hurts were still festering. And now they had been made worse by this business of a marriage contract and his betrothal to her. What a mess she had walked into. Would she be able to do anything to put any of it right?

But this was not the time for such thoughts. She had not diverted his mind or his intentions after all. He meant to kiss her. She turned away from him, drawing her hand free of his. There was no need for this. This was not what she had meant.

But he stepped up behind her, wrapped his arms about her waist from behind, and drew her against him until the back of her head was nestled against his shoulder. She could feel all of his warm man's body against the curves of her back and thighs. And it felt good, she admitted with an inward sigh of resignation. It gave the illusion of romance, the illusion of closeness, of intimacy. So much of life, by its very nature, had to be lived alone. Some of it—too much—in loneliness.

She *had* asked for adventure. Impulsively, without any forethought. She had never known that she wanted it. And what was it exactly she *had* wanted? What had she meant by adventure? This? Had she wanted to be kissed again? To be held again? She had never craved physical closeness with any man. Oh, with Neville, perhaps. But with him it had been more ... affection, companionship, comfort that she had sought. She did not know what made life a vivid experience for some people—like Lily. That was what she had wanted to discover.

Lauren closed her eyes as the old unwilling hatred washed over her. What did Lily have that she did not? What did Lily know?

She turned in Kit's arms, setting a little distance between them as she did so. She looked into his shadowed face and saw that he was watching her closely. She could never be like Lily. She could never be comfortable with the sort of embrace that had happened at Vauxhall.

She was afraid that all those unfamiliar feelings would overwhelm her—and more afraid that they would not, that she would feel nothing if he kissed her again, that she would discover with absolute certainty that she was frigid. That he would turn away from her with distaste. That he would regret his bargain with her almost before it had begun. That she would know beyond any doubt that she was forever unlovable, undesirable, unwanted.

"No, no," he said softly, leaning his head a little closer, his hands at his back, "don't retreat into that iceberg. I have worked out that it is a mere defense, you see. I am not going to hurt you. I am not even going to kiss you, in fact. I have changed my mind."

How absurd now to feel her heart plummet with disappointment and humiliation. It was better that neither of them discover the truth about her. But—he did not even *want* to kiss her?

Both his hands came up to unbutton her cloak, and one of them tossed it onto the bench where she had been sitting. The night air was cool on her bare arms. His hands, in contrast, seemed to brand her with heat as he moved his palms slowly downward from the scalloped hems of her short sleeves to the backs of her hands. He clasped them as she shivered, curling his thumbs into her palms, and raised them to set on his shoulders. Then he rested his hands lightly on her hips.

"Lean your body against mine," he told her. "From shoulders to knees."

It sounded shocking indeed—the more so as she was the one required to make the move, not him. There was no suggestion of coercion in his hands. He would not force the issue, she knew. She would not have that excuse. She felt a sharp, pulsing ache in her lower abdomen and swayed toward him, bracing herself with her hands until the tips of her breasts touched his coat and then pressed against it. She closed her eyes and set her forehead against his shoulder. She could feel his muscled hardness and his body heat with all of her upper body. She could smell his musky cologne and the very maleness of him.

He still did not move. His hands remained on her hips.

She leaned her thighs against his, and her abdomen and hips followed. His hands slid around to her back then, but lightly, without threat. She could have escaped at any moment.

He did no more than that. Neither did she. But her body felt and adjusted itself to the planes of his, soft femininity against hard masculinity, while her emotions were in turmoil. Behind her closed eyelids she could see him as he had appeared in the park that first day, stripped to the waist, splendidly muscled in his chest, shoulders, and arms, slender hipped and lithe in his skin-tight breeches and boots. Vital and virile and male. The same body against which she now leaned. She could hear his heartbeat. She thought she might well be on fire.

Neither of them moved for what seemed a long time. But she knew one thing before she finally stepped away and bent to pick up her cloak. She had no experience with such matters, but she understood that physically at least he desired her. And she had discovered something else too. With her whole body—with her hot cheeks, with her tender, swollen breasts and pulsing womb and slightly trembling thighs—she felt her femininity. She knew that despite the discipline of a lifetime, she was not just a lady. She was also a woman.

He did not touch her or say anything, for which fact she was enormously grateful. She turned after a few moments to look at him, her cloak clutched in one hand. He was standing on the exact same spot.

"So," she said in an attempt to restore some semblance of normalcy. "Your side of the bargain has been kept for one day. But I have mine to keep too, my lord. It would not do for us to be absent from the house any longer."

She wished she could see his face more clearly as he regarded her in silence for a few moments. Then he bent to take her cloak from her hand, wrapped it about her shoulders and buttoned it at the neck, and offered his arm.

"Yes," he said, his voice brisk and cheerful, "duty accomplished for one day. Tomorrow I will apply myself again. We will ride. Early. At sunrise."

She fought disappointment again at his tone. Could he not have said something a little warmer, more personal? Had she only imagined . . . ? But it did not matter.

"I very rarely ride," she said. "And I almost never rise early."

"Tomorrow," he said, "you will do both. I am going to give you an enjoyable summer if I kill both of us in the process."

"How absurd," she said.

"Tomorrow morning early," he told her as they made their way along the terrace. "Appear voluntarily—and alone—or I will come into your bedchamber and get you myself."

"You would not dare," she said indignantly.

He looked at her sidelong. "That is one word that is inadvisable to use in my hearing," he said, "unless you are quite prepared for me to take you up on it. I would certainly dare."

"You are no gentleman," she told him.

"Why is it," he asked her as they ascended the marble steps, "that you still say that as if you had just now made the discovery?"

9

*K*it was out in the stables when Lauren appeared there. It was
only a little after six o'clock in the morning. Before leaving
the house he had sent his valet to instruct her maid to wake
her, but she must have been up already to have arrived here so soon—
and looking like elegance itself in a forest green riding habit with a
matching hat set just so on her carefully styled dark hair, its lavender
feather curling invitingly about one ear.

He had been looking forward to going to wake her himself. He
would have dared. Her outrage would have been something to behold.

"Good morning." He grinned at her. "I have had the quietest mare
in the stables saddled for you. The only tamer animal would have to
be lame in all four legs. I will be riding beside you. You have nothing
whatsoever to fear."

"I am not afraid of riding," she said. "I just do not enjoy it as an
exercise. I resent this, you know. You are supposed to give me an enjoyable summer—enjoyable to *me*—not force me into doing things I
distinctly dislike, like rising at this hour to ride."

"No, no," he said, chuckling. "I promised you a *memorable* summer, and I always keep my promises. But if it will make you feel better, I can tell you that we will be riding only a short distance. I have something altogether more pleasurable planned for you. We are going to swim."

"*What?*" She looked disdainfully at him instead of recoiling in horror as he had expected. It was very difficult to ruffle the outer feathers of Lauren Edgeworth. Good Lord, he had been aroused by her last evening, and she had been standing flush against him and must have realized it unless she was more of an innocent than she could possibly be at her age. Yet she had appeared as cool as a spring breeze when she drew away from him and informed him that his duty was done for one day. "I absolutely do not swim, my lord."

"Kit."

"Kit. I do not swim, *Kit.* That is my final word."

"Two strokes and a bubble?" he asked sympathetically, cupping his hands for her booted foot and tossing her up into the saddle. "You sink like a stone?"

"I really would not know," she said, arranging her skirts and sitting so gracefully that she looked as if she might have been born in the saddle. "I have never tried."

Never tried. Good Lord! What kind of childhood had she had? Or had she skipped childhood altogether? Perhaps she had been born a lady.

"Then you will start this morning," he told her, swinging up onto his own mount and leading the way out of the cobbled yard. "I will be your instructor."

"I will not." She rode after him. "And you will not."

If Vauxhall had not happened, he might have been repelled by her. So coldly dignified. So perfectly ladylike. So lacking in spirit and humor. So absolutely joyless. Though even then, perhaps, he would not be able to resist goading her. But Vauxhall *had* happened. And he knew that somewhere beneath layers and layers of cool decorum, behind mask upon mask of gentility, lay a woman desperate to come out into the light but not knowing the way. Like a child waiting to be born but clinging to the familiar, confining safety of the womb.

Keeping his promise to her was the one redeeming act he could do in his life. One small act, which would bring him no personal absolution, but which might set a fellow mortal free. He could teach her to embrace joy. It was something he could never do for himself, though his acquaintances might be skeptical if ever he were to say so. He wore very different masks from Lauren's. But it was possible to teach what one could not practice. It must be possible.

He led the way down the drive and across the bridge before turning to his right onto the path that followed the river and then skirted the bank of the lake. The trees were denser on this side than on the side closer to the house. Sometimes the path wove deeper into the wood so that the water was lost to sight altogether for a minute or two. He stopped at one such point and looked back to make sure Lauren was having no trouble following.

"What do you think?" he asked her.

She looked reproachfully at him. "I think," she said, "that all civilized mortals are still in their beds at this hour. And I seem to remember that you promised to show me the formal gardens today, not the wild woods. If this is your idea of giving me enjoyment, I made a sad bargain."

He was getting under her skin, then. The oh-so-proper Miss Lauren Edgeworth had allowed annoyance to creep into her voice. Kit grinned.

His destination was the temple folly. It had been built close to the water's edge years ago for picturesque effect, mainly for viewing from the opposite bank, where its marble perfection could be seen reflected in the lake on a calm day. But it also had a practical function as a resting place for those energetic enough to stroll all about the lake's perimeter. It had been used by his brothers and his boyhood self as a bathing hut. Bathing had always been permitted in the lake—provided they were supervised by an adult. The catch had been that only very rarely had any adult been available and willing to accompany them, and even then there had always been an adult voice yelling at them not to dive off tree branches, not to swim underwater, not to go out of their depth, not to ambush one another or squirt water at one another or pull one another under. So they had bathed here, where they were out of sight from the house and were likely to remain undetected.

He dismounted when they reached the folly and tethered his horse to a tree branch. Then he lifted Lauren down before untying the bundle that he had secured behind his saddle. He led the way around to the front of the folly and up the shallow flight of marble steps to open back the double doors beyond four pillars.

A wooden bench lined the three interior walls. The floor was tiled, the walls plain except for an intricately carved frieze, across which naked, curly haired youths chased fleet-footed nymphs through unlikely groves of riotous flowers and ripe fruit. He and his brothers had more than once stood on the bench in order to ogle and snicker over the nymphs, whose flimsy, diaphanous garments hid nothing whatsoever of the feminine charms beneath. Small wonder that the youths were in eternal pursuit.

"Have a seat," he offered, and Lauren sat against the inside wall, facing out toward the lake view, her feet set neatly side by side, her hands cupped one on top of the other in her lap. Kit set his bundle down and seated himself on one of the side benches. She looked severe and somewhat brittle.

"Newbury Abbey is close to the sea, is it not?" he asked her.

"Yes," she said. "The beach is part of the park."

"But you never swam there?"

She shook her head. "I have never liked the beach," she said. "Sand gets in one's shoes and clothes, and the salt wind off the water dries one's complexion. And the sea itself is . . . wild."

"Wild." He looked curiously at her. "You do not like wild nature?" Did not everyone love the sea? Was there really, perhaps, nothing but primness to the very core of her?

"Not the sea." She gazed out at the lake, which this early in the morning was like a smooth mirror reflecting the rays of the sun. "It is so vast, so unpredictable, so uncontrollable, so . . . cruel. Nothing comes back from the sea."

What or who had not come back? Had someone she knew drowned? And then he had an inkling.

"When your mother and your stepfather went away on their wedding trip," he asked her, "did they go overseas?"

She turned her head to look at him, rather startled, as if he had changed the subject.

"They went to France first," she said, "during a lull in the wars, and then gradually south and east. They were in India the last time I ever heard from them."

The sea had not brought her mother back.

"I am told that my uncle and aunt took me to see them on their way," she said. "Apparently I waved my handkerchief until the ship had disappeared beyond the horizon. It must have taken a very long time. But I have no memory of the event. I was only three years old."

No memory? Or a memory pushed so deep that it could not surface into her conscious mind?

The sea had never brought her mother back.

But this was not the sea, and he had not brought her here to make her melancholy. He got to his feet and stood in the doorway, looking out.

"Did none of your childhood playmates swim either?" he asked her. "Even in that pool you told me about?"

"Oh, yes," she said. "Neville and Gwen both did. It was forbidden, of course, but whenever they arrived back at the house with wet hair on a particularly hot and sunny day Aunt Clara would pretend not to notice and my uncle would purse his lips and ask if it was raining."

"But you never broke the rules yourself?"

"It was different for me," she said.

He looked back over his shoulder. "How so?"

"I was not their child," she explained. "I was not even a blood relation. I was a stranger foisted upon them by circumstances."

He felt angry on her behalf. "They treated you like an outsider, then?" he asked.

"No." Her answer was very firm. "They showered me with love. They treated me no differently than the way they treated their own. I was as much Neville's sister as Gwen was. And Gwen and I were bosom friends almost from the day of my arrival. You must have seen yesterday that Aunt Clara and Gwen both hold me in affection. They came *here* with me. But they . . . Well, I owed them so much, you see. How could I disobey my uncle and aunt? How could I not every day of my life do everything in my power to show my gratitude, to prove myself worthy of their affection?"

He believed that Lauren Edgeworth had just presented him with an answer to some of the questions he had about her. *This* was why she had shaped herself into being the woman she was—no, not woman. *Lady* was a far more appropriate word. In order to earn acceptance and love? This was why her whole life until a year and a half ago had been devoted to Kilbourne, who apparently had told her when he went off to the Peninsula that she was not to wait for him? Because her adopted parents had planned a match between them? Because in a marriage to Kilbourne she had foreseen final acceptance, final security?

But that security had been cruelly destroyed.

Was she in fact, despite all her control and dignity, the most insecure person he had ever known?

"Do you have much to do with your father's family?" he asked her.

"No. None whatsoever," she said. "After my mother had been gone for a year or so, my uncle wrote to ask if my own family wished me returned to them until she *did* come home. Viscount Whitleaf, my uncle, who succeeded to the title after my father's death, said no. But I did not know this until after I wrote to him myself when I was eighteen and he wrote back to tell me that—that it was a practice of his never to encourage hangers-on or indigent relatives."

Kit stared at her over his shoulder, but she was looking at the hands spread in her lap, as she had done at Vauxhall, he remembered. *What the devil?* He certainly wished he had known this two weeks ago.

"My grandfather would have taken me, I believe, if he had been asked," she said, looking up at him again, a slightly defiant tilt to her chin, as if she expected him to argue the point. "But he would have thought, correctly, that I was better off with children of roughly my own age."

Galton had never offered to take her, then?

Kit grinned at her suddenly. "We are wasting the best part of the morning," he said, "when the water is at its calmest and freshest."

"Go and enjoy it, then," she said somewhat tartly. "I will sit here and watch you, though I would ask that you not remove your shirt. It would be most improper."

He laughed outright. "For propriety's sake," he said, "I must bathe in my coat and boots, then, and you in your habit and feathered hat? We would ruin perfectly decent clothes and look like a couple of drowned rats at the end of it all."

"I am not bathing at all," she said. "You may get that notion out of your head, my lord. And you might have the decency to do that outside where I will not have to watch you."

He had stripped off his coat and flung it onto the bench. He was tugging at one of his boots.

"What are you more afraid of?" he asked. "Getting your toes wet? Or allowing me to see them bare?"

Her cheeks turned slightly pinker. "I am not afraid of anything," she said.

"Good." He tossed his one boot under the bench and tackled the other. "You have five minutes to get down to your shift. After that you are going to be tossed in, ready or not."

"*What?*"

"Four minutes and fifty seconds."

"My sh-shift?" Her cheeks were flaming.

"I suppose," he said, "you are wearing one. I perceive a slight problem if you are not. I may not be able to restrain my blushes."

She stood up, all polar righteousness as his second boot disappeared beneath the bench. He was unbuttoning his waistcoat.

"I am going back to the house," she announced. "I begin to see that I should have listened to my relatives in London after all. Stand out of the doorway, if you please, my lord."

He grinned, and his waistcoat landed on top of his coat. He began tugging his shirt free of his riding breeches. "Four minutes."

Her nostrils flared. "You would not dare."

"Ah. That ill-advised word again." His shirt came off over his head and he wondered if she would swoon.

But she was made of sterner stuff. "You are no gentleman, my lord."

He tipped his head to one side as he mentally debated with himself whether he would bathe in his breeches or—far more sensibly—in his drawers. "You really ought to aim for some originality, you know. Three minutes fifteen seconds." He decided reluctantly on the breeches. He had brought an extra pair with him, after all. He lifted one leg to peel off his stocking.

"Please," she said quietly, "let me go."

Would he really toss her in, fully clothed? Probably not, he decided. Undoubtedly not, in fact.

"You wanted an adventure, Lauren," he said. "You wanted a summer quite different from any other you have ever known. You wanted to know what it feels like to live as other people live—people who do not have to earn the respect and love of those who nurture them. You wanted to know exuberance and happiness and freedom from restraint. You cannot have it both ways. You cannot expect these things to drop into your lap if you do not reach out to embrace them. I cannot keep my side of our bargain if you will not allow me to."

"I do not know how to swim," she said.

"I will teach you," he told her. "The water is not even very deep at this point. It is less than shoulder deep."

"I cannot remove my . . . I *cannot*," she said.

It was a definite problem. He could see that, given the type of woman she was.

"I'll jump in and swim for a few minutes," he said. "I'll not even glance in this direction. I'll not even know it for a while if you decide to steal off back to the house. When you are ready, wrap one of the towels about you—they are large—and come to the bank. I'll help you into the water. Or you can jump in unassisted if you prefer and I'll not see you at all."

"Kit," she said, "I did not know it was going to be like this. I did not *mean* this."

"Or kisses. Or passion. Or riding. What *did* you mean, then?" he asked her. "Go back to the house if you wish. I will not stop you."

He turned and strode away to the bank. He dived in headfirst and came up a short distance out into the lake, gasping from the shock of the water's coldness. He shook the drops out of his eyes and then put his face back under and began a slow crawl in the direction of the opposite bank.

"Kit?"

Several minutes had passed and, though he had not looked back to the folly, he was convinced that she must have started back to the house, probably on foot. But before he could turn his head to look, she called his name again.

"*Kit.*"

She was huddled over at the edge of the bank, kneeling, all except her head from the chin up wrapped inside the blanket in which he had rolled the towels. He swam a few strokes closer to her.

"The water is freezing," she said. "I cannot do this. Please don't make me."

What she could not do, he guessed, was take off that blanket and expose herself to his view, clad only in her shift. He felt his temperature rise a notch, cold water notwithstanding, at the realization that she must indeed have removed most of her clothes. He swam the rest of the distance and stood a couple of feet from her, both his hands outstretched.

"The moment of truth," he said. "How strong *is* your desire for adventure? How great *is* your courage to attempt something new and different? And undeniably daring. This is it, Lauren. Now or never."

She drew the blanket tighter about herself, if that were possible.

"Take my hands," he said. "Or go back home."

Back *home*, he had said deliberately. Not back to the house. He could see from the look in her eyes that she understood him. If she wished it, the whole charade could be over with this morning, almost before it had begun. She could return to Newbury or to London with her aunt and cousin.

She moved into a crouch and set first one and then the other hand in his, and with nothing left to hold it about her, the blanket slipped to the grass. Her cheeks flamed, he tightened his grasp on her hands, and she jumped—the lesser of two evils, he supposed, since her slim, shapely legs had been suddenly exposed from the knees down as well as her arms and shoulders and a generous expanse of bosom. She looked a good deal younger than usual.

And then she was gasping convulsively and clawing at him with both hands in utter panic. He grasped her waist and drew her under with him until the water covered their shoulders and she would have only its temperature to contend with and not the morning air as well. He was laughing—mainly at the impropriety of what he had coaxed her into. Her bare legs brushed against his and he was very aware that there was almost nothing between his hands and bare, inviting flesh.

"You are not going to drown," he assured her, "or freeze to death. You will be used to the water soon. It is not so very cold. Hold your breath."

He drew her down with him until they were fully submerged. He felt her fingernails dig into his arms and saw that her eyes were tightly closed and her hair floating in a dark cloud about her face. He lifted them both to the surface almost immediately.

She surprised him then. She opened her eyes, stared at the bank and at the water, and then into his eyes, droplets gleaming on her thick lashes. "I did it," she said. And then again, as if it were a moment of immense triumph, "I *did* it."

He threw back his head and laughed.

He began her first lesson, teaching her how to put her face in the water without panicking, how to blow out through both her nose and her mouth. She was a surprisingly apt pupil. Though perhaps it was not so very surprising. He suspected that she had always been diligent in her efforts to master whatever she set out to accomplish.

Finally he taught her how to float on her back. Once he had convinced her that she would not simply sink like a leaden weight to the bottom and neither be seen nor heard from ever again, she relaxed and followed his instructions. But she would do it only as long as he had a firm hold on her back beneath her shoulders. The last time she tried, he kept his hands braced beneath her until he knew she was re-laxed and buoyant, then he slipped them away. She floated alone, her arms stretched out to the sides, her eyes closed. After a few seconds he stepped away and waded around until he was a little way in front of her feet.

"The sky is lovely this morning," he said. "There are just enough fluffy white clouds up there to accentuate the blue."

She opened her eyes and gazed upward. "Yes," she agreed—and then realized where he was. She sank, came up sputtering, and wiped water from her eyes with both hands.

"I might have drowned!" she scolded. And then she lowered both hands, fixed him with a wide gaze of astonishment from her lovely vi-olet eyes, and . . . *smiled.* A full, sunny smile that lit up her face and made her suddenly and radiantly pretty. "I *did* it, Kit. *I floated alone.*"

She came wading toward him and somehow—his mind did not follow the full sequence of events—her arms were twined tightly about his neck and his about her waist and he was twirling her in the water, taking them downward as he did so, and covering her mouth with his own just before they went right under.

Sounds were muted. Time was suspended. There was body heat and there was mouth heat and for the timeless moments while they were submerged there were triumph and exuberance and pride and even joy all mingled together with raw lust.

And then they broke above the surface and were drawing apart and she was herself again—and he was himself once more.

"Your first adventure, ma'am," he said, deliberately careless laugh-ter in his voice, "safely accomplished and duly rewarded."

"*Scandalously* rewarded," she said, eyeing him warily. "But what could I expect from the infamous Viscount Ravensberg? It must be getting late."

"Lord, yes," he said. "And any or all of our relatives might be given the impression that you have been out enjoying the morning air with your betrothed. That would be shocking indeed."

"I came to Alvesley to lend you countenance," she reminded him, "not to embroil you in further scandal."

He chuckled and pulled himself up onto the bank. He ran the few steps to the temple and came back with one towel wrapped about himself and the other in his hand. It was devilish cold out of the water.

"Take my hand." He bent to haul her out.

She might as well have been wearing nothing at all. He was uncomfortably reminded of the nymphs on the frieze inside the folly—and of his reaction to them as a boy. Clothed, she was a beautiful lady. Wearing only a soaking wet shift, which clung to every slender curve, she was woman and wanton and siren—and eminently beddable. He tossed her the dry towel, stalked off to fetch his clothes from inside, and without a backward glance took them around into the trees in order to dress and leave her some privacy to do the same.

They were on their way back to the house ten minutes later, her horse ahead of his. Apart from the fact that her hair was damp and curlier than usual, she looked like the elegant ice maiden to whom he had grown accustomed. Her towel was rolled up in front of her sidesaddle. She had refused to give it to him, probably, he thought, trying not to dwell on the images that came to mind, because her wet shift was wrapped inside it. Which meant, of course, that she was wearing nothing beneath that very fetching riding habit.

It was all very well, he thought, to have agreed to give her a memorable summer and even a taste of passion. It was quite another thing to find himself with lascivious designs on a woman whose avowed ambition was to live an independent existence as a spinster. His mind needed some distraction.

"Did Lady Muir hurt herself recently?" he asked her. "Or is the limp habitual?"

"She was thrown from her horse," she told him, "while she was married. Her leg was broken and apparently not set properly. She also suffered a miscarriage."

"And widowhood not long after?" he asked. "She cannot be any older than you."

"One year older," she said. "Lord Muir died as the result of a horrible accident in their home. He fell over a balustrade into the hall below. She was with him at the time. As you may imagine, it took her a long, long while to recover—if she has fully recovered even now. It was a love match, you see."

Kit did not comment. What was there to say about a young woman whose life had been so dogged by tragedy? Apart from the limp, one would not know she had suffered at all. She smiled a great deal and was charming and personable.

How impossible it was, he thought just as if he were making a startling new discovery, to know people from their outer demeanor. How myriad were the masks people wore.

Lauren Edgeworth's back was rigid with ladylike dignity. Yet less than half an hour ago she had smiled with sunny exuberance and flung herself into his arms. Simply because for the first time in her life she had floated on her back.

He smiled with silent amusement and at the same time felt a curious ache in his throat, almost as if he were on the verge of tears.

10

Lauren was not late for breakfast, as she had feared she would be. There was even time for her maid to do something to disguise the dampness of her hair after she had changed her clothes. She went down with Gwen and her aunt, both of whom called at her room first to tell her how favorably impressed they were with their welcome to Alvesley, and how well they liked Lord Ravensberg. And how happy they were for her, of course.

The whole family was assembled for breakfast, with the exception of the dowager, who always remained quietly in her own apartments for most of the morning before going out for her daily walk, the countess explained. The earl himself seated the ladies, placing Lauren to his right, Aunt Clara to his left.

"You went riding with Ravensberg this morning," he observed to Lauren. "I saw you leave the stables."

"Yes, my lord." She smiled. "The early morning air was fresh and invigorating. We rode through the woods to the temple folly on the far bank of the lake. The view from there is quite splendid."

"Yes, indeed," he said.

"You have been on an outing already this morning?" Aunt Clara asked, all astonishment. "*You,* Lauren? *Riding?*"

And swimming too, Lauren thought. How terribly mortified she would be if the earl had witnessed that too. But she had *floated. Alone.* And then she had lost her head—something a lady never did—and launched herself at Kit in her excitement. And he had kissed her. Or had she kissed him? But that possibility did not bear thinking of.

Gwen was laughing. "Lauren has never been an early riser," she said. "And riding has never been her favorite form of exercise. I believe you are having a positive influence on her, Lord Ravensberg."

"I do hope so. But perhaps, ma'am," he replied, mischief in his eyes, "it was merely the effect of coercion. I threatened to haul her out of bed in person if she did not appear in the stables of her own volition."

Lauren felt her cheeks flame.

"Kit!" his mother said reproachfully.

Aunt Clara laughed.

"That would do it," Gwen said gleefully.

"The exercise has whipped a healthy glow into your complexion, Miss Edgeworth," the earl told her. "Sydnam, will you be ready after breakfast to help me inspect the new roofs on the laborers' cottages?"

"Certainly, sir," his son replied.

Kit, Lauren noticed, was not invited to join them. Neither did he suggest it himself. Of course, Mr. Butler was his father's steward. But even so . . .

The countess planned to call on her neighbors during the morning to deliver personal invitations to the festivities for her mother-in-law's birthday.

"Kit will attend you this morning," she said to her guests.

"But may I not be of some assistance to you, ma'am?" Lauren asked.

"That is extremely kind of you." The countess looked approvingly at her. "Yes, thank you, Miss Edgeworth. It would certainly be appropriate for me to introduce Kit's betrothed to the neighborhood. Lady Kilbourne, Lady Muir, would you care to accompany us too?"

It was decided that all four of the ladies would go visiting.

It was Sydnam Butler who introduced an awkward note into the discussion of the various morning plans. "Will you be calling at Lindsey Hall, Mother?" he asked. "Will you be taking an invitation there?"

"It is rather far," she said. "I believe I will have a servant take over a card."

"When all the other invitations are to be delivered in person?" Kit said. "It might be construed as something of a slight, might it not, Mother?"

"I daresay," she said briskly, "they will not be able to attend anyway. Though of course an invitation must be sent. Now, I believe we ought—"

"I will ride over there and be your messenger," Kit said. "It will give me something to do this morning."

There was an awkward little silence.

"But I would like to come with you, Kit," Lauren told him. "Can you wait until after we return? It would appear strange that I have been introduced everywhere else except Lindsey Hall."

The earl cleared his throat but then, when everyone looked his way, appeared to have nothing to say.

"I do understand all the awkwardness of the present relations between Alvesley and Lindsey Hall," Lauren assured the earl and countess. "I know what has happened, and I have explained it to Aunt Clara and Gwen. I really do believe that Kit and I should do our best to prevent any permanent estrangement. We should go together this afternoon. How the Duke of Bewcastle receives us and whether he and his family attend the birthday celebrations will be their decision."

"Oh, my dear." The countess sighed. "There is really no need for you to do this. The duke and his family can be very . . . Well, they do not take kindly to having their will crossed. This is entirely a problem for us to handle."

"But I am to be one of your family, ma'am," Lauren reminded her.

"It is certainly the right thing to do. I applaud your courage, Miss Edgeworth." The earl was looking at her with considerable respect. "Ravensberg will wait for you."

Kit, Lauren saw when she looked across the table at him, was re-garding her with steady, unsmiling eyes.

The rest of the morning was busy, but it offered nothing beyond the range of Lauren's experience. They called upon six families, three in the village, three in the country beyond it. Partly in fulfillment of her bargain with Kit, partly because it was second nature to her any-way, she made herself agreeable and charming. She was, of course, the focus of everyone's curious attention as the affianced bride of Lord Ravensberg. She had her main reward when for a few moments as Mrs. Heath showed off her flower garden to Aunt Clara and Gwen before they returned to the barouche, she walked at the countess's side.

"You are an extremely pleasant surprise," the countess said.

Lauren looked inquiringly at her.

"We have heard very little that is good about Kit since his return to England last year," his mother said. "We were quite dismayed when he came home two weeks ago and told us about you. We expected the worst, I must admit. It is an enormous relief to discover that he has chosen a perfectly charming lady."

"Thank you, ma'am." Lauren flushed with pleasure. "But were you very disappointed? About Lady Freyja Bedwyn, I mean?"

"Redfield and the Duke of Bewcastle—both this man and his fa-ther before him—have always dreamed of an alliance between our two houses since our lands adjoin," the countess explained. "Our el-dest son died before he could marry Lady Freyja. Redfield thought a match with her would suit Kit. We both did. We were taken entirely by surprise when he came home with news of his betrothal to some-one else. I cannot say I am entirely disappointed, especially after meeting you. I think you will do very well for my son. Perhaps you will be able to persuade him to settle down at last." She sighed. "And to be happy again."

There was no time for any further conversation together. Soon they were in the barouche and Aunt Clara was exclaiming over the beauty of Mrs. Heath's garden.

Lauren was left to deal silently with her guilt. How were Kit's parents going to feel when she broke off the engagement at the end of the summer? They were real people. They were not the heartless tyrants she had imagined when Kit had told his story in Vauxhall, but parents who wanted the best for their son. They wanted his happiness.

How could she have agreed to this deception? No—how could she have *suggested* it?

The need to confide in someone was suddenly almost overwhelming. She met Gwen's eyes across the barouche. Gwen was smiling at her and looking happy—happy for *her*. She had been terribly hurt for Lauren's sake by the events of last year. She felt disloyal, Lauren knew, for loving Lily and for feeling happy about her brother's happiness. She thought now that Lauren had found her happily-ever-after.

But a bargain was a bargain, Lauren decided. She could not tell anyone the truth until this was all over.

Less than two hours later Lauren was sitting beside Kit in his curricle. It was a perfect summer afternoon, but Lauren, shielding her complexion beneath the shade of a parasol, was in no mood to enjoy it. She was uncomfortable for two particular reasons. She kept remembering the early morning with considerable embarrassment, and she was more nervous about the coming visit than she cared to admit.

Kit seemed disinclined to talk as he drove along the country lane at a pace that seemed far too recklessly fast to Lauren. But she would not reprove him. She just wished he would talk about the weather or some other safe topic. Had she *actually* been in the lake with him this morning *in her shift* while he had worn nothing at all above the waist? Could it possibly have been merely a dream? But no, her dreams had never been that bizarre. She twirled her parasol.

"I have realized," he said without turning his head, "that it is a sign of emotion even when you are looking perfectly composed."

"What is?" She looked blankly at him.

"You send your parasol for a spin," he said, "and fan my cheek with the breeze it whips up. It is a sign of emotion. It betrays you."

"How utterly foolish," she said, holding her parasol quite still.

"Are you nervous?"

"No, of course not."

"Then you should be," he said.

An ancient wagon top-heavy with a load of hay was lumbering toward them. Kit deftly drew his curricle to the side of the road so that the hedgerow brushed alarmingly against the wheels, and grinned in acknowledgment of the farmer, who was bobbing his head and pulling respectfully at his forelock while his wrinkled face was wreathed in smiles. The horses did not reduce speed. Lauren slowly released her death grip on the handle of her parasol as they drew clear and had the narrow road to themselves again.

"There are six Bedwyns," Kit continued just as if between two sentences he had not put both their lives at risk, "none or most of whom you may be about to meet. And not a one of them will be feeling kindly disposed to either of us. They are, in order of birth, Bewcastle himself, who succeeded his father to the title when he was just seventeen, Aidan, Rannulf, Freyja, Alleyne, and Morgan. Their mother was apparently a voracious reader of the history and literature of old Briton—hence their outlandish names. Bewcastle is Wulfric, though not many people outside his own family have ever called him that. We were all friends and playmates during our growing years except for Bewcastle, who was too superior, and Morgan, who was too young. Aidan is doing his bit in the Peninsula. The others are all at home this summer, I believe. They are all hellions, Lauren, regardless of gender. It has occurred to me since this morning that in agreeing to your offer to accompany me here I have perhaps agreed to feed the lamb to the wolves."

It all sounded dreadfully alarming. But she had been taught that civility and gentility were the answer to all of life's ills, that the outer demeanor was all-important, any inner uncertainties being something to be kept strictly to oneself.

"I am not afraid," she said. "I came to Alvesley to help you establish yourself here on your own terms. It was part of our bargain. The attempt to mend the breach between your two families is necessary."

They had turned off the narrow country road they had been following for several miles and were proceeding up a wide, straight avenue lined with elm trees toward an imposing stone mansion, which appeared to be a blend of so many architectural styles that it was impossible to label it with one word. Yet it was magnificent. It was Lindsey Hall, Lauren supposed. She ruthlessly ignored the queasiness in her stomach.

"It occurs to me," Kit said, "that you are fulfilling your side of our bargain with single-minded devotion, Lauren. I am going to have to apply myself more diligently to mine. I will owe you some exhilarating adventure after this afternoon. And some grand passion."

"I am not going swimming again today," she said hastily. "Or kissing you again—ever."

He chuckled. "Actually," he said, "I had tree climbing in mind."

Her mind exploded with alarm, but there was no time to pursue the matter. The avenue divided into two branches close to the house and circled about a large and magnificent flower garden with a marble fountain at its center. Water spouted thirty feet into the air, creating the impression of a million diamonds and an array of rainbows against the summer sunshine. Kit helped Lauren down before the front doors and relinquished his horses and curricle to the care of a groom, who had come running from the stables.

"The house is a hodgepodge of various architectural styles," Kit explained as he rapped the knocker against the door. "All courtesy of generations of dukes and earls before them who extended and improved without pulling anything down. The great hall, as you will see, is pure Middle Ages."

He was quite right, Lauren saw as soon as they stepped inside. The ceiling was oak-beamed, the plain walls hung with weapons and coats of arms and faded old banners. One huge fireplace dominated the wall opposite the door, and a massive oak table took up most of the central floor space.

"I will see if his grace is at home, m'lord," the elderly butler said as he admitted them.

If the duke was at home, he certainly kept them waiting a long

time. Of course, he might well refuse to see them even if he *was* here.
But Lauren refused to feel apprehension. They had made this necessary courtesy call, and that was what mattered. Kit was silent. He
stood inside the outer doors, his booted feet slightly apart, his hands
clasped at his back, looking rather grim.

There was a minstrel gallery at one end of the hall, with an intricately carved oak screen reaching from beneath the protruding
balustrade of the balcony to the floor below. Lauren wandered closer
so that she could more easily examine the details of the carving. And
then a voice spoke from directly above her.

"Well," it said—a deep man's voice, pleasant enough and yet with
some indefinable edge of unpleasantness too, "Lieutenant-Colonel
Lord Ravensberg in person."

Kit looked sharply upward while Lauren stayed where she was beneath the overhang of the gallery. "Ralf?" He nodded curtly.

It was Lord Rannulf Bedwyn, then? He spoke again. "A social call,
Kit? Not the wisest thing you have ever done, old chap. Do yourself a
favor and take yourself off back to your Friday-faced bride. You
should suit each other. An alliance of the jilted, I understand."

Lauren felt acutely uncomfortable and quite undecided whether to
show herself or not.

"Pardon me," Kit said, just as pleasantly as the invisible man, "but
I have not been informed that you are master of Lindsey Hall or have
any authority to give the orders here, Ralf. My business is with
Bewcastle. I have come to present my betrothed to him since it ap-
pears we will be neighbors in the future."

Lord Rannulf laughed softly. "Is the prospective bride cowering
beneath my feet?" he asked. "I have lived at Lindsey Hall most of my
life and have been embarrassed in just this way so many times one
would think I would have learned by now to search beneath the
gallery before unbuttoning my lips. Accept my apologies, ma'am. My
quarrel is with Kit, not you."

Lauren stepped away from the screen and looked upward. He was
leaning nonchalantly on the balustrade, a great giant of a man with
thick, unruly fair hair and strong, handsome features. He put her

powerfully in mind of Viking warriors she had read about in her history books.

"Your apology is accepted, my lord," she said. "It is always shocking, is it not, to be overheard being spiteful by the very person concerned? Especially when one reflects upon the fact that one does not know that person at all—has not even met her, in fact. But there are none of us who cannot benefit from lessons in discretion and kindness."

He grinned appreciatively down at her. "Present me, Kit," he commanded. "I do believe I have just been dealt a withering setdown by a lady who is going to remember in a moment that it is unladylike to address any remark to a gentleman to whom she has not been properly introduced."

"Meet Lord Rannulf Bedwyn, Lauren," Kit said, "who would not recognize good manners if they reared up and punched him in the nose. The Honorable Miss Edgeworth, Ralf. To whom you owe an apology."

The giant continued to grin at her. "A beauty, by gad," he said. "The Friday-faced remark was quite unjustified, ma'am, and would not have been uttered if I had set eyes on you first. My humblest, most abject apologies. But it would appear the *master* of Lindsey Hall is about to grant you an audience. Or, I suppose, to have you informed that he is from home. Which is it, Fleming?"

The butler ignored him. "Follow me, my lord," he instructed Kit, bowing deferentially and turning to lead the way across the hall in the opposite direction from the gallery.

Lauren could hear Lord Rannulf's soft chuckle as she took Kit's arm. A very dangerous gentleman indeed, she thought. Kit had described him as a hellion—and all his brothers and sisters too.

One would not have guessed it from the scene that met her eyes in the drawing room. It was a huge, long room, and all its occupants were gathered at the far end of it. All were silent and absolutely still as Kit and Lauren progressed along the length of the room. Deliberately so, Lauren guessed. The size and splendor of the room itself seemed designed to awe guests, to reduce them to size and at the same time to a quivering mass of humble subservience. The tableau presented by its occupants was intended to complete the process. But Lauren was made of stern stuff. She looked about her instead of directing her eyes downward to the Persian carpet beneath her feet, as she suspected she was meant to do.

The Duke of Bewcastle—the man standing before the fireplace in the end wall must surely be he—was tall, forbiddingly dark, thin-lipped, and unmistakably haughty. There was no hint of a smile in his hooded eyes, no sign of welcome in his demeanor. A thin young girl, as dark in coloring as the duke, sat stiff and unsmiling to one side of him beside an older lady in black. At the duke's other side, one ringed hand resting on the back of a sofa, stood a slender, dark young man, whose resemblance to the duke was unmistakable though he was extremely handsome and did have an expression on his face—one of cold mockery. It was matched by the lady who sat on the sofa. Lauren knew immediately that she must be looking at Lady Freyja Bedwyn, even though this first glance was a shock. Despite Kit's warning about the family, she had somehow pictured a pale, pretty, timid, abject creature, who was powerless before the will of her brother.

Lady Freyja Bedwyn was wearing riding clothes, including boots, in the middle of the afternoon and in the drawing room. She was not at all pretty or dainty or softly feminine in demeanor. She wore her fair hair in a mass of loose, unruly curls about her shoulders and halfway down her back. She sat with one leg crossed over the other in a shockingly unladylike posture and was swinging the dangling foot while looking Lauren over from head to toe with narrow-eyed thoroughness.

Their progress down the room took only a few seconds, Lauren supposed. It seemed to take five minutes at the very least. His grace inclined his head when they were close.

"Ravensberg," he said. His voice was soft and quite arctic in tone.

"Bewcastle?" Kit replied with his usual good humor. He might even, Lauren realized suddenly, be enjoying this reception his neighbors and erstwhile friends had obviously orchestrated for his discomfort. "I have the pleasure of presenting my betrothed, the Honorable

Miss Lauren Edgeworth of Newbury Abbey. His grace, the Duke of Bewcastle, Lauren."

Lauren found herself being regarded from a pair of keen, heavy-lidded silver eyes that had her thinking of wolves. A matter of association, perhaps? Had Kit not said that his given name was Wulfric?

"Miss Edgeworth," he said in the same courteous, arctic tone as she curtsied. "May I present Lady Freyja Bedwyn, Lady Morgan with her governess, Miss Cowper, and Lord Alleyne."

Yes, she had correctly identified Lady Freyja, Lauren saw as she curtsied to each of them and Lord Alleyne Bedwyn bowed to her, his eyes doing to her what his sister's had just done, except that this time she felt as if garments were being stripped away with the progress of his eyes.

"We have come on an errand from my mother. She requests that all of you attend my grandmother's birthday celebrations," Kit said cheerfully. "Though we would be happy to have you put in an appearance any time before then too. A houseful of family guests will be arriving tomorrow, and we already have with us the Dowager Countess of Kilbourne and Lady Muir, her daughter."

"Lady Redfield is kind," his grace said. "Miss Edgeworth, have a seat. Miss Cowper, see to it that the tea tray is brought up."

The governess got to her feet, curtsied without lifting her eyes to her employer, and hurried from the room.

Lauren took the chair indicated.

"Kilbourne," Lady Freyja said, frowning, one long-nailed forefinger against her chin. "There is a familiarity. Ah, yes. Did not the present countess appear at Newbury under rather spectacular circumstances to prevent the earl from making a bigamous marriage?"

"In the nick of time, Free, I understand," Lord Alleyne said with languid hauteur. "The wedding service had begun. The bride was already blushing."

"Ah, yes, I remember now," Lady Freyja said—and then looked arrested. "But the abandoned bride . . . Not *you*, Miss Edgeworth?" Malice gleamed in her eyes.

"You have been quite correctly informed in the matter," Lauren said.

"But how unpardonably rude of me inadvertently to have reminded you of such a humiliation," Lady Freyja said, still nonchalantly swinging her booted foot. "Do forgive me."

It was just such mockery as this that Lauren had feared when she went to London. This was the first time she had actually to face it. "There is nothing to forgive," she said. "We all speak rather too hastily on occasion." She smiled and turned her attention to the duke. "I had time to admire the oak screen in the hall below, your grace. The carvings are remarkably well preserved. Are they original?"

For fifteen minutes, almost until the moment when they could decently take their leave, Lauren skillfully led the conversation, focusing it upon impersonal topics in which they could all participate, refusing to be cowed by the deliberate reluctance of the Bedwyns to allow the chilled atmosphere to warm by a single degree.

"Do you ride, Miss Edgeworth?" Lady Freyja asked suddenly in the very middle of a discussion on the merits of spending at least a part of the year in town.

"Of course," Lauren said.

"To hounds?"

"No, I have never done so."

"But you consider yourself an accomplished horsewoman?"

"It depends upon what you mean by accomplished," Lauren said. "Of course I can—"

"Do you gallop across country?" Lady Freyja asked. "Do you jump hedges rather than find a gate to open? Do you risk your neck for the sheer thrill of feeling horseflesh between your thighs?"

One's training as a lady could sometimes be a boon indeed. The vulgarity of those final words had been intended to shock, and they had succeeded. How could Lady Freyja speak so in the presence of gentlemen? And did she really ride *astride*? But not by even the flicker of an eyelid did Lauren display her intense discomfort.

"No," she said, smiling. "In that sense I am afraid I am not at all accomplished."

"Do you swim?"

"No." This was not the time to boast of being able to float.

"Or play cricket?"

A gentleman's sport? "No."

"Or shoot?"

Gracious! "Indeed not."

"Or fish?"

"I have never tried it."

"Or play billiards?"

"No."

"What *do* you do, Miss Edgeworth?" Lady Freyja asked, open contempt in both her voice and her eyes, having succeeded in making Lauren seem as dull and helpless as it was possible for a fellow human to be.

No one rushed to help out—not even Kit, who merely looked curiously at her. Everyone else focused upon her incredibly dull self with cold courtesy, except perhaps Miss Cowper, who looked anxious, as if she knew what it was like to be an object of Lady Freyja's scorn.

"I have a number of the accomplishments expected of a lady of good *ton*," Lauren said, looking Lady Freyja directly in the eye, "though I do not boast of genius in any one of them. I am adept at various kinds of needlework, I keep household accounts, I speak French and Italian as well as English, I sketch, play the pianoforte, sing, write letters that my family and acquaintances find legible and interesting and prompt, read books to improve my mind and conversation. Ah, and I have learned the difficult art of courtesy under all circumstances. In particular I always consider it my duty when at home to set my guests at their ease and to lead the conversation into topics that will neither embarrass them nor expose their ignorance."

Lord Alleyne sat with pursed lips, his eyes alight with laughter, Lauren saw as she got to her feet to take her leave and the gentlemen followed suit.

"We will hope to see you all at Alvesley soon," Kit said.

"It has been a pleasure, your grace," Lauren said, addressing the duke. "Thank you for your kind hospitality."

He inclined his head without taking his eyes from her. "The pleasure has been all mine, Miss Edgeworth," he said.

Kit offered his arm and they walked the length of the drawing room again, both the silence and the eyes directed at their backs this time.

"A milk-and-water miss!" Lady Freyja said with unconcealed contempt almost before the drawing room doors had finished closing behind the departing guests. "Kit surely cannot be *serious!*"

Lord Alleyne chuckled. "But I believe the lady won the first round of hostilities, Free," he said. "Quite resoundingly, in fact. She left you with your mouth gaping."

"Nonsense!" she said crossly. "She will bore him silly within a month. Needlework, sketching, household accounts, French, Italian, singing—yawn, yawn! What can someone who looks as if she has just swallowed a prune and who sits oh-so-correctly, without touching the back of her chair, and who sips from her teacup as if she had never heard of such a thing as an honest-to-goodness thirst, and who converses on—on medieval screens, for the love of God—what can such a sorry creature have to offer *Kit?*"

"A word of advice, Freyja," the duke said in the soft, pleasant voice that somehow succeeded in sending shivers of apprehension along the spines of most of the people who ever came within earshot of it. "It is always wise when one engages in any sport to look to one's defenses and not set oneself up for an unnecessary hit."

"I did *not*—" she began.

But even Lady Freyja was not proof against the haughtily raised eyebrows and steady silver gaze of his grace.

"And it is never worthy of a Bedwyn," he concluded before vacating the fireplace and the room, "to wear the heart upon the sleeve."

Freyja's nostrils flared and her mouth opened. But she knew better than to fling defiance at her brother's back. She waited until he had left before venting her fury upon a more vulnerable object.

"Do wipe that stupid grin off your face," she commanded her younger brother, "or I may feel compelled to do it for you."

Lord Alleyne presented her with an instant poker face that further incensed her.

"And *you*," she said, stabbing a forefinger in the direction of her younger sister, "ought to be in the schoolroom. I cannot imagine what Wulf was thinking, to allow you down to receive visitors he ought not to have received at all."

Miss Cowper rose to her feet in instant alarm.

"I daresay, Freyja," Lady Morgan said placidly, not moving, "he expected to derive some satisfaction from watching Miss Edgeworth fall into a dither at the sight of so many sober, silent Bedwyns. I daresay he will be annoyed with Ralf for eluding the summons. But I do believe, with Alleyne and Wulf, that she is going to be a worthy foe. She did not collapse at all, did she? And Kit was laughing the whole while. I could see it in his eyes."

"Lord Ravensberg to you," Freyja said sharply.

"He told me," Lady Morgan retorted, "when I was five years old and he carried me on his shoulders one day when I could not keep up to all of you, that I was to call him Kit. So you never mind, Freyja."

She got to her feet and made a triumphant exit, Miss Cowper trotting along in her wake while Lord Alleyne chuckled again.

"Little spitfire," he said. "She may outshine us all yet, Free."

11

"Lady Freyja has been hurt," Lauren said.

"No." Kit took her by the hand and drew her arm through his. "I think not. Her pride has been bruised, that is all."

They zigzagged their way along the gravel paths of the formal parterres, the hem of Lauren's light sprigged muslin dress brushing against the floral clusters that spilled over from the borders. They were headed toward the wilderness walk among the trees, from which Kit had emerged a mere five minutes before with Lady Kilbourne and Lady Muir. His grandmother had walked as far as the rose arbor with them and had then tried to insist that they all leave her there to enjoy the fragrant air while they continued their walk. But Lauren had insisted upon staying with her to keep her company.

There was a quiet kindness about Lauren Edgeworth that one might well not notice unless one was observing closely. Kit was observing.

"Are you sure that is all?" she asked now.

They had spoken very little on the way back from Lindsey Hall, as if by mutual consent they had decided to keep their impressions to themselves until they had properly digested them. But now they had been thrown together again by his grandmother, who had insisted they stroll for a time while the other ladies accompanied her back to the house.

"We shared a brief romance three years ago, Lauren," he said. "It was very brief after a lifetime of being simply friends and playmates. Then she betrothed herself to Jerome, I made an ass of myself by fighting both him and Ralf, and I went off back to the Peninsula, where I belonged. It would be absurd to imagine that she has worn the willow for me ever since. That simply is not Freyja's way."

"Is it yours?" They stepped beyond the parterres to cross the narrow stretch of lawn to the little humpbacked bridge spanning the stream that gurgled its way down over a stone-studded bed to join the river.

"Have I harbored a secret passion for her all this time, do you mean?" he asked. "No, of course not. It was briefly conceived, soon forgotten. Besides, Lauren, I would hardly admit to stronger emotions for her in your presence, would I? It would be in execrable taste."

"Why?" she asked. "Our betrothal is only a temporary thing, after all. There is no need to hide the truth from me out of tact. *Did* you love her? *Do* you?"

His boots clattered over the boards of the bridge in contrast to her lighter footfall. *Had* he loved Freyja? He had called it love at the time, though he remembered his feelings now more as a desperate hunger to lose himself in the body of a woman who could perhaps bring him a moment's forgetfulness. Not that their passion had ever been consummated, of course. She had more than once allowed him to come close, only to whisk herself away with laughter at the last possible moment. He had not thought of her as a tease at the time, but looking back now, he wondered if she had ever taken his attentions seriously.

"It is impossible," he said, "to put a label upon remembered feelings. They are colored too much by all our subsequent experiences. I was desperate to marry her, to carry her off to the Peninsula with me. But I was a desperate young man in many ways that summer. And it all seems a long time ago. How could I love her now? She was unpardonably rude to you."

He turned north with her in the direction that would take them uphill on a route that curved beside and behind the house. He had taken her aunt and cousin in the opposite direction earlier, on the shorter, easier route that ended at the riverbank.

"I was not offended," she said. "I understood her motivation, having felt it myself. Though I was never able to bring myself to be that blatantly rude to Lily."

But she had wanted to be? Because Kilbourne had hurt her?

"Were you offended," he asked, "when I did not rush to your rescue this afternoon? I did rather cast you to the wolves, did I not? But if you cannot stand up to the Bedwyns on your very first encounter with them, you see, they will make a meal of you at every encounter thereafter. You acquitted yourself magnificently, by the way. And if you did not notice, you won the respect of Ralf even before we went upstairs, and of Bewcastle, Alleyne, and Morgan after we did."

"She rides and swims and shoots and does all those things she asked me about, does she not?" Lauren asked. "She knows how to enjoy herself, how to have fun. She knows how to face life with vitality and passion. She is your perfect counterpart, Kit. I think perhaps you should use this time while I am here to consider your future carefully. It might be unwise to reject the idea of marriage with her just because you bear a grudge from three years ago."

They were walking along a narrow, fragrant alleyway, whose walls were high rhododendron bushes. Tall trees beyond them on both sides offered a canopy overhead as shade from the late-afternoon sun. She had left her parasol in the rose arbor. She was gazing straight ahead up the path, Kit saw when he dipped his head to look into her face. Sometimes he almost forgot that theirs was not a real betrothal.

"Perhaps I *should* use the time wisely," he said. "Perhaps I should woo *you* into making it a real betrothal."

"No." She shook her head. "We would not suit in any way at all. You must see that. No, Kit, I am going to be free when all this is over. Wonderfully free at last."

It was rather humbling to realize that even if he employed all his very best skills to charm her, even if he should come to the point of really wishing to wed her, even if he should fall in love with her, she might truly prefer a solitary spinster existence to marriage with him. Freedom, as she called it. Well, it was hardly surprising, perhaps. Women had precious little freedom. And he was not such a prize.

"I think perhaps you misunderstood your father earlier this year," she said. "You believe that he promoted a match between you and Lady Freyja purely for dynastic reasons, that he was demonstrating his power and showing no concern whatsoever for your happiness. But perhaps he thought to make you a peace offering with his plan, Kit. Perhaps he thought you would be very pleased indeed."

"What makes you say that?" he asked, frowning.

"Your mother said it this morning," she said. "Kit, sometimes we just see things from the wrong perspective. Because you quarreled with the Earl of Redfield three years ago, and because he banished you, you cannot conceive of the idea that perhaps he loves you, that perhaps he wants your happiness."

A peace offering? Or the autocratic assumption that a son, even one who was almost thirty years old, was subject to one's will, with no right to feelings or preferences of his own? Two vastly different perspectives indeed.

Up ahead the main path continued its gradual curving rise toward the high point north of the house. But there was another path, narrower, steeper, and stonier, that branched off sharply to the right. It led to the top of a wooded hill and a ruined tower, which looked ancient but was in reality just another folly. Kit turned Lauren onto the steep path and slid his arm clear of hers so that he could grasp her hand the better to assist her in the scrambling climb. She gathered up the front of her skirt with her free hand and labored onward, as dignified as ever.

"Kit," she asked, "was it a whole year after you returned to the Peninsula before your brother died?"

"Almost exactly," he said. "He caught a chill. There was a solid week or so of torrential autumn rain and the river flooded close to some cottages, marooning their occupants and threatening to drown them all. They were not our own laborers, but Jerome rode to the rescue anyway. There were not enough boats, so he did a great deal of swimming and saved a number of lives. No one died, as it happened—except him, two weeks later."

"Oh," she said. "He was a hero, then."

"Absolutely." A damned hero, who had not even lifted his fists to defend himself before Kit broke his nose and had not fought back afterward. A bloody hero, who had not even waited for Kit to come home again before dying. A shining hero, who had stranded his brother on this side of the grave without first shaking his hand and making peace with him.

"Where is he buried?" she asked.

"In the family plot in the churchyard, I suppose," he said abruptly. And no, he answered silently though she did not ask, he did not know exactly where. And no, he had no intention of visiting the grave. Ever. It had been a damned fool thing for Jerome to do, recklessly risking his life like that and losing it. He had not written one letter all that year to his brother in the Peninsula. Not one. Neither had Kit written to him, of course. The first word he had had from Alvesley after his banishment was the black-bordered letter addressed in his father's hand.

He had walked out beyond the camp after reading it, out into open countryside, and he had howled at the empty sky and shaken his fists at the cruel, invisible God. And then, even though it was less than two hours since he had returned from one exhausting mission, he had volunteered for another. He had not stopped for sleep or even for food. Not even for a shave. In action lay some hope of control over this malevolent thing called life. And perhaps—though improbably—forgetfulness.

"Oh," Lauren said breathlessly, stopping on the path, her feet firmly planted on a large, flat stone. "This is steep." She turned to look back the way they had come. They were surrounded by trees, but the main path was visible far below and through the tree branches beyond it some of the brightly colored flowerbeds of the parterres.

"Catch your breath for a moment," he said.

He wished they were back in London. He wished he had his own bachelor rooms to return to and his clubs to attend and his friends to spend his days and nights with. And Lauren to tease. It had been a mistake to come home, to believe that it would be possible to do if he brought a wife, or even a temporary betrothed, with him to somehow insulate himself from all that had set him adrift from his family and his boyhood self three years ago.

Jerome was dead and could never be brought back. And Syd . . .

"Why were your brother and Lady Freyja still not married after a whole year of being betrothed?" Lauren asked.

At first he had assumed that they *had* married, that Freyja was Jerome's widow. It was only after he was back in England and had sold out that he learned the truth. He had been puzzled—and deeply shocked.

"I have no idea." He shrugged. "A banished son is not fed a great deal of family information, you know."

They resumed their climb. Lauren's breathing was labored and her cheeks flushed. Her thin slippers must find the going rough underfoot. But she uttered no word of complaint. She was quiet dignity personified, he thought, and felt an unexpected wave of affection for her. He chuckled aloud at the memory of the wonderful setdowns she had dealt first Ralf and then Freyja. He had been very much afraid that like a lion with a mouse they would be able to devour her whole and spit out the remains.

But strength did not always show itself in boldness and physical action alone, he was discovering.

"What is funny?" she asked.

"Nothing is *funny*," he replied. "Just joyful. It is July and a hot, sunny day. We are in a country that enjoys peace within its borders. We are young and in good health and surrounded by the beauties of nature." His mood swung from depression to exuberance, and he tugged at her hand. "I want to show you something."

"That tower?" she asked breathlessly, glancing upward. "I suppose it has one of those steep, winding stone staircases leading to the top, does it? And you are going to insist that I climb it. I would really rather not. Going up is always relatively easy. Coming down is sheer terror."

"Not the tower." He pointed. "The best view to be had is not from the top of the tower, you see."

She stopped and looked, still laboring for breath. "Oh, no," she said firmly. "No, Kit. I have never in my life climbed a tree. It looked dangerous when Gwen and Neville used to do it, and it looks dangerous now. Besides, it would be a childish thing to do. We are quite high enough for a view, thank you very much. I can see the roof of the house quite clearly from where we stand. I am not—I am absolutely, definitely *not* climbing that tree."

It took all of ten minutes to reach the branch he had in mind. It was not as high up the ancient oak tree as he had often climbed as a boy, but it was definitely higher than the tower, and it was a broad, sturdy limb. It was easily reached by numerous perfectly safe foot- and handholds. But each move, particularly the first one that took them off the ground, had to be coaxed out of Lauren. He went up behind her, one arm linked about her waist, but she would not allow him literally to carry her up.

"I will do it myself, thank you," she told him curtly the only time he tightened his hold and would have hoisted her upward when she seemed to be paralyzed with indecision. "This is *not* what I meant at Vauxhall, Kit. There is nothing remotely enjoyable about this."

"But it *is* memorable, you must admit," he said into her ear with a chuckle. "Swimming in your shift and climbing trees all on the same day. You are in sore danger of becoming a notorious hoyden."

The branch was as broad as many of the trunks of lesser trees.

"You could not fall off if you tried," he said not quite truthfully as he sat down on it, settled his back against the trunk, and drew her down to sit between his spread legs, her back against his chest, his arms protectively about her waist.

"I do not intend to try," she assured him. "Kit, how are we ever going to get down?"

He could feel her heart thumping against his hand. She was over-warm and panting from the climb—and from fear too, he guessed. He noticed that her gaze did not move downward by even a single degree. She pressed her head back hard against his shoulder—her bonnet had been abandoned at the foot of the tree.

"Trust me," he said against her ear.

"Trust the man famous or infamous for all sorts of reckless and foolish exploits?" she said, closing her eyes. "Trust the officer mentioned in several official military dispatches as a particularly daring spy?"

"But I came back from every mission in one piece," he said.

Her heartbeat was beginning to slow to normal. She was beginning to relax. She was half reclined along the tree branch, her legs slightly bent, her feet flat. They were long, slender legs, clearly outlined by the flimsy muslin of her dress. Her feet were slim, her ankles trim. It was strange what a change an acquaintance with someone could bring to one's perceptions. Lauren Edgeworth seemed far more youthful to him now than she had appeared when he first saw her. And less classically beautiful and more femininely pretty.

"If you can ever persuade yourself to open your eyes," he said, "you will see that the view has made the climb worthwhile."

"*Nothing* could do that," she assured him. But she opened her eyes and looked.

It really was an impressive vista. There was a clear view over the treetops to the stream and the parterre gardens, which from here could be viewed in all their geometric precision, and the eastern front of the house. But they were high enough to see far more than that. There were the cultivated, tree-dotted lawns surrounding the house, the river with the lake in the distance, the deer forest and the spire of the village church, the hills in the opposite direction, farmland in the far distance.

A feast for the eyes and the other senses too. There were birds singing. There was a suggestion of coolness in the slight breeze. And there were bars of sunlight and shade across their bodies from the branches and the sun, which was descending in the late afternoon sky.

There were the heavy smells of heat and vegetation and . . . a soft, fragrant soap.

"Nothing could make the climb worthwhile," she said severely, "though the prospect is a good one, I will concede."

Well. Cool praise indeed. But a moment later she ruined the effect of her words. He felt a slight tremor beneath his hands, and then she was laughing softly. Lauren Edgeworth was laughing!

"I am up in a tree," she said. "Gwen and Aunt Clara will not believe it even if I should tell them. *No* one who knows me would believe it. Lauren Edgeworth up a tree, without a bonnet."

She seemed to find the idea enormously tickling. For a few moments her laughter was almost silent. But she could not contain it. She burst into peals of glee, gales of merriment. And Kit, holding her safe, joined her.

"And loving every moment of it?" he asked when he could.

"Now *that* I will never admit to," she said and laughed again. But finally they were both quiet, and when she spoke again her voice held more wistfulness than humor. "I will remember today. All of it. For the whole of the rest of my life. Thank you, Kit."

He settled his cheek against the top of her head—her hair was warm from the sunshine. The pleasures he had given her today—*if* they had given her pleasure—were such simple things. But she would remember them for the rest of her life? Strangely enough, he believed he would too.

He bent his legs at the knee, braced his feet against the branch on either side of her, and relaxed. When had he last done this? Just sat, that was, soaking up sunshine and heat, feeling the sheer comfort of another human presence? It seemed that perhaps he had never done it. Certainly not in recent years. He was always busily intent upon filling in every idle moment, avoiding every chance that he might inadvertently come face-to-face with his own thoughts. He even avoided lying in bed at night until he was too exhausted to do anything but fall into instant sleep. Though even then there were the dreams. . . .

But he abandoned all thought, all his cautious defenses, as he closed his eyes.

He had always favored small women, not being a particularly tall man himself. He had always been attracted to voluptuous women. And passionate women. He had had several affairs over the years, most of them tumultuous in nature, intensely satisfying, soon over. His summer with Freyja had followed much the usual pattern, though he had always denied it to himself, the only real difference being that his passion had not been satisfied physically and therefore had never been slaked. It had been over before he was ready to see it end. At the time he had thought he never would want it to end, that she was the woman to whom he could pledge his lifelong devotion. But had he not thought so with numerous mistresses before her?

Lauren Edgeworth was tall for a woman. She was slender. She was cool in nature. Not frigid. No, not that. But probably incapable of hot physical passion. She should have been unattractive to him despite her undeniable beauty.

But he desired her. He turned his head slightly, buried his nose in her hair, breathed in the scent of her. He desired her in an unfamiliar, controlled way. Without the usual burning need to mount her body to satisfy his hunger. It was a curiously uncarnal desire. And yet it *was* physical. It was desire he felt, not just admiration or affection.

He nudged her hair back from her face with his cheek and kissed her temple, her cheek, her jaw. He kissed her earlobe and sucked it gently between his teeth.

She sat motionless, her eyes closed again. Yet not quite motionless either. She tipped her head slightly toward his arm, allowing him easier access to the side of her face closer to him. He kissed her neck, nuzzling it softly.

She somehow fit him like a glove, he thought. A comfortable kid glove. And yet he felt definite desire—an invigorating surging of the blood and tightening of the groin. Desire mingled with tenderness, two feelings that had never coincided in him before now. He was on unfamiliar ground.

He settled his cheek against her head again and spread his palms over her waist and abdomen. They were flat, and yet soft and womanly too. He lifted his hands to cup her breasts lightly. He paused, giving her a chance to protest, to push his hands away, to break the drowsy spell of desire he was exploring. Drowsiness and desire as simultaneous feelings? Strange indeed! She spread her hands over his Hessian boots, just above the ankles.

They were small breasts, but firm and lovely. They fit his hands as if made for them. She seemed perfectly relaxed, yet her nipples, he found, touching them lightly with the pads of his thumbs, were peaked and hard. He lowered his head once more to kiss her in the warm hollow between her neck and shoulder. He opened his mouth, licking her, tasting her, breathing warm air against her silky flesh.

For the first time she made a sound—a soft whimpering sigh deep in her throat. She may not be a woman of passion, he thought, but she was certainly capable of desire. Loving her would be a somewhat tender experience. One would need to awaken her slowly, patiently, with gentle consideration. One would need to cherish her, to subdue one's own need in order to nurture hers. One would need to make love to her in ways he had never before made love. There was something strangely arousing in the thought.

He slid his palms downward and curved the fingertips of one hand into the soft, warm juncture of her thighs. She drew in a breath, not noisily but with slow deliberation, and pressed her head more firmly back against his shoulder. The soft muslin of her skirt gave before the pressure of his fingers, and he rubbed her lightly.

It was as well, he thought, that they were where they were. They were not really betrothed. They were not going to be married. And though he was honor-bound to try to persuade her to change her mind during the coming weeks, he had no wish to coerce her. He would not violate her and so give her no choice in her own future. The knowledge of where they were was its own limit on how far he could carry this encounter. He ran his palm along one of her inner thighs but made no attempt to reach down for her hem to lift her skirt.

He wanted her. He desired her. It would feel good to be inside her body. And yet his desire was curiously lacking in physical urgency. It felt more like a yearning of the heart. For her innocence, perhaps?

For the sweet, quiet discipline that could so easily be mistaken for cold passivity?

"Kit," she said, "no. Really you need not."

"*Need* not?" Reluctantly he wrapped his arms safely about her waist again. "What do you know of my needs?"

"Enough to be quite certain that I am not the woman to satisfy a single one of them," she said. "You have been wonderful to me today. Horrid but wonderful. I *will* remember swimming and climbing trees, you see. I will remember with pleasure. But I did not ask for passion, not of—not of this nature anyway. It is improper. We are strangers really, are we not? We *will* be strangers in future. If our families knew that we were not really betrothed, they would never allow us to be alone together like this. And it is easy to understand why. I have never . . . Kit, I have never done these things before. And I must not again. Please."

"You must not be a woman?" he murmured against her ear. "Only a lady?"

She did not answer for a few moments. "Yes," she said at last. "I choose to be only a lady."

"You cannot be both?"

"Only if I were married," she said. "To someone I loved and to someone who loved me in return."

"You believe Kilbourne loved you?"

He felt her swallow. "He did," she said. "He always did. We always loved each other. Not as he loves Lily or as she loves him, but . . . Kit, I do not want to be having this conversation. I cannot ever love you, that is all. And you certainly could never love me. Without love, what we have been doing is wrong. Even perhaps a little sordid, though it did not feel that way. Take me home, please. But how on earth are we to get down?"

"Now that you mention it," he said, "how *are* we?"

She turned her head sharply to regard him with wide, dismayed eyes. He grinned at her and waggled his eyebrows.

"I am s-s-scared," he wailed.

"Oh, Kit!" And she laughed again, as she had earlier, her whole face lighting up with glee as she punched his shoulder with the side of her fist. "Never fear. I will rescue you. I will open my mouth and screech for help." She laughed again—no, she giggled. Like a girl. Like the child she had never been, perhaps. She drew breath as if she were an operatic soprano about to hit a high C, and he clapped a hand over her mouth.

"If it comes to a choice between breaking both my legs on the one hand and watching an army of gardeners charge up here to the rescue," he said, "I think I will sacrifice my legs. Here we go, then. Hang on tight and trust me. Sir Galahad is my middle name."

She laughed once more.

12

We have scarcely had a private moment together. But I daresay I must accustom myself to losing you." Gwendoline linked her arm through Lauren's. "It is all in a good cause, fortunately. I like Lord Ravensberg exceedingly well."

"Do you, Gwen?"

They were on the wilderness path, taking advantage of a quiet morning before the expected onslaught of arrivals later in the day. Kit had gone off with his father to inspect the hay crop on some distant field. Lauren was pleased about that. She just hoped they would *talk*. She had maneuvered them together last evening. The earl had been turning the pages of her music at the pianoforte, and after finishing her piece she had smiled deliberately at Kit, who had been talking with Gwen and his grandmother, almost forcing him to her side. She had known that he was reluctant to come—and that his father too would be feeling somewhat trapped. They always avoided each other as much as they could, father and son, even though Lauren had witnessed no open hostility on either side.

She had folded her music, turned on the bench, smiled at both Kit and his father, and asked the latter questions about the home farm while they stood awkwardly side by side. Fortunately she had not had to suggest quite blatantly that Lord Redfield show Kit some of its operations. The earl himself had suggested that, and Kit had agreed. Oh, she was very skilled indeed at conversation, at steering it in directions she wished it to take. She knew it was one of her best accomplishments.

Perhaps they did not even realize they had been maneuvered. But it was one reason she had come here—to reconcile Kit with his family.

"He is such a perfect foil for you that your meeting must be considered a happy stroke of fate," Gwendoline said while Lauren shortened her stride to accommodate her cousin's limp. "His carefree, laughing manner balances your quiet good sense and makes for one pleasing whole. I am very happy."

"Thank you." Lauren was not sure the steep path she had taken with Kit the afternoon before would be good for Gwen, but she turned onto it anyway and they labored slowly upward.

Gwendoline laughed merrily. "Oh, so grave, Lauren," she said, "just as if you were not bubbling with happiness inside. This is me, Gwen. And I noticed your damp hair at breakfast, just as I noticed it yesterday. I thought then that you had got up early to wash it until Lord Redfield mentioned seeing you ride out with Lord Ravensberg. I am quite capable of adding two to two and coming up with a sum of four. Lauren, you have been *swimming*. Oh, this is famous!"

"And not at all the thing," Lauren said, pausing on a large, flat stone so that they could catch their breath. "But he insists that I be made to enjoy myself. Can you imagine anything more absurd, Gwen, than the notion that I might find riding in the early morning and swimming in the lake enjoyable?"

"Oh, Lauren," Gwen said, "I love him. I do. You had better marry him quickly, or I will steal him for myself."

"Gwen," Lauren said, resuming the laborious climb, "I can *float*. On my back and even on my stomach—with my face in the water. I sink like a stone, though, when I try to kick my legs to propel myself forward. He laughs at me." That was not strictly true. He had laughed *with* her. She must have laughed more in the last two days than she had done in her whole life before, in fact. Not just the laughter of polite amusement, but the helpless, straight-from-the-stomach merriment that had her doubled over and helpless with mirth, tears streaming down both cheeks.

"Oh, goodness," Gwen said, stopping and glancing upward. "Look at that tower. Is it a real ruin, do you suppose?"

"A folly," Lauren said. "It was built to look like a ruin. But it is rather picturesque."

She had had to come back here. She had to free her mind of a certain spell that appeared to have been cast over it. There had been nothing magical about yesterday afternoon. They had merely sat on a tree branch looking at the view. She had merely allowed him to fondle her in a manner that was so startlingly improper that even now she could not believe she had not stopped him far sooner than she had. It was ridiculous to remember that hour together as one of the most enchanted hours of her life. It was pathetic, if the truth were known.

Poor deprived twenty-six-year-old virgin!

She might have been a mother by now, almost sixteen months after her wedding. The duties of the marriage bed might have become routine to her by now. She might have been proof against such foolish unidentified yearnings as had kept her awake half the night before. Though she had not been the only one up. She had seen Kit walking in the darkness outside, striding down the driveway and across the bridge until he had passed from sight.

"We came up here yesterday," she told Gwen. "We climbed high enough to see over the tops of the trees."

Gwendoline looked up. "The view from the top must be breathtaking," she said. "But I would rather imagine it than see it. I believe I will sit down on the grass for a while."

She was looking at the tower.

"I mean the tree," Lauren said. "We climbed up the tree." The branch on which they had sat did not look so very high when viewed from the ground, but it was certainly high enough. Higher than the tower. Her knees turned weak.

Gwen looked and chose to be amused again. "You really *are* in love," she said. "Neville and I could never persuade you to do anything remotely daring when we were all younger. Oh, Lauren, what a relief it is to be able to mention his name to you without fear of seeing that stricken look in your eyes, so quickly veiled even from me. And to be able to mention Lily. She really is a joy, you know. I saw them the day after they announced to Mama and me that she is increasing. They were down on the beach, and Lily was twirling about and about on the sand, her arms stretched to the sides, without either a bonnet or shoes and stockings while Neville stood against the great rock, his arms crossed over his chest, laughing at her. I did not intrude."

Lauren drew a slow breath and set her palm against the great trunk of the old oak. It was not painful. It was *not*.

"She will be a good mother," she said.

The magic was still here this morning. She closed her eyes. He was not nearly as big as Neville. She had always thought she liked big, tall men. But she fit against Kit so very comfortably. He had lovely hands—not large, but nimble, strong, expressive. They had felt good. . . . He ought not . . . And she ought not to have allowed it. He had held her breasts, and for a moment it had felt so *right*. And he had put one of his hands *there*. But instead of feeling horror she had felt . . . pleasure. And something more than pleasure.

But that had not been the magic. Not really. There had been the exhilaration, the sense of daring and achievement, the sense of safety despite danger. She would trust him with her life, she realized suddenly. And there had been the laughter. Ah, yes, the laughter.

The seductive enchantment of sheer joy.

"*Shall* we sit for a while?" Gwendoline suggested.

Something Lauren had not noticed the day before was that both the hill and the trees fell away behind the slope they had climbed. The drop was a steep one, allowing for only a few hardy shrubs to cling to its side. Below and for miles into the distance was rolling farmland bordered with neat hedgerows, some of the fields under cultivation, some dotted with sheep. It was like a patchwork quilt, interrupted here and there by little cottages with accompanying clusters of farm buildings.

"What a blustery day after yesterday," Gwendoline said. "And cooler too. I hope those clouds do not intend to bring rain later. This is a lovely place, Lauren. Your future home. And not too far distant from Dorsetshire, thank goodness. We will be able to see each other occasionally."

"Unless you marry someone who will carry you off to the farthest Hebridean island," Lauren said. "Or to the westernmost coast of Ireland."

"I think not," Gwen said. "Indeed I *know* not."

"You cannot forget Lord Muir?" Lauren asked sadly. "No one can ever take his place in your affections?"

"I will never forget Vernon," Gwen said with quiet conviction. "I will never remarry. But Neville is happy and you will be and Mama needs companionship. And so I will be content. I *will*, Lauren."

Lauren lifted her face to the wind, heedless of the danger to her complexion. Yes, Alvesley was lovely. Rural and peaceful and beautiful and vast. But not her future home. That would be somewhere in Bath, she hoped. She would make a place for herself in the restricted, staid society of the spa, which was no longer as fashionable as it had used to be. It was inhabited mainly by the elderly. It would suit her. It would be safe.

"Now *that* looks rather dangerous," Gwen said, nodding in the direction of the land below them.

Three riders were moving like toy figures across the landscape. They were not following any road or lane but were riding a more or less straight course across the fields. They were moving at speed, galloping neck or nothing, in fact. If they encountered a stone or a rabbit hole in the uneven ground that was common to most fields they would be down in a moment, injured and very possibly killed. Even as they watched, the riders made straight for a hedge and soared over it.

Gwen sucked in her breath, but they landed safely on the other side and galloped onward.

"One of them is a woman," Gwendoline said.

With long, fair hair streaming out behind her.

"Lady Freyja Bedwyn," Lauren said. "With Lord Rannulf and Lord Alleyne, if I am not mistaken. They are riding in this direction. They must be intending to call at Alvesley."

"The lady Lord Redfield intended for Lord Ravensberg?" Gwendoline asked, shading her eyes with one hand and squinting more intently at the riders. "Gracious, Lauren, she is not wearing a hat, and her hair is down. Will she call on the countess looking like that?"

"I believe so." She was riding sidesaddle, but she was doing so with consummate skill. Lauren felt unwilling admiration.

"Is she beautiful?" Gwen asked.

"No, not beautiful," Lauren said. Indeed her first impression had been that Lady Freyja was remarkably ugly. "She has a bold, dark-complexioned face with a prominent nose and dark eyebrows quite at variance with the color of her hair. She is . . . handsome." That was not quite the right word, either. There was something about her, some charisma that Lauren knew she herself could never acquire even if she lived for a million years.

"And so are her brothers, if my guess is correct," Gwen said. "Are they really going to Alvesley? If so, Lord Ravensberg's insistence upon calling in person at Lindsey Hall yesterday and yours upon accompanying him seem to have brought about the desired results."

"I am glad, then," Lauren said. "Neighbors ought not to be at variance with one another."

She could picture Lady Freyja and Kit riding side by side. Galloping stride for stride, soaring over hedgerows together, laughing, careless of danger. They were surely perfect for each other. And surely must still love each other. Certainly Lauren felt no doubt that the lady's behavior yesterday had been occasioned by severely disappointed hopes.

But perhaps not disappointed forever, she thought, watching the riders disappear around a bend in the hill in the direction of the Palladian bridge. Once the summer was over, they would be free to rekindle their love without the direct interference of either the Earl of Redfield or the Duke of Bewcastle. By Christmas they would probably be married. He would be happy. He would have made up his quarrel with his father and would have overcome the awkwardness with his brother. He would have recovered the love of his heart.

By Christmas she would be established in Bath.

The thick band of clouds, which had been drifting closer for an hour or more, finally obscured the sun. Lauren shivered in the sudden chill.

The Earl of Redfield had decided to take his son, not just to the hay field, as planned, but on a general tour of the home farm. He talked determinedly and impersonally for most of the morning about crops and drainage and cattle and wages and a dozen other related topics. They stopped occasionally to talk to workers. Kit had the distinct impression that his father was uncomfortable with him and did not know how to deal with him on any personal level.

But he understood. He felt the same way.

He had been a cavalry officer for ten years. He knew, of course, how to take orders. Even as a lieutenant-colonel for the last year and a half of his service there had always been superior officers. But in the main he had been the one in charge, the one who issued orders, the one who bore all the responsibility of seeing them executed. That had been particularly true of his numerous missions as a reconnaissance officer, when he frequently had to make his own difficult and momentous decisions. He had made a name for himself in that capacity. He had been daring and ruthless, but utterly practical and trustworthy. He had been the one chosen for all the most seemingly impossible tasks. He had always found a way to do what had to be done. He had felt like a man very much in command of his own life.

It was only with his family that he had ever felt gauche and worthless. With his family he had been a massive failure—beginning with

Sydnam's intrusion upon his other life. But only beginning there. It had culminated, he supposed, in the year he had just wasted in London, behaving more like a callow youth than the Lieutenant-Colonel Lord Ravensberg known to his colleagues in the army. Almost as if he had felt compelled to prove to the whole of the fashionable world just how worthless he really was. Almost as if he had wanted word to get back to Alvesley so that his father and the rest of his family would be confirmed in their opinion of him.

He had never even tried to think this all out before. Was he really so immature?

"Does Syd always ride out with you on business?" he asked abruptly when they were finally on their way home. *Except this morning.*

"Usually," his father said.

"I am surprised he is able to ride," Kit said, broaching a topic he had no wish to pursue, except that it could not be avoided forever. *Syd had no right arm.*

"He has always been stubborn," the earl said. "He was out of his sickbed long before the doctor advised any movement at all. He kept walking, even though he had to grit his teeth against the pain, until he could do it without limping. And he bruised himself over and over—and caused your mother many a bitter tear—until he could ride without losing his seat and falling off. He practiced for long hours until he could write legibly with his left hand. And he started spending whole days together with Parkin, learning the duties of a steward. When Parkin retired at the end of last year, Sydnam asked me if he could have his position."

"But Syd was not cut out to be a *steward*," Kit protested.

"He has made a life for himself," his father said firmly. "He will accept no salary from me, of course, but he has been talking to Bewcastle about employment on one of the numerous Bedwyn estates. It seems that an opening is to be expected in the autumn—a salaried position even though Sydnam has independent means and does not need it. He is determined to be his own man. He does not wish to stand in your way here."

But Alvesley would need a steward. Why not Sydnam if he was already doing the job? It was at least something he could do at home, where he had family to care for his needs. But of course that family now included Kit. That was explanation enough for Syd's determination to leave.

"Why did he not come with you this morning?" Kit asked, though the answer was, of course, obvious. *Because I am with you.*

"The account books needed bringing up to date," his father said.

They were riding past a neat row of freshly thatched cottages, and the earl pointed them out as some of the laborers' homes, which had been leaking during the spring. He hailed and exchanged pleasantries with a woman who was outside sweeping the threshold of her home while three young children played in the grass nearby.

"Your mother and I would like to have the first banns for your nuptials read on Sunday," his father said abruptly as they rode on. "Our family members and Miss Edgeworth's can be persuaded to stay on here for a month, I daresay, to attend the wedding. I suppose that after what happened at Newbury last year, she will not wish to be married there. There is no reason for delay, is there? We approve of her. She is a true lady. The embarrassment over Lady Freyja is an unfortunate one, but there is no point in dwelling upon what cannot be helped. What do you say?"

Kit had been listening in dismay—the more so, perhaps, because his father appeared to be asking rather than telling him. Another of the olive branches Lauren had spoken of yesterday?

"I would not wish to rush her, sir," he said. "There will be bride clothes to shop for, and there are many other relatives she will want at her—at *our* wedding. The Duchess of Portfrey, her aunt, for example. The lady is to be confined soon—within the next month or so, I believe. We were thinking more of a winter or perhaps a spring wedding."

"I just do not want your mother or your grandmother disappointed again," the earl said.

Again? Was he talking about Jerome and Freyja? Of course, he must be. But no one had mentioned Jerome's name since Kit's return home. He could not mention it now. Neither, it seemed, could their father. They rode through the village in heavy silence and spoke with false cheer to the porter, who opened the gates for them and delayed them for a few moments while he squinted upward at the heavy clouds and speculated upon the likelihood of their lordships getting rained upon before they reached the stables.

"I would rather not have the idea of banns pressed upon Lauren too soon, sir," Kit said as they rode onward into the darker shade of the deer forest. "She suffered a severe and humiliating disappointment last year. I want all to be perfect for her this time."

"Hmm. The thought does you credit," his father said.

God help him, but he really did want that, Kit thought. Absurdly, he believed he would gladly give his life to make something perfect for Lauren. Perhaps he would find pardon and peace if he could bring about her happiness. But he could do just that, he thought rather bitterly. He could set her free.

By the time they rode clear of the trees an occasional large spot of rain splashed down onto them. Pretty soon it was going to be raining in earnest.

"We had better make a dash for it," the earl said, looking upward. He added rather stiffly, "It has been a good morning, Ravensberg. She is a true lady."

Yes. It had not escaped Kit's notice, either, that they owed this morning together, earl and heir together as they ought to be, to Lauren's gentle maneuvering last evening.

He smiled ruefully as he urged his horse to a gallop and clattered over the bridge in his father's wake.

The guests began arriving in the rain soon after luncheon. Lauren spent much of the afternoon in the great hall with the earl and countess, with the dowager countess and Mr. Sydnam Butler, and with Kit, receiving the visitors, being presented to all of them, trying to impress names and exact relationships upon her memory.

It was not easy. It might have seemed impossible if she had not trained herself long ago, when she had expected to spend her adult life as the Countess of Kilbourne with all the duties of a hostess. She would remember Lady Irene Butler, the late earl's unmarried sister, because she was white-haired and frail and severely bent over. And she would remember Viscount Hampton, the dowager's brother, because of his shiny bald head and loud laugh, and Mr. Claude Willard, his son, who closely resembled him. Then there was Daphne Willard, Claude's wife, and their three not-quite-grown children, two sons and a daughter—three young people who were on their very best behavior, doubtless in the hope of being included with the adults rather than with the nursery group during the coming days. Then there was the placid and smiling Marjorie, Lady Clifford, the Earl of Redfield's sister, and her florid-complexioned, wheezing husband, Sir Melvin. Boris Clifford, with the eyeglasses, was their son, the buxom Nell his wife. This latter couple had three infant children, who were whisked up to the nursery after a brief inspection by the dowager, their great-grandmama.

There was a lull in the arrivals before Lauren had to memorize more names and faces and relationships. Mr. Humphrey Pierce-James arrived next with his wife, Edith, their daughter Catherine and her husband, Mr. Lawrence Vreemont. The latter couple also had two infant children. Mr. Pierce-James, Lauren understood, was the dowager's nephew by a deceased sister. Last to arrive were Mr. Clarence Butler, the earl's younger brother, with his wife, Honoria, their daughter Beatrice and her husband, Baron Born, and their brood of unwed offspring, varying in age from Frederick, who must be Kit's age, to Benjamin, who was eight. Doris, one of the daughters, had her fiancé, Sir Jeremy Brightman, with her.

Lauren did not promise herself that she would remember every name and face and relationship immediately—there were so many of them—but she thought she would within a day or so. She smiled with some relief when it seemed the last guest had arrived and disappeared upstairs to freshen up before tea. Everyone had been amiable. If any of them knew about the projected engagement to Lady Freyja Bedwyn, none of them looked as if they held a grudge.

She had not had a chance to ask Kit about his morning. But he had spent the whole of it with his father about estate business—a promising sign indeed. Neither of them had been at home to receive Lady Freyja Bedwyn and her two brothers, but they had indeed called and spent fifteen minutes with Kit's mother and grandmother and with Aunt Clara. They had expressed their intention of riding over again before the day of the birthday celebrations. A permanent rift had been avoided, it seemed.

It must be time to go back upstairs to the drawing room, Lauren thought. But the butler, peering discreetly through a window, announced that yet another carriage was approaching across the bridge.

"Perhaps *this* time," the countess said, speaking to the earl but smiling at Lauren. "Do have a seat, Mother. You will be exhausted from having been on your feet all afternoon."

"I will not . . . sit," the old lady said. "Miss . . . Edgeworth, let me . . . take your . . . arm again."

But Sydnam Butler stepped forward and offered his instead. The newly arrived carriage was drawing up before the steps, and the butler himself had gone down with a large black umbrella to escort the gentleman who was alighting from it indoors. Two footmen held the doors wide open. Lauren shivered from the chill of the wet, windy outdoors. But she donned her sociable smile again and prepared to be presented to yet another member of Kit's family.

And then the butler removed the sheltering umbrella and stood to one side while the visitor stepped over the threshold into the hall and looked about expectantly.

Lauren forgot her famous dignity in the surprise of recognition and the welling of joy. She hurried forward, both arms outstretched.

"*Grandpapa!*" she exclaimed.

"Lauren. There you are, my dear!"

She was enfolded in his embrace then and inhaling the snuffy, leathery scent she always associated with him. And swallowing and blinking her eyes and trying—in vain—to hold her tears in check.

He had come.

He had come!

"I did not know," she said, drawing back from him and gazing into his lined, dearly familiar face. "I did not expect..." She turned to look with tear-bright eyes at the earl and at Kit. "Who did this? Whose idea was it?"

"Mine," Kit said. He was grinning. "As soon as Mother and Father asked me which of your relatives should be invited."

"Thank you," she said, smiling at each of them in turn. "Oh, *thank* you."

"Present me, please, Lauren." Kit stepped forward and brought her back to a sense of duty.

She proceeded to present them all, her arm linked through Baron Galton's—her very own relative—her heart brimming with happiness. They had invited him for her betrothal celebrations, and he had come all the way from Yorkshire. Just for her! Surely because he loved her. And it had been Kit's idea to invite him and surprise her in this way. What a delightful surprise it was.

It was only as she led him up the grand staircase a short while later to the room that had been prepared for him, Kit on his other side, that she remembered something. Amazingly, alarmingly, it had totally fled her mind for all of ten minutes.

It was not a real betrothal.

13

For the rest of that day and all of the next Lauren felt that she would have been entirely happy if she had not kept remembering that she was living a lie. She pushed the thought aside as much as she could. She had committed herself to doing just what she was doing, and it was too late now to withdraw. There would be time enough to deal with her guilt over the deception when she had put an end to it.

She set herself the task of acquainting herself with Kit's relatives. It was not difficult to do. They were a close and basically cheerful family and were quite prepared to take Kit's betrothed into the fold and to be kind to her family too. Aunt Clara was appropriated by Lady Clifford and Mrs. Butler, Kit's aunts, and by Mrs. Vreemont. Viscount Hampton, who had a previous acquaintance with Baron Galton, was pleased to renew it. Gwen became an instant favorite with Baron Born's numerous offspring, especially with Frederick and Roger, who were soon vying with each other over her smiles and attention.

Lauren was everyone's favorite, simply because, she thought, Kit was everyone's favorite too. The quarrel with his family three years ago had certainly not tainted his relationship with his numerous aunts, uncles, and cousins. It felt seductively pleasant to be the focus of attention much of the time. Lady Irene Butler liked to pat her hand and tell her what a pretty child she was. The aunts and older cousins liked to talk to her about London and the latest fashions. The uncles liked to tease her about anything they thought might draw her blushes. The younger female cousins wanted to know who her modiste was, who chose the lovely fabrics and the elegant designs and the perfectly coordinated colors of her clothes. And how her maid styled her hair so perfectly just so. They wanted to know what she was planning for her bride clothes. The younger male cousins paid her compliments, some of them very extravagant and foolish indeed. They called Kit a lucky dog and he agreed with them wholeheartedly, his eyes twinkling at her. The young mothers took her to the nursery to meet their children, assuming that she liked infants. She was rather afraid of them, in fact, having had little to do with children during her adult life. But she learned all their names and was touched when they wanted to ask questions and show her their treasures and be picked up and played with.

She was careful to give much of her attention to Kit's immediate family since it was his full reconciliation with them to which she had pledged herself. The Earl of Redfield was inclined to look favorably upon her, she believed. And he and Kit were no longer avoiding each other even if they were still treating each other with a somewhat stiff cordiality. The countess was pleased to accept the help she offered. Apart from all the plans for the birthday itself, there were meals and activities and floral arrangements to think of each day with such a large number of guests. Although she was perfectly capable of handling everything alone, she seemed grateful to listen to a second opinion on some details and even a few new suggestions. The countess seemed well inclined to treat her elder son with affection.

Lauren had grown truly fond of the dowager countess. It was never any trouble to walk with her or to sit and listen to her. The old lady's left hand was stiff and curled inward as a result of the apoplexy she had suffered. But it was not quite paralyzed. Lauren took it in both of

hers the evening after everyone's arrival and massaged it gently, opening the fingers back with her own. It felt good, Kit's grandmother said,
and they smiled at each other. It was for her sake that Lauren felt most
guilty, for she believed that her affection was fully returned.

It was only with Sydnam Butler that she had so far failed to set up
any rapport—or any communication with his brother.

She did not see a great deal of Kit. Or rather, she *did* since it
rained for the rest of that first day and most of the second and everyone was forced to remain indoors, but she did not spend much time
in his company and none at all alone with him. Her swimming lesson
had to be canceled on account of the weather, though why it should
be when they were going to get wet anyway he did not know, he had
added over her protests. She missed the morning outing, though, the
sheer *fun* of floating and splashing in the water. She wondered how
she was going to do without such activities when the time came, but
she determinedly pushed such thoughts aside.

They played charades in the drawing room during the second
evening, a game in which most of them participated and which gave rise
to a great deal of noisy animation and laughter. The younger people
were not willing to see the game end, with the result that they were all
rather late going to bed. Lauren sat with Gwen for an hour after that,
as she did most nights, talking. It was after midnight when she returned
to her own room, and even after that she did not go immediately to bed,
but blew out the candles and stood at the window, brushing her hair,
enjoying the sight of the moon and stars again. The rain had stopped
late in the afternoon and the clouds had finally moved off.

Was he sleeping? She knew that, like her, he suffered at least sometimes from insomnia. She had seen him more than once outside the
house after everyone was in bed. On that one occasion he had walked
off down the driveway until he had been lost to sight. He did not
seem like the sort of man who would have trouble sleeping. He
seemed always to be cheerful and laughing. But she knew too that the
outer appearance was in some ways not the real Kit. There were
depths to his character that he hid carefully from the view of most of
his acquaintances.

What troubled him enough that he could not sleep?

It was as if her thoughts conjured him. He appeared below her on the terrace, wearing breeches and topboots and a riding coat rather than the evening clothes he had been wearing an hour or so ago. He walked across the terrace to the edge of the lawn and stood there, his feet slightly apart, his hands behind his back, gazing out into the darkness. He looked lonely.

Perhaps he wanted to be lonely or at least alone. Perhaps he treasured times like this, when everyone else was supposedly asleep and finally he could enjoy an hour of solitude. Or perhaps insomnia had driven him outside, and perhaps that sleeplessness was caused by a troubled mind. Perhaps he was tired, restless, unhappy. In need of a kindred soul to listen to him or be silent with him—a sympathetic presence.

Or perhaps it was she who needed company.

It would be terribly improper to go down and join him. Even if they were truly betrothed it would be improper before they were wed. But she was growing mortally tired of propriety, of her prim devotion to a way of life that put all the emphasis upon what was correct rather than upon what one's heart knew ought to be done. Perhaps the heart was a poor and unreliable guide for behavior, but so surely was cold, blind propriety.

She was hurrying into her tiny dressing room even as she was thinking. If he did not want her, he could tell her to go away. She would not stay out long anyway. She would just stand beside him for a while and they would talk. Perhaps then he would be able to sleep. Perhaps then she would.

Descending the stairs and crossing the hall in the dark was no easy matter. And all the time she was afraid that perhaps he had gone out a different way and she would find the doors bolted and impossible to open. But when she turned the great handle of one of them, it opened easily, and she stepped outside onto the marble steps.

He had gone.

There was only empty space where he had been standing a short while ago. So much for her boldness, she thought, descending the steps slowly, holding the ends of her shawl crossed at her bosom. He had gone. But even as she thought it she saw him. He was striding across the lawn in the direction of the driveway. He was walking rather fast, she thought. She hesitated for one moment before going after him.

"Kit."

He was on the driveway already, not far from the bridge. Lauren was half running over the grass. She could feel its wetness about her ankles and the hem of her dress.

He stopped abruptly and turned toward her even though she had not called out loudly.

"Lauren?"

He sounded surprised. Was he also displeased? Had she done entirely the wrong thing? She came up to him in a few moments but stopped several feet away.

"I saw you from my window," she said. "It is not the first time. Could you not sleep?"

"And could *you* not?" It was impossible to tell from his tone whether he was annoyed or not.

"I thought I might walk with you," she said. "I thought it might be . . . comforting to have some company."

"Do you have trouble sleeping, Lauren?" he asked.

"Sometimes," she admitted. She had not used to. But despair after her aborted marriage had robbed her of the oblivion of sleep she had so longed for, and then sleeplessness had become a habit. It was the time when she most ached with nameless yearnings. She could usually keep herself well occupied during the day, but at night . . .

"We should stroll back to the house," he said. "You would not want to come with me where I was going."

"Where?" she asked.

"A gamekeeper's hut in the forest actually," he said. "I suppose I have spent too many of my adult years alone, living under rough conditions. A civilized home, especially one filled with other people, oppresses me. I feel that I cannot breathe freely. Since I came home I have equipped the hut with the bare necessities, and sometimes I go there at night. It somehow soothes my mind. Sometimes I sleep there."

"Ah," she said, wishing she had not acted so hastily. "You *do* wish to be alone, then. I am sorry. And you do not need to walk back to the house with me, Kit. Really you do not. Good night. I will see you in the morning. Will we—will we swim?"

He did not answer immediately. She felt awkward, rather humiliated. She turned to hurry away. But his voice stopped her.

"I would *like* you to come with me," he said.

"Truly?" She looked back at him. "You need not say so just to be polite, Kit. I do not wish to intrude."

But he was smiling at her and looking his usual self.

"Truly."

She walked beside him, holding her shawl. He did not offer his arm.

"What sort of troubles keep you from sleep?" he asked her.

She shook her head. "I don't know."

"What happened last year?" he suggested.

She shook her head again. "I don't know."

"What masks we wear," he said. "No one looking at the beautiful and dignified Miss Lauren Edgeworth in Lady Mannering's ballroom a couple of months ago would have suspected that she nursed an utterly shattered heart. I am sorry that I did not have the sensitivity to know it or even suspect it. I am so very sorry, Lauren."

"It was my *life* that was shattered more than my heart," she said. "But looking back, I am not sure . . ."

"Of what?"

They were walking through the Palladian bridge. She could hear the water rushing beneath it.

"I am not sure it was quite the disaster I thought it at the time," she said. "I was only half a person at that time. Don't ask me to explain, Kit. I am not sure I know quite what I mean myself. Life was lived by a rigid set of rules. It had a set pattern. But that is not real life, is it? At some time surely I must have woken up to that fact. Life could not have continued placid and perfect to the end." And maybe placidity and perfection did not go hand in hand, anyway, although she had used to think so.

He looked curiously at her, but they did not speak again. Soon after they crossed the bridge they reached the trees, and he took her arm and turned off the driveway. It was very dark among the trees. She would have been totally lost and not a little frightened if his own steps had not been sure. As it was, all she had to do was put her trust in him—a remarkably easy thing to do. She would always feel perfectly safe with him, she believed, even if a hungry wild beast were to step into their path. She smiled to herself at the thought.

She had no idea how he found the hut in the dense darkness, but he did. He felt along the top of the lintel, produced a key, and turned it in the lock. He left Lauren standing on the threshold and went inside. A few moments later the feeble light of a lamp sprang to life, and she stepped into the small wooden cabin and closed the door. He was on one knee, setting a light to the fire that was laid in the small grate.

It was a remarkably cozy interior. There was a low bed covered with blankets, an old wooden rocking chair, and a roughly hewn wooden table with a single chair pushed beneath it. There were two books on the table, and the lamp. Apart from those things and a rush mat on the floor, the hut was bare.

"Take the rocking chair," Kit said. He had pulled the top blanket from the bed and was spreading it over the bare wood.

"Thank you." She sat down and the chair rocked gently beneath her weight.

Kit sat on the side of the bed, his arms across his spread knees, his hands dangling between. It was an informal, relaxed pose. Lauren smiled at him, relaxed back in the chair, and closed her eyes. It was not a cold night, but the warmth from the fire felt good. She listened to the crackling of the kindling.

"Why do *you* have trouble sleeping?" she asked.

"Sleeplessness is a defense against nightmares, I suppose," he said, "though not always a conscious one."

"Nightmares?"

"You would not want to know, Lauren," he said. But he continued speaking anyway. "I became a military man because it was what my father had always planned for his second son. And it was my personal choice too. I cannot remember a time when I did not dream of becoming an officer and distinguishing myself on the battlefield. I was not disillusioned after my commission was purchased for me, either. The life suited me. The tasks at hand were ones I could do and do well. I jumped at the opportunity to become a reconnaissance officer when it came my way, and I never regretted my choice. Selling out last year was a hard thing for me to do. In some ways I felt that I was giving up a part of my identity. And yet . . ."

The rockers of the chair squeaked. It was not an unpleasant sound. It was almost lulling.

"And yet?" she asked.

"And yet it involved killing," he said. "I lost count long ago of the number of men I have killed. There are all sorts of ways of justifying killing in war, of course. It is a kill-or-be-killed situation. It is most comforting, though not often possible, to think of the enemy merely as a mass of evil monsters who deserve no better than death. Certainly when one is a soldier one must find a way of overcoming one's scruples and simply do what must be done. But the faces of dead men come to me in my nightmares. No, not dead. Dying. The faces of *dying* men. Ordinary men with mothers and wives and sweethearts at home. Men with dreams and hopes and worries and secrets. Men like me. In my worst nightmares the man who is dying has the face of the man I see in the mirror every day."

"And so you prove that you are human," she said. "War would be truly monstrous if it destroyed all horror of killing."

"But it would be easier to sleep if one were an unfeeling monster," he said.

She had never thought to wonder if men's minds were permanently damaged by the atrocities of war. She had always considered that Englishmen fought for right and justice and so would have nothing on their consciences.

"If I am thankful for one thing," he said, "it is that you and my mother and grandmother and those children in the nursery have never been in the path of warring armies. I am grateful for that, at least."

She opened her eyes and turned her head to smile at him. It was time to change the subject, she thought, time to lighten the gloom, to make it possible for him to return to the house and sleep dreamlessly.

"What a delight the children are, Kit," she said. "I have not encountered many since I was a child myself. I was a happy child, you know. Were you?"

"Yes." He smiled back.

"That is something we have in common, then," she said. "It is rare, I believe. I do not often think back to my childhood, but there were so many happy times. I was fortunate to have Gwen and Neville for companions, and there were cousins too that we used to see quite frequently."

They began exchanging stories of their childhoods, as she had intended. Stories full of humor and adventure and nostalgia—and of mischief on his side. At first their stories alternated with no pause between. But eventually Lauren put her head back and closed her eyes again, and when the pauses between stories grew longer, they were not at all uncomfortable, but were filled with warm thoughts and a cozy companionship that had no need of words. The fire, which he had built up once, burned down again, spitting and crackling a little as it did so. The rocker squeaked with slowing rhythm.

Yes, she had had a happy childhood, which she might not have had if her mother and stepfather had returned from their wedding trip and taken her off somewhere to live alone with them, away from her adopted brother and sister. Yet she had spent much of her childhood pining secretly for the mother whose face she could not even remember. Strange!

She sighed deeply.

Kit was still sitting upright on the side of the bed, even though he had been growing sleepier by the minute. The squeaking of the rocker on the old chair should have been annoying but was not. It was lulling him before it stopped altogether.

Lauren, he guessed, had fallen asleep. She had not spoken for several minutes, and she had not responded to the last story he had told.

He had stopped thinking of his childhood during the past few years. There were almost no memories that did not include Jerome and Syd, and very few that did not involve the Bedwyns. But tonight he had opened up the memories again and had found them pleasant, surprisingly free of pain or bitterness. Despite all that had happened three years ago, those had been happy years. The friendships and the brotherly love had shaped him, nurtured him, made him the man he was now, he supposed.

Lauren's head had tipped to the side. It was an endearing pose, so different from her usual disciplined dignity. He should wake her up and take her back to the house. He rather thought he would sleep peacefully himself for what remained of the night. Indeed, he could nod off right now if he allowed himself to. The thought of the walk back was daunting.

She had done that deliberately, he thought, gazing at her. She had allowed him to talk about his nightmares, but she had not let him wallow in them. She had changed the subject. She had done it so deftly that he could not recall now how they had suddenly found themselves talking about their childhoods. What had created the link from his talk of war and killing? He could not remember, but he was convinced that she had done it deliberately and skillfully. So that his spirits would be lifted, so that his thoughts would be softer, brighter, more conducive to sleep.

He yawned widely.

If he did not wake her soon, she was going to have a sore neck. He got to his feet and reached out a hand to shake her shoulder—and then returned it to his side without touching her. He looked at the bed and then pulled back the two remaining blankets. They were alone together in the middle of the night in a room with a bed—a potentially dangerous situation if ever he had heard of one. Though strangely enough the thought of seduction had not once crossed his mind since they had come inside the hut. And even now the desire he knew he could feel for her was not dominating his mind.

He turned back to the rocking chair, bent down, and scooped her up gently into his arms. She woke up, of course, but she was too sleepy for resistance. He set her down on the bed, as far to the inside as he could. He removed her shoes and then his boots and lay down beside her. He drew the blankets up over both of them. She watched him sleepily the whole while. It was not a wide bed. It was impossible to leave any gap between them.

"Go back to sleep," he said.

He thought she might already have been asleep before he spoke. He could smell that fragrant soap smell of her hair again. He could feel the soft contours of her body all down his right side, and her body heat. Strangely, although he was half aroused, it was merely a pleasant, easily controlled feeling. He did not want to desire her any more urgently. He did not want this to be turned into a sexual orgy.

It was too precious for that.

She was too precious.

She had worked her way into the affections of his mother and grandmother—he believed Grandmama adored her, in fact. She had won the respectful regard of his father. And all of it with quiet dignity. His own life here had been immeasurably more comfortable since her arrival—somehow he was finding it easier to relate to his family again, except for Syd, of course.

He had taught Lauren to be a little more outgoing. He had taught her to bathe in the lake and to climb trees. He had coaxed her into unbending enough to smile and even laugh. But it was not just the changes in her that were precious to him. It was the insight she had allowed him into the person behind the cool façade. The person who did not demand much for herself but worked quietly and tirelessly for everyone else's comfort.

He was surprised most of all, perhaps, by the fact that such a woman—apparently without any great charisma—attracted him.

She *did* attract him.

He turned his head, rubbed his face against her soft curls, and kissed the top of her head.

He was asleep within moments while the lamp burned itself out on the table and the last embers of the fire faded.

For just the merest moment when she awoke, Lauren did not know where she was. But then she remembered that she was still inside the hut in the woods where she and Kit had talked last night. She had been sitting in the rocking chair, growing more and more sleepy, finding it harder and harder to concentrate upon what he was saying. And then ...

She was lying on the bed, she realized without opening her eyes. The pillow beneath her neck was warm and comfortable. She was lying on her side pressed against something equally cozy. One of her legs was wedged between ...

She was not alone on the bed, she realized in a flash. She was in Kit's arms. She could hear his heart beating. She could smell his cologne. For a moment she stiffened in alarm, and indeed a tentative wiggling of the toes on her free foot told her that she was without her shoes. But when she moved a hand slowly to touch herself on one hip, it was to the reassuring discovery that she was fully clothed. She was on the inside of the bed. There would be no wriggling her way out without waking him.

But did she want to? Wriggle her way out, that was?

What on earth would they think at the house?

Whatever had she done?

She had done nothing, that was what. Nothing to be ashamed of. She had talked with Kit, and they had comforted each other and made it possible to sleep peacefully. This was just one more incident in her summer to tuck away for future memories. How she would remember this night!

"You are awake?" he asked softly.

She opened her eyes, tipped back her head—it had been wedged between his shoulder and neck—and looked at him in the faint early morning light beaming through the hut's one small window.

"Did I fall asleep in the middle of one of your stories?" she asked.

"The very best of them." He shook his head in apparent sorrow.

"Kit," she asked, suddenly anxious despite herself, "did—"

"No," he said firmly. "This was one occasion on which I was the perfect gentleman. Well, almost perfect. I would have woken you and taken you back to the house to be quite perfect, I suppose. I could not face the walk back."

"Did you sleep?" she asked him.

"Like a baby." She saw the flash of his grin in the near-darkness. "Thank you, Lauren. Both for listening and for . . . being here."

He was a man who needed to be listened to, she thought. He was not the uncomplicated, carefree man she had judged him to be on first acquaintance.

"However are we to get back to the house without being seen?" She could feel herself flush.

"Why would we arouse suspicion by even trying to creep in unseen?" he asked her. "We will walk boldly up the driveway, and anyone who sees us will assume we have been out for an early walk."

He withdrew his arm from beneath her head and rolled away to sit on the edge of the narrow bed, his back to her. He set his elbows on his knees and pushed the fingers of both hands through his hair. He looked rumpled and . . . undeniably attractive.

Lauren could hardly believe she had spent the night in bed with a man. Even more amazing was the fact that she was feeling no shock, no horror, no sense of humiliation.

It would be as well for this masquerade to end as soon as possible, she thought as he got to his feet and she felt beside the bed for her shoes. She was turning into a wanton.

He smiled at her as he held open the hut door and she stepped out to the freshness of the morning air and the sound of the birds chirruping a dawn chorus from the treetops. It was his smile—and his laughter—that she would remember long after her other memories had faded, she thought. It was a memory that would surely bring a smile to her own lips down the long years ahead.

He took her hand in his as they began to walk.

"For the benefit of anyone who happens to be watching," he explained. "There is no more tender sight than that of a betrothed couple holding hands."

"Kit," she said reproachfully, but she made no effort to pull her hand away.

14

The sun was shining the next day and it was possible to seek amusement outdoors. Lauren herself did not go out until afternoon—if one discounted a walk with Kit back to the house from the gamekeeper's hut at a little after six in the morning. She helped the countess look over her plans for the birthday celebrations and offered to take over some of the responsibility for the daytime events. She spent an hour in the nursery at Nell Clifford's invitation. And she sat conversing for a while, first with her grandfather and then with the dowager and Lady Irene.

A group of the younger people had agreed to go riding in the afternoon. They were loud in their insistence that Gwendoline and Lauren accompany them. Gwen was quite firm in her refusal, but Lauren's objections were overridden.

"Oh, *do* come," young Marianne Butler begged. "I want to see your riding habit. I'll wager it is *ravishing.*"

"Ladies do not make wagers," her brother Crispin reminded her and won for himself a rude, cross-eyed stare, which Lauren pretended not to notice—and which she was surprised to find amusing.

"Of course you will come," Daphne Willard said briskly. "If it is to be just the very young things, I will have no one sensible to talk to."

"And Kit will pine away if you are not there," Frederick Butler added, "and likely fall off his horse."

"We would have to carry him back on a door," Phillip Willard said, adding to the nonsense.

"Of course Lauren will be coming," Kit said with a grin. "I have promised to make this summer more enjoyable for her than any other she has known. How can one enjoy oneself if one does not get out for at least one respectable gallop?"

She looked reproachfully at him, but he was his usual merry-eyed self today and there would be no reasoning with him, she knew. Her stomach fluttered with awareness when she remembered that she had spent the night with him, pressed against his warmth, listening to his deep, even breathing the few times she surfaced to near-consciousness. She had *slept* with him. How much more scandalous could her behavior become this summer? And how much more enjoyable, added a little inner voice that she was beginning to recognize as her emerging rebellious self. It had been the most wonderful night of her life.

"Oh, very well," she said weakly. "I will ride. But I will *not* gallop, Kit. The very idea! I would be the one coming home on a door."

Kit winked at her and the cousins chose to find her words amusing. The dowager and Aunt Clara, both of whom were present, smiled indulgently.

The pace set by Claude Willard, who led the way out of the stables, was reassuringly sedate. Lauren rode between Marianne, who lamented the fact that she did not have the figure to wear anything as divinely elegant as Lauren's riding habit, and Penelope Willard, who wanted to know—among numerous other things—if the gentlemen in London were more handsome than those in the country. It was a novel, rather pleasant experience to Lauren to be the admired idol of young girls who were not yet "out."

Kit was riding a little way ahead, in the midst of a group that was indulging in a great deal of laughter. He did glance back quite frequently, though, to smile. And to check to see that she was still firmly planted on her horse's back? Lauren wondered. But she was beginning to enjoy both the ride and the company.

Until, that was, Lady Freyja Bedwyn and Lord Rannulf hove into sight, also on horseback, and chose to join the party after exchanging loud greetings with the group, with all or most of whose members they appeared to have an acquaintance.

Suddenly, and without knowing quite how, Lauren found herself riding between the two of them.

"You really *do* ride, then, Miss Edgeworth," Lady Freyja observed, controlling with consummate skill her magnificent, spirited mount, which was clearly accustomed to a far quicker pace.

"And with a remarkably elegant seat," Lord Rannulf added, his mocking eyes sweeping over her and making of his words a double entendre.

"I expected to find you at Alvesley, hard at work on your sampler," Lady Freyja said.

"Indeed?" Lauren replied coolly. "How very peculiar."

"You are exposing your ignorance, Free," her brother told her. "Even I know that only very little girls work on samplers. Miss Edgeworth doubtless graduated long ago to tatting and weaving and lace-making and knitting and knotting and all those other fascinating accomplishments that true ladies spend their time so usefully about."

"Oh, *do* you do all those things, Miss Edgeworth?" Lady Freyja asked. "How you put me to shame. I always find them *so* dull."

"Fortunately," Lauren said, "the world offers enough variety of activities to suit every taste."

"Well, *my* taste does not run to crawling over the earth's surface when I have a good mount beneath me," Lady Freyja said. "If we were to go any more slowly we would be in danger of going backward. Race with me, Miss Edgeworth. To the top of *that* hill?" She pointed with her whip across the pasture they were traversing to a hill maybe a couple of miles distant—Lauren rather thought it was the hill behind Alvesley on which the wilderness walk came to an end.

"I am afraid I cannot oblige you," Lauren said. "This pace suits me admirably."

"I must confess, Miss Edgeworth," Lord Rannulf said, lowering his voice, the mockery in his eyes turning to laughter, "that a slow ride can occasionally be every bit as satisfying as a vigorous gallop to the finish. Provided the mount is worth the effort of restraint, that is."

He could not possibly mean . . . But Lauren had no chance to digest her shock.

Lady Freyja had raised her voice to command the attention of the whole group. "Miss Edgeworth will not race against me," she cried. "Will no one accept my challenge? Kit? You could not possibly say no. Though on *that* horse you would not be able to beat a mule to the top of the hill."

"Ah, a challenge," Lord Rannulf murmured.

Kit was grinning. "You are going to have to eat those words within a few minutes, Freyja," he said. He made an extravagant gesture with one arm. "Lead the way."

A few of the cousins whooped with enthusiasm as Lady Freyja dug her spurs into her horse's side and, bent low over her sidesaddle, went streaking off in the direction of the hill. With a laugh, Kit went after her.

"She always was an outrageous hoyden," Daphne Willard remarked cheerfully.

"And more often than not Kit's equal," Lord Rannulf added.

Lauren watched them go in a race that had been deliberately orchestrated for her benefit, she knew. It did not matter. They looked just as she had imagined them that day up on the hill with Gwen. They were galloping side by side, flying like the wind. They looked magnificent together.

They would *be* magnificent together once this summer was over and they were both free and under no pressure to make a dynastic alliance. They were each other's equal in passion and daring.

She did not mind, Lauren told herself. She had no claim on Kit herself. She had no wish to have any claim on him. She wanted only to be free herself. But she could not stop remembering last night—the shared stories, the gentle, shared laughter, the rhythmic squeaking of the rocking chair, the lazy wonder of waking to find him lifting her out of the chair and laying her on the bed, the cozy comfort of sleeping with her body pressed against his.

The racers were sitting side by side at the bottom of the hill when the rest of the group came up to them. Their horses were grazing untethered nearby. Lauren met Lady Freyja's glance and saw challenge and triumph and faint malice there.

"Well, who won?" Claude Willard called.

"Kit did," Lady Freyja called back. "He would have pulled back at the end to let me win, but I told him I would shoot him between the eyes if he ever stooped to such condescension."

"What was the prize, Kit?" Lord Rannulf asked.

"Alas," he said, getting to his feet, mounting his horse, and riding toward Lauren, "we did not agree upon anything in advance. Now, if no one has any objection, my betrothed and I would like a little time alone together."

Lauren turned her horse without comment and rode off with Kit while Daphne behind them was suggesting that they all climb the hill and rest on the summit.

"Were Freyja and Ralf annoying you?" Kit asked.

"Not in any way I could not handle," she said.

He looked across at her, a smile in his eyes. "No," he said. "I have realized that about you. Has this afternoon brought you any enjoyment at all?"

"Of course it has," she assured him. "I like all your relatives, Kit. I like their company."

"But it has not been the sort of memorable stuff I promised you." He grinned at her. "We will pass sedately through that gate into the pasture, and then we will see."

"Kit!" she protested. "Please don't get any ideas. I am quite perfectly happy as I am."

But he would only chuckle.

"Now." He closed the gate behind them a couple of minutes later and gazed off into the distance—it seemed a vast expanse of distance. "There is another gate at the other side, which you may remember even though it is not visible over that slight rise in the land. We will race to it."

"Kit!"

"And this time," he said, "we will agree upon a prize in advance. A kiss if I win. And—*what* if you win?"

"There is not even any point in naming anything," she said indignantly. "*Of course* you will win, or would if I were to be foolish enough to accept your challenge. I never race, Kit. I never take a horse to a gallop."

"Then it is time you did," he said. "I will be sporting about it, though. I will give you an early start. I'll count slowly to ten."

"*Ki-it!*"

"One."

"I will not do it."

"Two."

"You will not be satisfied until I have broken my neck, I suppose."

"Three."

She took off.

She knew her horse could gallop at least twice as fast as it did. She did not by any means give it its head. Even so, it felt to her as if the ground were flying by beneath its hooves, as if the wind would whip off her hat despite the pins, as if she had never done anything nearly as dangerous or exhilarating in her life before.

He did not pass her. It was quite a while before she realized that he was just behind her left shoulder—in position to catch her if she fell? She started to laugh.

By the time the gate came into sight—reassuringly close once they had topped the rise—she was laughing helplessly, and she could hear Kit laughing behind her.

"I am going to beat you," she shrieked with just a few yards to go. "I am going to—"

He went past her as if her horse were standing still.

She bent forward until her nose almost touched the horse's neck. She could not seem to stop laughing.

"If you would just raise your head," he said at last, "I could claim my prize."

"Unfair!" she said, straightening up. "You were just *toying* with me. *I* should be the one putting a bullet between your eyes. Oh, Kit, that was such *fun!*"

"I always thought," he said, riding up alongside her until one of her knees was pressed against his thigh, "nothing could be lovelier than your eyes. But they can be lovelier than themselves when they sparkle, as they do now."

"Oh, foolish," she said at the silly flattery, warmed through to the very center of her heart by it.

And then his mouth was on hers, firm, warm, his lips parted. He took his prize with slow thoroughness while she thought again of the loveliness of last night and realized in some shock that she was in danger of coming to care rather too much for comfort.

"There!" she said briskly when he had finished. "The debt is paid, you foolish man."

She expected him to grin. He smiled softly instead.

"Foolish," he murmured. "Yes, I suppose I am that."

She was in grave danger indeed.

The family gathering in the drawing room that evening was a merry one. Two tables of cards had been set up for the older people. Several of the younger people took their turn at the pianoforte while others gathered around the instrument to listen, to sing, to joke, and to laugh. Still others stood or sat in groups, sipping their tea, catching up on family news and other assorted gossip.

Kit's grandmother was at the heart of it all, in her chair beside the fire, nodding and contented despite the fact that she had used to enjoy playing cards. Lauren sat on a stool beside her, massaging her bad hand, as had become her daily custom. She was a pretty child, the old lady told her, not for the first time.

"Hardly a child, ma'am," Lauren said in her usual quiet, matter-of-fact way. "I am six and twenty."

"But very definitely pretty, Grandmama," Kit said from his standing position before the fireplace. "I am in full agreement with you on that point. Not on the other, though. What, might I ask, would I want with a child bride?"

His grandmother chuckled. She had become deeply attached to Lauren already, he knew.

Baron Galton was at one of the card tables, partnered by Kit's mother, while the Dowager Lady Kilbourne and Uncle Melvin Clifford pitted their skills against them. Lady Muir was conversing with Sydnam in the window embrasure, his usual spot in the evenings.

Kit dared to feel contentment. Lauren's family fit in well with his. He liked all three of them who were here, and they all appeared to approve of him. None of them had spent any time in London during the past year, of course, to have had their opinions tainted by the reputation he had courted there. Kit smiled as he remembered the interview Baron Galton had requested on the day of his arrival. He had subjected Kit to a far more thorough grilling than Portfrey had, asking about his military credentials, his present aspirations, and his future prospects. Kit had even found himself—rather foolishly, under the circumstances—asking the old man formally for Lauren's hand. Just as formally Baron Galton had granted it.

She really would be a perfect wife for him, a perfect countess, a perfect member of his family. He had become convinced during the past few days that he could find contentment with her. As for passion—well, passion had never worked for him. At best, it had never lasted longer than a week or two; at worst, it had caused him intense misery. He would be able to trust contentment, relax into it, grow old with it. With *her*. If only he could persuade her during the next week or so . . .

But his thoughts were interrupted by the sound of young Marianne's voice, demanding everyone's attention. They simply *must* have dancing, she declared, her hands clasped to her bosom, her pleading gaze directed at Kit. The other young cousins gathered about the pianoforte murmured their support and also gazed hopefully at Kit.

"Dancing? A splendid idea." He grinned and strode forward. "Why has no one thought of it before tonight? We do not have to wait for the birthday ball, do we? We will have the carpet rolled back immediately."

The murmur rose to a faint cheer, and his grandmother smiled and nodded.

While Kit supervised two footmen in the task of rolling back the Persian carpet, Marianne wound her arms about her mother's neck and wheedled her shamelessly into providing the music.

Eight of the cousins began the dancing with a vigorous jig, which aroused much laughter among them and applause from the spectators. The next dance was to be a Roger de Coverly, Aunt Honoria announced from the pianoforte. Kit extended a hand for Lauren's and winked at his grandmother.

"Come and dance with me, Lauren," he said. "We will show these young sprigs a thing or two."

They led off the set, which boasted six couples this time. He had only ever waltzed with Lauren before. But she was an accomplished country dancer too, he soon discovered. She smiled and her cheeks flushed and her eyes sparkled as they moved down between the lines, she along the gentlemen's side, he along the ladies', twirling each member of the line about alternately with each other. It was only after they had led the lines around the outside of the set and had formed an arch with their hands for everyone else to pass beneath that he realized all other activity in the room had been suspended— the card games and the conversations. Everyone was watching, not just the dancers in general, but him and Lauren in particular. The newly betrothed couple. Kit with his beautiful bride-to-be.

He sensed approval and affection emanating from them. And he felt something a little warmer than contentment as he remembered her helpless laughter, her flushed cheeks, and her bright eyes this afternoon—and her softly acquiescent kiss.

He really must prevent her from breaking off their betrothal.

They were at the far end of the line again when the dance ended, close to the windows. Young Crispin Butler, fresh down from Oxford and fancying himself an experienced man-about-town, was already demanding a waltz tune of his mother, and the dancers were eagerly taking new partners.

"Miss Edgeworth?" Sir Jeremy Brightman, Doris's betrothed, took her hand to lead her into the dance.

"Lady Muir?" Kit bowed to Lauren's cousin, who was still sitting on the window seat. Too late he remembered her limp and hoped he had not just embarrassed her unpardonably. But she smiled and rose to her feet and set her hand in his.

And then Cousin Catherine came dashing up, all bubbling energy.

"Sydnam," she demanded, grabbing his hand with both of hers, "do come and dance with me. You surely cannot intend to sit there all night."

Kit froze. Catherine had never been known for tact or tender sensibilities, but even for her this was a howler.

"I beg to decline, Catherine," Syd replied. "Ask Lawrence. He needs the exercise."

"I can dance with my husband any night of the year," she said. "I want you. You were always a divine dancer, I remember. Do come—"

"*Catherine!*" Kit spoke far more sharply than he had intended, unconsciously addressing her as he might have addressed a recalcitrant private in his regiment. "Can you not take a civil no for an answer? Syd cannot dance. He—"

"*Yes. Thank you.*" Sydnam was on his feet, his face pale and set, his voice quivering with barely suppressed fury. He bowed to their cousin and completely ignored his brother. "Thank you, Catherine. On second thought, I suppose I can shuffle about with sufficient competence to avoid banging you into furniture or other cousins."

It was a tense, nasty moment, a brief flaring of passion, most of it unspoken, which had attracted the attention of everyone in the room. Kit was well aware of the awkward silence behind him, and then the rush of sound as everyone pretended they had not noticed anything untoward.

He closed his eyes briefly. He felt suddenly dizzy and even nauseous. He had been trying to *help*, to protect Syd from embarrassment. But he seemed to have accomplished just the opposite—and had been soundly rejected in the process. Again! The prospect of turning around to face the room, of smiling at Lady Muir and dancing with her as if the past minute had never happened, was so daunting as to be quite impossible.

"Excuse me, ma'am," he said, bowing hastily to his partner. "Please excuse me."

He turned and hurried from the room without looking at anyone as he passed.

15

He turned upstairs rather than down, though he had no particular destination in mind. His room, where he could hide out for the rest of the evening? He was at the top of the flight when a voice stopped him.

"Kit."

He turned and looked down. She was standing with one slippered foot on the bottom stair, one slim hand on the banister. He was feeling grim and humiliated—and grief-stricken, as if he had just lost all that was nearest and dearest to him. His first instinct was to tell her to go back to the drawing room. He was no fitting company for her or for anyone else at the moment. But he did not want to be alone, he realized suddenly. He could not bear to be alone.

"Come," he said.

He watched her until she was halfway up and then turned to take a candle from a wall sconce. He knew where he would go, where he would take her. He did not wait for her to reach his side, but strode away from the bedchamber wing toward the western wing and the family portrait gallery, which stretched the full width of the house.

The door was kept locked, but he knew that the key was kept in a not-so-secret hiding place inside the large marble urn that stood on the floor nearby. He reached inside for it, unlocked the door, and stood aside while Lauren preceded him into the room. He locked the door behind them.

His single candle threw darting, ominous shadows across the floor and up the walls. It was quite inadequate to light up the whole gallery. And it was cold up here. Sometime during the evening the wind had come up. He could hear rain lashing against the windows. All Lauren had with which to cover her arms was a thin cashmere shawl. He strode along the room, shadowy, barely visible ancestors gazing silently down at him from their heavy ornate frames on the walls, and Lauren followed. Neither of them spoke until he came to the great marble fireplace in the center of the long wall, flanked by wide, velvet-covered benches with low backs.

A fire had been laid in the hearth. He knelt down and lit the kindling with the flame of his candle and then set it on the mantelpiece. He stood looking down into the feeble flames, listening to the crackling of wood, feeling the first thread of warmth.

He was reminded of the night before. There was a strong similarity of circumstances but a far different atmosphere. There would be no comforting and lulling exchange of stories tonight. Tonight he was staring deep into the abyss of all his worst and most frequent nightmares. The ones he had not told her about last night. The ones he had shared with no one for three interminable years.

Lauren, he sensed rather than saw, sat down on one of the benches. She made no attempt to speak to him. He had not expected that she would. She was one of a rare breed, he had learned. She was a giver rather than a taker. And God help him, he was about to take from her. He was about to use her as an audience, as he had begun to do last night. He was about to force her to hear what he was compelled to say. He had bottled it inside for too long. He would surely go mad—literally insane—if he did not tell her. He would not allow himself to consider the impropriety of telling such a tale to a gently raised lady.

"It was I who first suggested that Syd purchase a commission," he said abruptly. "I had come to England on official business and dashed home for a week's leave. I accused him of softness and inactivity. A military life would toughen him up and make a man of him, I told him. It was said as a joke. I did not mean it, and he knew I did not. I was inordinately fond of him—and he of me, more is the pity. But I had planted the seed in his mind, and before I knew it, he was urging our father to purchase him a commission. At first I joined the chorus of protest and told him not to be an idiot, that there were more important things for him to do than brandish a sword at Frenchmen. But when I saw that his mind was made up, I was—God help me, I was taken with the idea. When Mother pleaded with me to talk him out of it, I told her it was Syd's decision, that I would not interfere. I could easily have done what she wanted. He would have listened to me. But I did not do it."

Flames were licking about the larger logs wedged above the kindling. Warmth was beginning to radiate beyond the hearth.

"I was good at my job as a reconnaissance officer," he continued. "It was a lonely, dangerous job, but I had the physical stamina and the mental fortitude for it as well as a well-developed love of a challenge. It was a job that needed a will of steel and a heart of flint. There was no room for fear, for indecision, for pity, for any of the finer sensibilities that a gentleman might permit himself in more civilized circumstances. Too many lives depended upon me alone. But I did it willingly and well. Honor and duty were all that mattered. They were right and good. I did not ever expect to have to choose between honor and love. They ought to be on the same side, ought they not? On the side of right? It should be not only possible to choose both but impossible to separate them. What would you do if they *were* on opposite sides? Which would you choose?"

He did not expect an answer even though he paused for several moments to gaze into the dancing flames. He had almost forgotten that he had an audience, except that he felt all the uncertain relief of finally unburdening himself to another human being. He would take any judgment that might follow. He would take any punishment. God grant only that it be harsh enough and painful enough to bring him some absolution—provided it was not everlasting, as the guilt was now.

"Syd persuaded Colonel Grant to allow him to accompany me on one of my missions," he said. He did not want to continue. He *could* not continue. But neither could he stop. He leaned one arm along the mantel, bowed his head, and closed his eyes. "I don't know how he did it, but he did. I raged and stormed at both of them, but to no avail. Grant was his usual inflexible self, and Syd merely went quietly and cheerfully about his preparations. Two things were wrong about that mission—three if one counts the fact that I had my brother with me. First, the nature of the task made it imperative that we travel without uniform. It was very rare. I had done it only two or three times before. Second, I had papers with me—usually there was nothing written, nothing tangible, but this time there was. If they had fallen into French hands . . . Well, they simply could not be allowed to do so, that was all. But on our second day out we became trapped in the mountains of Portugal by a French scouting party—something that had never happened to me before."

He curled his hand into a fist and rested his forehead against it. His heart was beating so loudly he could hear it hammering against his eardrums.

"There was one slim chance of breaking out," he said. "Syd was the one who saw it. If one of us created a diversion, something that would mean certain capture, the other might be able to get away. The choice of which of us would court capture and which would continue on his way with the papers was mine to make—I was the superior officer. Syd had no experience. Even if he had broken free, the chances were slim that he would successfully complete the mission. It *had* to be completed. Honor dictated that I do all in my power to serve the allied cause. Honor dictated that I be the one to escape the trap. Love dictated that I choose the more painful role. Which would you have chosen, Lauren?"

She spoke for the first time. "Kit," she said softly, "Oh, Kit, my dear."

"I chose honor," he said, pressing his forehead so hard against his fist that he felt—and welcomed—pain. "God help me, I took the chance of escape and assigned my brother the role of scapegoat."

From a position high in a mountain pass, after he had broken free of the encircling trap, he had looked back to see Syd being led away captive. He had continued on his way and had completed his mission successfully. He had been highly commended afterward, mentioned in dispatches, hailed as a fearless hero. One of God's bizarre jokes.

"It was war," Lauren said.

"It was worse than war." His nightmares were clawing at his waking self. He was about to face the dreaded images quite deliberately. He was about to verbalize them to a lady, who should be protected from the harsh realities of life and war, not deliberately exposed to them. But his own need to achieve some sort of catharsis overwhelmed his sense of decorum. "War is a game, you see—a vicious game. If a British officer is captured in uniform, he is treated with honor and courtesy while held in captivity. If he is not in uniform, then he is treated with all the ferocity the French and the Spanish and Portuguese partisans show one another's captives. I knew that before my decision was made."

He had known it. *He had known it.* It had been in the forefront of his mind when he had hesitated for the merest fraction of a moment before making his decision. He had known what would be facing the one of them who was caught. There had been time for only a quick bear hug . . .

"I met up with a group of partisans the same day," he continued. "I could have sent them back to rescue Syd. They could have done it—they outnumbered the French. But I needed them—all of them. My *damned* mission had need of them. Two weeks passed before we were finished and could find Syd and spring him free. I did not expect to find him still alive, but he lived—barely."

If only memory were not such a starkly visual thing. He closed his eyes more tightly. If only it were *only* visual. But there were sounds.

And smells. Who would have guessed that in one's nightmares one could *smell* burned flesh?

"They had started on his right side," he said, "and worked their way gradually downward with exquisitely wrought tortures of burning, crushing, and gouging. They had reached his right knee before we found him. Our surgeons saved his leg, but his arm had to be amputated after we had got him back to base. That journey!" He sucked in air slowly and audibly. "He had given away nothing under torture—not my name or my destination or the purpose of my mission. Only his own name, rank, and regiment, repeated over and over again, night and day, even after we had him back. They had not broken him, except in body. Had he broken, of course, and told them what they wanted to know, they would have granted him a swift and merciful death."

He heard a soft expulsion of breath behind him, but she said nothing.

"I sacrificed my brother," he said, "for honor. And then I had all the glory of success. I was trained, you see, to have a heart of flint, to be ruthlessly opportunistic and selfish in the accomplishment of my duties. I sacrificed my brother, and then I brought him home and created mayhem here with the lives and sensibilities of the rest of my family. I behaved badly that summer, Lauren. *Shamefully.* It is a good thing you have insisted upon a temporary betrothal. I would not be a good lifelong bargain. I amputated myself, you see, in exchange for becoming a glorious hero. There is nothing of *me* left." He laughed softly. "Nothing but honor."

"He is alive," she said. His sensible, matter-of-fact Lauren. "Kit, he is *alive.*"

"He breathes." He spoke harshly. "He is not alive, Lauren. He will never be that again. He is my father's *steward* here, for God's sake. He plans to accept the salaried position of steward on one of Bewcastle's properties. You do not understand, of course, the dreadful nature of such a fate. How could you? Sydnam was an *artist.* No, is—he *is* an artist. His landscape paintings were the most extraordinary canvases I have ever seen. There was craftsmanship there and an eye for color and atmosphere and detail and . . . Ah, how can an ordinary mortal like me describe the—the *soul* that was there? His painting breathed with what even a layman like me could sense was the very meaning of the scene he depicted. He was a gentle man and a dreamer and a visionary and . . . And now he is serving a life sentence inside the prison of a ruined body, capable of nothing loftier than being someone's steward."

"Kit," she said, "you must not do this to yourself, dear. It was war. And you did what was right. You made the right decision. You did your duty. It was what you had to do."

"How could it be right?" he cried. "When I see him so maimed and scarred, when I see my sweet-natured Syd shut up deep inside himself, rejecting my every overture of sympathy, hating me, how can I believe that what I did was right?"

"It just was," she said. "Some things have no neat explanation, Kit. Life is not like that, unfortunately. One can spend all of one's life doing the right things and going unrewarded in the end. One can find oneself forced into making a choice between two courses that seem equally right but only one can be chosen. You made the right choice."

A part of him knew with the utmost certainty that if he had the choice to make over again he would take the same course—and suffer the same hell of remorse and guilt afterward.

" 'I could not love thee, dear, so much/Loved I not honor more,' " he said quietly. "Who wrote those lines? Do you know?"

"Richard Lovelace, I believe," she said. "One of the Cavalier poets."

"Never believe it," he said. "It is a lie. *Nothing* should come before love."

"If you had made the other choice," she said after a short silence filled with the howling of the wind and the lashing of the rain, "and if hundreds, perhaps thousands, had suffered as a result, Kit, you would never have forgiven yourself."

He laughed softly. "I would not have needed to. I would be dead."

"You did your duty," she said softly. "It is all any of us can do, Kit."

He kept his eyes closed and his forehead pressed to his fist. He allowed her words to envelop him, to soothe him, to comfort him, very much—for the moment at least—like absolution.

For the past several minutes Lauren had been feeling very much as if she were going to faint. She had always tried to avoid any sight or mention of violence, believing that ladies should have no dealings with such sordid realities. It had never been particularly difficult to do. Most gentlemen seemed to hold the same belief. She could remember an occasion when Lily, newly come to Newbury, had launched eagerly into a conversation about the wars—she had grown up in the train of the armies, first in India, then in the Peninsula, as the supposed daughter of an infantry sergeant. Lauren, consumed by secret hatred at the time, had tried to appease her conscience by instructing Lily in what would be expected of her as the Countess of Kilbourne. She could recall advising Lily that a lady did not speak of the wars or listen to any conversation about them.

She had been so very righteous in those days, so convinced that she was right. So much the perfect lady. So unbearably prim.

But now she could not shake from her mind the horrifying images of torture that Kit had conjured up, though he had given no details. Or the image of the regimental surgeon plying his trade, saw in hand, amputating a man's arm. She could almost smell the blood.

At one point she had considered trying to change the subject, as she had done so successfully last night. But the two occasions, so similar on the surface, were in fact entirely different. Tonight the unfortunate incident in the drawing room with Sydnam Butler had ripped away everything he had put there to cover the gaping wound of his deepest agony. Tonight it would have been cruel, unthinkable, unpardonable, to have tried to stop him. Tonight he had needed to unburden his conscience more, perhaps, than he had needed anything else in his life before.

And so she had sat straight and still on the wide velvet bench, her feet neatly side by side on the floor, her hands clasping the ends of

her shawl, determinedly clinging to consciousness, fighting the ringing in her ears, the coldness in her head. The fact that she was a delicately, correctly nurtured lady was of no significance. She had resisted
the urge to shift the focus of her hearing to the wind and the rain
outside. She had listened carefully to every single word.

She had not cringed or allowed herself to faint. She knew what it
felt like to lock up everything that was most painful inside oneself,
not sharing one's hurt even with one's dearest friend. She knew all
about pain and loneliness and even despair. Perhaps that was why he
had chosen her as his audience, even if it had not been a conscious
choice. Perhaps he simply recognized in her a fellow sufferer.

There was no doubt that he had done what was right. She had
told him that, and of course he must know it for himself. But she realized too that knowing it would not really ease his pain. She knew he
would never forgive himself for not doing the wrong thing. It was
pointless to add words to words. She sat quietly and waited, giving
him all the time he needed. She was glad he had locked the gallery
door behind them. There was no danger of anyone rushing in before
he was ready to face the world again.

After a while, when she sensed somehow that the time was right, she
got to her feet without speaking and closed the distance between them.
She set her arms about his waist from behind and rested her cheek against
his shoulder, intent upon giving him all the comfort of her physical presence, for what it was worth. She felt him inhale slowly and deeply. She
both felt and heard the breath shudder out of him. And then he turned
and caught her to him, crushing her against him with arms that felt like
iron bands. She felt all the breath rush out of her, but it did not occur to
her to feel alarm or to struggle to be free. He needed her.

Plainly and simply stated, he needed her. And it did not occur to
her for a single moment to resist his need.

When his mouth found hers, it was hard and urgent, grinding her
lips against her teeth, bruising them, pressing them apart. His tongue
plunged deep into her mouth. One of his hands, spread over her
lower back, jerked her hard against him, leaving her in no doubt of
the sexual turn his need had taken.

She felt curiously detached. The part of her that was the Lauren Edgeworth, perfect lady, stood some distance away, coolly analyzing, admonishing her with the reminder that *this* was the inevitable consequence of all the impropriety that had characterized her dealings with him from the very start—from the very moment she had looked back over her shoulder at him in Hyde Park. This was the consequence of being repeatedly alone with him, having deceived her family and his into allowing it on the assumption that they were betrothed. This was the sort of unbridled, dangerous passion one must expect to be unleashed by the unseemly talk of violence she had allowed when they were alone together behind locked doors.

This had to be stopped *right now.*

The other, less familiar, formerly unsuspected part of herself that had been born at Vauxhall—or perhaps much earlier than that, in the park—stayed present in his arms and recognized that she was a woman, that he had need of her, that she had warmth and femininity and *humanity* to offer him in his need. And the freedom to give all if she chose. Choices again. Until recently—ah, until *now*—choices had never been difficult. She had always known, by the rigid code of gentility, what was right. She had never known the code of the heart. Honor or love? They were opposed, as they had been for him. But this time it was love that could—and should—triumph.

She chose love, though she did not perhaps use that word to herself since her thoughts were not verbal ones.

This, she thought quite clearly—*this* was what she had meant at Vauxhall. She knew it with a sudden blinding intuition. *This* was what she had meant. This coming alive to the woman who had been locked away all her life inside the lady who was Lauren Edgeworth.

His mouth was against her throat, on her shoulders, at her breasts. His hands were moving urgently against the flimsy fabric of her evening gown, pushing it off her shoulders and down her arms, exposing her breasts. She did not flinch even though there were both firelight and candlelight to make her feel doubly exposed. She was a woman and he needed her. She would give, then. She needed too— she needed to be a *woman.* She shivered with mingled fright and excitement as his mouth closed warmly over one breast and suckled her, his tongue flicking over her nipple and suffusing her from head to toe in raw desire. She cupped a hand with infinite gentleness over the back of his head and set a cheek against his soft fair hair.

He moved his head to set his forehead against her shoulder.

"Stop me," he said, his voice both rough and husky. "For God's sake, Lauren, stop me."

"No." She lifted his head with both hands and looked into his face, her fingers gently stroking through his hair. "This is what I choose, Kit. What I freely choose. Don't stop. Please don't stop." She could not bear it now if he did. "This is not just for you. It is for me too." She feathered light kisses over his face as she spoke, kissing his cheeks, his eyes, his mouth.

He was holding her again then, just as close, and kissing her just as deeply as before except that the frenzied urgency had gone, to be replaced by hot passion mingled with what felt very like tenderness. As if she had become for him not just a woman, but Lauren too. Her naked breasts pressed against his coat.

She was giver and gift. He was gift and giver.

It was upon one of the velvet benches that he laid her down after another minute or two. It was quite wide enough to make a narrow bed, she realized. She reached up her arms for him, but he was raising her gown to her waist, removing her silk slippers, her stockings and her undergarments, unbuttoning the front flap of his breeches. His eyes, heavy-lidded with desire, roamed over her. His hair was disheveled, his cheeks flushed. He looked beautiful beyond belief.

Lauren Edgeworth, that disciplined lady, stood apart again for a moment and informed her other self that she was simply not *thinking*, that she would forever regret what would happen unless she put a stop to it *now*. But the point was that she *was* thinking. This was not mindless passion. It was not even passion, in fact. It was something more primal, more deeply emotional than that. It was something she knew with absolute certainty she would never regret.

He knelt beside the bench, kissing her face with light, feathering kisses. With his hands he fondled her, doing exquisite things with her breasts, holding them, stroking them, rolling the hardened, tender nipples between thumbs and forefingers. And then with one hand he fondled her *there*, his fingers nimbly probing her naked flesh, parting folds, stroking, lightly scratching, pulsing, finding the most intimate part of her and sliding inward.

She closed her eyes and inhaled slowly.

She knew what happened between a man and a woman. Aunt Clara had explained it to her before her planned wedding to Neville. She had sometimes tried to imagine it, though more often she had tried *not* to. It must be embarrassing, utterly distasteful, she had always thought. She had imagined it as a purely carnal thing, totally stripped of emotion or even of any tactile sensation apart from the humiliating penetration of her body that must occur.

She had never suspected that there would be this ache, this yearning, this eagerness to be penetrated, to be joined. This need—emotional as well as physical—to give and to be gifted. Was *this* passion? If so, it was not mindless at all.

"Lauren." His mouth was warm over hers. "It is not too late to stop me."

"Don't stop." She did not open her eyes. "Kit . . ."

He had removed his coat and waistcoat. His shirt felt warm and silky against her naked breasts. So did his breeches against her inner thighs as he pushed between them and spread them wide. His weight bore her down into the velvet cushions of the bench. It made her feel more defenseless, on the verge of alarm. Open and vulnerable. And pulsing with a heightened need that was almost unbearable.

She felt him then, pressed against the place where his finger had been just moments before. But much thicker, harder . . . She breathed in slowly as he came inside her, slowly, stretching her, filling her with a terrifying sort of exultation. There was no going back now, no stopping him. It was too late, and she was *glad* it was too late. She gripped his shoulders and concentrated upon not showing either fear or pain. There *was* pain. There was no more room. He was going to hurt her—but she had been *told* it would hurt. Then something tore inside her, something that for a moment threatened unbearable pain and then was gone, just as the barrier of her virginity was gone. He pushed deep.

"Lauren," he murmured against her ear. "Sweet. So very sweet. Have I hurt you?"

"No." Her voice sounded shockingly normal.

She should lie still and relaxed, Aunt Clara had advised, until her husband had finished. *Her husband.*

Finished? Had he finished now?

He drew out of her and she felt a pang of regret. This was all? Once in a lifetime and it was over already, to be relived only in dreams for the rest of her life? Over so soon? But at the moment she expected him to withdraw altogether he pushed back inward. There was soreness. There was also an exquisite silken feeling and the knowledge that there were to be a few moments longer. She wanted to beg him to do it again, but even at such a moment she knew a lady's reluctance to appear gauche or to make foolish demands.

He did it again. And again. She lay still, holding his shoulders as if they were the only anchor of her existence, quietly absorbing all the forbidden delights of her shocking fall from virtue.

She was *glad*. What reward had virtue ever brought her? Virtue was its own reward, she had always believed. But it was *not*. Virtue was no reward at all.

Did he know how good it made her feel, this repeated thrust and withdrawal, which had become smooth and rhythmic? Did he know? Was that why he did it? To delight her? But she could hear his labored breathing, and she could feel his increased body heat, and she knew that of course he did it because it delighted him. *She* delighted him.

She *delighted* him. She, Lauren Edgeworth. She smiled and focused all her thoughts, all her feelings, downward. She would drink this cup of pleasure to the very dregs. The memory would last her a lifetime.

His hands slid beneath her before she was more than halfway down the cup, holding her buttocks firm, tilting her upward, and his thrusts became harder, faster, deeper. A sharp ache of pure pleasure came swirling upward through her belly to focus in her breasts, but before it could be repeated, far too soon, it seemed—how greedy she was!—he strained deep into her and she felt a warm liquid gush.

Ah. He was finished.

And she was not.

Did women ever finish? Did they ever begin? Was there only the delight and the reaching for something beyond one's grasp? But the delight was enough. She was not sorry. She would never be sorry. She would not allow her conscience to scold her later tonight, tomorrow, for the rest of her life. She was glad this had happened. It had been one of the loveliest experiences of her life. No—it was *the* loveliest.

She thought he must have fallen asleep for a few minutes. She ran her fingers through his hair and turned her head to gaze into the fire, which was sending crackling sparks up the chimney as the logs burned down. She listened to the cozy sound of rain against the window.

"Mmm," he said after a while, and he lifted his head to look down at her. "I do not have to say I am sorry, do I, Lauren? I did not force—"

She set the fingers of one hand over his mouth. "You know you did not," she said. "I will not be on your conscience, Kit."

He smiled—a sleepy, warm smile. "I will say thank you instead, then," he said. "Thank you, Lauren, for such a precious gift. Was it very painful? I have heard it is so the first time."

"It was not very," she assured him.

He lifted himself off her then and stood up to adjust his clothing, his back to her. He held his handkerchief out to her without turning.

"Use this," he said.

She had been wondering how she would manage. There was blood, she discovered. But even now, though her hand shook as she cleansed herself, she could not bring herself to a full realization of the enormity of what she had done. That came only after she had put herself to rights and was sitting on the edge of the bench, all neat and respectable again, the soiled handkerchief balled in one hand.

"Well," Kit said, turning and smiling cheerfully at her, "we are going to have to decide upon a wedding date, aren't we?"

16

*T*he rain stopped during the night, though it was the middle of the morning before the sun shone and dried the grass and promised summer heat for the afternoon.

Kit suggested and organized a game of cricket out on the long front lawn. It was intended originally just for the children, but all the young people and even some of the older gentlemen greeted the idea with such enthusiasm that the scope of the game was quickly extended. And almost everyone who was not playing—all except the dowager, Lady Irene, and Baron Galton, in fact, who retired for an afternoon nap—agreed to play the essential role of spectator.

The men busied themselves setting up the pitch while Kit divided the prospective players into teams of roughly equal ability and experience. Lauren, Gwendoline, and Daphne meanwhile spread blankets on the lawn for the spectators, a safe distance from the wickets. Several of the younger children dashed about, getting under everyone's feet, tolerated only because the sun was shining and soon their energies would be channeled into the game. In all the noise and bustle no one noticed three riders approach up the driveway and onto the terrace until Daphne Willard hailed them.

Lord Rannulf Bedwyn had already dismounted and was lifting Lady Freyja to the ground. Lord Alleyne was surveying the chaos before him.

"Ah," he said. "A cricket match, I perceive, and not yet begun. Good afternoon, ma'am." He addressed himself to the countess, sweeping off his hat and inclining his head as he did so. "Might one be permitted to join the fun, even though one came merely to pay one's respects?"

The countess introduced them to Gwendoline, whom they had not yet met. Lord Rannulf bowed over her hand and retained it while he exchanged civilities with her.

"You are quite sure you will not play?" Kit asked, coming toward Lauren and grinning down at her.

It seemed to her suddenly that last night could not possibly have happened—none of it. He looked so normal, so much his usual self. And she was very much *her* usual self.

"Quite sure," she said firmly. "I would not have the smallest idea what to do."

"You can catch a ball, surely?" he coaxed. "You can run. I can teach you how to wield the bat."

"Kit," she said, "if this is another of your ideas for forcing me to enjoy myself, you are going to forget it right now. I am going to enjoy myself *immensely* sitting here. Besides, not one of the other ladies over the age of eighteen is out there to make a spectacle of herself."

But even as she spoke Lady Freyja Bedwyn strode out onto the lawn with Lord Alleyne and announced her intention of playing on whichever side was *not* Kit's. Lord Alleyne joined Kit's team.

"There is no persuading you?" Kit laughed and turned his attention back to the cricket match, which was about to begin.

Lauren adjusted her wide-brimmed straw hat to shade her complexion more effectively from the sun and permitted herself a sigh of relief. She had feared for one moment that he was going to insist. She needed to think. No, she did not! Not now. She felt color flood her cheeks at the memory of last night. She must not think about any of it until she was alone again—or of the fact that she had said no. God help her, she had said no.

The cricket match was lively and merry. Kit, whose side was fielding first, did a great deal of yelling and laughing. He was bowling, and he was annoying some of the more serious members of his team by deliberately allowing the smaller, weaker players to score against him while reserving his more lethal skills for the experienced players. When young David Clifford, standing at the wickets closest to him, his bat almost as big as himself, had to run the length of the pitch in order not to be thrown out by Sebastian Willard, a member of Eton's first eleven last term, Kit picked the child up bodily and ran with him, laughing gaily all the way. They raced the ball by perhaps half a second.

"Dear me. Thus far Kit is the star of both teams," Lord Rannulf remarked. "He must be inspired, like the knights of old, by the admiring eye of his lady. Do you wear his favor in your bosom by any chance, Miss Edgeworth? But we are about to see what he can accomplish against Freyja."

Crispin Butler having just been bowled out, it was indeed Lady Freyja who had come up to bat. Lauren had been very aware of her from the start, standing on the sidelines some distance from the blankets with the rest of her team, bareheaded, her mane of unruly hair shining golden in the sun, smiling occasionally in the direction of the spectators, a challenge in her eyes as they met Lauren's.

She was, of course, perfectly at her ease on the cricket pitch. She settled her bat before the wickets and squinted off in the direction of Kit, who was running in to the far wickets to bowl to her. It was clear that he knew her to be an accomplished player. He bowled his best ball at her. She hit it for a six. The ball arced up into the sky and landed way off on an undefended expanse of lawn. Benjamin went racing after it while the spectators applauded, the fielders groaned, Claude's team jumped up and down with loud, unrestrained glee, and Lady Freyja hitched her riding habit with one hand and dashed between the wickets, laughing triumphantly, her hair streaming out behind her.

Kit was laughing too. "That was your free hit," he called to her. "After this one we get serious."

"Serious is not nearly good enough for me," she called back. "Bring on a better bowler."

Flushed, animated, and magnificent, she turned her head in the direction of the blankets again and her eyes mocked Lauren's prim, ladylike presence.

"Ah, a gauntlet has been tossed down," Lord Rannulf murmured. "This is quite like old times."

Lady Freyja blocked the next ball and the wickets stood.

She got a hit off the next one, a perfectly catchable hit, but it sailed in the direction of four-year-old Sarah Vreemont, who watched it come in evident dismay, clapped her hands together at just the wrong moment while her teammates screamed at her to catch it, and burst into tears as the ball thudded onto the grass at her feet.

Lauren, twenty-two years her senior, knew just exactly how she felt.

"Hmm." Kit trotted toward the child. "That was a mis-hit, Freyja. It was not Sarah's fault at all that she did not catch it. You had better hit it again."

Someone threw the ball back to Lady Freyja, and she tossed it up and hit it in a slow arc. Kit scooped up Sarah with one arm, cupped her little hands in his free one, and caught the ball.

"Out!" he yelled, and all his teammates cheered wildly.

Lady Freyja made a fuss—a loud one, as did the rest of her team. She stood, hands on hips, her bat dangling from one of them, her head thrown back, complaining that Kit was sly and conniving while he laughed at her and accused her of being a poor sport. But it was perfectly clear to Lauren that there was nothing serious about the quarrel, that they were deliberately insulting each other for their teams' amusement, that they were really enjoying themselves. They were a perfectly matched couple, in fact, as she had seen from the start.

It was an undeniably depressing realization. Not because she was in any way in competition with the lady, despite the mocking glance

Lady Freyja threw her way as she stalked off the field, apparently in high dudgeon. But merely because—again!—Lauren knew that she never could be in competition even if she wished to be. She had looks and breeding, yes, but she was completely lacking in that certain something that could win and hold a man's admiration and arouse his passion. Despite last night, when all was said and done she was merely Lauren Edgeworth.

Sarah, her moment of triumph over, came wandering toward the blankets, looking for her mother, who had already gone back indoors out of the heat. There were still tears on her cheeks. Lauren drew her handkerchief out of an inner pocket and dried the child's eyes.

"That was a wonderful catch," she said. "Are you tired of cricket?"

The child nodded. "Come and play," she invited.

Lauren hesitated. She had been to the nursery a few times during the past few days and had been surprised to find that children seemed to take to her. But she had not been alone with any of them.

"What would we do?" she asked.

"Push me on the swing." Sarah had hold of her hand now and was tugging at it.

"There is a swing?" She got to her feet.

There was indeed. It was suspended on long ropes from a high branch of one of the great oak trees close to the parterre gardens. Lauren had not noticed it before. Sarah, who held her hand as they crossed the lawn, climbed on, and Lauren pushed her, at first tentatively, and then higher at the child's urging.

Sarah whooped with glee. "Higher."

Lauren laughed. "If you go *too* high," she said, "you will kick your way right through into the treetop land and I will be left with an empty swing and no Sarah."

And then she noticed that their progress across the lawn had not gone unobserved. Other small children, bored with cricket, were approaching and demanding their turn on the swing. Lauren was soon busy pushing the swing, making sure that everyone had an equal turn, helping the idle ones climb onto the lower limbs of the tree, jumping them down to the ground so that they could scramble up and do it all over again, and laughing with them. At least they were in the shade here, she thought gratefully, sheltered from the full force of the sun.

"The swing goes to a magic land at the top of the tree," Sarah announced after a while.

"Who *says* so?" Henry Butler demanded scornfully.

"I say so." Lauren looked at him, all amazement. "You mean you have never heard of it? You did not know there is a magic land above swings?"

"Tell us."

"*Tell us.*"

All five children took up the chant and Lauren laughed again. *Now what had she started?* It was years since she had entertained herself and helped lull herself to sleep with stories in which little girls were never left behind by their mothers, in which life was always a vivid adventure, in which one could sail beyond the farthest horizon and always come back safely again, in which there was always a happy ending. She had never told such stories aloud. And yet there was a time when she had dreamed of doing so, of sitting on the side of her own child's bed—hers and Neville's—telling bedtime stories.

"I am going to sit down here in the shade," she said, suiting action to words. "Gather around if you want to hear."

The children sat on the ground and raised eager faces to her. The youngest, three-year-old Anna Clifford, came and cuddled into the crook of her arm.

"Once not so very long ago . . ."

She began to spin a tale of two young children—a boy and a girl—who had sat side by side on the swing and swung themselves so high that they had pushed aside the branches and the air and slipped between the curtains of the world straight through to the magic treetop land, which could not be seen from the ground, and which was different in every possible way from the land below—the grass was different and the houses and animals and people. It was a place of eye-popping novelty and hair-raising adventure and heart-pounding danger.

"And then in the nick of time," she said at last as they all gazed at her, spellbound, "they spied the empty swing come soaring up through the red grass and they climbed on quickly and clung to the ropes and each other's hand and came swooshing back down to the foot of the tree, where their mama and papa were waiting anxiously for them. They were safe again and had *such* a story to tell."

There was an audible sigh of satisfaction from the children.

"Did they ever go back up?" Sarah asked.

"*Did* they?"

"Oh yes, indeed," Lauren assured them. "Many times. And had all sorts of exciting adventures. But those are stories for another time."

"Ahhh," the children protested while Lauren laughed and hugged Anna to her side.

"Which we must all hope will come very soon."

Lauren looked up to see Kit standing bareheaded out in the sunlight, still in his shirtsleeves, his arms crossed over his chest. He looked as if he must have been standing there for a while. The lawn behind him was deserted, she could see. The cricket match had ended without her noticing. He was smiling at her, a look of unmistakable affection in his eyes.

Her stomach performed a complete somersault—or felt as if it did—and left her feeling slightly breathless. She recognized that it was desire she felt. She knew too in that moment that it was more than just desire. It was knowledge. She *knew* that lithe, handsome body. More, she knew the man inside. She knew him as a complex person, who hid so much of himself away behind the surface gaiety. And yet the gaiety was real too. It was not just a mask.

"Everyone has rushed off to the lake for a swim," he said. "Is anyone here interested?" He grinned about at all the children, who were on their feet and dashing off in the direction of the water almost before he had finished speaking.

"Not me," Lauren said hastily.

He stood where he was, still smiling. "You continually surprise me," he said. "I did not know you were so wonderful with children."

"Oh, I am not," she assured him. "I have never had anything to do with them."

"Allow me to contradict you," he said. "You have been playing here for almost an hour with five toddlers—no easy task on such a hot afternoon. I observed no sign of any quarrel despite the fact that there is only one swing and there are *always* quarrels over it."

"Has it been that long?" she asked. "And how do you know there were no quarrels? You have been playing cricket."

"Oh, I know," he assured her, causing that strange somersaulting in her stomach again. He came closer and offered his hand to help her to her feet. "Where did the story come from? A book?"

"No, of course not," she said with a laugh. "I made it up as I went along. It is not difficult to create a magic land in which anything can happen and usually does."

"I do believe," he said, "you have been enjoying yourself and I cannot claim any credit for it."

"Yes, you can," she said earnestly. "I would still be in London, Kit, if you had not brought me here. I would still be fending off all the worthy gentlemen the Earl of Sutton and Wilma consider eligible for me. And hating every moment."

"They are a pair of prize idiots," he said. "They thoroughly deserve each other."

She laughed again.

"There are enough supervisors and to spare for the children at the lake," he said. "Let's play truant for an hour or two, Lauren."

"Is . . . Are . . . Is *everyone* swimming?" she asked. "The visitors too?"

"I daresay." He grinned. "A little matter of propriety will not deter Freyja, you may be sure. The other girls will doubtless follow her lead and give their mothers heart palpitations. But it is a hot day and we all used up a great deal of energy playing cricket."

"Are you sure you would not rather be there with h—with everyone else?" Lauren asked.

He tipped his head to one side as she brushed grass and twigs from her skirt. "I think we should go somewhere quiet together," he said. "It is what everyone will expect of us, you know. No." He held up one hand as she looked up at him. "Don't stop smiling. We *are* betrothed. And despite the firmness of your answer last night, we *are* going to be married, I believe. But we need not discuss that again yet. Play truant with me?"

Yearning hit her hard, low in the abdomen. Caution knocked on the door of her mind at the same moment. She had gone too far last night. She did not regret it in the obvious way—she had been unable in all the hours since to be morally shocked by what she had done. But she regretted it in another way. Her femininity had been dragged out of hiding last night. She had given in to needs she had kept carefully locked inside herself before her wedding day and since, needs she had ruthlessly denied, needs she had always believed only Neville could satisfy.

The need to be fully and openly a woman.

She could very easily come to need Kit. She could very easily fall in love with him. It was a new and alarming possibility. She had never doubted until last night that she was a one-man woman, that she could never love any man but Neville.

She could fall in love with Kit.

But she must not allow herself to do so. For she was not at all the right woman for him. She was as different from Lady Freyja Bedwyn as it was possible to be. Yet Lady Freyja was so patently right for him. It was with her he had laughed and come vibrantly alive this afternoon. She must not fall in love. She must not risk having to cope again with the sort of heartbreak she had hardly expected to survive last year.

Besides, she had promised him that she would release him from their engagement at the end of the summer. She could not break a promise even though last night had changed things sufficiently that his honor would make him try to insist. She had not intended to trap him into marriage. She would not do it.

What she *had* come here for was to have one small adventure, one brief fling of pleasure before settling down to her chosen future. And what she had found here so far *was* an adventure. She *was* enjoying herself. She wanted more. She wanted to drink this cup to the dregs, to the last wonderful moment before she must leave.

"Just for an hour then," she said, reaching out her hand for him to clasp in his own—and then wondering why she had done something so uncharacteristic of her. There was instant connection, both physical and emotional. Walking hand in hand with a man was far more intimate, she discovered, than walking arm in arm.

And more youthful.

More joyous.

17

He knew exactly where he would take her. It involved walking beside the lake on the house side and passing all the children and youngsters and a few adults splashing and shrieking in the water while others stood or sat on the bank watching. As he had fully expected, Freyja was in the water, swimming with strong strokes farther out than anyone else. Ralf was leaning indolently against a tree trunk, talking with Lady Muir. Both turned and lifted a hand in greeting.

Kit was surprised to discover that he had no wish to jump in and frolic with everyone else, that he felt no urge to race Freyja to some predetermined point. He had wondered—yes, indeed he had, even after two visits to Lindsey Hall. Even after the horse race. He had wondered if seeing her again would rekindle his passion for her. He had wondered it even this afternoon when she had ridden up with Ralf and Alleyne and had thrown all her considerable energy into playing cricket. He had wondered even as he had known that now he *must* marry Lauren.

But a strange thing had happened during the course of the match. He had thoroughly enjoyed the competition with Freyja, the bantering challenges and exchange of insults. He had felt almost as if time had regressed and he was a boy again, she a girl. He had felt for her all the exuberant camaraderie of old with none of the madness that had gripped him during those dreadful weeks three years ago. He had enjoyed the cricket match, yet all the time as he concentrated on making the game fun for the children and challenging for his older cousins, he was aware of Lauren. He was aware of her sitting cool and ladylike on the blanket, pretty in her light muslin dress and straw bonnet, watching the game. He was aware of her the moment she got to her feet and was tugged off in the direction of the swing by Sarah. He was aware of her playing there with the child and attracting other little ones into her orbit.

He had been amazed by the tenderness of his feelings for her. He was not accustomed to feeling tenderness for women. He did not quite understand the feeling. Yet he liked it. Perhaps, he thought, this was what women meant when they spoke of romance—something warm and gentle and enticing. Perhaps he was involved in a romance with Lauren Edgeworth. His first. Though of course there was more to it than just that—there had been last night.

"Are you sure you do not wish to swim with everyone else?" she asked him. "I do not mind if you do. You must not feel honor-bound to remain with me. I am dull company for someone like you, I know."

For someone so beautiful and with such impeccable manners and breeding she had a remarkably low image of herself.

"Allow me to be the judge of that," he said, adjusting their clasped hands so that their fingers were laced. "Lauren, did Baron Galton make no attempt to learn of the fate of your mother? Did the late Earl of Kilbourne make none to discover what happened to his brother?"

She shook her head. "How would it have been possible to discover anything?" she asked. "The world is a large place to search."

But two members of the British aristocracy would not go unnoticed wherever they went.

"So there was no finality for any of you," he said.

"It does not matter. I do not think of it." A lie if ever he had heard one. She was looking down at the grass over which they walked, her face hidden behind the wide brim of her straw bonnet.

"I have connections, you know," he said. "Men whose business it is to uncover what is hidden, to learn what is seemingly impossible to know. I could call in a few favors. I could set an inquiry afoot. Shall I do it?"

She turned her head sharply then. Her eyes were wide and very deeply violet. "You would do that," she asked, "for me? Even though if there *is* anything to discover, it could not be done until long after we part?"

She had been quite adamant last night that she would not marry him even though she had lain with him. Foolishly adamant—she might be with child.

"You have done a great deal for me," he said. "Allow me to do something in return."

"Have I?" She had stopped walking. Her eyes were brimming with tears. "But I wish there did not have to be so much deception involved, Kit. I like your family so very much—your mother, your grandmother. Everyone."

"There is no need for any deception at all," he said gently. "We could announce our wedding date at Grandmama's birthday. Not an imaginary occasion. The real thing."

She shook her head.

"Are you so irrevocably attached to him, then?" he asked. He was beginning to be irritated no end by the Earl of Kilbourne, though he had never met the man.

She shook her head again. "It was our bargain," she said. "A way out of a tangle for you, freedom for me. Don't spoil everything, Kit. All I wanted of the summer was a little adventure."

It was rather lowering to know that she would not marry him simply because she did not wish to do so. But she had never pretended otherwise. He was the fool if he was allowing himself to be beguiled by a summer romance.

He smiled at her and began walking again. "You cannot blame a gentleman for having a conscience," he said. "We will devote ourselves to the adventure, then. You see that piece of land jutting into the lake up ahead?" He pointed toward it. "It is an island actually. Man-made, of course, as is the lake. We will go there. There is a boat."

"Thank you," she said.

He did not know for what he was being thanked. But he was content to stroll onward in companionable silence and to look forward to relaxing on the island with her. The boat was still in its accustomed place, he discovered when they arrived at the little boathouse, and it was in good repair. The pile of towels that had always been kept on a shelf was still there too, and they looked fresh and clean. He took two of them. He rowed the short distance across the water while Lauren sat, relaxed and elegant on the narrow bench opposite him, one hand on the side of the boat for balance. He helped her out on the other side and dragged the boat clear of the water.

On the side of the island farthest from the house there was a wide bank, almost like a small meadow, sloping gently to the water's edge. It was grass-covered and carpeted with daisies and buttercups and clover. They waded ankle-deep through the wildflowers, and Lauren sat down in the midst of them, clasped her arms about her knees, and gazed about her.

"I was never really fond of the outdoors," she said with a contented sigh.

"But now you are?"

"Yes." Her eyes squinted at the bright water.

Kit did not sit down. It was a hot afternoon. He had engaged in an energetic game of cricket, they had walked some distance, and he had just rowed the boat across the lake. He peeled his shirt off over his head, dragged off his boots, and pulled off his pantaloons. He hesitated only a moment before removing his drawers too. Lauren watched him lazily. Just a few days ago, he thought, she would have been bristling with embarrassment and outrage.

"You are very beautiful," she surprised him by saying.

He chuckled. "Despite all the scars?"

"Yes," she said.

He splashed into the water and immersed himself. It felt deliciously cool against his hot, naked flesh. He swam several strokes underwater and then surfaced and shook the drops from his eyes. She was still sitting among the flowers, as pretty as any picture, looking cool and unruffled, her face shaded by the wide brim of her bonnet. But she untied the ribbons beneath her chin even as he watched, and let the hat fall backward to the grass while she shook out her dark curls.

He had swum out beyond his depth. He trod water, his arms spread to the sides, watching her take off her shoes and stockings and then get to her feet to unbutton and remove her dress. Her shift clung to her slender curves. He gazed appreciatively at her, marveling that today there was none of the maidenly modesty that had had her undressing inside the folly and then huddling under a blanket to the very water's edge on the two mornings they had bathed.

And then his lips pursed in sudden shock as she crossed her arms and drew the shift off over her head before dropping it onto the small pile of her other clothing. Naked, she was perfection itself—youthfully taut flesh and muscles; firm, uptilted breasts; long, slender legs, dark hair at their apex. She came down the bank and waded into the water, her eyes on it rather than on him, though she made no attempt to cover herself. Her flesh was pure alabaster in the bright sunlight. He felt his mouth turn dry and moistened his lips before diving under again and surfacing beside her.

He did not touch her. She did not touch him. They smiled at each other and she closed her eyes and lay back on the water. She floated easily and kicked her feet lazily to propel herself backward. He swam a slow crawl at her side.

Did she realize, he wondered, how much she had changed during the short time she had spent at Alvesley? How far she had stepped out from behind her ice maiden mask? Lauren Edgeworth bathing naked in broad daylight with a naked man? Her friends and his would not believe it possible. Could it really be true that she wanted this for only a brief summer out of her life, that she would freely choose to return to her old self as soon as it was over?

"If I try to put my feet down," she asked, turning her head to look at him after a few minutes, "will I be able to?"

He gauged their distance from the bank. "Probably not," he said. "But don't be afraid. You will not sink unless you choose to do so. And I will rescue you even if you do."

"I am not afraid," she said. "Kit, teach me to swim like that. Let me try again."

He turned her over onto her front, his hands skimming sleek, cool flesh. It was as if she moved in that charmed, magic world she had been spinning for the children. This afternoon she could put her face in the water without panicking and breathe without gulping in water instead of air. And today she could kick her feet close to the surface so that her efforts to move forward were not in vain. She learned the arm motions for a crawl in a trice. Within ten minutes she was actually swimming—in water that was at least eight feet deep.

"At this speed," he said, swimming beside her, "you could probably make it across to the main bank in twenty-four hours. Twenty-three if you did not stop for a rest halfway."

"Mock on," she said breathlessly. She probably had more to say, but she needed all her breath and concentration for the task at hand.

He turned her onto her back again after a while, and they floated side by side, her hand in his. He could not remember feeling so relaxed, so contented, so filled with a sense of well-being since . . . Well, perhaps he had never felt this way.

He closed his eyes and soaked up the warmth of the sun on his face and its brightness on his eyelids.

"Some moments," he said, "should be made to last forever."

"Mmmm," she agreed.

But the moments and the truant hour would pass all too quickly, of course. Although their status as a newly betrothed couple gave them much license to spend time alone together, there were limits. Soon enough they must return to the house and all the busy merriment of the house party.

The air felt cool against wet flesh when they came out of the water and climbed the bank. Cool but not cold. The heat of the sun would dry them in no time at all. He spread their towels on the grass and lay down on one. He expected that now she no longer had the water for cover Lauren would wrap the towel about herself and perhaps sit a little apart from him, prim and self-conscious again. He half ex-pected that she would dress as quickly as possible and want to return to the boat.

But she lay down naked on the towel beside him, covered her eyes with one arm, and raised one leg to set her foot flat on the ground, an inviting pose that was undoubtedly unconscious. He turned his head and then raised himself on one elbow for a better look. All the mis-tresses he had ever had and all the casual amours had been volup-tuously built—it was one criterion by which he had chosen them. Generous curves and full, heavy breasts aroused him sexually—and of course mistresses were for sex.

Lauren Edgeworth was slender and long-limbed. When she lay on her back her breasts appeared even smaller than usual, though they were nicely shaped and rose-tipped. Her abdomen was flat. Her legs were slim and shapely. He felt a pleasurable tightening in his groin and realized with rueful humor that if she removed her arm from her eyes she would surely understand her danger in a moment.

She was without a doubt one of the loveliest women he had ever set eyes upon. But he had known that even as far back as Lady Mannering's ball—no, farther back. In Hyde Park, despite the fact that he had had only one functioning eye, he had noticed and appre-ciated her extraordinary beauty.

But she was more than beautiful. She was . . . sexy. Was there such a word? If there was not, there should be. Without any of the obvious allure of a courtesan, her body nevertheless invited a man to sex. Yet there was nothing erotic about either her body itself or her character. What *was* it?

Was he the privileged witness to long-repressed womanhood blos-soming forth into glorious femininity? Was he the instrument through which it was happening? Did he have that *honor*? He knew for a certainty that she had never done anything remotely resembling this ever before. Even if he had been in any doubt of that fact—though he had not—he had encountered the proof of it last night. She had been a virgin.

His eyes moved down her slim, quite unvoluptuous, sexy body. He desired her every bit as much as he had ever desired a woman. Perhaps more. But she would not marry him. She did not want to. He must not ... He had already endangered her once last night. He must not trap her into losing the freedom she clearly prized. He must not be that selfish, that undisciplined.

She moved her arm away from her eyes and turned her head to smile up at him.

"Kit," she said, her lovely eyes warm and dreamy, "*this* is what I meant at Vauxhall. Just this, though I did not even know it myself at the time. This—the sunlight on my face. I have never allowed it there before—it might ruin my complexion. The sounds of water and birds and insects—thousands of them chirping and droning away. Sometimes I forget that the world is *alive*. Sometimes I think there are only humans here and maybe horses and cows and sheep. And the smell of water and grass and flowers. The *flowers*, Kit. They are *weeds*—daisies and clover and buttercups. But they are more lovely than anything else in the universe. And ... and myself a part of it all. I have always been a spectator of life, you know, never a participant. Never. But now I am. *Today* I am, and I am awed and deliriously happy. This is the adventure I asked for, the adventure I am having. I will be forever grateful to you."

He swallowed. He felt absurdly close to tears. He fought his arousal and hoped she had not noticed. She had spoken the simple truth. He could tell that just by looking into her eyes and seeing her as part of her surroundings. She *was* a part of it all, one with the sunshine and water, with the grass and flowers, with the birds and the chirping insects. Like a wood nymph or a water nymph. Like a sprite or a goddess.

He knew beyond all doubt that this was one of life's precious moments and that it would remain with him for the rest of his life. It was one treasure that his memory would hoard for future comfort. He must do nothing to spoil it.

"Kit." She reached up a hand and touched his cheek with light, cool fingertips. "Do what you did to me last night. I want it again. Just one more time, here among the flowers, under the summer sun. It would be lovely here, would it not? If you want to, that is. Perhaps you do not."

He leaned over her and set his lips to hers. She tasted of cool lake water and warm summertime. She tasted of innocence and awakened womanhood. She tasted of the enchanted land beyond the treetops. He ought to remind her of reality—of the fact that women were frequently impregnated during the act of sex. That pregnant women must marry their seducers even if they loved elsewhere, even if they craved freedom.

But that enchanted land beckoned him too. Indeed, he was already immersed in it, in flower-dappled grass and clover fragrance and warm summer sunshine and bee-song. This was what she had meant. This was what she had yearned for. Just this fleeting, magic moment—to be grasped or to be lost forever. He raised his head an inch or two above hers and she smiled dreamily at him. He smiled back.

Last night had been for him. He had poured out all his deepest pain to her, telling her Syd's story and his, and then he had reached out to her for physical comfort, which she had given generously, warmly, unstintingly, gifting him with her very self. This afternoon would be for her.

He loved her slowly with his hands and with his mouth, using all the expertise learned over the years with other women, but adapting it all just for her. She was not a woman of wild passion—not yet, at least. She was a woman who needed tenderness and gentleness. He gave her both as his hands and mouth roamed her body, feathering, stroking, lightly scratching and pinching, licking, sucking, gently biting—choosing the erotic spots that would give her most pleasure. Her hands roamed his shoulders, his back, his chest—gently, inexpertly. He was accustomed to women who knew unerringly how to heighten and satisfy his passion. Lauren knew not a single one of their many tricks. But her very inexpertness brought him to full-blown, almost painful arousal.

He loved her with almost desperate tenderness. He kissed her mouth with soft, deep kisses, licking warmly inside while the fingers of one of his hands explored the moist heat between her legs, parting folds, seeking, penetrating, feeling her muscles close about him. With his thumb he found the secret part of her womanhood and stroked her there until she whispered a surprised exhalation into his mouth and shuddered into a spasm of pleasure.

"Do you want me inside?" he murmured to her.

"Yes." She circled him with her arms. "Oh, yes. Do it to me—like last night."

"Not quite like last night." The long grass and nodding flowers might give the appearance of a soft carpet, but they would make a hard mattress for a woman in the act of love. "Come." He lifted her over him and parted her legs to straddle his own. "Kneel up on the grass. Trust me."

"Yes." She kneeled astride him and braced herself with her hands on either side of his head. She looked down at him and smiled, her eyes heavy with desire.

He raised his knees and set his feet flat. He positioned her carefully, nestling himself against her opening before bracing his hands over her hips and guiding her down onto him. He watched her eyes close as she first frowned and then relaxed. Her muscles tightened about him as he held deep in her for a few moments to allow her time to adjust. She was hot and wet and exquisitely feminine. He drew a few steadying breaths. He was unaccustomed to having to impose control on himself after making his mount. It was the point at which, after long minutes of vigorous foreplay, he usually gave himself up to a frenzied climax.

Except last night. But then last night had not really been about sex at all.

Neither was this afternoon. This was not sex—not as he knew sex, anyway. This was . . . what was it? A warm, intimate, tender sharing of—of what?

He raised her a little with his hands and began to pump slowly, smoothly, in and out of her. She held still, though her inner muscles picked up his rhythm, responded inexpertly at first, and then matched it. The sensation was delicious and painful both at once. He wanted to prolong the pleasure indefinitely. He wanted to give in and explode into her right now.

Most of all, he wanted to give her all the pleasure twenty-six years of living had denied her. He wanted this to be for her. Not for himself but for Lauren. He wanted to see her totally, utterly happy.

He stroked her with smooth, deep strokes for many minutes, not attempting to hasten the ending, as he might easily have done by touching her again in that small, secret place. He could see from her closed eyes and parted lips and look of concentration that all her attention was focused in the passage that he worked, and that she was greatly enjoying the sensations. Perhaps that was all she would experience, but he would not shatter it until he could sense that she was ready.

Then she frowned again and her eyes clenched more tightly shut and she drew her lower lip between her teeth. She lost rhythm and tightened hard about him. She opened her mouth and gasped.

"Relax now," he told her. "Relax those muscles and let yourself go." He tightened his hands over her hips and worked her with harder, faster thrusts. "Let it all come. Trust me."

But there was no need for instruction, no need for him to coach her to climax. She cried out and shattered about him and collapsed her weight onto him. He wrapped both arms protectively about her. She was still pulsing and trembling.

"Let it all go," he murmured against her ear. "Let it all come."

He had never had to concern himself with feminine orgasms. He was usually too intent upon his own.

She finally lay still and hot and damp on him. Now, finally, he was free to complete his own pleasure. He moved his hands back to her hips and braced his feet more firmly against the ground—and paused a moment, gritting his teeth.

Then he lifted her off him and turned to set her gently on the towel beside him.

"Mmmm." The sound was a satisfied purr from deep in her throat as she rolled onto her side and curled in against him and promptly fell asleep.

Kit lay back down and breathed deeply and evenly, clenching and unclenching his hand on the side farthest from her. Several minutes of sheer agony passed before his erection began to subside. He chuckled ruefully when the worst of it was over. In her innocence she doubtless was quite unaware that she was the only one who had completed the act.

As probably he had been last night.

He might well have impregnated her last night. Only time would tell. But if she had escaped during that encounter, then she was still safe today. She would still have choices left when the house party ended. She would still be free to leave him.

He set one arm over his eyes and sought and found her hand with his other. This must not happen again. They were not really betrothed—by her choice. And Lauren Edgeworth was not the sort of woman with whom one indulged in an illicit affair.

Last night she had given to him in his need.

This afternoon he had returned the favor.

That was all. It was completed, this unexpected physical bond forged of both their needs.

Yes, it was completed.

He drew in a slow lungful of clover-fragrant air and let it out on an almost audible sigh.

18

The following morning presented Lauren with an opportunity to talk privately with Sydnam Butler, something she had not accomplished before. He was not often visible during the day, and during the evenings he invariably sat in the drawing room window, his very posture discouraging company. She had no real wish to talk with him at all, but she had come here to help Kit be reconciled with his family. The deepest hurt of all, she had discovered two nights before, involved his younger brother.

A number of the men and boys had gone fishing with Kit, Lauren's grandfather among them. Several of the ladies, including Gwen and Aunt Clara, had gone into the village to see the few shops and to view the Norman church. Lauren had stayed behind to wander among the flowerbeds and through the hothouses with the countess and help her make final plans for decorations for the birthday. When that task was completed she accompanied the dowager on her morning walk to the rose arbor and back.

Mr. Sydnam Butler was riding alone up the driveway, Lauren saw as they slowly climbed the steps on their return to the house. He appeared to do it very well considering the fact that he had only one arm. She felt very sorry for his disabilities, but she did not feel particularly kindly disposed to him. He had been unfair to Kit.

The dowager took the arm of her favorite footman, a stout, good-natured young man, for the climb up the stairs to her room. Lauren excused herself and went back outside. She hardly knew what she intended to do as she stood on the steps again, her eyes on the stables. Kit's brother came walking out onto the terrace a few moments later. He limped ever so slightly, she noticed, perhaps as a result of stiffness from his ride. The limp disappeared after a few steps. He hesitated for a moment when he noticed her, and then came onward.

"Good morning, Miss Edgeworth," he said when he was close enough. He touched the brim of his hat with his whip.

"Mr. Butler."

She felt dislike—and guilt. But why feel guilt merely because he was maimed? She *did* dislike him. He had consigned Kit to a sort of permanent hell for no good reason. Yet Kit still loved him.

He smiled his crooked smile when he came to the foot of the steps and would have gone on past.

"Mr. Butler, will you walk with me?" Lauren asked.

He looked at her in evident surprise. He drew breath—to offer some excuse, she guessed. But he closed his mouth again, bowed, and turned to walk with her across the terrace and out onto the wide lawn on which the cricket match had been played the day before.

"The weather is not quite as lovely as yesterday," he remarked.

"No, there are some clouds today."

She almost lost her courage. But their bargain aside, she was concerned about Kit. She cared about him—she cared *for* him. Much too deeply for comfort. She clasped her arms behind her and drew breath.

"Mr. Butler," she asked, "why will you not forgive him?" It did not occur to her that perhaps he would not know what she was talking about.

"Ah," he said softly. "Is that what he has told you? Poor Kit."

"Is he mistaken, then?" She frowned.

He said nothing for a while as they strolled diagonally in the direction of the trees. Then he sighed.

"It is far too complicated an issue," he said at last. "You need not concern yourself with any of it, Miss Edgeworth. And you need not fear that I will be here indefinitely to blight your happiness and Kit's. I will be leaving within the next month or so, I believe. I will be taking a post with the Duke of Bewcastle."

"As a steward?" she asked. "That upsets Kit, you know. He tells me you were not made for such a life, that you were—*are*—an artist. He loves you. Do you not realize that?"

He stopped walking and gazed at the grass ahead of them before turning his head and looking directly at her. Lauren was shockingly aware of how very handsome he had been, of how terribly disfigured he now was. But her dislike of him had not waned.

"And you think I do not love him?" he asked her.

"I think you cannot," she said, "or you would offer him some comfort. Do you believe he has not suffered just because he does not carry around your wounds?"

He was angry then. Furiously so, judging by the sudden hardness of his eye and tensing of his jaw and flaring of his nostrils. But he brought himself under control before he spoke again.

"Yes, I believe he has suffered," he said curtly. He turned to look back at the house. "This walk was not a good idea, Miss Edgeworth. Not unless we agree to talk about the weather. I like you. Very much indeed, though I realize the feeling is not mutual. You are kindness and patience itself with my grandmother. You are gracious and amiable with everyone else. You have an obvious affection for my brother. I wish you happiness—both of you. But I must leave. I doubt you will see much of me once I have gone. It will be best for everyone that way. Shall we return?"

But she had heard more than his words alone conveyed. She had heard another sad and lonely soul, too far withdrawn into himself for happiness. Kit, for all his deep misery, had found an audience in her two evenings ago and some comfort. In whom did Sydnam Butler confide his deepest griefs? Was there anyone? He seemed such a very solitary figure.

"There is one thing I am good at," she told him, ignoring his gesture back in the direction of the house. "I am good at listening. *Really* listening, instead of hearing only what I want or expect to hear. Tell me what happened. Tell me *your* version of what happened."

Kit had told her facts. She did not believe he had lied or tried in any way to mislead her. But sometimes even facts did not tell the complete story. Sometimes there were unconscious omissions or shadings that could change the whole perspective on an event. Get three people to tell what had happened on some tumultuous occasion—her wedding at Newbury, for example—and the chances were that one would get three similar but essentially different stories.

He looked steadily into her eyes for a few moments before turning to continue their stroll away from the house.

"Yes, I was the artist," he said, "the dreamer, the little brother who was small for his age until he shot up to a gangly height at the age of fifteen. I wonder if Kit has ever noticed that I grew taller than he. Jerome was the solid one, the responsible one, the one who would inherit and be earl one day. He was confident, active, strong. Kit was the mischief-maker, the daredevil, the one at the center of any trouble, the one most often summoned to our father's library. He was the charismatic one, the bright, laughing one. My boyhood hero. I adored him."

Lauren said nothing. A largish cloud had just moved off the face of the sun, and there was a flood of welcome brightness and warmth.

"I was everyone's favorite," he said. "Sweet little Syd, the gentle dreamer. The one to be protected against all danger, all potential enemies, all punishments." He chuckled suddenly, and Lauren realized that he had almost forgotten her presence. "One time when I took the boat out and did not secure it properly on my return so that it drifted off into the middle of the lake—even taking it out unsupervised was strictly forbidden, you must understand—Kit confessed to the misdemeanor and was caned. Then after I had heard about it and insisted upon telling the truth and was feeling rather proud of my own stinging rear, Kit got caned again for *lying*. They both did it—Jerome and Kit. They were forever protecting me. But I was a dreamer, you see, not a weakling."

"They were *over*protective?" Lauren asked.

"Yes." They had reached the little stream that bubbled over its uneven stony bed on its way to join the river. They turned to walk beside it. "Because they loved me, of course. Love can be an infernal nuisance, Miss Edgeworth. Did you know that?"

It was a rhetorical question. She did not attempt to answer it.

"I wanted so desperately to be like Kit," he said. "Self-knowledge is far more slowly learned than any of one's other lessons. Indeed, some people never come close to learning it, and perhaps none of us fully succeeds. I suppose the boat episode must have been an attempt on my part to be as bold as he. My insistence upon becoming a military officer was another. It was utterly foolish. I was not, of course, cut out for such a life. But I had something to prove. To Kit and my family. Most of all to myself."

"And it ended badly," Lauren said. "I am very sorry about that. But it was not really Kit's fault, was it? He did not insist that you purchase a commission. He actively tried to prevent you from joining him on that disastrous spying mission. And his promise to protect you was unrealistic."

"Of *course* it was not his fault," he said fiercely.

Lauren looked curiously at his perfect left profile. "Why then," she asked him, "do you refuse to forgive him? There is not even anything to forgive, is there? He made the right decision. Didn't he?"

He looked angry again. They walked onward while Lauren listened to the brook and looked across it to the path of the wilderness walk, just visible among the trees opposite.

"I owed obedience to officers of superior rank," he said at last. "At that time I was a lieutenant while Kit was a major, two ranks above me. He was my superior. More than that, on that particular mission he was my commanding officer. Had he ordered me to stay and be captured, I would have obeyed him without question. He did *not* so order. I volunteered. Did he tell you that?"

"No," she said after a brief, silent moment. "He did tell me that you were the one to spot the possibility of escape for one of you."

"He *never* ordered me to do it," Sydnam said. "I volunteered. He was horribly silent, wasting precious moments after I had suggested it, knowing very well as a loyal officer himself that there was no alternative. But he could not bring himself to give the order. I volunteered again. I insisted. And then I hugged him and I ordered *him*—a superior officer—to get out of there. I *chose* to stay. Even though he would have ordered me to do so eventually—because duty *must* come before a brother, you will understand—I would not burden him with having to do it. I *volunteered*."

"Then why . . ." Lauren frowned. *"Why?"*

"Kit will have told you that I was tortured," he said. "I will not horrify you with any of the details, Miss Edgeworth. I hope he has not. I will say only this. For days and days on end death seemed the most attractive, desirable gift ever dangled before my eyes. I could have grasped that gift at any moment for the price of a little information. I did not do so because I was an officer, because it was my duty to keep silent. I did not break because I was capable of *not* breaking. I surprised even myself, because hell could not possibly be worse than— Pardon me. Eventually I knew—beyond a certain point I *knew* that I would have the strength of will to die the hard way. I knew it and a part of me exulted in the knowledge. I was so very proud of myself." He laughed softly. "And then Kit and a gang of partisans rescued me."

Lauren understood suddenly. He did not need to complete his story. She understood. But having begun it, he needed to tell it. They had come to the junction of the stream and the river and had stopped walking. Lauren gazed off into the deer forest beyond and waited.

"Again I was poor Syd," he said. "I went through amputation and other painful procedures. I went through the delirium of fever and the ordeal of the voyage home. And all the time I was poor Syd. I arrived home and Kit took all the blame on himself. I was just poor Syd, who should not have been allowed to go in the first place. I was poor Syd, whom my brother had failed to protect. Kit came very close to madness that summer—because he had sacrificed his young brother, because he could not take the wounds and the sufferings of poor Syd upon himself. Pardon me for being bitter. I could not make any of them understand. I gave up trying."

"They would not simply rejoice with you?" Lauren asked quietly.

He looked at her sharply. "You *do* understand?"

She nodded, and her eyes filled with tears, something that seemed to be happening to her rather too often these days.

"Yes, I understand." She set one hand tentatively on his arm and then stretched up to place one gentle kiss against his good cheek. She hesitated only a moment before kissing his withered, purple-skinned right cheek as well. "You were every bit as much a part of the success of that mission as Kit was. No, you were the greater part, because your role was so much more dangerous and painful and lonely. There is nothing sad or pathetic about you, Sydnam Butler. You are a great hero and I honor you."

His grin was lopsided and rather sheepish.

"Yes indeed," she said severely, "love can be an abomination when it insists upon wrapping the loved one in cotton wool, when it will not trust the strength of the one it loves. I am quite sure you have made yourself into the world's most competent steward."

They laughed together and turned to walk back to the house.

"You are going to have to talk to Kit, you know," she said as they approached the terrace. "Even if you have to tie him down and gag him."

"I think not," he said, though he chuckled at her words.

"Please?" she begged softly.

Baron Galton had come by gig with Sir Melvin Clifford to the stretch of riverbank where all the men and boys had gathered to fish, but he chose to walk with Kit back to the house, relinquishing his place in the vehicle to the earl.

"A dashed good spot for fishing," he said.

"We have always had pleasure from it," Kit agreed. "There are few more relaxing ways to spend a morning."

The others strode on ahead, talking all at once, it appeared, and bearing the morning's catch with them. Kit reduced his stride to accommodate the slower pace of the elderly gentleman.

"I am planning, sir," he said when there was no longer any possibility of their being overheard, "to institute an inquiry. I was a reconnaissance officer for a number of years, as you know, and have several useful contacts at both the Foreign Office and the War Office. I know many officers who are still active in the field too. I believe you should be aware of what I plan to do. I hope to discover exactly where, when, and how Mrs. Wyatt, Lauren's mother, your daughter, died."

"Why?" Baron Galton looked at him sharply. "What the devil do you want to know that for?"

Kit was somewhat taken aback by his almost hostile tone. "You have never been curious yourself, sir?"

"Never!" the old man assured him. "They met with some misadventure and died and word did not get back to us. That is all. People—sons, daughters, parents—die every day, Ravensberg. We can do nothing to bring them back once they are gone. It is pointless to spend time and money and effort simply to discover what we already know. It is best to leave them in peace and get on with our own lives."

A sensible attitude, perhaps, but it did not seem quite natural for a father to be so unconcerned about his daughter's fate.

"You made no inquiries at the time, sir?" he asked.

"At what time?" the baron asked. "They never did write often. How were we to know they were even missing until years had gone by? By then any inquiry would have been fruitless."

"Did the Earl of Kilbourne make no attempt to locate his brother? Or discover what had happened to him?"

"Look here, Ravensberg." Baron Galton had stopped walking and was regarding Kit sternly from beneath bushy eyebrows. "I have no doubt you are a clever young man and are eager to impress your betrothed by discovering what no one else has discovered in ten or fifteen years. But take my advice and leave it. Let sleeping dogs lie."

Kit looked steadily back at him. "Good God, sir," he said with sudden insight, "you *know*, do you not?"

The old gentleman pursed his lips and looked broodingly at him. "Leave it," he said again.

Kit leaned slightly toward him, his hands clasped at his back. "You *know*," he said. "But Lauren does not. Why? What happened?"

"She was a *child*, that was why," the baron said irritably. "She had a good home with Kilbourne and his countess. She was happy and secure. She had companions of her own age and good prospects. She was only three when her mother left, little more than a baby. She quickly forgot her, as children do. Kilbourne and his wife became her parents. She could not have asked for better. You can see for yourself that the Dowager Lady Kilbourne loves her every bit as much as she loves her own daughter."

"You believe that Lauren did not miss her mother?" Kit was still frowning. "That she did not feel abandoned? That she did not suffer when the infrequent letters and gifts stopped coming?"

"Of course she did not." Baron Galton spoke firmly and turned to resume walking. "She never once asked. She never spoke of her mother. She never stopped being as serene and happy as she had always been. You may wonder how I can be so sure when I visited her only rarely. I love my granddaughter, Ravensberg. I dote on her. She is all I have of my own. I would have had her to live with me at the snap of two fingers, but it would have been selfish of me. She was happier where she was. I wrote weekly to Kilbourne until his death and he wrote weekly to me. Lauren was a model child and then a model young lady. She was rarely if ever disobedient. She never neglected her lessons or her other duties. She was never discontented or demanding. She was less trouble than either of Kilbourne's own children. There was no need to upset her unnecessarily with news of a mother she had long forgotten."

"Kilbourne knew the truth too, then?" Kit asked.

"Of course he did," Baron Galton replied. "Forget about your inquiries, Ravensberg. And forget about upsetting my granddaughter by dredging up what is long in the past. Leave it be."

"What *did* happen?" Kit asked.

The old gentleman sighed. "I suppose," he said, "you have a right to know. I would have felt it my duty to inform you before you committed yourself to a betrothal to Lauren, had you given me an opportunity to do so. But I was presented with a fait accompli instead. My daughter was as unlike my granddaughter as it is possible to be, Ravensberg. She was always a great trial to her mother and me. She married Whitleaf just to be free of us, I believe, though I approved the match. She led him a merry dance. It was something of a scandal when she married Wyatt a mere ten months after Whitleaf's death. By some miracle, though, that very marriage gave Lauren a good, steady home, where she was soon loved for herself. I never heard one murmur from either Kilbourne or his countess about bad blood. And they were quite as eager for the match between their son and my granddaughter as I was."

They walked in silence for a while. Kit offered no comment that might distract his companion's train of thought.

"Their wedding trip turned into a permanent way of life," Lord Galton continued eventually. "She—Miriam—was forever wanting Lauren to join them, but I flatly refused to send her, and Kilbourne backed me on that decision. She was no fit mother, and they lived no fitting style of life for a child. There were forever rumors about their wild excesses and debaucheries, brought home by other travelers. Finally, Ravensberg, when they were in India, she left Wyatt in order to take up residence with some fabulously wealthy Indian potentate, and he resumed his travels with a Frenchwoman of questionable reputation. He died five years later—ten years ago—somewhere in South America. Kilbourne did not go into public mourning—mainly for Lauren's sake. He did not want to have to hurt her with explanations. She was sixteen years old at the time—an impressionable age."

"Good God! And Mrs. Wyatt?" Kit asked.

"The last I heard, she was still in India, with some official of the East India Company," Baron Galton said curtly. "She writes once or twice a year, usually to Lauren. She is dead to me, Ravensberg, and by damn she will remain dead to my granddaughter if I have any say in the matter."

"You—or Kilbourne—have kept her mother's letters from her?

You do not believe she should know the truth?" Kit asked. "That her mother is still alive?"

"I do not."

The house was well in sight. It had been a lengthy walk for an elderly gentleman who obviously did not indulge in a great deal of exercise. He was breathing heavily.

"Perhaps," he said sternly, "you feel you have made a bad bargain in your choice of bride, Ravensberg. But it was your choice to rush into a betrothal. And by God you will treat her kindly, or you will have me to answer to for as long as I am spared from my grave."

"You need not worry about that, sir," Kit said. "I love your granddaughter."

The lie was spoken without thought, but it could not be recalled. And it was not such a great untruth, was it? He had grown enormously fond of Lauren. He had lain awake half the night before, thinking about her, wishing she were there in the bed beside him, curled warm and relaxed and asleep against him as she had in the hut and on the island, realizing that after she left there was going to be a yawning emptiness in his life for some time to come. The idea of actually marrying her was becoming more and more appealing to him. The need somehow to persuade her to marry him was becoming more and more imperative, quite aside from the fact that she might be with child by him.

Yet how could he coerce her when it seemed that the greatest gift he could give her was her freedom?

"Then you will protect her from the sordid truth," Baron Galton said, "as I have done. As the late Kilbourne and his countess and their son have done. If you love her, you will never breathe a word to her of what really happened to her mother. She is far happier in her ignorance."

"Yes, of course, sir. I will do all in my power to protect her."

But she was *not* happy, he thought. All those who had loved her all her life were wrong about that. She had cultivated obedience and gentility and placidity in order to hide the hurt of being a child unwanted by her own mother. She had made herself into the perfect lady to win the love of her adopted family—so that they too would not abandon her. She believed her grandfather had not wanted the bother of caring for her. She believed—rightly, it seemed—that her father's family had openly rejected her.

She was *not* happy. She had lived behind the mask for so long—for at least twenty-three of her twenty-six years—that even those nearest and dearest to her seemed to believe that the mask was the reality. Perhaps he was the only person on this earth who had seen the eager, vital, laughter-loving, sensual, truly beautiful woman who was the real Lauren Edgeworth.

But it was indeed a sordid story. Under the circumstances perhaps her grandfather and the Kilbournes had made the right decision to keep it from her. What would it do to her to discover now that her mother still lived, that she was, apparently, promiscuous?

That she had never stopped writing to her daughter?

That she had wanted Lauren to live with her?

"No." Kit stopped walking again. They were very close to the house. "No, sir, I cannot agree with you. Lauren has suffered from not knowing. She would suffer too from knowing. Perhaps it *would* be a kindness to keep the truth from her, to protect her because she is a lady and has lived a sheltered life. But I don't believe so. I believe she has the right to know."

"You would tell her, then," Baron Galton asked, clearly angry, "when I have spoken to you in strictest confidence?"

Kit looked steadily back at him. "Yes, I believe I will, sir," he said, "if I am given no alternative. I will tell her the truth after I marry her. Not before then. I beg *you* to do it. The story should come from you. She *needs* the truth. You need to trust her with it. You need to set her free."

"Free?" The old gentleman frowned. He drew breath to say more, but closed his mouth again.

"Please, sir?" Kit asked softly.

19

*L*auren had fully expected the day before the dowager's birthday to be a busy one since she had committed herself to helping the countess with the last-minute preparations. But
looking back on it later, she marveled that any day could be so eventful and still contain only twenty-four hours. She had never lived
through a more tumultuous, emotion-packed day.

It began after breakfast when she was already busy with the countess in the latter's private sitting room, drawing up a written schedule
for the next day's division of labor. The earl and countess would offi-
cially greet all comers during the afternoon—outdoors if weather
permitted—and judge all the contests that had been announced in
the village and the surrounding countryside a month or more ago. Kit
and Lauren would organize and run the children's races. The countess
would . . .

But there was a knock on the door and at the countess's summons
it opened to reveal an apologetic Aunt Clara, with Gwen behind her.

"I am *so* sorry to interrupt you, Lady Redfield," Aunt Clara said, lifting her right hand to reveal an opened letter, "but I simply could not wait to let Lauren know the news."

Lauren got to her feet. She had noticed Gwen's suppressed excitement at the same moment as she saw the ducal crest at the head of the letter—the Duke of Portfrey's crest, that was.

"Elizabeth has been delivered safely of a boy," Aunt Clara announced before they all disgraced themselves by falling into one another's arms and laughing and crying and exclaiming.

"The Duchess of Portfrey?" the countess asked, getting to her feet and hugging Lauren. "Well, this news is as good an excuse for an interruption of work as any I have heard. Do sit down, ladies, and I will have a pot of chocolate brought up. I am quite sure Lauren is ready to hear every sentence of that letter. If she is not, *I* am."

The duke had written that his son and heir had arrived earlier than expected, but with ten fingers and ten toes, a powerful set of lungs, and a voracious appetite. Elizabeth was recovering well after a long and difficult delivery. As soon as mother and child could safely travel, he was intending to take them to Newbury Abbey so that the newborn Marquess of Watford could become acquainted with Lily, his half-sister, and Elizabeth could be fussed over by her own family for a month or so.

"Oh, Lauren," Gwen said, tightening her grasp on her cousin's hands, "Mama and I must go home early to prepare for their arrival. Not that we will need to do anything, of course. Lily and Nev will have everything well under control. The duke is Lily's father, after all, and the baby her half-brother. And Elizabeth is Neville's aunt as much as she is mine. But—" She smiled, still dewy-eyed.

"But of course you will want to be there when the Portfreys arrive," the countess said. "That is perfectly understandable. I just hope you will remain for the birthday celebrations tomorrow?"

"We would not miss them for any consideration," Aunt Clara assured her. "But perhaps the day after tomorrow we will be on our way. Lauren, you must stay and—"

"But of course she will stay." The countess leaned over to pat Lauren's knee. "I am beginning to wonder how I ever managed without the help and support of a daughter. I am going to find it difficult to relinquish her, Lady Kilbourne, though I must eventually allow her to return to Newbury to make plans for the wedding."

"Yes, indeed," Aunt Clara agreed, and the two older ladies indulged in a comfortable coze on the subject of weddings while Gwen winked and smiled fondly at Lauren and Lauren felt wretched. If only she had stopped to *think* during that infamous tête-à-tête in Vauxhall.

It was later in the morning, as Lauren was returning from the rose arbor with the dowager and Lady Irene, that she found Kit and her grandfather standing out on the terrace, obviously awaiting her approach, both looking almost grim. Aunt Clara's decision to return home the day after tomorrow with Gwen had made Lauren very aware that her task here had been completed and there was really no further need to linger. But seeing him now, knowing that she must leave soon and then never see him again, made her feel decidedly queasy. She smiled.

"Take a little walk with us, Lauren," her grandfather said after exchanging courtesies with the older ladies.

"Of course, Grandpapa," she said, taking his arm and looking inquiringly at Kit. His expression gave nothing away.

They turned in the direction of the stables.

"Aunt Clara has had a letter from the Duke of Portfrey," she said.

"Yes, so we have heard," her grandfather said.

Kit walked silently at her other side, his hands clasped behind him.

"I have been anxious about Elizabeth," she said. "She is rather advanced in years to be having a child." And perhaps she herself was with child, she thought, not for the first time. What would happen if she was? She would have to marry Kit. He would have to marry her.

They walked in silence until they were on the lawn beyond the stables, on their way to the lake.

"What is wrong?" she asked.

Her grandfather cleared his throat. "You have always been happy at Newbury Abbey, have you not, Lauren?" he asked. "They always treated you well? You never felt that the earl and countess resented you in any way? Loved you less than their own children?"

"Grandpapa?" She looked at him, puzzled. "You know I have always been happy there. You know they have always been kindness itself to me—all of them. Last year was unfortunate. Neville had *told* me not to wait for him when he went to war. He truly believed when he came back that Lily was dead. He would not in a million years have hurt me deliberately. Why are you—"

But he was patting her hand and clearing his throat again.

"Did you ever think of your mother?" he asked her. "Ever feel sad that she was not there with you? Ever feel hurt that she did not return? Ever feel that she had abandoned you?"

"Grandpapa?"

"Did you?" he asked.

She thought of denial. Denial was second nature to her. What had made him even ask the questions? And why was Kit with them, a silent presence at her other side? She was tired of denial. Mortally weary of it. And of so much else in her life too.

"Yes," she said. "Yes to all of your questions."

He drew in his breath and let it out on a sigh. "And did you ever think I did not want you with me?" he asked.

Ah. Sometimes the truth was impossible to tell. Sometimes it would hurt.

"You were alone, Grandpapa," she said, "and not a young man. Having a child with you all the time would have been a heavy burden. I did not blame you. I never did that. I have always known that you love me."

"Sometimes I ached to have you with me," he said. "When I used to visit you, I used to dream of taking you home with me, of your asking me to take you so that doing so would not have seemed so selfish. But you were far happier where you were, among younger people, with other children."

"Grandpapa—"

"Sometimes," he said, "children are quiet and obedient and good-natured and one assumes they are perfectly happy. Sometimes one can be wrong. I was wrong, was I not?"

"Oh, no," she cried. "I *was* happy, Grandpapa."

"I have to tell you about your mother," he said.

They had reached the bank of the lake, the spot where everyone had bathed after the cricket match. It was quiet now, deserted. What did he mean—*I have to tell you about your mother?*

They were standing side by side close to the water's edge. She was no longer holding his arm. Kit had strolled away to lean against a tree trunk, but he was well within hearing distance.

Lauren felt cold and inexplicably frightened suddenly.

"What about her?" she asked.

And then he told her.

There was a slight breeze, enough to cause ripples on the surface of the lake. It had been like glass all three times she had bathed in it.

The sky was dotted with moving clouds. It was amazing how variegated the colors of water could be. And of sky.

Someone must have taken the children out for a walk. Their voices, shouting, shrieking, and laughing, were coming from somewhere far off.

Kit, propped against the tree, did not move except to cross his arms over his chest.

Her grandfather cleared his throat but did not speak. It was Lauren who broke the silence that had succeeded his story.

"She is alive?" A rhetorical question.

He answered it anyway. "Yes, or was until recently."

"There have been letters from her ever since I last heard from her when I was eleven?"

"It was better that you thought her dead, Lauren. Kilbourne and I were agreed on that."

"She wanted me to join them during their travels?"

"You were far better off where you were."

She was alive. She had wanted Lauren with her. She was alive. She had kept on writing. She was in India, where she had lived with at least two men who were not her husband. She was alive.

She was alive.

"The letters?" she asked, suddenly frantic. "The *letters*, Grandpapa? Did you destroy them?"

"No."

"They still *exist*? All her letters to me? Fifteen years' worth of letters?"

"Thirty-two of them," he said, his voice flat and heavy. "I have them all, unopened."

She pressed one hand to her mouth then and closed her eyes tightly. She felt herself swaying, then felt strong, steadying hands close about her upper arms from behind.

"I think it would be best if you were to return to the house, sir," Kit said. "Go and rest. I'll take care of her."

"You see?" Her grandfather's voice was distressed, accusing. "It was the wrong thing to do. Damn you, Ravensberg, it was the wrong thing."

She pulled herself back from what felt like a long, dark tunnel down which she was falling. But she did not open her eyes.

"It was not the wrong thing, Grandpapa," she said. "It was not wrong."

She could sense rather than hear him walk away. Then Kit tucked one arm very firmly about her waist and drew her against his side before strolling with her farther along the bank of the lake. She dipped her head sideways to rest on his shoulder.

"She is alive," she said.

"Yes."

"She wanted me. She loved me."

"Yes."

"And she has never stopped loving me."

"No."

She stumbled and he tightened his arm even more firmly about her. They had come to a stop on a particularly lovely stretch of the bank, with cultivated beds of anemones beyond the grassy bank, and trees beyond them. Across the lake the temple folly was visible.

"Kit," she said. "Kit."

"Yes, my love."

She wept. Long and helplessly, a storm of weeping. Grief for the lonely, wounded child she had been, for the girl who had felt so very alone even though she had been surrounded by love, showered with it at every turn. For the terrible cruelty of love—from people who had loved her. For the mother who was not dead. Who had loved her enough to write thirty-two unanswered letters over fifteen years. Who could never come home because she had behaved in ways that were unforgivable in English polite society.

Kit scooped her up and sat down on the grass with her. He held her on his lap, cuddled her, cradled her in his sheltering arms, crooned nonsense into her ear.

She was quiet at last. The sun, peeking out from behind a cloud, shone full on the white marble of the folly. Its bright reflection shivered in the water beneath.

"*Was* it the wrong thing to do?" Kit asked softly.

"No." She blew her nose in her handkerchief, put it back in her pocket, and settled her head against his shoulder again—he must have removed her bonnet when they sat down. "The people we love are usually stronger than we give them credit for. It is the nature of love, perhaps, to want to shoulder all the pain rather than see the loved one suffer. But sometimes pain is better than emptiness. I have been so empty, Kit. All my life. So full of emptiness. That is a strange paradox, is it not—full of emptiness?"

He kissed her temple.

"It was you, was it not?" she said. "You talked Grandpapa into it?"

"I advised him to tell you," he admitted.

"Thank you." She snuggled closer. "Oh, Kit, *thank* you."

He kissed her temple again, and when she lifted her face, he kissed her mouth.

"I must look a dreadful fright," she said.

He drew his head back and looked closely at her. "Good Lord," he said, "you do. I am going to have to muster all my courage not to run screaming back to the house."

She laughed. "Silly!"

He was going to have wrinkles at the corners of his eyes long before he was an old man, she thought as they crinkled with laughter.

And that was only the beginning of her eventful day.

Tomorrow was going to be a day for guests and organized celebrations. Today would be for family. It was what they all agreed upon during luncheon, though it was Sydnam who suggested a picnic out at the hill where the wilderness walk ended. The idea was greeted with enthusiasm and immediately acted upon.

The mothers of young children went up to the nursery to get their children ready, most of the other adults retired to their rooms to change their clothes, Sydnam strode off to the stables to have the gig prepared since he had persuaded his grandmother—with the help of a chorus of supporting pleas from various cousins—to come too, and Lauren and Marjorie Clifford descended to the kitchens to cajole the cook into preparing a picnic tea and a couple of footmen into conveying it out to the hill.

The top of the hill was the highest point in the park and afforded a wide prospect over the surrounding countryside in every direction. For that reason the designer of the park and the wilderness walk had decided that there would be no trees up there and no elaborate folly to obstruct the view. What he had done instead was build a hermit's cavern into the side of the hill, close to the top. There never had been a hermit, of course, but the children loved it. They were first to scramble to the top.

Everyone else toiled up more slowly. The whole family had come, without exception. Frederick and Roger Butler cupped their hands together at the bottom of the slope and carried their grandmother to the top—despite her protests—after she had been helped out of the gig. Boris Clifford had set up a chair for her on the summit, and Nell had plumped up a cushion for her back. Lawrence Vreemont and Kit carried Lady Irene up while Claude and Daphne Willard prepared her chair. The elderly sisters-in-law sat side by side, like twin queens on their thrones, Clarence Butler remarked. Lauren raised their parasols for them and Gwendoline helped Marianne spread blankets on the grass for any other adults who cared to sit and recover from the walk.

Kit sat down and prepared simply to enjoy himself. Lauren, he noticed, was pink-cheeked and bright-eyed and looking remarkably pretty. After they had returned from the lake earlier, she had gone up to her grandfather's room and remained there with him until luncheon. She had come down on the old gentleman's arm, and had been looking noticeably happy ever since.

He could not stop himself from remembering some of the words she had spoken—*I have been so empty, Kit. All my life. So full of emptiness.*

It was such a relief to know that he had done the right thing in persuading Baron Galton to tell her what he knew of her mother. To know that he had done some good in his life.

But there was not a great deal of time for reflection—or recovery from the walk and climb. The children, who were perfectly well able to play with one another, could not resist the attraction of a whole host of idle adults, who surely could not possibly have anything better to do than play with them. Before many minutes had passed it was no longer good enough for bandits and crusading warriors to creep up by foot on dragons and kidnapped maidens and hidden robbers in the cavern. Horses were required, and of course adult male cousins and uncles and occasionally fathers made splendid steeds.

Kit galloped around the hilltop for all of half an hour with an assortment of youngsters on his back. But the ladies were not exempt, he saw just before the older children tired of that particular game. Lauren and Beatrice and Lady Muir had been coaxed to their feet by some of the infants and were playing some circle game with them, all their hands joined—ring around the rosy, he guessed when they all fell down. Lauren was laughing, and little Anna jumped on her, followed by David and Sarah. She wrapped her arms about them while their mothers scolded and told them not to hurt Lauren.

But their attention was soon distracted. Young Benjamin had discovered that the slope behind the hill was broken halfway down by a wide, flat ledge before it continued its descent to the plain below, and that the upper slope was just long enough and smooth enough and grassy enough to be perfect for rolling down. He tested his theory with shrieks of exuberance, and soon all the tiring human horses were abandoned in favor of the new game. Even the little children could join in this one and did.

And then Sarah was tugging at Lauren's hand, while Kit watched, grinning, from a short distance away. She laughed and shook her head, but then David was pulling at her other hand, and she was walking closer to the edge of the slope.

"Do it!" Frederick called, distracted from the conversation he was having with Lady Muir.

Sebastian put two fingers to his lips and whistled. Phillip whooped. Everyone turned to look.

Lauren was laughing.

"I dare you!" Roger said.

She took off her bonnet, sat down on the grass and then lay down, and rolled to the bottom, all light muslin skirts and bare arms and trim ankles and tumbling dark curls and shrieking laughter.

Kit stared after her, utterly enchanted. But it was Lady Muir, moving to his side and setting one hand on his sleeve, who voiced his thoughts.

"*That* is Lauren?" she said. "I can scarcely believe it. Lord Ravensberg, I bless the moment she met you."

Lauren was up on her knees, brushing the grass from her dress, looking upward, and still laughing.

"It would be a great deal easier," she said, "if one did not have arms to get in one's way."

Yes, there had been that moment when they had met—that first moment in Hyde Park when their eyes had met. And there was this moment, when the truth finally burst in on him. Of course she had become precious to him. *Of course she had.* He was head over ears in love with her.

He loved her.

Sydnam was standing watching too.

"Oh, well," he called down cheerfully, "if a lack of arms makes for easier rolling, I should be halfway decent at it." And surrounded by shrieking, exuberant children, who were absorbed in their own pleasure, he rolled down the hill to come to rest a few feet from Lauren.

Kit tensed while all around him the relatives whistled and applauded. And then as Syd scrambled to his feet and offered his hand to Lauren, he looked up at Kit and their eyes met. He was *laughing*.

They toiled up the slope, hand in hand, while the children continued the game and most of the adults turned their attention to the approach of their tea from the opposite direction. They stood before Kit, still hand in hand. There was a moment of awkwardness.

"I need to tell you," Sydnam said, his voice pitched low so that only Kit and Lauren would hear, "that I lied to you, Kit. When I told you the night you came home that I wanted nothing of you, you asked me if that included your love. I said yes. I lied."

Kit swallowed hard, terrified that the sudden ache in his throat would translate into tears that everyone would see.

"I see," he said stiffly. "I am glad."

This, he thought, was the first time Syd had spoken voluntarily to him since that night three years ago when he had told Kit to leave and not come back. *Why was he holding Lauren's hand?* He released it even as Kit thought it, smiled rather awkwardly, and would have turned away.

"Syd," Kit said quickly, "I . . . er . . ."

Lauren, looking most unlike her usual immaculate self—bonnetless, her hair untidy and strewn with grass, her cheeks flushed, her eyes bright—linked one arm through Syd's and one through his and turned to stroll away from the chairs and blankets and rolling, noisy children.

"I have been thinking," Kit said, "about something Lauren said this morning. I have not been able to get it out of my head, in fact, even though she was not talking about either you or me, Syd. She said that the people we love are usually stronger than we give them credit for. *You* are, are you not? And God knows I love you."

"Yes," Syd said.

"And I humiliated you the other night, coming to your defense when Catherine wanted you to waltz with her."

"Yes."

"I suppose," Kit said, "it happens over and over again—with Mother and Father, with all your old friends and neighbors."

"Yes," Syd admitted. "But with you most of all, Kit."

They did not descend the slope. They stood looking out across the fields below, across the pasture where Kit and Lauren had raced a few days before.

"You are an *artist*, Syd." Pain was back in his throat and chest, the terrible, impotent pity for the brother he had adored from childhood on. "But you are condemned to be a *steward*."

"Yes," Syd said. "It has not been easy to adjust. Perhaps the adjustment will never be fully made. Perhaps being an excellent steward will never quite make up for the fact that I can never paint again. But it is *my* problem, Kit, *my* adjustment to make. This is *my* body, *my* life. I'll cope with it. I have done rather well so far. I would appreciate a little credit. I don't need your pity. Only your love."

Lauren still had an arm linked through each of theirs, creating a physical connection between them, a sort of bridge, Kit thought, realizing suddenly that it was quite deliberate. Her hand crept into his, and she laced her fingers with his.

"I can't forgive myself," Kit said. "I can't, Syd. You ought never to have been in the Peninsula. You certainly ought not to have been on that mission with me. It was my carelessness that led us into that trap. And then I left you to suffer . . . *this* while I escaped. Don't tell me it is your life and not my concern. It *is* my concern. I doomed you to half a life and got off scot-free myself."

"I would find that almost insulting if I did not recognize your agony," Sydnam said. "Kit, I *chose* to become an officer. I *chose* to be a reconnaissance officer. The trap was unforeseeable. I *volunteered* to be the decoy."

Was that true? Of course it was. But did it make a difference? Had Syd had any choice? If he had not volunteered, Kit would have had to command him to take that role. Syd had saved him from having to do that.

"I'll not say I enjoyed what followed," Sydnam continued. "It was sheer hell, in fact. But I was *proud* of myself, Kit. I had finally proved myself your equal, and Jerome's. Perhaps I had even surpassed both of you. In my conceit I expected *you* to be proud of me too. I expected when you brought me home that you would tell everyone here how proud you were. I thought you would have extolled my courage and endurance. It was very conceited of me."

"And instead I belittled you," Kit said quietly, "by taking all the blame and focusing everyone's attention on myself as I went noisily mad. I made you seem no better than a victim."

"Yes," Sydnam said.

"I have always, *always* been proud of you," Kit said. "You did not have to prove anything, Syd. You are my *brother*."

They stood gazing out across the countryside, the breeze at their backs, the noise of merry voices and laughter behind them.

Kit chuckled softly. "You *were* talking about me, Lauren," he said. "What else did you say this morning? 'It is the nature of love, perhaps, to want to shoulder all the pain rather than see the loved one suffer.' In some ways, Syd, my role was as hard as yours. That may seem insulting, but there is truth in it."

"Yes, I know," his brother agreed. "I have always been thankful that I was not the one appointed to escape. I could not have borne to see *you* like this. It *is* easier to suffer something oneself than see a loved one do it."

"I don't know about either of you," Lauren said after a short pause, "but I am very hungry."

Kit turned his head to smile at her and then met his brother's eye beyond her. He wondered if he looked as sheepish as Syd did, and decided that he probably did.

"Come on, Syd," he said, "let's see how well you can eat chicken with just one hand—and the left one to boot."

"I have one distinct advantage if it is greasy," Syd replied. "I have only one hand to wash afterward."

Kit pressed his fingers tightly about Lauren's and blessed again the moment he had looked up from kissing the milkmaid to find himself locking glances with a prim, shocked Lauren Edgeworth.

Except that she might yet break their engagement.

20

*L*auren stood at her bedchamber window, still in her night-gown, gazing out on what promised to be a lovely day. There was not a cloud in the sky. The tree branches were still, suggesting that if there was a wind at all it was the merest breeze. All the anxiously conceived alternate plans for the day's festivities if it rained could be abandoned. The countess would be *so* relieved. All was going to be perfect for the dowager's birthday.

Tomorrow Aunt Clara and Gwen were returning to Newbury. Grandpapa too had decided to return home to Yorkshire. He was going to send the bundle of letters from Lauren's mother by special messenger—to Newbury. She had asked him to send them there rather than here.

She had come here to help Kit avoid an unwanted betrothal. She had done that. She had come to help reconcile him to his family, who had rejected him and sent him away three years ago. She had done that. She had done it in time for this birthday and could feel confident that Kit would be able to celebrate fully and happily with his family and they with him. There was really nothing left to do.

She had come for a little adventure, for a taste of life as other people lived it, those who had not disciplined all spontaneity, all joy, out of their lives. She had found adventure in abundance. She had bathed and swum in the lake—once, naked; she had climbed a tree to the higher branches; she had raced on horseback; she had played with children and rolled down a steep slope with them. Very tiny adventures indeed.

She had gone outside alone one night and spent what remained of it in a hut with Kit. She had *slept* with him on a narrow bed. She had lain with him on one of the velvet benches in the portrait gallery and given him her virginity. She had lain with him among the wildflowers on the island and made love with him. A momentous adventure.

The sound of laughter and voices had her leaning closer to the window and peering downward. Phillip and Penelope Willard, Crispin and Marianne Butler, were on their way out for an early morning walk. The day was beginning.

The last day.

There was no more to be experienced. Already there had been too much. Far too much. There was no point in prolonging the inevitable. Tomorrow she would leave with Aunt Clara and Gwen, though she was not going to tell anyone until today was over. If she did not go soon then she might stay forever, and that would be dishonorable.

She would not cling to what she had found. All her life she had clung with all her might to her only hope of permanent belonging and security, a marriage with Neville. And when that anchor had been snatched from her, she had drifted on a vast, dark, threatening ocean, frightening in its emptiness. She would not cling now, even though she knew Kit's honor would urge him into encouraging her to do just that, even though she knew he had grown fond of her. She did not need to cling. Not to anyone. She could and would stand alone.

This time her heart would not break, even though it would hurt and hurt for a long time to come. Perhaps for the rest of her life. But it would not break. She had the strength to go on alone.

She had learned something of limitless value here at Alvesley. And she had Kit to thank. It was such a simple, such an earth-shatteringly profound lesson. The world, she had discovered—*her* world—would not explode into chaos if Lauren Edgeworth laughed.

There was a scratching on the door behind her, and she turned with a smile to watch her maid come in with her morning cup of chocolate.

The morning was to be for the family alone—the calm before the proverbial storm, as it were. They all went into the village for a celebratory service at the church. The plan was that the dowager would then return home in the first carriage in order to rest quietly in her private apartments for a few hours before the afternoon festivities began.

It was a return that was delayed by nearly half an hour. Almost the whole village had spilled out of doors to gather about the churchyard gateway to cheer the dowager and pay their respects and pelt her with flower petals. She would see them all again during the afternoon, but she insisted upon stopping to talk to a number of them—no easy feat for her—and to hand out coins to the children.

Finally she was on her way, Lady Irene beside her. A long line of carriages, barouches, and curricles moved steadily forward to pick up the rest of the family.

Kit took Lauren by the elbow. "Will you mind walking back to the house?" he asked.

"Of course not." She turned her head to smile at him. Her bonnet and the ribbons that trimmed her light muslin dress exactly matched her eyes. She looked very fetching indeed.

"I want to look at something," he told her.

He had sat down with his father the night before, after everyone else had gone to bed—and Syd too had stayed on his window seat, a silent listener through most of the conversation that had followed. Kit had begun it by apologizing for his behavior three years before.

"It is best forgotten," his father had said. "It is over."

But Kit had disagreed, and they had talked, awkwardly at first, with growing ease as time went on.

"I sent you away," his father said at one point. "I never meant it to be forever. I never used the word *banishment*. That was your interpretation, Kit. But I was content to let it stand. I was as stubborn as a mule. You take after me there. When you did not write, your mother wanted *me* to do it. But I would not. Jerome pleaded with me to do it, but I would not. Neither would he, of course—or your mother. What a parcel of fools we all were. All of us—you too. Family quarrels are the very worst kind. They are so very difficult to end."

"*Jerome* wanted you to write to me?"

There had been an understanding between Jerome and Freyja for several years, apparently. It had been one of those courtships that no one had been in any particular hurry to bring to fruition. But then Kit had come home, half raving and in a towering rage at the whole world, most of all himself. His family had watched helplessly as he flung himself into passionate pursuit of Freyja, which in their opinion had nothing whatever to do with love. Jerome had been particularly alarmed and had ridden over to discuss the matter with Bewcastle—and with Freyja herself. His announcement of their betrothal at dinner had been the result—followed, of course, by Kit's fight, first with him and then with Rannulf.

"He never blamed you or held a grudge, you know, Kit," the earl said. "He blamed himself for going about things entirely the wrong way. He should have had a talk with you, tried to explain, he used to say afterward. He should have tried to get you to vent your anger, brother to brother. Though there was really no talking to you that summer, Kit. After you were gone, he kept putting off the nuptials. He wanted you here. He wanted peace with you before he married Freyja. He wanted to know that you had realized she was not the woman for you. He wanted me to write to you. But he was too stubborn to do it himself."

"And then," Kit said, "we all ran out of time."

"Yes."

"He never stopped loving you, Kit," Syd said, speaking up at last.

"None of us did. And you must stop punishing yourself now. It has gone on long enough. For all of us."

It was years since Kit had been to the family plot behind the church. His grandfather had been his childhood idol. Kit had visited his grave regularly for a number of years after his death. But he had not been here since he was eighteen, since his commission had been purchased.

"This is where the family ancestors are buried," he told Lauren, leading her through the gateway between the two halves of the low, neatly clipped hedge that separated the plot from the rest of the churchyard. "I have not been here for eleven years."

He found his grandfather's grave immediately. There were fresh roses in the marble vase before the headstone—his grandmother had come here after the picnic yesterday with her two sons and her daughter. There were roses in the vase before another headstone too—the one that had not been here eleven years ago. Kit moved toward it and stood at the foot of the grave, reading the headstone. Only two words out of all those written there leapt out at him.

Jerome Butler.

His hand was in Lauren's, he realized suddenly, their fingers tightly laced. He was probably hurting her. He eased his hand free and set his arm lightly about her shoulders.

"My brother," he said unnecessarily.

"Yes."

"I loved him."

"Yes."

He had been afraid that, standing here, he would be overwhelmed by bitter regret, remembering their last encounter, knowing that they had been unreconciled when Jerome died. But it really did not matter, he found now. Love did not die just because of a quarrel. And a relationship was not a linear thing, the last incident defining the whole of it. They had been close, the three of them—Jerome, Kit, Syd. They had played and fought and laughed together. They had been brothers. They *were* brothers.

He had been afraid he would break down with inconsolable grief at seeing finally the indisputable evidence of Jerome's nonexistence. He was dead. His remains were beneath the ground here.

Kit smiled. "He used to tease me," he said, "when I came home on leave and he would have heard of yet another dispatch in which I had been singled out for commendation. I would die a gloriously heroic death, he used to say—when Mother was not around to hear him say it, of course—and there would be no living down my memory. It would be insufferable. I think it might have amused him if he could have known that *he* was the one destined for the heroism. And the death."

"There are worse ways to die, Kit," Lauren said.

"Yes, there are." He had seen too much of death to cling to any illusion that it was reserved for old age. "Good-bye, brother. Rest in peace."

He had to blink then, several times. And he had to release the pressure of his grip on Lauren's shoulder. She was leaning against him. Her arm was about his waist.

Perhaps after all, he thought, he had not lost the right to grasp hold of whatever remained of life and live it to the best of his ability. Jerome had lived his life. Syd was living his. They were his brothers and he would love them both to his dying breath, but when all was said and done he could live only his own life. He had done his share of foolish, even wrong things—but who has not? He had the freedom to live on and try to do better. It was all he could do.

He felt suddenly, strangely happy.

"Let's go home," he said.

"Yes."

He took her hand in his and drew it through his arm.

The afternoon brought friends and neighbors and tenants and laborers and villagers—people of all classes from miles around, in fact— to the lawns of Alvesley for a garden party that was enlivened with contests of all descriptions for all ages.

Lauren had her part to play—almost her final part—and played it to the full. While the earl and countess judged the needlework and baking and woodworking contests and the dowager listened to the poetry contestants proclaim their verses but refused to judge them because all the poems had been written in her honor—they were drawing a great deal of attention and much laughter—Lauren and Kit organized the races and other physical contests.

There were footraces and sack races and three-legged races for the children, though Kit ran the latter too with young Doris, there having been an uneven number of would-be contestants. There was a batting contest for the young boys with a cricket bat and ball. There was a wood-chopping contest for the young men and an archery contest too, though the winner of that was the sole female entrant, Lady Morgan Bedwyn, who had ridden over to Alvesley with Lord Alleyne. She would not be at the ball in the evening, she admitted haughtily when pressed, because Bewcastle had the Gothic notion that at six-teen she was too young. She threatened to put an arrow between Lord Alleyne's eyes when he laughed.

There was tea for everyone when it was all over, and Lauren circulated among the visitors, plate in hand, making sure that she had a friendly word with almost everyone who had come. But she was feeling hot and nearly exhausted. How was she ever to find the energy to dance during the evening?

It was a feeling shared by others, it seemed. The earl, after the final visitor had left, suggested that they all retire to their rooms for a rest. He would see to it that a bell was rung loudly enough to rouse them all in time to dress for dinner and the ball.

"Come for a walk?" Kit asked Lauren, taking her hand in his.

A walk was the last thing she needed. But it was her final day and already it was late afternoon. There could be panic in the thought if she allowed herself to dwell upon it. But there was still a little time left, this evening and . . . the rest of this afternoon.

She smiled.

He did not take her far. At first when he set out in the direction of the lake she hoped that perhaps he would take her to the island again. She hoped that perhaps they would make love one more time. But although part of her longed for it, she was not sorry when he led her only as far as the secluded spot where they had stood yesterday, across from the temple. The sun was in such a position in the sky that the surrounding trees shaded the bank.

"What a busy day!" she said, sinking to the grass beside him. "I hope it will not prove too tiring for your grandmother."

"She is lapping up every moment of it," he said, stretching out on his back and closing his eyes.

Lauren took off her straw bonnet and lay down beside him. He felt for her hand and held it in his. It felt so natural now, she thought, to be alone together like this, and to touch each other with casual gestures of affection. And seductively comforting.

He did not want to talk, it seemed. Neither did she. She wanted to concentrate on this, perhaps their final time alone together. She wanted to memorize it so that she could call it to mind anytime she wished to in future. It was a memory she would avoid for a long time, she suspected, as being just too painful a reminder of a brief summer when life had come vividly alive and love had been born with startling unexpectedness. But eventually she would remember this lazy heat, the cool springiness of the grass, the smell of flowers, the droning of insects, the warmth of his hand.

She slept.

She swatted at the ant or whatever it was crawling across her nose and trying to wake her when she had no wish to awake. But it was a persistent insect and trailed boldly across her nose again. She brushed it away crossly and then someone chuckled softly and kissed her warmly on the lips.

"It was you!" she accused sleepily, seeing the telltale blade of grass in his upraised hand. "Horrid you."

"There is a ball to attend, Sleeping Beauty," he said.

"That was Cinderella." Her eyes drifted closed again. "Wrong story. Sleeping Beauty did not attend any balls. She was allowed to sleep for a hundred years."

"I wonder," he said, "if she was this cross with the prince who kissed her."

She opened her eyes and smiled at him again. "Was I really sleeping?"

"Snoring like thunder," he said. "I could not snatch a wink myself."

"Silly." She sighed with contentment. For the moment she had forgotten that this was the final day.

"Lauren," he said, "I would like to have our wedding date announced tonight."

She was finally, irrevocably awake.

"No, Kit."

"Why not?" he asked. "We *are* betrothed, and I thought you had perhaps grown fond of me—and of my family. You must know I have grown fond of you."

"Yes." She lifted a hand to push aside a lock of hair that had fallen over his forehead. It fell back as soon as she had removed her hand. "But it was not part of our bargain, Kit."

"To hell with our bargain."

"Don't talk like that," she said. "It is not nice language."

"My abject apologies, ma'am." He grinned at her. "Neither was it a part of our bargain that we indulge in carnal relations. We must marry, you know. You may very well be with child."

"I hope I am not," she said. "It would spoil everything. I think a wonderful thing has happened here, Kit, much more than we could ever have anticipated. I believe we have helped set each other free. Really free, not just of certain social restraints, but of all that has held us back from happiness—for years in your case, all my life in mine. We must not snare each other now before we have even had a chance to test our wings."

He stared down at her, his eyes suddenly blank and unfathomable.

"Is that what you really think?" he asked her. "That we have found our separate freedoms? That marriage with each other would be an undesirable trap?"

Yes, it *was* what she believed—with her intellect. Her heart was a different matter altogether. But her heart had no part at all in their bargain. And it would be grossly unfair to explain that *fondness* was no basis for marriage. It had been altogether enough for her once. But Kit was not Neville. He was not someone with whom she had grown up as a sister grows up with a brother. Kit was *different*. Fondness would not be enough with him, not when there was something much different from fondness on the one side.

"It is what I really think," she said, forcing herself to look steadily back into his eyes. "It was our bargain, remember? That for you the betrothal would be real, that in your gallantry you would try to persuade me not to break it. That for me it would be a charade. That I *would* break it when the time was right."

"Not yet," he said quickly.

She drew breath to tell him she would be leaving tomorrow, but did not say the words.

"Not yet," she agreed softly, and he lay back on the grass again.

She did not turn her head, but she knew that he stared at the sky as she did, sleep and relaxation forgotten, even though it was a long time before he got silently to his feet and reached down a hand to help her up.

21

After dinner Lauren stood with Kit and the earl and countess in the receiving line at the ballroom doors. The dowager was seated on a comfortable chair inside surrounded on three sides by great banks of flowers—her own private bower, she had said when she saw it. There she was greeted and kissed by everyone who passed and showered with gifts.

There had been no rest at all for Lauren after returning from the lake. Apart from having to bathe and dress and have her hair done, she had taken it upon herself to help the countess check the decorations the servants had worked upon during the afternoon. The ballroom was like a garden. It had been Lauren's idea to confine the colors to varying shades of pink and purple, together with white. And green, of course, so often neglected in floral arrangements. She definitely had a gift for color and design, the countess had told her approvingly.

It was not exactly the squeeze of a London ball. But the room was pleasingly full nonetheless before the dancing began. Most of the guests were not quite as fashionably dressed as their London counterparts would have been, or as bedecked with costly jewels, but all were wearing their best and looked bright and festive. She liked country gatherings better than town ones, Lauren decided as Kit led her into the ballroom and onto the floor to signal the imminent opening of the ball. There was something warm and intimate about them.

Kit looked very handsome in shades of gray and silver and white. She was wearing the violet gown she had worn to the Mannering ball, a deliberate choice. It seemed fitting somehow that she should wear it the last time she danced with him as she had worn it the first. More than one of the guests, as well as a few family members, had commented on how well they complemented each other in appearance, on what a handsome couple they made.

She was going to enjoy the evening, Lauren decided as other couples gathered around them. Every single moment of it. Her maid was above stairs, packing her trunks. But there was this evening left.

"You look particularly lovely tonight," Kit said, leaning a little closer so that only she would hear his words. "And do I mistake, or— No, indeed I do not. Your gown really does match the color of your eyes." His own eyes laughed into hers.

"Absurd." She smiled back. How much had happened since the first time he had spoken those words to her! And yet not so very much time had passed. He had been a roguish, unwelcome stranger then. Now he was . . . well, now he was Kit. And achingly dear to her.

The music began and she concentrated on the steps and figures of the quadrille. She could never be happier than she was at this moment, she thought—and realized in some shock that it was precisely what she had told herself on her wedding eve ball when she had been in company with Neville.

The day following that had been the bleakest of her whole life. . . .

She smiled more brightly and noticed that the Duke of Bewcastle had just stepped into the ballroom with his brothers and Lady Freyja.

Sleeping Beauty, Kit had called her this afternoon. She felt more like Cinderella, dancing at the ball with her prince—with the knowledge that midnight would inevitably come and turn everything into rags and pumpkins.

But she had no glass slipper to leave behind on the stairs.

Lauren had taken to the floor with Bewcastle, who was looking elegant, austere, almost satanic in black and white. Kit had never seen him dance at any assembly or ball before this. He did so now, it would seem, to allay any lingering suspicion there might be in the neighborhood that he nursed some resentment against the Earl of Redfield and his family. Ralf was leading out Lady Muir while Alleyne bent his head close to Kit's grandmother to hear what she was saying.

"May I have the honor, Freyja?" Kit bowed to her and extended his hand. She was looking particularly handsome tonight in gold satin overlaid with blond lace. Her hair was tamed and dressed high on her head with gold ornaments that gleamed in the candlelight.

She was small—smaller than Lauren, but fuller figured. Quite voluptuous, in fact. And she had the boldness, the energy, the vitality, to which he had always responded. As they danced without talking, he tried to re-create in his mind and his emotions the madness that had possessed him three years before when he had been consumed by passion for her. He could do it with his mind. She had always been his friend—and he had needed a friend that summer. A male friend would not do, as he had discovered when he had tried pouring out his woes to Ralf, and Ralf had told him rather impatiently not to be an ass. He had done his duty and also saved Syd's life, had he not? And brought him home? What did he find to blame himself for? Freyja had shown no greater sympathy, but Freyja was a woman. All his grief, all his anger, all his guilt, had been converted to physical, sexual passion and focused on her person.

If he had anything to remember with guilt from that summer, it was surely the way he had used Freyja. It had been unconscious and quite unintentional, of course. But that was what had happened. She had been there, and he had used her.

"It is too warm in here," she said when the set was almost at an end. The words, typical of Freyja, were issued almost like a challenge.

"It is," he agreed. "It has been a hot day. It probably still is warm outside."

"At least," she said, "the air must be fresh out there."

"Do you want to find out?" He grinned at her. "You are not about to faint, are you?"

She looked at him with mingled haughtiness and contempt.

The ballroom was at the east side of the house, on the ground floor. The east entrance was close to it, and on such a warm night the doors stood open and several guests had stepped outside, some merely to stand in the cooler air, a few to stroll among the parterres of the formal gardens. There was no one in the rose arbor, toward which Freyja turned. Kit walked beside her, hoping she would turn back before they actually reached the arbor.

"We need to talk," she said.

The arbor it was, then. She sat on the very seat where Lauren had sat the evening of her arrival at Alvesley, and Kit stood looking down at her, his hands clasped at his back.

"What is it?" he asked. But he did not wait for her to reply. "Freyja, allow me to apologize—for three years ago. You never did say you loved me, did you? You never did say you would marry me and come with me to follow the drum. It was all in my imagination. I had no right to come banging on the door at Lindsey Hall and to force that fight on Ralf and create such an atrocious scene. Please forgive me."

She looked at him coolly. "How foolish you are, Kit," she said. "How utterly foolish."

"You had an understanding with Jerome," he said. "You would not have married me."

"Of course I would not," she said impatiently. "You were a younger son. I am the daughter of a Duke of Bewcastle."

"Well, then." How devastating those words would have sounded to him three summers ago. How relieved he was to hear them now.

"There was no permanent harm done, then, was there? Did you love Jerome?"

"Oh, fool, Kit," she said softly. "Fool!"

He had known her for a long time. They had been close friends. Sometimes meanings did not have to be spelled out in words.

"Freyja—" he began.

"For what are you punishing yourself this time?" she asked him. "Still for Sydnam? For Jerome? Because you broke his nose and had no chance to beg his pardon before he died? You have become a bore, Kit. Just *look* at her! If you had chosen to flagellate yourself with a nail-studded club you would not have been picking a worse punishment. She is primness and dullness personified. You have made your point, believe me. Now, what do you plan to do to extricate yourself?"

For a brief moment he closed his eyes. Ah, he had not expected this. He moved a little closer, fearful suddenly that they might be overheard. He lifted one foot to the seat beside her and draped one arm over his raised leg.

"Freyja," he said, "you are mistaken. *Very* mistaken, I'm afraid."

There was one thing about Freyja—she had never been slow of understanding. And it was quite against her nature to grovel, to beg, to weep, to make any sort of scene. She stared up at him, all cold haughtiness, and then she moved to jerk to her feet.

"No, don't." He grasped her shoulder. "Don't hurry back without me. It might be noted and commented upon. Take my arm and we will return together. Perhaps we can smile?"

"You, Kit," she said, getting to her feet more slowly and linking her arm through his, "may go to hell. I hope you burn there. Better yet, I hope you live well into your nineties with your lady bride. I cannot imagine a more hellish sentence for a man of your nature."

She lifted a smiling face to his. Freyja had always been mistress of the feline smile.

He did not respond. There was no point. Besides, he was reminded that if he *did* live into his nineties, sixty or so of those years were going to have to be lived without Lauren. Unless even yet he could get her to change her mind. Surely he could. Once this day was over he would be able to concentrate all his efforts upon coaxing her to love him.

We must not snare each other now. . . .

He would not remember that she viewed marriage with him as a sort of imprisonment, as a loss of all her newly won freedom.

He would teach her that there was more than one kind of freedom.

Kit was nowhere in sight when the dance with the Duke of Bewcastle was over. But Gwen was approaching on Lord Rannulf's arm. Lauren smiled at them both. She would suggest to Gwen that they slip away for a few minutes to find a cool drink. It was a warm night. But Lord Rannulf gave her no opportunity to make the suggestion. He bowed to Lauren and asked for her hand in the next set.

He was one of the few gentlemen of her acquaintance, she thought after she had accepted, who could make her feel almost diminutive. He really was a giant of a man.

"You are looking becomingly flushed, Miss Edgeworth," he said with that look in his eyes that she had never been able quite to interpret. Was it mockery or simply amusement? "But one would hate to force you into further exertions too soon. Do come and stroll with me outside."

She had absolutely no wish to walk outside with him even though she knew there were several other guests out there to make all proper. But it was not a request he had made, she realized. He had drawn her arm through his and was moving purposefully out of the ballroom and toward the outer doors. Well, she decided, a little fresh air *would* feel good.

He could be an amusing companion. He pointed out several of the neighbors and told her brief anecdotes about them. He was a keen observer of human nature, it seemed, and yet none of his observations were quite malicious. Lauren found herself feeling well entertained. They were strolling above the parterres, in the direction of the rose arbor.

"Ah," he said softly when they were close, "foiled! There is someone there before us—two persons actually. We must walk into the flower gardens instead." And he turned her into the parterres.

He must have known even before coming out here, she realized, even before asking her for this set of dances, who was in the rose arbor. He had wanted her to know, to see for herself. Probably Lady Freyja wanted it too.

She was sitting on one of the seats. Kit, in a characteristic pose, stood close to her, one foot on the seat, one arm draped over his leg. The other hand was on her shoulder, bringing his head very close to hers.

Lord Rannulf was recounting some other anecdote, to which Lauren was not listening. He stopped, obviously without finishing.

"I beg your pardon," he said. "I would not for worlds have had you see that."

"Would you not?" she asked. Ladies did not call gentlemen liars.

"It is not what you think," he said. "They have been friends all their lives, you know. They are still friends. You have seen for yourself how much they have in common, how they love to challenge each other and compete against each other, how much they come alive in each other's company. But there is no more to it than friendship, I do assure you."

"Lord Rannulf," she said, "you were in the middle of a story. Please finish it. You need not concern yourself with what I think. My thoughts are private. You could not begin to guess their contents."

Despite herself she had been wavering in her resolve. She did not even realize it until now when her determination to leave in the morning was strengthened, when staying even one more day was finally no option at all. It was a good thing this had happened, she thought as Lord Rannulf at her side, far from completing the story he had begun earlier, fell silent.

She had known that it *would* happen, of course, that it was inevitable. But now she had seen for herself and could entertain no niggling doubts. No faint hopes.

She would not let it upset her. It would be vastly unfair—to both Kit and herself. She had had her adventure and now it had come to an end. It was understandable that her spirits were rather flat after such a splendid adventure. But she would soon cheer up once she was back at Newbury. There would be her mother's letters to read, Elizabeth and the baby to fuss over, Lily to rejoice with—oh, yes, finally, *finally*, she would be able to rejoice with Lily—and her future to plan. There would be her new freedom to enjoy. How many women had the freedom she now had?

"I am sorry," Lord Rannulf said softly, and for the first time it seemed to Lauren he spoke with sincerity. "I am truly sorry, Miss Edgeworth. You have not deserved this."

"Deserved what, Lord Rannulf?" she asked him. "Trickery? But life is full of tricks and lies and masks. One would be foolish not to be armed against them."

Especially when she herself was the biggest perpetrator of deception.

He took her to where Aunt Clara was talking with the Countess of Redfield in the ballroom, bowed over her hand before raising it to his lips, and walked away without speaking another word to her.

Lady Freyja was back in the rose arbor when Lord Rannulf found her. She was sitting on the same seat she had occupied a few minutes before.

"Go away," she said ungraciously when she saw him coming.

The Bedwyns rarely did as they were bidden. He moved closer and sat beside her.

"Well?" he asked.

"Bloody hell and a thousand damnations," she said, quiet venom in her voice. "No, make it a million."

He clucked his tongue but attempted no other admonition. Years ago none of a long string of governesses had ever been able to impress upon their headstrong pupil the reality of the fact that she was a lady and must learn to conduct herself accordingly. Her brothers had never made much effort to reinforce what the governesses had tried to teach.

"I want to go home," she said. "I want to raid Wulf's wine cellar. I want to get foxed. Blind drunk. With you. You can drink with me."

"That is very generous of you, Free," he said. "It is very tempting too after what you have just put me through—I *like* the woman, damn it. But Wulf and Alleyne would not appreciate being stranded here without the carriage. And it would offend my sensibilities to haul up the best liquor with the sole purpose of drinking ourselves three sheets to the wind with it. Inferior liquor would serve the same purpose but Wulf does not keep any."

"Wulf be damned," she said.

Her brother raised his eyebrows. "Drinking like a fish is no cure for what ails you, you know," he said. "All you will get out of it is a crashing headache and a fervent wish that you were dead."

"When I need your advice," she said with woeful lack of originality, "I will ask for it."

"Quite so." He shrugged. "It was foolish to fall in love three years ago and never fall out again, you know."

He saw it coming despite the darkness. But he thought it might do her more good than drinking herself under the nearest table. She clenched her right hand into a tight fist, drew back her arm, and punched him hard on the chin. His head snapped back, but he was not swayed from his comfortable posture on the seat.

"Ouch!" he said quietly after a few moments. "If you really insist upon getting foxed, Free, we will steal two horses from the stables here and be on our way. Or we could go back inside and dance. You could show everyone what you are made of. Show that you don't care a fig for Kit or any other mortal so far beneath the notice of Lady Freyja Bedwyn."

"I *don't* care for him," she said, getting to her feet. "I hate him if you want to know the truth, Ralf. And as for that mealymouthed *lady* he has brought home with him, well—I would have to say he richly deserves her. And that is *all* I have to say. Are you coming or are you not?"

"I'm coming." He got to his feet and grinned down at her. "That's the girl, Free. Up with the chin. The Bedwyn nose can be a priceless asset on occasions like this, can it not?"

Freyja looked at him along the length of hers as if he were a worm beneath her dancing slipper.

Country balls, even when they were of the elaborate nature of the one at Alvesley, did not continue until dawn as the most memorable of London balls did. Supper was served at eleven and was followed by the first and only waltz of the evening for the relatively few couples bold and skilled enough to dance it. After that the dancing continued, but the guests began gradually to drift away. And the Dowager Countess of Redfield retired to bed.

Kit and Lauren took her up to her room. They had just waltzed together, and Kit had been powerfully reminded of their first waltz, when he had been struck by her beauty, daunted by her apparently cold dignity, and challenged to try to shock her out of her complacency.

His grandmother was tired. There was none of her fierce independence tonight. Instead of clutching her cane with her good hand, she had one arm linked through Lauren's and the other through his, and she was leaning heavily. But Kit knew it had been an extraordinarily happy day for her.

"Good . . . night." She relinquished Lauren's arm when Kit had opened her dressing room door and her dresser had come hurrying to assist her. "P . . . recious boy."

"Good night, Grandmama." He hugged her gently as she kissed his cheek.

"Good night." She turned to kiss Lauren, who leaned down to hug her too. "Sweet . . . child."

"Good night, ma'am. Happy birthday." There were tears in Lauren's eyes when she took Kit's arm again.

"We have just danced together," he said as they made their way back downstairs. "If we return to the ballroom, we will have to take other partners."

"So we will," she said. "It is the polite thing to do."

"Would it be *impolite* to walk outside together?" he asked her.

She shook her head. "Everyone has a partner for this set anyway."

There were still a few other people outside, mostly the young cousins, who were chattering and laughing together in a group. Kit led Lauren past them, exchanging cheerful greetings as they went. They strolled without talking through the parterres and across the lawn below until they came to the little wooden bridge across the stream. They stopped there by unspoken assent and rested their arms along the wooden rail. There was the sound of water bubbling below, though it was invisible in the darkness cast by the trees. In contrast, the lawn and flower beds and house were bathed in moonlight.

Kit sighed. "A long day almost over."

"But a wonderful day," she said. "It has been perfect, has it not? Perfect for your grandmother and perfect for everyone else too."

"Yes," he agreed.

He could hear distant laughter from the direction of the house. And the faint sound of music. It was good to be alone with Lauren. She was a restful companion. He had not realized until recently how important a component of friendship the ability to be quiet together was. And to feel as comfortable as one felt when alone. No, *more* comfortable.

"Kit," she said softly, "we did the right thing, did we not?"

He understood the question immediately.

"If you had come here alone," she said, "you would be feeling now that you had been forced into a betrothal without any freedom of choice. You might always have resented it, and your family would have sensed it even if you had not put it into words. There would be awkwardness and friction and hostility whereas now there are peace and love and harmony. It was not wrong, was it?"

"It was not wrong," he said, finding her hand with his own on the rail and covering it.

"After it is all over," she said, "the harmony will remain here, and you will be free to choose your own future."

"From tomorrow on," he said, "I am going to be free to woo you more aggressively. I am going to do it. Be warned. I am going to convince you that the best ending for what had been started here is going to be our wedding. Happily ever after and all that."

"Kit," she said after a short pause, "I am going to be leaving with Aunt Clara and Gwen tomorrow."

"No!" His fingers closed tightly about hers. Panic gripped his insides.

"It will be the best possible solution. You will surely agree when you think about it," she said. "They are from my own home. They accompanied me here as my chaperones. They are eager to return home because Elizabeth is coming with the new baby. It will be the most natural thing in the world for me to leave with them. And your mother and Aunt Clara between them have assumed that our wedding will take place at Newbury. It will seem, then, that I am going in order to start the preparations. No awkward explanations will need to be made. By the time I write to put an end to our betrothal, your family guests will all have returned home and you will be able to break the news quietly to the earl and countess. And to your grandmother and Sydnam."

Her voice was quiet and sensible. There was no trace of regret there, of pain, of any emotion whatsoever.

"Stay a little longer," he said. "A week. Give me one week to persuade you. Don't leave tomorrow, Lauren. It is too soon."

"I have accomplished everything I came here to do," she said. "And I have had my adventure, my summer to remember. There is no good reason to prolong it and every reason to end it. It *is* time, Kit. You will soon realize it for yourself."

"Stay," he urged her, "until we know for sure whether or not you are with child."

"If I am," she said just as coolly as before, "I will write to you immediately. If I am not, I will write to cancel our betrothal. I will wait until I know, Kit. I can do that just as easily at Newbury. And I really believe I am *not*. There were only two occasions, after all."

One. There had been only *one* occasion when she might have conceived. "I hope you are," he said, gripping her hand even more tightly. "I hope you *are* with child." Did he? Was he so desperate that he wanted her to be coerced?

"Why?" she asked.

Because I love you. Because I cannot bear the thought of life lived without you. But he could not hang that albatross about her neck. It would be horribly unfair. She might somehow feel honor-bound to stay with him, to marry him, to give up the life she dreamed of, now so close to being in her grasp.

"It is because you have . . . possessed me, is it not?" she said. "As a gentleman you feel you must persuade me to marry you at all costs. There is no need—not unless I am with child. It was not seduction. What I did, I did freely. It was part of the adventure, part of the memorable summer. I will never regret it. I will always be glad that I—that I *know*. And that it was with you. And that it was so . . . wonderful. But you owe me nothing, certainly not a lifetime of devotion. You are free, Kit. So am I. *Free!*"

She made freedom sound like the most desirable state of the human condition. He might have agreed with her a month or so ago.

He tasted defeat. How could he argue against a plea for freedom?

"There is nothing I can say to change your mind, then?" he asked.

"No."

He lifted her hand, set his forehead against it, drew a slow breath.

"Thank you," he said. "For all you have done for me and my family, thank you, Lauren. You have been sweetness and patience and generosity and unfailing dignity."

"And thank *you*." She set her free hand on his arm. "For my adventure, Kit. For the swimming and riding and tree-climbing. For the—for the laughter. And for persuading Grandpapa to tell me the truth about my mother. That is a more precious gift than I can put into words. Thank you."

He felt her lips against his cheek and fought the urge to pull her into his arms, to use his superior physical strength, to flatly refuse to let her go—ever.

"Tomorrow morning, then?" he said, his eyes tightly closed. "We will need to be cheerful, will we not? Regretful for the brief parting, but cheerful because wedding plans are being set in motion. Basically cheerful, yes. I'll kiss you, I believe. On the lips. It will seem appropriate."

"Yes," she agreed. "There will be others gathered to see us on our way, I daresay. There will be others watching."

"But now," he said, bringing her hand to his lips, "we are alone together. For the last time. Good-bye, then, my friend. Good-bye, Lauren."

"Oh, my dear," she said, and for the first time it seemed to him that her voice faltered and emotion crept in. "Good-bye. Have a good life. I will always remember you with—with deep affection."

He stood there for several silent moments, his back to the house, his eyes closed, her hand to his lips, memorizing the feel and the soap fragrance of her and the gentle aura she seemed to cast about him, before escorting her back for what remained of the birthday ball.

22

*S*ummer had lingered on through the hot, lazy days of August and well into September. But it was finally giving place to autumn, it seemed. There was a distinct chill in the air and clouds were gathering overhead, low and heavy. It was going to rain.

She was in the very worst place she could be on such a day, Lauren thought. She was on the beach at Newbury Abbey. Not only on the beach, but perched on the very top of the great rock that appeared for all the world as if a giant must once have hurled it there from the cliffs above to land in the middle of the wide expanse of golden sand. She was sitting with a cloak wrapped warmly about her, her arms clasping her updrawn knees beneath its folds. But she was hatless—her bonnet lay at the foot of the rock, wedged into a narrow cranny with her gloves, where they would not blow away. The wind—no, it was more like a gale—whipped her hair back from her face and tasted of salt. The sea, on the ebb and halfway out along the sand, was slate gray and rough and flecked with angry white foam.

She was feeling almost happy. She allowed herself the qualifier of *almost* because she had accepted the fact that self-deception was also self-destructive. She would not deceive herself any more or hide behind any mask in an attempt to shield herself from the reality of her life.

Hence the beach, which she had never liked until recently, especially on a wild day. And hence her perch on top of the rock, which she had never climbed before today. Climbing it had been forbidden when she was a child, and so of course both Neville and Gwen had scaled it several times. Equally inevitably, she never had. Climbing it more recently had been unladylike. She could remember her shock at seeing Lily sitting up here one day, not long after her arrival at Newbury.

And hence too her bonnetless state. The wind and the sea air would do dreadful things to both her complexion and her hair. She tipped her face higher into the air and shook out her tangled hair with smiling defiance.

Hence also the fact that the likelihood of rain was not sending her scurrying back to the dower house for shelter. If she got wet, she would also feel cold and uncomfortable and might ruin her bonnet and her good shoes. She looked up at the clouds and challenged them to rain torrents on her head.

She was not with child. She had wept in the privacy of her own room when her courses had begun less than a week after her return from Alvesley. She had grieved for the child who had never been and the marriage that would never happen. At the same time she had been overwhelmingly relieved. She had written the next day to Kit, breaking off their engagement—the most difficult task she had ever undertaken in her life.

The thought of it—of the moment the letter had left her hands—could still make her chest tighten with an almost unbearable pain. She would not allow herself to think of it. At some time in the future—still rather far in the future, she believed—she would be able to look back on the brief summer at Alvesley and remember with pleasure what had surely been the happiest time of her life.

But not quite yet. At this precise moment in her life she was *almost* happy. She accepted with quiet patience that she was not entirely so.

Tomorrow she was going to Bath. Oh, not permanently yet, but the wheels were being set in motion. Gwen and Neville were going to accompany her. An agent had found four different houses he considered suitable residences for a single lady of modest fortune. She was going to view them all and make her choice. Against the advice of everyone except Elizabeth, but with the reluctant support of all, she was about to embark upon the rest of her life. Not a passive observer any longer, but an active participant.

The mist of spray from the sea—or perhaps it was the beginning of the rain—was dampening her face. Her hair was going to be impossibly curly when she got back home and her poor maid was called upon to do something with it. Lauren closed her eyes and felt enclosed by wind. Exhilarated by the wildness of it. Empowered by it.

She had read fifteen years' worth of letters from the stranger who was her mother. Cheerful, careless, untidily scrawled letters from a woman who was clearly enjoying her life even though she complained freely about anything and everything—particularly about the men on whom she had heaped rapturous praises in an earlier letter, and consistently over the fact that her beloved Lauren never wrote back to her, never came to live with her. They were letters that would have shocked Lauren to the core even a few months earlier. But she had acquired a new tolerance, an acceptance of the myriad ways in which other people coped with the one life allotted them. She felt an aching love for the mother she remembered so dimly that none of the memories was concrete. She had written a long, long letter and sent it on its way to India. She could not expect any reply until sometime next year, but she felt a connection with the woman who had borne her.

She should climb down, she supposed, looking with some misgiving at the footholds and handholds that had appeared perfectly manageable when she had examined them from the beach. But she had been looking up then, not down. If she waited until the rain was falling in earnest, the rock might become slippery and she would be stranded.

For a moment her mind touched upon the memory of Kit helping her descend the tree at Alvesley, his body and arms cradling her protectively from behind, though she had forbidden him to touch her or carry her down. She pushed the memory aside. She was not ready for it yet. It was still too painful.

Something caught at the edge of her vision, and she turned her head to look. There was a steep path down from the cliff top to the valley where the waterfall and pool and cottage were, just out of her range of vision from where she sat. But she could see the bridge that crossed the river as it flowed the last few yards to the beach and the sea. He was just stepping onto the bridge, his long drab riding coat billowing out to one side, his tall hat pulled low over his brow.

A mirage, she thought foolishly, whipping her head downward to rest on her knees. Her heart thumped uncomfortably, as if she had been running too fast. It was just Neville, sent by Aunt Clara to discover what kept her so long on the beach. But it was not Neville. The Duke of Portfrey, then, sent by Elizabeth and Lily on the same errand. No. No, it was not he. Besides, none of them would have come looking for her. She had told them she wanted to be alone.

She lifted her head again and turned it casually, so as not to disappoint herself when she saw empty beach and bridge and path.

He was on the beach, striding toward her.

Lauren clasped her knees more tightly.

All the guests had left Alvesley within two weeks of the birthday party. Sydnam had left a week after that, bound for one of the Duke of Bewcastle's larger estates in Wales. He had been very cheerful about it. Doing a good job as someone else's steward was a challenge he needed to take on, Kit had realized. Syd certainly had no need of the extra income.

Life at home would have been tranquil and happy except for one thing. His relationship with his father was better than it had ever been. They could communicate man to man. They could relate as father and son. His father was eager to teach; he was eager to learn. And he brought with him skills acquired during years of commanding men and shouldering life-and-death responsibilities, and a young man's energy to complement his father's slower, more deliberate wisdom. His mother was cheerful and affectionate. He was once again his grandmother's favorite, though he had little competition, of course. He had come face-to-face with Rannulf when both were out riding alone one day. They had talked for a few hours, Ralf turning his horse to ride alongside his erstwhile friend since neither of them had had any particular destination in mind. They had fallen back into the easy camaraderie they had enjoyed throughout their boyhood years. They had met several times since then. Their friendship had resumed.

There was only one thing to mar the tranquillity, though to call it *one* made it sound small, insignificant, unimportant. It was the consuming fact of Kit's life. Lauren had written a formal little note from Newbury, breaking their engagement, citing incompatibility and personal fickleness. Right to the end she had kept her part of the bargain, careful to assume all the blame for the breakup. And the letter was designed for other eyes in addition to his own. There was not a whisper of a mention of pregnancy. He had to assume from the nature of the letter that she was not with child. He had opened it not knowing which of two quite opposite fates he was going to be facing.

After reading it he had stridden down to the lake, torn off all his clothes—even though it had been daytime and total privacy had been by no means guaranteed—and swum the whole length of the lake, using every last ounce of his energy so that by the time he reached the far side of the island he had had to half stagger, half drag himself up the sloping bank to fall in a panting stupor facedown on the grass among the wildflowers. He did not even know for how many hours he had lain there.

The foolish part—the really stupid part—was that after he had returned to the house he had not immediately told anyone. He could not face the questions, the explanations, the emotion, the recriminations, the sympathy, the whatever it was he would have been called upon to face if he had told. He had postponed the telling until the evening, and then until the next morning, and then . . .

He had not told at all.

One morning when they were riding home from an inspection of the ripening crops on the home farm, his father admitted to him that he had arranged the marriage with Freyja only because he had thought it would please Kit. Left to himself, he had added, Kit had chosen far more wisely and well than anyone else could have done for him. He had matured into a sensible, dependable man despite the wild oats he had been sowing in London even as late as this spring. Miss Edgeworth would be a fine viscountess and a worthy countess when the day came.

The day Syd left, their mother linked an arm through Kit's after drying her tears and strolled with him in the parterre gardens. She had had misgivings at the prospect of sharing a home with Freyja, she admitted, though she was very fond of her and of all the Bedwyns, who had suffered only from not having had a mother through their most formative years to curb their wildness and teach them some restraint. But she simply loved Lauren. She had done almost from the first, though she confessed that she had been predisposed to dislike her intensely. Lauren already felt like the daughter she had never had but had always longed for.

Kit's grandmother spoke of Lauren when she got up in the mornings and Lauren was not there to accompany her on her walk, when she sat by the fire in the evenings and Lauren was not there to listen to her or to entertain her with conversation or massage her bad hand, and whenever she fancied that Kit was looking restless, which was almost every time she set eyes on him.

He had been able to find neither the courage nor the heart to tell them that the engagement was over, that they would never see Lauren again, that he would not either.

By the middle of September, with his mother asking almost daily when the wedding date was to be set and his grandmother urging that it be before Christmas so that they would have Lauren with them for the holiday—and so that they could start airing out the family christening robes—he knew that he was going to have to do something decisive. He was going to have to tell them.

It was during a lapse in the conversation at dinner one evening that he finally steeled himself and drew breath to speak.

"I'll be going down to Newbury Abbey," he said abruptly. "Tomorrow, I think. I need to . . . see Lauren."

His words surprised him as much as they did his family. More so, in fact. They were all delighted. They had been expecting it, in fact. They thought it was high time. Lauren would be thinking he was having second thoughts.

It was only when the unexpected, unplanned words were spoken that he understood why he had not broken the news to his family, why he had been unable to let go of the charade. He had learned something of infinite value during the summer—he and Lauren had both learned it, he believed. He had learned the importance of openness, of talking to the people he loved, even when habit urged him to keep everything locked up inside himself. He had a good relationship with his father and with Syd today because Lauren had coaxed him into talking with them after a three-year estrangement.

Yet he had never spoken the full truth to Lauren herself. He had withheld it for her sake, because it was something she did not want to hear, because she might find the knowledge a burden, because it might influence her into sacrificing what was of greatest importance to her—her freedom.

But perhaps she had a right to the truth. Freedom surely involved the right to choose.

Or perhaps he was simply deluding himself into self-indulgence.

But if it was self-indulgence, he thought as he rode into the village of Upper Newbury two days later on a blustery day and took a room at the inn on the green, it felt remarkably uncomfortable. The village was picturesque, and there was another part of it—Lower Newbury?—at the bottom of a steep hill, he could see from his room, its small houses clustered about a sheltered harbor, which nevertheless could not disguise the roughness of the sea.

He was undecided about whether he should call first at the dower house or at Newbury Abbey itself. But the dower house, he found, was just a short distance inside the gates of the park. He went there first. The ladies were at the abbey, a servant informed him, and so he rode the rest of the way along a lengthy, winding driveway and presented his card at Newbury Abbey with the request that the Countess of Kilbourne receive him.

He was kept waiting for only a couple of minutes before being ushered up to the drawing room, where several people were awaiting his appearance, all on their feet. Lauren was not among them.

She had not been as reticent as he, he could see immediately. These people all *knew*. Lady Muir was looking pale, the Dowager Lady Kilbourne grave, Portfrey poker-faced. But the small, blond-haired, exquisitely pretty young lady who hurried toward him, her hand extended, was smiling.

"Lord Ravensberg?" she said. "What a pleasure this is."

"Ma'am?" He bowed over her hand.

"Ravensberg?" A tall, blond man, about Kit's own age, came up beside her and bowed without offering his hand.

"Kilbourne?"

He was in the presence, Kit realized, of the man who had meant so much to Lauren all her life, whom she had been within a few minutes of marrying, whom she had loved and probably still did. And of the infamous Lily, who had blighted all Lauren's hopes and dreams.

"What a pleasant surprise," the countess said. "Do come and have a seat. It is rather chilly outside today, is it not? You know everyone else, I believe?"

The ladies curtsied. Portfrey inclined his head. He was holding a small child against one shoulder, Kit noticed for the first time. The duchess smiled warmly.

"You have come, Lord Ravensberg," she said. "I am so glad as I have predicted it."

"And I," the countess added, taking Kit's arm and leading him toward a chair. "Lauren wrote to you before telling any of us—even Gwen—that she was going to end her betrothal. We have all been mystified and very sad because Gwen and my mama-in-law were both firmly of the opinion that it was a love match and very much approved of by your family. Lauren insisted that the breakup was all her idea, that none of the blame must be laid at your door, but of course we have been doing just that. We love Lauren very dearly, you see, and it is always easier to blame strangers. But now you have come, and you may defend yourself in person."

"Lily!" Kilbourne said. "Ravensberg owes us no explanation at all. We do not even know why he has come."

"I came," Kit said, "to speak with Lauren. Where is she?"

"What is it you wish to say?" Kilbourne asked. "She has ended the betrothal. None of us knows why exactly, but we can safely guess that she has no further wish to see or speak with you."

"She is best left alone, Lord Ravensberg," the dowager added. "She was quite adamant in her insistence that she had not acted out of impulse when she wrote to you. I do not know what happened at Alvesley, but she is quite determined not to have you despite the social stigma of a broken engagement. If this is a courtesy call, I thank you on behalf of my niece. If it is not, you see a formidable array of her concerned relatives before you ready to protect her from you."

"Poor Lord Ravensberg," the duchess said with a sympathetic laugh. "You will be thinking you have stepped onto an Arctic continent. We are being unfair to you. Lauren really has insisted that none of the blame for what has happened is yours."

"She is down on the beach," Lady Muir said quietly from some distance away.

Kit looked at her and inclined his head. He still had not sat down.

"Thank you, ma'am," he said.

"She said she wanted to be alone," Kilbourne said. "She said she did not want to be disturbed."

"And so, Lord Ravensberg," the countess added, smiling, "you will have all the privacy in the world to say to her what you have come to say."

"I'll not have her upset," Kilbourne said.

The countess relinquished Kit's arm in order to take her husband's. She smiled up at him. "Lauren is twenty-six years old, Neville," she said. "She is very sensible and has just spent weeks convincing us that she is in control of her own life and can make her own decisions. If she does not want to speak to Lord Ravensberg, she will tell him so."

When Kilbourne looked down into his wife's eyes, Kit realized two things. Lauren was very much loved here at Newbury Abbey, especially perhaps by the two who had caused her the most pain. And Kilbourne was consumed by guilt for what he had made her suffer. Consequently he was doing all in his power to see to it that she did not suffer again.

"I will walk down to the beach if someone will show me the way," Kit said.

"It is going to rain," Kilbourne said, glancing toward the window. "Tell her to come home without delay."

The countess smiled dazzlingly at her husband though she spoke to Kit. "Tell her to take shelter in the cottage, Lord Ravensberg. It is closer."

"Walk down over the lawn," Lady Muir instructed him, "bearing right as you go until you reach the cliff path."

Kit bowed to them all and made his exit.

It was not really raining when he reached the steep path down the side of the cliff. It was not even quite drizzling. But his face felt damp and his ungloved hands clammy. It was certainly going to be raining soon.

He realized where he was when he was halfway down. Lauren had described it once—the short valley with a waterfall and pool at the inner end and a picturesque cottage beside the pool. It was where she had once seen Kilbourne and his countess frolicking and had concluded that she was incapable of that kind of passion herself. There was no sign of Lauren. He turned his gaze to the beach and shaded his eyes as he looked along the wide stretch of golden sand.

And then he spotted her. And smiled. And knew beyond all doubt that the summer had not been in vain for her. Wearing a cloak but no bonnet on a blustery, damp day, she was in the middle of the beach, facing a wild, tumultuous sea, and perched at the very pinnacle of a great tall rock, which from this angle appeared to have almost sheer sides.

At the same time the scene chilled him. This she had done alone. She had not needed help or support—not from him or anyone else.

Seeing her thus, he knew that she had achieved self-knowledge and peace. That she was capable of living her life her way. That she needed no one.

That she did not need him.

Foolishly, he was tempted to turn back before she saw him. But he had something that needed to be said. Something he must say.

He thought the wind might blow him over when he stepped out of the relative shelter of the path onto the bridge over the shallow river. He lowered his head so that he would not lose his hat. He was on the beach, plodding over the sand, when he finally looked up again. She had seen him. She was watching him approach, sitting quietly at the top of the rock, clasping her knees. It seemed to take forever to walk the rest of the way.

He looked up at her and grinned. "Stuck?" he asked. "Do you need rescuing?"

"No," she said with all her characteristic quiet dignity, "thank you."

And she moved from her place to descend the other side of the rock. It was far more scalable than the side by which he had approached, he saw when he walked around it. Even so, she descended at a pace that would have put a tortoise to sleep. He would have climbed up to be close enough to catch her if she slipped, but something told him that it would be entirely the wrong thing to do. Finally first one foot and then the other was on firm ground—or on shifting sand, at least. She turned and looked at him.

He opened his mouth to speak and discovered that he had no idea what he would say.

She made no move to help him.

They stared at each other.

And because his mind really was quite terrifyingly blank, he leaned forward and kissed her instead of talking. Her lips softened and pressed back lightly against his.

"Lauren," he said.

"Kit." After a few moments she rescued him. "Why are you here? Why have you come?"

The dampness in the air had turned to drizzle.

"To instruct you to hurry back to the house," he said, "if you wish to listen to Kilbourne. To suggest the cottage as a closer destination if you prefer the advice of the countess." He grinned again.

"Kit." She frowned. "I did not want to see you again. I really did not."

He swallowed and set a hand against the rock beyond her shoulder. He lowered his head and noticed idly that the sand was destroying the shine on his riding boots—and he had come without his valet.

"You are still here," he said. "Still at Newbury." He had braced himself for the possibility that she would already be gone.

"Only until tomorrow," she said. "Tomorrow I will be going to Bath to choose a house. I am going to live there."

"Is that what you really want?" he asked.

"You know it is," she said. "Kit, why have you come? Where is Lady Freyja?"

"Freyja?" He looked up at her with a frown. "At Lindsey Hall, I suppose. Why?" But he understood before she could answer. "There is nothing between Freyja and me, Lauren. There was once very briefly, but it was a long time ago. Now there is nothing. Nothing whatsoever and never will be."

"Yet you suit," she said.

"Do we?" He considered the matter. "Yes, I suppose there is a similarity. That does not mean we would *suit*. We would not. Did this misconception have anything to do with your breaking off our betrothal?"

"Of course not." She sighed and leaned back against the rock. "It was all arranged even before I met Lady Freyja, remember? Kit, *why* are you here?"

"There is something I need to tell you," he said. "Something I should have told you before you left Alvesley. Something you ought to know whatever you decide to do with the knowledge. Once I have told you, you have only to say the word, Lauren, and I will walk back along this beach and up to the cliff top and into the village and I will never trouble you again, never try to see you again. It is a promise."

"Kit—"

He set one finger across her lips and looked into her eyes.

"I want to marry you," he said. "I want it more than I have ever wanted anything else in my life. For many reasons. But only one of them really matters to me. It is the one I did not tell you of because it seemed somehow dishonorable after you had carried out your side of the bargain so sweetly and so well. I *love* you. That is it, you see, the part I omitted. Just that. I *love* you. I do not believe it can really hurt you to know. It lays no obligation on you. I just needed to say it. I'll leave now if you wish."

She said nothing, just pressed her head back harder against the rock and gazed at him with her lovely violet eyes. The drizzle was turning to light rain. It was running in droplets down her face. But it was not raindrops that were welling in her eyes.

"Tell me to go," he whispered.

She started to say something and then swallowed. She tried again. "I do not *need* you, you know," she said.

"I know." His heart was down in his boots somewhere.

"I do not need anyone," she said. "I can do this alone, this living business. All my life I have shaped myself into being what others expect me to be so that I will belong somewhere, be accepted somewhere, be loved by someone. When I knew I could not belong to Neville, I felt as if I had been cut adrift in the universe. I anchored myself by retreating into an even more rigid gentility. I don't need to do any of that any longer. And I *do* have you to thank. But I don't *need* you any longer, Kit. I am strong enough on my own."

"Yes." He bowed his head and closed his eyes again. "Yes, I know."

"I am free, you see," she said, "to love or to withhold love. Love and dependence need no longer be the same thing to me. I am *free* to love. That is why I love you, and it is the *way* I love you. If you have come here, Kit, because you think you owe me something, because you believe I might crumble without your protection, then go away again with my blessing and find happiness with someone else."

"I *love* you," he said again.

She gazed at him for a long time, her eyes still swimming in tears, and then she smiled, very slowly, and very, very radiantly.

He wrapped his arms about her waist, lifted her off her feet, and twirled her about in circles, while she braced her hands on his shoulders, flung her head back to expose her face to the rain, and laughed.

Kit whooped, and because the echo from the cliffs was so impressive, he threw back his head too and howled like a wolf.

23

How is your grandmama?"

"Busy setting out the family christening robes."

"Oh."

"I am to marry you before Christmas, get you with child *by* Christmas, and be pacing the floors of Alvesley by this time next year, tearing out my hair in clumps and wearing out my boot leather while you deliver our first boy. Strict orders. Why do you think I *really* came? Just to tell you that I love you?"

"Foolish of me."

By the time sanity had returned down on the beach, it was raining in earnest and they had linked hands and made a dash for the cottage. Lauren had thrown off her cloak and shoes—her bonnet and gloves, she remembered too late, were still wedged in somewhere at the foot of the great rock. She was rubbing her hair with a towel and watching Kit, minus his drab riding coat, stooping down on his haunches before the fireplace, building a fire with the wood and kindling beside it.

If this were a dream, she thought, she hoped she would not wake up for a long, long while—like the rest of her life.

"Have you read your mother's letters?"

"Yes, all of them. She is not at all respectable, Kit. And that is a massive understatement. She sounds so delightful that my heart aches. But you may want to think twice about allying yourself with her daughter."

"Ah," he said, reaching for the tinderbox and setting a light to the fire, "that explains a few things. It was her daughter, I believe, who swam naked in the lake at Alvesley, almost casting me into a fit of the vapors and drowning me. It was her daughter who came after me on one occasion to spend the night alone with me in the gamekeeper's hut. Perhaps she *is* too shockingly fast for me."

"Ki-it—"

He got to his feet, brushed his hands together, and turned a laughing face to her. She rubbed harder with the towel.

"And just look at you now," he said.

She looked downward and saw in some embarrassment that her damp dress had molded itself to her body. She laughed.

"We cannot have you catching a chill," he said, glancing through the open doorway into the small bedchamber within, "and coughing and sneezing your way through our wedding. It would just not be romantic." He strode off into the bedchamber and came back with a blanket. "Come here by the fire."

She came and stood meekly before him while he stripped off her clothes, looking at her frankly and appreciatively as he did so and before he wrapped the blanket about her. He talked to her all the while.

"Portfrey was clutching an infant," he said. "They cannot afford a nurse?"

She chuckled. "The baby is absolutely adorable," she said, "and is shamelessly spoiled by us all. I have never seen Elizabeth happier or his grace so relaxed. And Lily can never have enough of her new half-brother."

"Are you now in charity with the countess, then?" he asked.

"I have always recognized that under other circumstances I would have liked her enormously," she said. "She is sunny-natured and unaffected and loving. She has always been unfailingly kind and sympathetic to me. Now I can love her."

"And Kilbourne?"

He drew her against him, opening back the edges of the blanket as he did so. She could feel his superfine coat, his riding breeches, his leather boots against her naked flesh and felt a rush of awareness more intense than if he had been unclothed.

"I love him too, Kit," she said. "I always have and always will. If we had married on that day, I believe we would have had a good marriage. I believe I would have been content and would have thought myself happy. I would never have realized that my love for him was that of a devoted sister. I would never have wondered why I could feel no—no *passion* for him. I would simply have thought that was my nature."

"But it is not?" She had tipped her face up, and he was bent over it, his eyes roaming it.

"No." She shook her head.

"Lord help me," he said. "You don't feel a passion for *me*, do you, Lauren? And expect me to *act* on it?"

She laughed. And she did something quite outrageous—she rubbed herself against him and gazed at him through half-closed eyes. Desire stabbed down along her inner thighs.

"Devil take that rain," he said. "It has trapped me in a deserted cottage with a woman who has conceived a *passion* for me. And no one is going to come riding to my rescue either. I distinctly remember someone up at the house telling someone else that you had asked not to be disturbed down here. And then someone telling *me* that I would have all the privacy I needed to say what I had to say to you. *Now* what do I do?"

She loved the way he could hold his features solemn, even alarmed, while his eyes danced with laughter.

"Absolutely nothing at all," she told him. She lowered her voice as her hands found the top buttonhole of his coat. "*Yet.*"

He shivered elaborately and his eyes danced.

"I begin to think," he said, "that I could grow to like women who are free to love."

"And I begin to think," she said, still in her low, velvet voice, "that you are about to be driven to the brink of madness by one of them, my lord."

"Oh, goody," he murmured agreeably.

She opened back his coat and pushed it off his shoulders and down his arms while he stood relaxed and unmoving. Waistcoats, she discovered then, had far too many buttons, all of them small, each with an accompanying buttonhole that seemed smaller yet. She did not hurry. She occupied herself while her hands worked by feathering kisses over his throat and neck above his cravat. She ran her tongue along the seam of the long scar beneath his jaw and surprised an epithet from him that was definitely not suitable for the ears of a lady. She kissed his mouth, which he held relaxed. She prodded her tongue beyond his lips, exploring the soft, moist inner flesh with its tip. She stretched her tongue deep into his mouth.

"I have won praise and commendation from high places," he said conversationally when his mouth was free, her eyes being needed to discover the secrets of the front flap of his breeches, "for military feats that required only half the courage and discipline I am displaying this afternoon. I hope you realize that you are in the presence of extraordinary heroism."

Sometime during the last ten minutes or so, she had lost her blanket, Lauren realized. It did not matter. The fire had burned up and taken the damp chill from the air. In fact the cottage felt almost uncomfortably warm.

"A word of advice," he said, "from a man who has been undressing me for almost thirty years. Tackle the boots first. Would you like me to be a participant yet? Shall I haul them off for you?"

"No." She knelt down on the floor.

"An erotically submissive posture," he commented with a sigh, raising one foot. "Entirely deceptive, of course. Yes, you have to tug hard. You are not about to break my ankle, I assure you. I feel inclined to urge you to hurry so that we can reach the good part. But alas, you are turning all my preconceptions on their head, Lauren. This tortoiselike seduction feels excruciatingly good."

"And this is only the beginning," she promised, looking up at him from beneath her lashes before pulling off the second boot and standing up again.

"Witch!" he said. "I strolled into Lady Mannering's ballroom that night all unsuspecting, poor innocent that I was. You looked like a perfectly harmless lady. Respectable, prim."

"Prudish," she said.

"Precisely."

"I should be calling for the hartshorn now, then," she said. "You look neither innocent nor harmless, Kit." She had pulled off first his breeches and then his drawers.

He looked down at himself and she touched him at the same moment, cupping him lightly in both hands, amazed at her own brazenness, half crazed with suppressed desire. He looked up and their eyes met.

"You can continue this game all afternoon and all evening if you wish, love," he said. "Sex games are delicious. I look forward to playing an infinite variety of them with you for the rest of our lives. But unless you have a definite preference for prolonging this, I think we might be better occupied on the bed in there. I would very much like to put that inside you."

The greatest surprise of all was the discovery that *not* being touched could be every bit as arousing as having his hands and mouth all over her. He was still standing motionless, his arms loose at his sides, his eyes, heavy-lidded, devoid of laughter, gazing into her own. But his words were her undoing. She was suddenly weak-kneed.

"I thought," she said, "you would never ask. A lady never invites a gentleman to bed."

His hands did not touch her until she had pulled back the blankets and lain down on her back on the bed and reached up for him. They touched her then only at her hips and beneath her buttocks as she spread her legs wide. He came down on top of her and mounted her with one deep, hard, satisfying thrust.

She drew a few slow breaths.

"We can do this the easy way," he said, raising his head and grinning down at her, all the old roguery back in his eyes, "or I can aim at the highest medal of honor and ride the long, hard route home. *Very* long and very hard. Which shall it be?"

"Which is the road to near madness?" she asked, hooking her legs snugly about his and tilting herself slightly so that she could receive him more deeply.

"The less easy road," he said.

"The long, hard ride, then, please," she said, using her low voice again and running her palms over the muscles of his shoulders as she watched the laughter fade from his eyes. "Please, my love."

It was very long. And very hard. It took a great deal of energy. After a while she became aware of the dampness of their sweat, the heat of their bodies, the heavy, labored sound of their breathing, the silken pounding of their joining, the erotic sound of wetness, the rhythmic squeaking of the bed.

For a while her enjoyment was tempered by the fear that it would end too soon, that she would not reach the startling explosion of pleasure she had experienced on the island bank among the wildflowers when he had touched her with his hand and then taken her on top of him. But after a while she knew with an instinct born of love and trust that he did indeed have the fortitude and the sensitivity to wait for her—as he had at the lake.

It came slowly. Achingly slowly, first with an intense physical yearning in the place where they rode together, and then swirling in slow spirals, down into her legs, back into her bowels, up into her stomach, her breasts, her throat, her nose. It came so slowly she feared there could be no ending, no climax, no fulfillment.

"Relax now, love," he murmured against her ear. "Let me do the rest for you. Let yourself open and I'll come to you. Trust me."

Words dimly remembered. Had he spoken them to her before? She was afraid. Mortally afraid. He might as easily have asked her to leap off a high cliff into his waiting arms. But she had known long ago that she would trust him with her life. She had given him her love since then and had accepted his this very day. All that was left to do was to trust him with her heart, to withhold nothing that was her-self—to believe with her heart, as she already did with her intellect, that he would never abuse the gift, that he would never hold her love imprisoned.

She launched herself forward off the cliff, trusting, never doubt-ing, that he would catch her.

"Ah, love." He was thrusting faster, deeper into her. "Oh, God!"

She was falling, shuddering out of control, never fearing for a mo-ment, never doubting. He cried out, and his arms and his body caught her at the bottom of her descent, wrapping firmly about her, pinning her safe and warm and sated against the mattress. She could hear her heartbeat pounding in her ears. And his too. They beat as one.

He was very heavy. She could scarcely breathe. Her legs were stiff from being pressed apart for so long. She was sore inside. And she had never been more comfortable in her life.

"We," he said, his voice sounding shockingly normal, "are going to have the first banns read next Sunday. It is high time I made an honest woman of you. Besides, it may be possible to pass off an eight-month child as an early bird, but a seven- or six-month child would look scandalously suspicious. It might even be whispered that we had an-ticipated our wedding night."

"Shocking indeed." She sighed with contentment. "Sunday it will be, then."

"A big *ton* wedding one month from now," he said. "Both our fam-ilies will be set on it, and frankly I do not have the energy to argue. Do you?"

"I would like a big wedding," she admitted.

"Good. That is settled, then." He kissed her temple. "I have just made a delightful discovery, considering the fact that we are going to be sharing a bed for the rest of our lives. You make a wonderfully comfortable mattress."

"And you make a tolerable blanket," she said, untwining her legs and stretching them luxuriously beside his. She yawned lazily. "Stop talking, Kit, and let's sleep."

"Sleep?" He lifted his head and grinned down at her. She was filled with instant alarm. "*Sleep,* Lauren? When we are both stale with sweat and sex and there is a perfectly decent pool out there, complete with waterfall?"

"Ki-it—"

He just grinned.

"I am *not,*" she said. "I am absolutely, definitely *not* going to swim out there. It is *raining.*"

"A definite problem," he conceded, disengaging from her and lifting himself off both her and the bed. "You might get wet."

Had she not giggled, she might have been saved. Though probably not, she admitted a couple of minutes later as her naked body plummeted into ice-cold water and she came up gasping, her hands with a death grip on Kit's. She wished fervently that she knew a few foul curse words. But her teeth were probably clacking too loudly for them to be heard, anyway.

She shook her head to clear the water from her eyes and laughed at him before doing the most foolish thing she had done all day. She challenged him to a race to the waterfall and—of course—he accepted, another bedding in the cottage to be his prize if he won.

If he won!

She was still getting her arms and legs organized when he was nonchalantly treading water right under the waterfall and grinning despicably.

A wedding eve ball had been the tradition at Newbury Abbey for a number of generations. It seemed rather strange to Kit when the bride and groom might be expected to want as much sleep as they could get the night before their wedding night, but perhaps the Newbury bridegrooms who had allowed the tradition to develop had not been particularly lusty men. Or perhaps it had been a clever ruse of Newbury brides to take the edge off their lust.

However it was, his own wedding eve ball and Lauren's was in full swing. The abbey was packed to the rafters with Kilbourne and Redfield family and friends. The dower house too, and the village inn. Even by the standards of a London Season, the gathering in the ballroom, on the balcony beyond the French windows, and on the landing and winding stairs beyond the ballroom might be called a very creditable squeeze. How everyone was expected to fit inside the village church tomorrow morning he could not begin to guess.

Lauren, with whom a mere bridegroom was expected to dance only once—and he had already been allotted his quota—was flushed and looking radiantly happy. She was also many times lovelier than the next loveliest lady in the room. She literally shimmered in a satin gown of such a deep violet that some might call it purple. The diamond necklace his mother and father had given her as a wedding present sparkled in the light of hundreds of candles. His ring—the diamond was so large and many-faceted that he had distinctly overheard one of his least favorite females, the former Lady Wilma Fawcitt, more recently the Countess of Sutton, describe it as vulgar—his ring glinted on her finger.

"You cannot get close enough for another dance, Ravensberg?" Lord Farrington asked him.

"An abomination, is it not?" Kit said cheerfully.

"Does the delectable Lady Muir dance?" Farrington asked. "One would hate to risk a faux pas when she has that limp."

"She dances," Kit said.

Farrington, it appeared, had escaped the clutches of the ambitious Merklingers during the spring. He was footloose again, his roving eye intact.

"I'll go and try my luck with her, then," he said, "and see if I can charm her away from that great handsome Viking."

"Ralf Bedwyn?" Kit grinned—and then turned his attention to a footman who had touched his sleeve. There was a gentleman newly arrived and waiting downstairs. He had requested a word with Lord Ravensberg.

Yet *another* guest? Kit strode off in the direction of the staircase.

The new arrival was a very young man. He was tall and overslender as if he had not yet quite grown into his body. He was also fresh-faced. If he shaved at all yet, it was clearly not a daily necessity. He was a good-looking boy, though. Kit assessed him in one quick glance, as he had once been accustomed to doing with scores and even hundreds of new recruits.

"Good evening," he said.

"Ravensberg?" The young man strode toward him, his right hand outstretched. "I read your invitation less than a week ago. By that time the notice of your wedding was in the papers. I came as quickly as I could." He flushed when Kit regarded him blankly. "I beg your pardon," he said. "I am Whitleaf. Viscount Whitleaf."

"Whitleaf?" Kit took his hand. "The invitation was to my *betrothal* celebrations at Alvesley Park. My grandmother's birthday party, actually." He had sent it off at the same time as he had sent one to Baron Galton, before Lauren had arrived at Alvesley, before he had known of her total estrangement from her father's family. He had been more relieved than disappointed when no one had shown up.

"I have been in Scotland ever since coming down from Oxford in the spring," the young man explained, "on a walking tour with my old tutor and a couple of friends."

And where have you been for the rest of Lauren's life?

Kit did not ask the question aloud. He clasped his hands behind him.

"I asked my mother who Lauren Edgeworth was after reading your invitation," Viscount Whitleaf said. "It was obvious she must be a relative. I am an Edgeworth too."

"You did not *know* who she was?" Kit asked.

"No, not really," the young man replied. "Maybe she was mentioned when I was a lad. I don't remember. I was sorry I had missed the celebrations at Alvesley. But when I read the notice in the paper, I thought it would be rather jolly to come down here to pay my respects to my cousin on the occasion of her wedding."

"Jolly?" Kit frowned.

The young man flushed again. "You are not pleased to see me," he said.

"How long have you held the title?" Kit asked.

"Oh, forever." Whitleaf made a dismissive gesture with one hand. "My father died when I was three. I was the last of six children—the only boy. I'll reach my majority in January. I'll be free of all my guardians then. *That* will be jolly, let me tell you. Are you really not glad I have come? Was my cousin offended when I did not even reply to the invitation? Should I leave?"

"Guardians," Kit said quietly. "Since you were three."

"Lord, yes," the young man said, grimacing. "Three of them. A humorless lot. Not one funny bone among the lot of them. And my mother too, though she does occasionally laugh, to give her her due. And mothers do not have a great deal of say in their minor sons' lives, you know. For some peculiar reason they are supposed not to have brains. Anyway, for most of my life I have had leading strings projecting from all parts of my body, like the spokes of an umbrella."

"Did you know," Kit asked, "that these guardians have been writing letters in your name? Declining the chance to take Lauren in as a child when her mother apparently disappeared during a long journey overseas, for example—even though her father had been a Viscount Whitleaf, presumably your uncle? Replying to her own overture of friendship when she was eighteen—eight years ago—with the information that you did not encourage indigent relatives or hangers-on?"

Viscount Whitleaf flushed and winced. "If ever I used to ask to see my correspondence or their replies," he said, "they would call me a precocious cub or something equally endearing and look at me as if I were a particularly nasty insect that had crawled out from beneath the nearest piece of furniture. But that sounds just like them—what you just described, I mean. My mother told me last week that my aunt, Miss Edgeworth's mother, was not highly regarded. She flirted with everything in breeches—according to my mother. And then she went off and married Wyatt before my uncle was cold in his grave. There was even a suspicion—er, perhaps I ought not to mention this.

It's doubtless nonsense, dreamed up by old tabbies who had nothing better to do with their time. It was even said, anyway, that her daughter—that is this Miss Edgeworth—was his. The new husband's, I mean, and not my uncle's."

Kit, inclined to fury, decided on amusement instead. "But you still thought it might be jolly to meet her?" he asked.

"Oh, I did." The young man smiled. "The family black sheep are invariably more interesting than the white sheep. *They* tend to be dead bores. Or worse."

"Stay here," Kit said. "Make yourself comfortable. Lauren is probably dancing with someone. I'll fetch her down as soon as she is free. I can assure you beyond any reasonable doubt that my bride is indeed a legitimate member of the Edgeworth family."

"Oh, I daresay," the viscount said good-naturedly. "But I really wouldn't care a fig if she wasn't, you know."

"She has your color eyes," Kit said, smiling. "I should have realized who you were as soon as I walked through the door. But the light was behind you then."

"Ah, the Edgeworth eyes," the young man said. "They always look better on the women than the men."

Kit chuckled to himself as he made his way back upstairs, greeting guests as he went, acknowledging their congratulations and good wishes. The stripling was surely going to discover within the next three or four years that women would fall all over themselves for just a single glance from Viscount Whitleaf's violet eyes.

24

Lauren's dressing room suddenly seemed rather crowded even though she had dismissed her tearful maid five minutes before. The silly girl had sniffed and wept all through the hour of dressing her mistress and styling her hair. She had never been happier in her life, she had declared while hiccuping woefully, and though she did not entirely fancy not seeing her mum, who lived in Lower Newbury, so often, she would be thrilled to move to Alvesley and call Lord Ravensberg master. He was the handsomest, kindest gent she had ever clapped eyes upon.

Lauren had made allowances for the fact that it was a day when emotions could be expected to run high.

It was her wedding day.

Aunt Clara was the first to come to her dressing room. Lauren had not breakfasted with all the guests in the dining room. A tray had been brought up to the bedchamber, laden with appetizing foods, all her favorites. She had not been able to swallow one bite.

Aunt Clara enfolded her in a light hug, so as not to squash either of their wedding finery.

"Lauren," she said. It was all she could say for a while, even though she smiled.

Oh, yes, it was a day for emotions. Lauren knew that her aunt was delighted for her. She had been dreadfully upset at the broken engagement, convinced as she had been at Alvesley that her niece had found happiness at last. She had actually wept—Neville and Lily had had to console her—when Lauren and Kit had walked into the drawing room at the abbey late on that wet afternoon a month ago. They had not needed to say a word. Everyone had known instantly that they were reconciled. It had been almost embarrassing. It must have been glaringly obvious why they had been so long down on the beach.

Gwen was next to come.

"Oh," she said, stopping in the doorway, "how absolutely beautiful you are, Lauren. No one else I know—except perhaps Elizabeth—can get away with simplicity and make it look like elegance personified. Some of us are *dumpy*."

Lauren laughed with true amusement. Gwen was small and curvy, but *dumpy* was the last word anyone would use to describe her.

And then Viscount Whitleaf—Cousin Peter—scratched on the door and peered inside, all eager flushes, when Gwen opened it.

"Oh, I say!" he said. "You do look splendid, Cousin. I am just off to the church. I thought I would poke my head in and say good morning and good wishes and all that, me being the only relative present on your papa's side. I hope this is not an impertinence. The ball last night was rather jolly, was it not?"

Lauren hurried across the room and took both his hands in hers.

"The ball was *very* jolly," she said, "in large measure because you came and I met you at last. You have made my happiness complete."

"Oh, I say!" he exclaimed, looking pleased. "But I must be off." He spotted Gwen beside the door and made her a bow. "May I thank you again, ma'am, for your extreme kindness in giving up your room for me last night?"

There had not been another available either at the abbey or at the dower house or at the inn. Gwen had slept on a truckle bed in Aunt Clara's dressing room.

And then, less than two minutes after he had left, Neville and Lily appeared.

"We simply had to run up and see Lauren on our way to church," Lily said by way of apology. "Oh, Lauren, how *absolutely* gorgeous you look. I am so happy for you. So *happy.*" She hugged Lauren, regardless of the danger to their finery—and of the growingly visible bulk of her condition.

Lauren hugged her back. "I love you, Lily," she whispered.

"Well, I would think so too," Lily said, quite unabashed. "If it were not for me, this would not be your wedding day, would it?"

Trust Lily to bring all that out into the open.

And then it was Neville's turn. Like Aunt Clara, he said nothing— not even her name. But he wrapped his arms tightly about her and hugged her close. She twined her arms about him and closed her eyes.

Neville. Her dearly beloved Neville. The dearest, dearest brother a woman ever had. She knew—though they had not spoken of it—just how much today meant to him. It was the day when he would finally see her happiness complete, the day he could finally let go of his terrible guilt.

"Be happy," he said, releasing her at last and smiling at her. "Promise me?"

"I promise." She smiled back. "I love him, you see."

"If we do not leave immediately, Neville," Aunt Clara said, "the bride is going to race us to the church. What a disgrace that would be."

They all laughed, and Aunt Clara bent one last, lingering look on Lauren as she left with Neville and Lily.

Lauren was left alone with Gwen. She turned and looked at her, her smile fading.

"Perhaps," she said, "I should have suggested Alvesley for the wedding after all."

Gwen understood. How could she not? They had been sisters and dearest friends for all of twenty-three years.

"No," she said. "Your dignity and your courage have not failed you for more than a year and a half, Lauren. They will not fail you now."

Lauren's maid tapped on the door then and poked her head around it. She was still looking tearful. Baron Galton awaited Miss Edgeworth and Lady Muir in the hall below, she announced.

It was all so very reminiscent. . . .

It had been spring the last time—March. It was late October this time. The weather was just as lovely, cool but sunny. The trees surrounding the dower house and lining the short stretch of driveway before the carriage reached the park gates and drove out to the village and the church beyond were decked out in all the glorious colors of autumn. The driveway was carpeted with leaves already fallen.

The village green was dotted with villagers. A denser crowd of them clustered about the churchyard gates. The roadway surrounding the green was lined with empty carriages of all kinds. Their coachmen stood idly about, gawking at all the excitement, their colorful liveries distinguishing them from the villagers.

Ah, yes, eerily reminiscent.

Standing inside the church porch a few minutes later while Gwen stooped to straighten her hem and arrange her train, Lauren could sense crowds of people filling the church just beyond the line of her vision. The vicar would be waiting at the altar rail. So would Kit and Sydnam. She could visualize all the people outside, waiting for the ringing of the church bells to herald the completion of the marriage ceremony, waiting to catch a glimpse of bride and groom as they came out of church, newly married.

And she could almost *feel* a small, shabbily clad woman dashing up the churchyard path and into the porch and brushing past Lauren to hurry on into the church to bring the world crashing to an end.

Her grandfather was waiting patiently, smiling benevolently at her.

She thought she would surely faint. Worse, she felt horribly bilious. Panic clawed at the edges of her control. Then Gwen looked up at her—and stood up to take her hand and squeeze it tightly in both her own.

"Lauren," she said softly, "it is all over now. The past is gone. The future awaits you. This is today—your wedding day. Your *real* wedding day."

The great pipe organ began playing. Lauren's grandfather offered his arm. And they stepped inside the church, into the long nave.

For a few moments she could see everything, as if it were all etching itself onto her memory for all time. Faces turned back to watch her approach, most of them familiar, almost all of them smiling. She even noticed individuals—Joseph, daring to wink at her, Claude and Daphne Willard, Aunt Sadie and Uncle Webster, the Duke of Bewcastle and Lord Rannulf Bedwyn, Elizabeth and the Duke of Portfrey, Cousin Peter, Kit's grandmother, nodding and beaming, Lily and Neville, Aunt Clara, the Earl and Countess of Redfield.

But only for a few moments. Then her eyes focused on the end of the nave, where a man stood watching her come. He was not as tall as either the vicar on one side of him or Sydnam on the other. But he was handsome beyond belief and dressed with consummate elegance in a black, form-fitting tailed coat with ivory satin knee breeches and embroidered waistcoat and sparkling white linen and stockings. Lace frothed at his throat and wrists.

Kit!

He looked formal and solemn. But no! As she drew closer, Lauren could see that his eyes smiled. Not with his customary merriment and roguery, but with something that took her breath away even though she had known beyond any doubt for a whole month that he loved her. He had written daily from Alvesley—sometimes twice daily, once three times—to tell her so, often in outrageously florid language that he knew would have her laughing.

His eyes drew her to him. They warmed her from head to toe, they devoured her, they made her beautiful and desirable and very much wanted. His eyes adored her.

She wondered suddenly if she was smiling and discovered that she was.

She was also as terrified as she had been all through a sleepless night, all through the dressing for her wedding, all through coming to church and standing in the porch. Terrified that even now, even now when Grandpapa was answering the vicar's question and giving her hand into Kit's, something would happen. The wedding service— *her* wedding—had begun, she realized, but she could not concentrate on it. She thought it altogether possible that she might be going to faint.

He had never seen her more beautiful. Her dress of shimmering white satin was unadorned except at the hem and around the bottom of the train, at the edge of the short sleeves and about the scooped neckline, where it was delicately scalloped and decorated with silver embroidery and hundreds—perhaps thousands—of tiny pearls. Her bonnet, slippers, and long gloves were all white, the former adorned with the finest lace veil, which fell over her face. The only touches of color were the violet ribbon beneath her bosom, its ends trailing to her hem, and the small posy of violets and dark green leaves she carried in one hand.

He had never expected his wedding day to be the happiest of his life. Weddings—with the possible exception of the wedding night— were tedious, rather embarrassing affairs for the man, he had always thought. But today he was prepared to concede that there was something to be said for the old cliché. A great deal, in fact. She looked rather like the old marble Lauren Edgeworth at first. But then, when her eyes focused upon him and she came closer, she smiled.

His heart turned over. Another cliché. Perhaps weddings were clichés personified. He had missed her during the past month. And yesterday he had scarcely been able to get near her. Today . . . well, to-day was the happiest of his life.

And then he saw the terror behind her smile and felt the rigidity in her hand. It was not simple nervousness. He knew her well enough, by God, to know that. And of course—of course! He had wondered about the suitability of the church at Newbury—the scene of her first wedding—for their nuptials. But he had concluded that it would be good for her to have it happen here, to be able to lay the final ghosts to rest. Foolish of him—*stupid* of him—not to have realized what an ordeal this part of today would be for her.

He tried to reassure her with his hands, with his eyes. He tried to wrap the security of his love about her. He stopped concentrating on the marriage service.

"I require and charge you both," the vicar was saying when Kit paid attention again—and he could see that Lauren was suddenly listening too, "as ye will answer at the dreadful day of judgment, when the secrets of all hearts shall be disclosed, that if either of you know any impediment why ye may not lawfully be joined together in matrimony, ye do now confess it; for be ye well assured that so many as are coupled together otherwise than God's Word doth allow, are not joined together by God, neither is their matrimony lawful."

Her hand stiffened further in his.

No, my love, no one will break the silence. There is no impediment. It will all be over in a moment now—all the irrational fear. Courage, my love.

"Wilt thou have this woman for thy wedded wife?"

It was *over*. It *was* over. She relaxed instantly and smiled radiantly at him. There was no impediment.

Soon—very soon—they were man and wife. Joined together as one until death did them part. He lifted the veil back from her face and folded it over the brim of her bonnet. He smiled into her eyes.

His love. His viscountess. His wife.

The terror—the foolish terror—was all forgotten. The register signed, the church bells pealing joyfully to the world outside, the organ playing jubilantly, the newly married couple made their way back up the nave, smiling at all their family and friends, who smiled right back at them.

But some of the congregation had not waited. Cousins from both families and a few others had slipped out and armed themselves before

Kit and Lauren stepped out into the bright sunshine and the villagers raised a cheer, almost all of them now clustered about the gateway and the open barouche—lavishly decorated with white ribbons and streamers—that would convey them to the abbey for the wedding breakfast. The cousins were lined up on either side of the churchyard path, all grinning maliciously, all armed with mounds of autumn leaves.

"Hmm," Kit said while Lauren smiled radiantly about her. *Nothing* had the power to mar her happiness for the remainder of her wedding day. "Shall we cower here and hope to be lost to sight among the crowd in a few minutes' time? Or shall we make a run for it?"

"It would be unsporting," she said, "to spoil their fun."

"Unsporting." He grinned down at her. "And so it would. But they will be sorely disappointed if we do not put our heads down and run for it. Shall we disappoint them?"

"Absolutely," she agreed, and she took his arm and walked sedately down the churchyard path with him, smiling and waving and being rained upon by gloriously colored leaves.

They waved again to the crowds as Kit handed her into the barouche and then vaulted in beside her. Their coachman yelled a good-natured command, the crowds parted to let them through, the carriage lurched into motion, and Kit tossed out handfuls of coins that had been lying ready on the seat. The wedding guests were beginning to spill out of the church.

Kit's hand found Lauren's and clasped it warmly. They looked at each other and smiled as the barouche slowly circled the green before moving between the gateposts into the park.

"Alone together at last," he said. "Or almost alone. This past month has been interminable."

"Yes, but it is over." Her eyes sparkled with sudden tears. "And this morning is over."

He squeezed her hand more tightly. "Everything was perfect," he said. "My wife. Always and forever my wife, Lauren. Always and forever my love."

"My love," she repeated softly. And then her smile grew more radiant. "Oh, Kit, I am *glad* you fought in the park that day and I walked there. I am *glad* you made that horrid wager with your friends. I am *glad*—"

He bent his head and kissed her.

From behind them came an increased roar of cheers. And a single piercing whistle.

The church bells pealed merrily on.

ABOUT THE AUTHOR

Bestselling, multi-award-winning author Mary Balogh grew up in Wales, land of sea and mountains, song and legend. She brought music and a vivid imagination with her when she came to Canada to teach. Here she began a second career as a writer of books that always end happily and always celebrate the power of love. There are over three million copies of her Regency romances and historical romances in print. You can learn more about her novels at her website: WWW.MARYBALOGH.COM.